Adele PARKS

TELL ME SOMETHING

headline
review

First published in Great Britain in 2008
by MICHAEL JOSEPH
An imprint of PENGUIN BOOKS

This edition published in Great Britain in 2012
by HEADLINE REVIEW
An imprint of HEADLINE PUBLISHING GROUP

1

Cataloguing in Publication Data is available from the British Library

ISBN 978 0 7553 9427 2

Typeset in Garamond MT

Printed and bound in Great Britain by
Clays Ltd, St Ives plc

Headline's policy is to use papers that are natural, renewable and recyclable
products and made from wood grown in sustainable forests. The logging
and manufacturing processes are expected to conform to the environmental
regulations of the country of origin.

HEADLINE PUBLISHING GROUP
An Hachette UK Company
338 Euston Road
London NW1 3BH

www.headline.co.uk
www.hachette.co.uk

For Bob Shevlin, Wilbert Das and Massimo Bianchi

I

I fell in love with Roberto twice.

The first time was twelve years before I met him.

I was on holiday with my parents in Padova, north Italy. I was fourteen, sulky, brooding and romantic. The second time was twelve years later, in a pub, in south-west London. He was watching a football match on the large screen. I was pulling pints. By then I was more gregarious and thoughtless but still astonishingly romantic.

Before Padova, holidays with my parents (and there was no other kind) had been limited to the British Isles. I grew up accepting that foreign holidays were something that everyone else did but, for me, they were out of the question.

My parents were a traditional pair and they were careful with their money. Both facts can be quickly explained and possibly excused if I tell you that my mother and father were forty-four and forty-nine respectively when the stork dropped me on their doorstep. Today they would not be considered horribly geriatric parents but back then they were regarded as such. Some of my mum's friends were grandmothers. Besides, they'd previously had two stork visits, nineteen and seventeen years earlier. My father always joked that the bird assigned to our family had no sense of direction or urgency and it had been late by about fifteen years. He maintained that he and my mother had always wanted three children and a little girl was especially welcome; which was very kind of him although unlikely to be strictly accurate.

No one in my family can have been particularly over-joyed by my tardy arrival. My brothers, Max and Thomas, must have felt vaguely uncomfortable with this obvious proof that their parents still indulged in sex. No doubt both of them were happy to rush off to university as soon as feasibly possible in order to put distance between themselves and the whole messy business. It would have been quite reasonable for my parents to have assumed that the broken nights' sleep and soiled nappies part of their lives was well and truly behind them, at least until grandchildren arrived. My father had just made partner at his accountancy firm and he was the captain of the golf club that year; both time-consuming, demanding roles. My mother had her bridge and now she had me.

Still, they made the best of it. I was healthy and my mother found pleasure in dressing me up in party frocks, something that had not been available to her while parent-ing Max and Thomas, obviously.

But family legend suggests I was not so much a bundle of joy, rather a bundle of trouble; a poor sleeper, picky eater and angry while teething. It wasn't a picnic. I grew up believing resentment silently slept with us all. I believed that their ideas were out-dated and overly fussy in com-parison to other parents. My father played the oboe and called boys chaps. He often corrected my friends' use of the auxiliary verbs 'can' and 'may'. My mother was more embarrassing still, just because her exposure to my classmates was more regular.

She was not as pretty as all the other mothers who

clustered at the school gate. Her clothes, shoes and complete ignorance about who Paul Young was set her a generation apart. Looking back I can see that she was a careful and concerned mother but at the time I gave her no credit for this, only grief. She regularly invited my friends around for tea but refused to serve fish fingers or Angel Delight, as the other mums would. Instead she made huge stews and persisted in serving sprouts or cabbage. She had no idea. She also insisted on collecting me from the school gate even when I was at senior school. Sometimes, if I thought I could get away with it, I pretended she was my batty grandmother (a batty grandmother being infinitely more acceptable than an interfering mother) and I would join the other children in laughing at her sensible shoes and practical mackintosh before I was in her hearing range.

I was always vaguely embarrassed by my parents and I was ashamed of myself for being so, which in turn made me even angrier at them for being the source of my ugly emotion in the first place. They weren't draconian; they were just wrong. While the pocket money they gave me was slightly below class average, they (theoretically at least) allowed me to spend it on whatever I chose. But their obvious disappointment if I chose a *Jackie* comic and a stack of sweets rather than an edifying classic novel always diminished the pleasure of those treats. Clothes were an issue. I was twelve before I was allowed to own a pair of jeans, fifteen before I was allowed mascara (although I secretly applied it at school long before that), seventeen before I was allowed to have my ears pierced. OK, I'm looking back at these grievances from a wiser age (just thirty-two) and I admit that my parents didn't exactly commit war crimes but, at the time, in my view, they might as well have done.

The main focus of contention was holidays. Other parents took their kids to Costa del somewhere or other or even (the pinnacle of cool) Disney in America. My classmates tried sticky liqueurs on holiday and spent their money on stuffed toy donkeys and jars full of coloured sand. Their sunbathing was injudicious and they often returned home with sore sunburnt limbs but exciting stories about flirtations with foreign boys to make up for the pain.

My parents were more interested in National Trust buildings than busy beaches. Their idea of a superb holiday was to hitch up the caravan to a site along the southern coast (preferably near a castle and a decent tea shop that sold a light sponge cake). I endured countless wet weeks watching my parents struggle with an Ordnance Survey map in an attempt to find the footpath that took us to yet another dull relic.

When I was fourteen it was my parents' thirty-fifth wedding anniversary, and Max and Thomas (who were already enjoying successful careers as a journalist and a doctor, respectively) thought that the anniversary was excuse enough to treat our parents to their first holiday abroad. My father had been to Germany to complete his National Service but my mother had only ever crossed the Channel to go to the Isle of Wight (terrific bird-watching, apparently).

My parents' reaction was guarded. Max spent hours drawing attention to the numerous places of historical and archaeological interest and Thomas calmed their fears about drinking tap water or attacks from mosquitoes, and slowly my parents started to accept – and then finally enjoy – the idea. I was to be included in my parents' anniversary trip, as they would never have allowed me to stay at home under the supervision of my big brothers, let alone by myself. My reaction was one of unequivocal joy.

I got a paper round and began regularly babysitting for neighbours' kids, as I longed for a wardrobe boasting bikinis and shorts. I was thrilled at the idea of owning a passport. I pored over maps and guidebooks. I became silly with excitement when my father and I finally visited the bank to exchange our currency. I marvelled at the strange money and couldn't resist sniffing it. It felt warm and peppery; somehow promising and mysterious. Obviously, I had less interest in churches or art galleries than my parents and I was more focused on getting a tan, eating ice-cream and making eye contact with Italian boys. My targets were modest – I wasn't even expecting to speak to anyone other than the hotel receptionist – and still I was fizzing with the excitement of the adventure.

By some miracle our holiday managed to surpass even my lofty expectations. I delighted in everything strange, new and foreign. The duty-free shops at the airport seemed glamorous beyond compare and I coveted the enormous Toblerone bars that were not so freely available in UK supermarkets in those days. I was disproportionately pleased with the wet paper towels that the friendly air hostess doled out with free (*free!*) drinks of cola on the flight. From the moment the aeroplane doors swung open when we touched down and the sun slammed into the plane and cocooned me, I was in love.

2

I wasn't in love with the guy ushering us down the plane steps and towards the airport bus, or anything prosaic like that (although he was cute). I was in love with *Italy*. A wall of thick heat slapped on to my pale, gangly limbs and I wanted to sing because suddenly I felt at home.

I lived in a clean, functional house which groaned with healthy food, music practice and educational games. We were comfortably off. We had everything we could ever have needed but nothing that I wanted. We had fitted carpets, a microwave, hot water bottles, silver cutlery (that had been handed down to my parents from my mother's grandmother), but we did not have a TV in the sitting room (just a very tiny one tucked away in the spare bedroom, pulled out on special occasions); we had a piano, we had net curtains, for goodness sake; the very epitome of a middle-class British existence in all its insipid glory.

Suddenly I felt warm, colourful and impassioned. I'd never got excited about anything in my life until that point. Without a TV I had no idea who Duran Duran really were, and had faked a crush on 'the drummer' to blend in at school, but I couldn't have picked him out in a line-up of Thai lady boys. I did not excel at a particular sport or a subject. I was not the type of child to have found solace in books. My few friends were equally dull and ill-defined. We didn't even choose to be one another's friends – we were sort of the left-over kids that no one really wanted to be pals with. I'd never had a boyfriend or even been kissed.

And suddenly there was Italy.

A country of warmth. A country that smelt of sweet, strong coffee. A country full of noise, chaos, chat and energetic and constant hand gestures. I was heartened by the abundance of flowers, festivals and flowing ribbons pinned to doors to announce the birth of a baby. It seemed to me that the Italians knew how to squeeze every ounce of juice out of life. And best yet – even better than the squeals of delight expelled from the kids chasing pigeons in the piazza – it seemed that every boy and man looked at me in a way that suggested I was interesting, appreciated and alive. In England my curly hair, fair skin and splattering of freckles were tragically unfashionable. But Italian men didn't seem to mind that I didn't sport a sleek, dark bob; quite the opposite.

My infatuation grew deeper and more serious with every espresso I gulped. For ten days as I wandered around the narrow medieval streets of Padova I did not feel the ghosts of Giotto, Dante or Petrarch, as my parents did; I felt the weight of appreciative glances from the city's Giovannis, Davidos and Paulos. While my parents discussed the beatific smiles great artists had given the Virgin and Jesus, I wallowed in the much more salacious smiles secretly bestowed on me by waiters and boys lounging outside souvenir shops. I was too shy to actually talk to anyone else, tourist or local, so for hours I licked ice-creams or drank coke and stared.

I watched the girls who giggled in gaggles yet managed to attain a level of sophistication that even the sixth-formers I knew could only long for. Was it their high heels? Or the tight belts? Their thin wrists or mascara? I did not know. All I knew was that I wanted to be one of them. I wanted to join an enormous, noisy family for the *passeggiata* parade at five o'clock; it was marvellous that even something as simple as an evening stroll seemed to be a celebration. I wanted to buy cakes as a Sunday morning gift for my friends; cakes that were presented in a cardboard box, wrapped with cheerful ribbons. I wanted to live among ancient history and serious style. I wanted their sociability to be mine. I wanted to eat their food and to bask in their civic pride and cultural interests. I wanted to live in Italy. I wanted to be Italian. It was obvious what I needed to do. I would marry an Italian.

I came back to England with bagfuls of *Oggi*, the Italian equivalent of *Hello!* magazine. I vowed to teach myself Italian from those glossy pages; it would do – at least until I could find a formal tutor. But, as my tan wore off, so did my keenness to self-teach. While I continued to nurture my passion for all things Italian in terms of food, style and coffee, I'm afraid I did nothing about actually learning to speak the language. I pushed the *Oggi* under my bed and they stayed there gathering dust for several years.

I did intend to study Italian at university, but my grade C at French GCSE didn't convince the necessary academic authorities that I had a talent for languages. The university admissions tutors were not in the least impressed when I tried to explain my motivation; apparently 'desire to marry an Italian' is not a compelling enough reason to be accepted on to a degree course. I considered moving to Italy to teach English. I'd heard about a course where the teacher doesn't even have to know the native tongue but instead can teach students through full immersion; but then I discovered that getting this TEFL qualification would cost thousands, so I decided that my best bet was to work for a year or so and save up. Mum and Dad were devastated when I told them I planned to move to London. My father said he feared I'd drift. He repeatedly pointed out that my brothers had always been terrifically motivated and decisive and had never presented him or Mum with a moment's worry. I was also motivated and decisive, but it was impossible to explain as much to my father. I was certain that he, like the university admissions tutors, would not accept my ambition to marry an Italian as a legitimate career plan. Luckily, that year Max's wife, Sophie, presented Mum and Dad with another grandchild and Thomas got married to a scary paediatrician, Eileen MacKinnan, who impressed and bossed my parents in equal measures. They had plenty to keep them occupied.

When I got off the National Express coach I immediately headed to Covent Garden, where I knew there were enough authentic Italian bars and restaurants to allow me to pretend I was in the country that flew the tricolour. I told myself that it would do until I'd saved up enough money to actually go there. I quickly found work waiting tables and pulling pints, yet somehow I never managed to gather together the money necessary for the teaching course. One year drifted into the next and then merged into another, almost without my noticing. My father got to say 'I told you so' on an indecent amount of occasions. If I ever gave any thought to my just-out-of-grasp TEFL qualification I reasoned that there was no particular hurry; there would always be Italians needing to learn English. I was happy as long as I earned enough money to buy fashionable shoes and handbags and pay the rent on a scruffy bed-sit in Earls Court which I shared with my friend Alison, a girl I met through one of the waitressing jobs.

Despite the ordinary jobs and the tiny, scruffy flat I remember my early twenties as marvellous years; it's criminal to do anything other. I may not have been committed to earning a TEFL qualification but I was still resolute in my vow to marry an Italian, and I soon discovered that there were plenty of Italian guys to date here in the UK; I didn't really have to have the upheaval and inconvenience of going abroad alone. I dated a series of Giancarlos, Massimos and Angelos. They did not disappoint. They flattered and were attentive; they fed me pasta and enormous compliments and I had a ball. Admittedly, sooner or later, they inevitably returned to Italy or the intensity burned out after only a few short weeks. This wasn't much of a problem; while I had a tendency to instantly fall in love with every one of these guys, I fell out of love relatively quickly too. I never allowed myself to be heartbroken for anything longer than a week. Alison called me shallow but I liked to think of myself as adjusted. I was aware that my youth was to be enjoyed and I saw so many girls wasting night after night crying into their pillows because of some guy or other. Ridiculous! There were always plenty more *pesce* in the *mare*.

Alison suggested that I try to date men who were more likely to stay in the country but she was missing the point. I was spoilt for life and found it disappointing to date anyone other than Italians. I didn't even want to. I did try, once or twice, but what came after was always *after*. English men simply didn't know about intense stares. They became tongue-tied when issuing compliments. By comparison, their dress sense was poor. Tailored shirts versus saggy football tops, reciting poetry or the words of some dated *Monty Python* sketch, drinking champagne out of my shoe or necking lager out of pint glasses; there was no competition.

So eight years passed, filled, but not punctuated, by a blur of intense but short-lived love affairs. Maybe I *was* shallow, or maybe I was perfectly average. I don't know. I just had a type.

Then Roberto walked into my bar and my life.

I watched him watching the football match on the TV screen. Even before he said a word it was instantly clear to me that he was Italian (his shoes shone and he was wearing a pink shirt with a confidence that eludes English blokes); besides, he had a unique energy and appetite that seemed to ricochet through the bar and then ping right into my being. I watched as he cheered his team when they made a decent pass, as he pulled at his hair when they let a goal slip through, as he hugged his friend with delightful, firm enthusiasm when his team equalized – and I was mesmerized.

The excitable and exciting stranger seemed to sense I was watching him. He turned and caught me undressing him with my eyes. I wondered whether he knew I was projecting way past the first carnal encounter, down the aisle and straight into the maternity hospital. I was defenceless; his deep, dark eyes stripped me of any ability I had to feign indifference. I fought my instinct to reach out and stroke his glorious bronzed skin. I wanted to run my hands over his well-defined and athletic body. While not especially tall, everything about his presence seemed purposeful and powerful. His being in the bar made me feel strangely safe and excited all at once.

He pulled himself away from watching the football and came over to where I was standing behind the bar. Alison would probably have described him as swaggering, I saw a saunter. He leaned close enough for his citrus cologne to drift into my consciousness.

'I take a beer and, you too, if you are available,' he said. He held my eye, and despite my best intention of dragging my gaze away from his, I found I could not. Did he mean he wanted to buy me a beer? Did he mean he wanted to take me somewhere? Could he mean he wanted to take me sexually? Could he possibly be being so brazen? I hoped so.

'Where would you take me?' I asked, choosing to understand his comment to mean more than an offer of a beer.

'Wherever you want. To a restaurant. To a movie. To a new sort of ecstasy.'

He dropped the last suggestion with indecent aplomb and waited for my response with a cool confidence. I should have been offended or outraged. At the very least I should have *pretended* to be one of those things; instead I offered my phone number.

'No. I won't take your number,' he said firmly.

'You won't?' Suddenly I was embarrassed. Had I got it completely wrong? Had I misheard him? Had I imagined the chemistry which was zinging between the two of us? Had the lethal dart of attraction just struck me?

'I wait here with you until your shift is finished.'

'But that's five more hours,' I objected gently, grinning, not trying to hide my amusement.

'I have forever. I know you are worth the wait. If you give me a number, I call, you might have met another man by that time. I can't risk it. Rather I wait for you. I must not let this go. I sense it is important.'

I had heard similar before. Italians are prone to this sort of impassioned announcement – it's one of the things I like about them. But I had never felt such chemistry before. Roberto's presence made my throat dry. He'd detonated a bomb of unprecedented excitement. I felt sparkling shafts of exhilaration shoot and spread through my body. Lust lodged in my skull. Desire drenched my innards. Longing shuddered down every nerve in every limb.

The bar rapidly receded. I didn't care if there were customers to serve or crisps to fetch from the storeroom. Suddenly there was only me and this Italian man; everything other was a dull, sludgy irrelevance.

We cleaved to one another for the following five hours. By turn we chatted, laughed and silently stared at one another. He told me of his love of fast cars and football. He introduced two or three of his pals but I could barely harness their names to my memory, as he was all-consuming and everything other was less. He told me that he'd only been living in England a week but already had an interview for a job in an advertising agency in Soho.

'And your family?' I probed.

'My family have a business in the wine trade,' he said simply; then he sipped his beer in a manner which suggested he found the turn in the conversation difficult.

'A vineyard, how amazing.' I imagined rows of green vine things, like soldiers in the sunshine.

He shrugged. 'Not really. Quite normal.'

I could not comprehend how he could describe running a vineyard as normal. It must be the most romantic thing in the world. I assumed he was attempting to be modest. I wondered if they still crushed grapes by stamping in them. Probably not, some European regulation doubtless prevents it, but maybe they still celebrated festivals by producing wine through the traditional methods. The Italians are big on festivals. Not that I was sure that I'd actually want to feel grapes oozing through my toes. I'm not really that earthy. Worse yet, someone else's toes. Yuk. It's enough to send you teetotal.

He sighed. 'Actually, I have come to England after terrible argues with my family. I need to prove myself. Make career here.' I admired his independent spirit and didn't need to ask for any detail on the nature of the arguments as he added, 'Sometimes families are stifling. I need to be away from my family for a time. You understand?' I nodded enthusiastically. Yes, yes, I understood. I understood everything about this man. 'I think you really do,' he said with a gravelly voice that shook with sincerity.

A sincerity that transcended all that had gone before.

3

I was a smug bride. We married within six months of meeting one another. My parents thought that was a little hurried but I pointed out that *they'd* only known each other for three months before they got engaged. Mum tutted and said things were different 'in her day', plus they'd had a two-year engagement. Privately I believed that Mum must have had time to waste or perhaps tiny doubts about my father which needed relieving; I had neither time nor doubts so didn't see a need for a lengthy engagement. Alison hinted that we might be in lust rather than love but I dismissed her cynical insinuations with a giggly laugh; secretly I pitied Alison for not having experienced such a glorious free-fall. By default my father was the most encouraging of our speedy nuptials; his only comment being that maybe if I married I'd finally start thinking about a *real* job. He never missed an opportunity to let me know that he didn't think working behind a bar was a particularly admirable way to fill the day.

My father was right, I was thinking about a real job: a series of *bambini* – one popped out straight after the next. I did not want to be an old mum, like mine had been, and while I had two siblings the age gap was such that I might as well have been an only child. I wanted a bursting, boisterous house full of kids. I didn't bother telling my folks that, they'd only have worried about whether Roberto's relatively junior job in advertising would bring in an adequate salary to support a family. Since everyone seemed intent on worrying and finding fault with our union I didn't want to add fuel to the fire. I abhorred the lack of romance in my nearest and dearest. That's why Roberto was so perfect for me. We were both very romantic and impetuous. We recognized and admired each other's daring souls.

To me, it was delightfully simple. We were desperately, totally, firmly in love. He, like all Italians, adored my curly blonde hair and freckles. He couldn't keep his hands off me and his constant physical attention seemed to have a material effect on my body. My breasts seemed fuller and more responsive; Roberto only had to walk into the room and my nips seemed to spring to attention like rookie soldiers in the presence of an officer. My waist appeared tighter, my stomach flatter. I existed in a constant state of heightened sexuality. He was charmed at the way I pronounced 'mobile' and 'potato', he liked it that I could explain English humour to him and he loved the way I smiled all the time. He didn't mind that I didn't have an impressive degree or job. He found my obsession with all things Italian charming, flattering. He agreed that I'd make a great mum. Everything about me delighted him, nothing about me irritated him. And it was so lovely to be so thoroughly approved of.

And for my part, I simply adored Roberto. He was the embodiment of everything I'd long dreamed of. I was mad about his voice (sort of huskily heartfelt but not cheesy). I worshipped his eyes, which always focused on me, and I loved his shoulders and back, which seemed strong and perfectly in proportion to his waist. His feet were neat. His cheekbones just the right side of angular.

His clothes were immaculate and his hair was glossy to the point where I found it a trial not to stretch out and touch some part of him every time we were in the same room. He was everything I'd ever fantasized about. Loving him was easy.

We married in the UK, which was not in fact my dream. I wanted to get married in Italy. I saw myself click-clacking through a piazza in a flowing white gown and high heels. I'd be holding Roberto's hand and giggling as we led the wedding party to a stupendous *trattoria* for the enormous wedding breakfast. Onlookers would cheer and clap, wish us well and throw rice. We'd drink fine wines and eat for hours. Then we'd dance in the street, the evening would be warm long after the sun had gone down. Except Roberto pointed out that I'm not Catholic and in those days there were requirements that had to be met in terms of instruction classes, etc. if I wanted to marry in a Catholic church. It wasn't practical for us both to leave our jobs for months before the wedding just to attend instruction classes. Besides, I couldn't speak the language (I kept meaning to take lessons but never found the time) and the service would be in Italian or even Latin.

The matter was settled when my father started to suffer from seizures thanks to his dicky heart. The seizures were mild and he was probably well enough to travel, but somehow I couldn't see him dancing in the streets and struggling to communicate in Italian with his new in-laws at seventy-five years old. I figured (or actually Roberto reasoned) a more sedate Church of England wedding in my parents' local village church was the most realistic option. I knew Roberto was being the perfect son-in-law by putting Dad's health first and so I could hardly stubbornly hang on to my dream. I comforted myself with the thought that we could have the children baptized in Italy and we could parade through a piazza then.

I was surprised so few of Roberto's family could make it to the wedding. His father had died when Roberto was fourteen, but his mother was still living with her very elderly father and Roberto's sister, Paolina. Apparently the row that had caused Roberto to come to England and pursue a career independent of his family's business could not be forgotten in just six months. Around the time of our engagement Roberto made a number of calls to his mother. Even without a degree in the Italian language I understood from his tones that Roberto begged and cajoled his mother to come to our wedding. To no avail.

I wrapped my arms around his neck and tried to comfort him.

'Maybe we should wait until you and your mother sort this thing out before we get married,' I offered, although secretly dying at the idea of delaying the wedding for a single moment.

'Pointless,' said Roberto. He didn't elaborate and I didn't pursue.

Still, I had expected a host of aunts and uncles, cousins and godparents to attend. Italians *do* family, don't they? None came. They pleaded the lack of notice as an excuse, but I suspected Roberto's row with his mother had sent shockwaves through the family. I pretended to accept their excuses at face value rather than force Roberto into another tricky confrontation. For all the hours we'd spent talking about just about every subject under the sun in the previous six months, I'd never found the right time to probe into the exact nature of the 'stifling' family or the need to be away from them. Roberto had assumed I understood. An urgency for gory detail would somehow taint that assumption of connection. I chose to leave well alone. It would all come out in the wash, eventually. I didn't have to concern myself. Thank goodness, four or five of Roberto's Italian friends did come to the wedding; most brought wives and multiples of children, so his side of the church didn't look too stark in the end.

Some brides say that their wedding day did not meet their expectations. Perhaps the stress and hype just proves too much. Not me; my day was blissful. I loved every moment from dawn to dusk and beyond. My hair gleamed, my husband was handsome, my dress flattering. The flowers were fragrant, friends delighted, relatives sober. It was perfect. As I stepped down the church steps I took a deep breath. Perhaps it's just because the air in the Midlands is cleaner than in London, but I swear that I breathed in a pungent smell of possibility and I whispered to myself, 'Bring it on. Happily ever after, here I come.'

4

When I close my eyes and think of the happily ever after shebang, there are at least a dozen plump *bambini* in the picture but our happily ever after has not produced offspring with thick dark curls and velvet eyes. Nor any other type, come to that.

I'd be a good mother. I know I would. I love babies, *all* babies. I've never come across one that I didn't think was just one hundred per cent adorable. I don't even mind if they are screaming, smelly or ugly. In fact I don't accept that there are ugly ones (although Alison swears there isn't any other kind) – I think there are just some that haven't grown into their looks yet. *And* I adore kids. Lots of women like babies but not kids – or the other way round – but I don't mind. I like them when they are tottering or tearing about. When they are lisping their first few words or when they are incessantly repeating the latest catchphrase from some awful cartoon. I even like teenagers. I just want a family. A noisy, messy, demanding, *big* family. It's what I've always wanted. Isn't the *passeggiata* parade at five o'clock with said noisy, messy, demanding, *big* family part of the Italian deal?

And Roberto is an ideal dad candidate, too. He also likes kids – Italians do, don't they? And as he is patient, kind and fun – all my friends' kids *love* him.

We've been trying for years, in fact we've always tried, right back from our very first carnal encounter, which might have been a tad irresponsible but at the time responsibility was not on my mind. The physical attraction between the two of us was so absolute that we got naked within about six hours of first clapping eyes on one another and pretty much stayed that way until I had to get up to put my wedding dress on. But still no babies.

Everyone knows someone who can't get pregnant. It's the latest epidemic, but its common or garden nature does not make the situation any less heartbreaking; I think it makes it more so. Sympathy is exhausted. Hearing that a couple are struggling to conceive (I'm very careful with the use of the word infertile) is a bit like hearing that a kid has food allergies. You're sympathetic but also slightly sceptical. I mean, there were no food allergies when we were kids, were there? Isn't it possible that food allergies are a modern paranoia? And childlessness the same.

I've read every article that has ever been written on the subject. I know that the decrease in childbearing is because women are now taking responsibility for contraception (already explained that this is not my case) or that they have selfishly put their careers before their family life (what career?) or that they have delayed too long because they were constantly at the hairdresser's or the beautician's or some other hopelessly indulgent pursuit (not true, not true!). The only conclusion I can reach is that I really ought to buy a different newspaper; something less misogynist would be nice. Other articles suggest that it might be the filthy Thames water lowering the sperm count, but Roberto drinks mineral water. Or the eight hours a day that he spends in front of a laptop might be to blame. Apparently something nasty is emitted and is gnawing at his manhood, but the guy at the desk next to his has four kids, including twins. It might be additives in convenience food (bad wife, lazy wife) or it might be our stressful lifestyles, but we are not a stressy couple, at least, we weren't.

Or it could just be bad luck.

It turns out it's just bad luck.

We've had all the tests. After two years of not conceiving we started the battery of examinations that many couples endure in order to discover why they aren't being blessed with a bundle. Poor Roberto – neither of us particularly enjoyed the experience but I always think men find medical intrusion much harder to bear. I'm not saying I enjoyed peeing into pots, giving blood and handing over all sorts of bodily samples but at least I'd had years of smear tests to erode my dignity by way of preparation. Before our fertility tests the most intrusive thing a doctor had ever done to Roberto was tap his knee to test his reflexes.

There's no need for me to go into exactly what we had to tolerate; as I said, everyone knows someone who has endured this modern torture. Everyone knows it's embarrassing, heartbreaking, painful, soulless and ultimately – for us at least – inconclusive. It turns out there's nothing wrong with either of us. When I first heard this I was delighted. If there was nothing wrong then we must be all right. We were told to take a holiday and have more sex. Naturally, we were happy to follow doc's orders. But after another year of going at it like rabbits and still no baby it dawned on me that being told there was nothing wrong with either of us was disastrous. If there was nothing wrong, how could we be fixed? And we did need fixing.

We returned to the doctors and asked for more tests. We wanted to know what our choices were; we wanted more options. We were given an explanation that under other circumstances would have been almost funny. Ultimately, after prolonged consultations with a large number of experts, the diagnosis they settled on was 'unexplained infertility'.

'What exactly does that mean?' asked Roberto. He didn't bother to hide his irritation and frustration. I took his hand in mine and gently squeezed. I wanted him to remain polite with the doctor. I wanted the doctor to know we were good and nice people who *deserved* a baby. I thought that showing any irritation might jinx us.

The doctor sighed and said, 'Unexplained is exactly that. It's self-explanatory.' He shrugged apologetically. 'Physically there's nothing stopping either one of you conceiving a child. Elizabeth is ovulating on time. Your sperm count is fine. There's no sign of tube damage or endometriosis. Everything is in order. You're a healthy young couple.' He pushed his glasses further up his nose and looked doubtful. 'Thirty per cent of infertility is unexplained.'

'That is ridiculous,' snapped Roberto. 'There must be more you can do.'

The doctor shrugged. He looked as tired and worn as we did. I wanted him to reassure and encourage, like some sort of sports coach, but I got the feeling that he knew we were dropping down the fertility league tables and he couldn't brook our relegation. He sighed.

'We could run a test and see if Elizabeth's vaginal fluids repel your sperm; that's often the answer in cases such as this.'

If he was intending to be more specific about exactly what this test would entail or whether he could offer us a treatment depending on the results of the test, he wasn't given the chance. Roberto leapt from the chair as though someone had put thousands of volts through it, grabbed my arm and dragged me from the surgery.

Out on the street it suddenly seemed miserably cold. An autumn wind scratched my skin and I watched leaves and litter skittering across the road. The doctor's ugly words stood on the pavement with us, more real than the longed-for pram with a chubby baby inside. Roberto swore, repeatedly and in Italian. He kicked a discarded, crushed can and then a wall. For a split second I wondered if he wanted to kick me or at least my hideous repelling juices.

'*Va fanculo* stupid doctor,' he muttered time and time again. 'He know nothing. *Nothing.*' Roberto finally dragged his eyes to mine. He stopped cursing and pulled me to his lips. The swearing and blaspheming was swallowed as he kissed me passionately. He flagged a cab, bundled me into it and gave our home address. I didn't realize I was crying until the tears splashed on to my hands, which were folded on my lap. I guess I was practising self-restraint. If my hands were free to flay I might have caused myself harm. What good was I? What was the point of me? Roberto resumed the muttering and vicious swearing and maintained it at a ferocious level for the entire journey. We were, most likely, terrifying. We must have been, because even the cabbie (normally an irrepressible breed) did not dare to pass bigotries or pleasantries.

We were barely through the door before Roberto started loosening his belt and pulling up my skirt. He yanked down my knickers and entered me almost immediately. We had sex on the stairs; urgently and angrily he rode me hard and fast. The sweat ran down his back and slipped between his buttocks. I clasped him tightly and tried to ignore the friction burns that were developing on my shoulders and elbows. He thrust over and over again, as though he was chasing something. Perhaps he wanted to go deeper than ever before. Perhaps he sought to be nearer than ever before. It was clear he thought that he was battling my murderous juices. His needy rutting was not exciting or fulfilling, it was desperate. It put me in mind of Alice chasing the crazy White Rabbit. *I'm late. I'm late.* I heard him repeatedly mutter the names of saints. He sometimes did this to delay orgasm, which I'd always thought sweet and amusing. I liked the fact that he found me so desirable he had to employ particular techniques to prolong our pleasure. That day I listened carefully and soon realized that this time he wasn't trying to counter the carnal by thinking holy thoughts; he was praying.

'This time, please God,' he whispered. Roberto and I locked eyes. His face was swimming through my tears. He kissed the wetness from my cheeks. 'This time please God. We *need* this baby.'

After he came he collapsed on to me. His body, a dead weight, desperate to make a new life. He lay still for some moments before he summoned the energy to struggle to stand. Still in his socks, with his trousers around his ankles, he impatiently kicked his clothes away and then carried me, like a new bride, to our bedroom.

There, we made love slowly and carefully for the entire afternoon. He kissed and caressed me, as though he was trying to wipe away the doctor's filthy words. With each stroke he tried to ease the misery of our uncooperative bodies and ward off the desolate thought of a childless future. His touch patched me and comforted me for brief seconds at a time and – when I let my self-hate recede – his touch excited me.

He expertly eased me from one position to the next, leaving me feeling delicate and ladylike (not true – I'm reasonably sturdy and solid); he appeared powerful and controlling. It was brilliant of him to know that I needed to feel feminine and he needed to feel masculine. The months of tests had eroded those roles and the doctor's words had desexed us in a final fatal blow.

He slowly took off the remainder of my clothes and his. He made a long, lingering trail of kisses up and down my body. He'd always been a conscientious and careful lover but that day he took us to a new level. He cupped my breasts as though he'd never held them before. He trailed his fingers along my spine and over my buttocks. He seemed to anticipate where I needed to be touched next and the pressure I required him to apply. Moaning softly, roving leisurely, so gently, as though he had all the time in the world to spend on me, his long fingertips finally provoked, and tugged, and spun me into overdrive. He made me feel wanted, needed. Thrilled and thrilling. I came and then came again. With each wave of orgasm we hoped, wished and prayed that we were creating. We wanted to believe that the doctor's hateful analysis could be willed away, that if we loved long enough, deep enough and hard enough we'd make a life. It was the best sex we'd ever had or certainly had since. It felt clean, purposeful and important. I felt passionate, consumed and joyful.

But there was still no baby.

5

We stopped talking about it. Roberto greeted the period after my right royal seeing-to in silence. He watched me throw a box of Tampax into the supermarket trolley but did not comment. There was nothing left to say.

Thirty-two with no children wouldn't actually be too bad if I wasn't married. Then people would satisfy their curiosity about my life by constantly asking me if I'd 'met anyone special?' Then you fast-forward six months and the same people would be able to ask, 'Have you named a day?' There's a natural progression to conversations about relationships. Everyone knows the script. After discussing bridesmaids' dresses and the honeymoon for a reasonable period of time, the next question is always, 'Are you thinking of starting a family, any time soon?' But Roberto and I have been married for six years and it's obvious to everyone if we were thinking of starting a family 'any time soon' then our plans are not panning out. It's embarrassing all around really. People don't know what to say to me any more. My barrenness renders them dumb.

So, for the last three years, I've pretty much confined my emotional meltdowns to the occasional outburst to Alison. If I have too much to drink or if yet another one of our mutual friends falls pregnant then I might have a moan or even a bawl, but largely I suppress my feelings of hideous self-pity which constantly battle with murderous envy and blind fucking fury and I manage to attend baby showers with a smile on my face. It's quite an achievement.

I'm still trying for a baby. Correction, *we* are still trying for a baby. Only we don't allow ourselves to indulge in imagining a family any more, at least not verbally. Roberto and I no longer talk about whether we need to move out of our small flat in order to have a proper-sized garden, we don't comment on other kids' behaviour and discuss what we'd do differently when we bring our own into the world. We don't talk about Roberto wowing our kids and their friends with his cooking skills, nor do we discuss how we'll spend family Christmases.

I still discreetly take my temperature every morning. I pee on a stick quite often too. I wait for the results. If I didn't feel ill before all of this became necessary, by now it would be easy to imagine that I have something seriously threatening. I try and have sex when there is (according to the books) the best chance of my conceiving but I know that Roberto can become resentful of this approach. So, while I know that my most fertile time is eight to eleven days after my period (and I try to have sex every night around that time), I still try to slip in a quick one at least once a week, just so he doesn't see a pattern develop.

Roberto continues to think that we should just have spontaneous loving whenever the mood takes us. He reckons that's more natural and what will be, will be. He has greater faith in the big guy upstairs than I do. My money is on the scientists. Or the natural herbalists. Or the nutritionalists. Oh, OK, I do still have the occasional word with the big guy upstairs as well. I'll take anyone's help. On the up-side, I think Roberto's grateful that we have an active sex life. Other couples who have been together as long as we have settle for once a week – tops. But then other couples who have been together as long as we have often have two kids demanding attention and breaking their sleep.

Lucky buggers.

Whenever I get my period I become insufferable. Many women are irrational, angry, spotty or greasy-skinned around this time; I realize that I am all of those things plus fat, clumsy, forgetful – oh yes – and heartbroken. Every period is a failed baby; each bleeding seems one step closer to a lonely old age. I've never enjoyed having to bleed like a split pig once a month; there was no great moment when my mum took me out to buy sanitary pads and high heels, or if there was, I've totally forgotten it. I can't remember my first time; it was not a magnificent rite of passage, it was just life. Or so I thought. I accepted the embarrassment and inconvenience and downright mess of the whole business because I thought it was a necessary evil leading to what I most wanted in life. Now the hideous hassle of having to own two wardrobes – one to accommodate fat days – seems particularly galling and pointless.

Children anchor you. I'm weightless. Floaty. Like a balloon on a string hovering above rooftops, I need my string to be held by a chubby child hand. Everyone who has ever seen a floating balloon knows it's going to burst any moment. Balloons need hands.

I wish I could embrace my childless state. After all, we're still young; lots of our friends haven't even started thinking about having babies yet. Many of our friends rent cottages for cosy weekends away in the Cotswolds in the winter and go scuba-diving in exotic locations in the summer. Many still sit in noisy bars and drink until they fall off their stools, but it's different for them. Those friends sit in noisy bars because they have a choice. They believe that the moment they do want to procreate they just have to stop drinking, pop some folic acid and zinc and then have a shag. And you know what? It normally turns out that way too. It seems that all my friends are as fertile as a 50 kilo bag of Miracle-Gro garden fertilizer.

Roberto and I do not have a choice. We sit in noisy bars because there's no point sitting at home, listening to the emptiness of rooms that should be filled with kids' chatter. I know I should probably train at something and then throw myself into my career. At the very least we should sling on backpacks and run around Australia. But I don't want to. I want to sling on a Baby Bjorn and stroll around Kensington Gardens with all the other yummy mummies.

My friends who have kids try to tell me that being a parent is not always all it's cracked up to be. They grumble about their lack of independence and the endless nights of broken sleep but then they undo all their work in one unguarded glance. I see them look at their kids and it's clear that they adore them. *Worship* them. They *love* being mothers and would not swap their babies for all the riches imaginable. I watch couples pushing kids in prams. I'm not insensible, I know that many of those couples are bewildered and bickering. Sleep-deprived and bitchy. But I long to have a domestic about who changes the next nappy.

Alison does not share my longing for a child. She stopped being a waitress when we were twenty-two and now she's got this incredibly well-paid, stimulating, meaningful role advising Britain's farmers about marketing their organic produce. PR director or something, for . . . oh, I forget. Not the Soil Association but a similar body. Anyway, it's very worthwhile and she makes a difference. I know that much. She's always being asked for comment in the *Guardian*. My brother, Max, couldn't hide the fact that he was genuinely impressed and somewhat bemused by our friendship. He doesn't credit me with serious friends, or anything serious, come to that, except maybe a serious overdraft. He couldn't help himself, he actually asked me what we find to talk about. I told him mostly we talk about lipstick and her lesbian lovers. This isn't strictly true. We do talk about lipstick and Alison is a lesbian but we talk about other things too. I just wanted to shock him into being less patronizing. Just because I don't have a child my family think I am one.

I once asked Alison if she thought it was her fulfilling job or her sexuality that made her disinclined to have kids.

'My job, I think. Oh, yes, and lack of partner. I wouldn't fancy doing it alone. I'd want to be with someone who wanted to co-parent. But maybe it is my sexuality that means I don't have the same desire to subjugate all my needs, to care for someone else or several someone elses, in a set-up that has been crushing women's creativity and eroding their independence since time began.'

I can't believe the way she talks about family life.

Alison and I agree to differ on this issue and many others. Sometimes I think Max has a point, and even I wonder how the hell we've managed to stay friends for so long. We are so dissimilar. She thinks marriage and family life are the devil's work; a family home – modern take on hell. Or at least she would think that if she didn't completely reject any concept of an afterlife as anything other than superstitious nonsense, fence-sitting or delusion. I really think there's a possibility that there's life on other planets, Jesus seemed a nice man and I'd never walk under a ladder. I haven't got the confidence to go it alone without superstition and conjecture. I don't see any appeal in being a corporate slave, not even for a worthy corporation (although I do think she wears lovely suits). She's Old Labour. I'm a floating voter who often forgets to vote at all. She can point out any city in the world on a map and she can tell you most of the main historical events that have taken place there. My under-standing of geography is limited to which act each country is putting forward for the Eurovision Song Contest.

Yet we love each other.

I think she appreciates the fact that I wasn't freaked out when she slipped out of the closet, aged twenty-three. Unlike many of her friends, I did not avoid her calls, make jokes about wearing dungarees or try to convince her that she just hadn't met the right man yet. Nor did I exclaim that she is too pretty to be a lesbian (as her mother insisted). Alison *is* very pretty, but if anything, only a woman would appreciate her true beauty. My best friend being gay has never been a problem for me, although it does cause other people more than a moment's discomfort. Her girlfriends (few and far between) are suspicious of me, as she always prioritizes our relationship over her latest lurve interest. She is not the sort to fall off the friendship radar only to reappear again a few months later, shamefaced and in need of a box of tissues.

Alison and I defy stereotypes. She is gay, but despite clichés, she's not in the slightest bit promiscuous (this has always disappointed my old boyfriends and even Roberto, who secretly long for me to fall off the heterosexual log just long enough for them to film something saucy); Alison rarely gets any action at all. I, however, have not gone longer than a few weeks since I was eighteen. I'm not promiscuous either, but I have always been a serial monogamist. The most generous way of describing the pair of us is I'm romantic, she's choosy.

Time counts. The fact that we have known each other for eleven years means a lot. Neither of us has any family in London. Roberto and I are her adopted family, she's ours. We've seen one another through the good, the bad and the ugly. She's probably the person who knows me best in the world, including Roberto, which is something he'd be horrified to hear. She's the person I ring when I get my period.

'Hiya,' I mutter. I don't bother to introduce myself, the mobile does that, and anyway of course we know each other's voices.

There's a pause. I can hear Alison type something. I bet she's checking her electronic diary.

'You got your period,' she says with sympathy. I nod but can't trust myself to speak. For the last two months I've been struggling to swallow a herb called agnus castus (also known as chaste tree berry, which seems a bit odd to me considering it's a herb that's supposed to assist in impregnation). The herb tastes like a witch's vile brew and smells so badly that Roberto threatened to divorce me if I continued stewing the thing in the kitchen. Alison knows all of this and she's been supportive of me as I tried this latest fix. Occasionally she lets her guard slip and I catch her throwing out a glance which is clearly questioning my sanity, but most of the time she manages to pretend to be optimistic.

'This month's herb of choice didn't cut it, hey?' Alison states the obvious. I appreciate the effort she makes in keeping up with my treatments and remedies. She gets me a great discount on my organic veg boxes too. 'Isn't agnus castus supposed to help restore hormone imbalance?' she asks. She really must take notes when I blub.

'Yes,' I mumble.

'But you don't have a hormone imbalance, honey. The doctor said there was nothing wrong like that.'

'Well, he might have been mistaken,' I groan. 'Something is wrong, clearly. I'll try anything.'

I'm in an internet café and I'm looking at a web page entitled '*The Natural Way to Assist Fertility*'. When I first discovered the site a few months back, I'd been quite excited. I know most of the sites related to my problem and have digested all the advice available. This site was new and therefore whispered possibility. There's a picture of a lady doctor wearing a white coat and a big smile. She's quite curvy, subliminally suggesting that she's given birth at least a dozen times. She's sat in the middle of a green alpine forest and exudes an aura of calm and confidence. I believed in her.

'The herb also helps increase fertility, it says so here,' I hiss-whisper to Alison. I'm aware that I am in a public place but I'm not as embarrassed as I probably should be. I've cried in much busier places.

'The website *claims* that the herb *might* assist. There's a difference.' I know what she's doing. She's trying to blame the website for my raised hopes so that I don't feel like a fool or a failure. 'Are there any statistics to back up this claim?'

'In one study forty-eight women, diagnosed with infertility, took agnus castus daily for three months; seven of them became pregnant during that time and twenty-five regained normal progesterone levels.'

'Right.' She doesn't comment that the survey was conducted with an insubstantial number of women to be considered scientifically robust. She doesn't point out that forty-one of the candidates did not fall pregnant. Or that we have no idea about these women's case histories or records of fertility. She doesn't say that basically I'm clutching at straws; she doesn't have to.

'Fancy a coffee?' she asks.

'Have you got time?'

'I can make time.'

We quickly decide on a coffee house near Alison's office. As I put the phone down and grab my purse and Oyster Card I consider for a moment that it must be fantastic to be Alison. She is so important she can make her own agenda at work and just pop out to see her weepy mate whenever she likes, she just has to tell her PA to field her calls. Then I consider that until I go into the restaurant tonight I am my own boss and I don't even have calls to field. I must have the better deal.

6

Alison's office is just off High Street Kensington. On a good day that's a twenty-five-minute bus ride from our flat in Chiswick; when the traffic gods are feeling cranky it can take up to an hour. Luckily, while it's a week before Christmas, it's not snowing or raining and there are extra buses to accommodate Christmas shoppers. Even so I arrive after Alison. She's already ordered two cappuccinos and two large slices of cake; hers is carrot cake, mine is chocolate. She knows I always need chocolate when my period starts.

'I'm sorry,' she says, as she pushes the gooey cake across the table towards me. The plate drags through someone else's coffee spillage.

I thank her and try to ignore the fact that the café is heaving with new mums and young children. Groups of women, about my age or younger, sit flaunting their fertility; probably just to spite me. I must not cry. It would embarrass Alison. I blink furiously and try to bash back the tears and sadness. I can't help myself, I automatically make a tally; there are three toddlers, one baby sleeping in a pushchair, one baby hooked on to its mother's veiny boob and a pregnant woman. I'd put her at thirty-two weeks, as she's blooming. Alison follows my gaze. I see her shudder involuntarily. She just doesn't get it.

'Maybe we should have gone somewhere else,' she says.

'No point, it's the same everywhere,' I admit with a

sigh. 'Mums and kids are teeming all over the place. Besides, it's not just women with bumps or babies that I envy. It's every woman who has ever produced. I envy the middle-aged ones who brag about their kids' A-level results and grandmothers who link arms with their grandson as they mooch across the road. Mothers are everywhere and they just go on and on.'

Whereas I don't see a way of continuing. Don't cry. Just don't bloody cry, I silently and fiercely instruct myself.

'Mums and babies don't frequent my kind of bar,' says Alison with a rueful grin. She means the type of place where people spill drinks down your back as they hassle to get to a seat.

'I wish I was more like you,' I tell her as I bite into the cake. Chocolate oozes around my mouth and a large blob falls on to my lap. I don't care. I greedily cram more into my mouth. I want everything to be sweeter.

'You mean you want to start fantasizing about having sex with Kylie Minogue?'

I consider it for a fraction of a second, Kylie is such a good dresser she deserves that sort of respect. 'No, not that. I envy your serenity. You don't know how painful it is to long for something so badly.'

Alison shoots me a warning look. I know I test even her patience. I guess it is a bit presumptuous assuming that she doesn't understand the meaning of longing. I know that she's coveted jobs or women in the past but my point is she's never wanted anything for *six* consecutive years. I try to joke off my previous comment.

'Some women long for strong stomach muscles or thinner thighs; I just want a swelling belly and leaky boobs.' Alison doesn't interrupt, which is encouragement enough. I fiddle with the strap of my handbag and add, 'I just feel I'm missing out.'

'How can you miss what you've never had?'

'There's nothing easier. Did this have to happen just before Christmas?' I wail.

'Well, there's always next month. New year, new start. Everyone hates January, it's a miserable month; nothing but debt and diets. You can spend the entire month in bed making babies.'

I can't be cheered. It's not that easy. Alison reaches for my hand and gives it a little pat. 'Kath, at work, miscarried.'

She's telling me this to make me feel if not better, at least not alone. She wants me to know that there are hundreds – no thousands – of women out there in the same or similar boats to mine but she doesn't know that I've even sunk so low as to loathe women who are lucky enough to have miscarried; how sick is that? My reasoning is at least they know they can conceive. I'm brutal, debased. I should be sad for this Kath, who I've only met once, and all the other women like her. I should empathize with their acute grief but my desperation has driven me past the ability to be decent.

I manage to mutter, 'I'm sorry to hear that,' but then I feel compelled to turn the conversation back to me.

'I feel I'm letting everyone down.'

'Roberto?'

'Certainly.' I shudder.

Now here's the thing, the one thing I haven't managed to confide in a soul, not even Alison. I dwell on the issue of my childlessness incessantly. I continually consider possible methods of conceiving, anything from IVF to sex on a pagan burial site in the light of a full moon. I spend hours fantasizing about giving birth, naming, dressing, feeding the child. I have my day-dreams developed to such a detailed level that I can imagine her room in college and his first car. But when it comes to Roberto, my mind goes blank. I cannot think about him and the baby, or rather the lack of baby. I cannot think what I'm depriving him of. It's just too hideous. The doctor said my juices repelled his sperm. Thinking about his valiant, battling sperm and my hideous murdering juices leaves me struggling for breath. I try to push the thought away but it's too late, a tear slaps down on to my crumb-filled plate. I'm like a leaky ship.

'You can't go on like this,' says Alison crossly. 'You can't spend the next fifteen years of your life living round twenty-eight-day cycles, punctuated with nothing other than peeing on sticks and weeping into your coffee. Something has to change.'

I know. I sniff and nod, not risking words that would surely be accompanied by a torrent of tears. I know she's right. But knowing something is sometimes harder than not knowing.

7

'I've been fired,' says Roberto the moment he walks through the door.

I am trying to dash out of the same door and I'm already fifteen minutes late for work. I'm meant to be helping out in the kitchen tonight before I start on the tables. The sous chef (a grandiose title for dogsbody) resigned yesterday, in a blur of knives and insults. We have three office parties booked in for their Christmas do. It's going to be manic. People are depending on me. I can't be late.

I sink on to the nearest chair.

'What?'

'Well, fired, redundant, let up. What is it you English say when you don't want to say what you mean?'

'Let go?'

'Yes, that's it. Regrettable, valued employee, etc., etc. Reasonable package but there's the door. Effective from immediately.'

'The week before Christmas!'

'Quite a gift, hey?'

'Why?'

'It wasn't just me. Nothing personal. Mark, Ella, Drew. A whole gang in production and someone in accounts too. We've lost three major clients in ten days.'

Roberto works (or, I suppose, rather more accurately, *worked*) in a trendy advertising company. It's all glass walls, unisex loos and flat-screen TVs in the reception. I'm too intimidated to visit often, let alone socialize with his colleagues, so I have to confess I'm not exactly certain how it all works. I know he's in the account management department. And I know that he's not the guy who comes up with the idea, or the guy that writes the ad, or the guy that films it, so I suppose he does the other bit. He calls it the client interface bit, i.e. he is paid to make the client happy and encourage said client to spend money. It's a serious blow to the agency's revenue if three clients have withdrawn their business in a short space of time; I can see that question marks will have hovered over the account management department's performance.

It would be disloyal to say so. Instead, I rush to hug him. He accepts the hug for a brief moment, then brushes me away and heads towards the fridge.

'I need a drink.'

Roberto's job is not what my parents consider a serious job and it's not what anyone would consider a well-paid job. Or at least it wasn't until last month, when Roberto was promoted from an account manager (paid a pittance, treated like dirt) to an account director (paid a wedge, treated to lunch). It was only three short weeks ago that he came home with champagne and a bonus to celebrate. I curse the fickle nature of the industry. Mark, Ella and Drew are all account directors too. I see that they have all become too expensive to save.

'Oh well, it's not the end of the world,' I comment. The end of the world is getting your period; nothing much else bothers me. I accept the glass of wine Roberto is proffering; it's clear that I can't go into work now, Roberto needs my support.

Roberto shoots me an odd look. 'You are right, Elizabeth, it is not the end of the world but I am very disappointed.' He's clamping his mouth together and I can see the pulse in his neck flicker. He looks like he's swallowed a frog.

'Well, it's not like we had time to get used to the salary, we're used to managing on not much.' And it's not like I'm pregnant or we have school fees to find.

'I'm sick of managing and getting up,' snaps Roberto.

'You mean getting by.' I correct Roberto automatically and then I consider he might mean getting up. I sometimes don't want to get up but, surely not; Roberto isn't the depressed type.

'I'd like a car and a decent stereo. I'd like to live in a home with more than one bedroom.'

I'm startled. I suppose it's true to say that when Roberto and I stopped discussing trying for a baby we gave up a number of other big conversations as well.

'You want to move?'

'Yes. I find it depressing that I can sit on the loo in the bathroom and touch all four of the walls.'

Odd, the things men get up to in the bathroom. But then, I do most of my praying there. Each to their own.

'We have never talked about moving because we have not the money, but since my promotion I started to think it was a possibility.'

Roberto opens his laptop bag. There's no laptop in it. I suppose he had to hand that back. The bag is stuffed full of details of properties, some obviously collected from a handful of estate agents, others looking as though they've been printed off from a web page. It's funny to think that Roberto has been spending hours on the web pursuing his dreams, like me; but not like me.

I pick up the top sheet. It's a small terraced cottage, typical of Chiswick. It has a pretty blue door and white shutters. But the sweet door opens out directly on to the street and I know I wouldn't be happy bringing a child up in that house. I say so and Roberto looks at me as though I ought to be committed.

'It doesn't matter now because we can't afford this house. Or any house in London.' He flings the papers in the bin. I watch the lid swing to and fro.

'You'll get another job.'

'Not as an account director.'

'As an account manager then.'

'Elizabeth, I am thirty-four. You earn nuts. I cannot be a man that is the earner of bread on that salary. Men my age are running companies.'

'*Pea*nuts and bread earner,' I correct. 'Earner of bread just sounds funny.'

I'm not sure if he hears me because he storms out of the room and slams the door behind him.

8

28 December

'You're moving to *Italy*?'

Alison sounds amazed, delighted and then wary in one sentence. Perhaps this is a record. I wonder if there are entries in *The Guinness Book of Records* about how many emotions a person can spin through in one sentence. How would you measure it? I think I'd have quite a chance at winning that, particularly when I'm hormonal; it would be nice to win something.

'When?' she demands

'Mid Jan.'

'That soon! Whereabouts in Italy?'

'Veganze, Roberto's home town. We're going to move in with Raffaella, Roberto's mother; at least to start with. We're going to help out with the family business.'

Alison's eyebrows jump up above the crown of her head. 'You're kidding,' she yells. She's so surprised that she nearly knocks over her cocktail.

'Not at all.' I try to sound calm and composed although I know exactly what Alison is going to say.

'But Roberto hates his mother. It won't work.'

Yup. Had that nailed. Wish I'd placed a bet. Of course, I anticipated Alison's reaction because mine was just the same when Roberto first suggested moving back to Italy to live and work with his family. I try to recall his argument so that I can play it back to Alison.

'Hate is far too strong a word. OK, so they had a massive falling out when Roberto came to the UK. All families have rows. From what I understand Raffaella felt abandoned but now he's going back to Italy, so there's nothing for them to fight about any more.'

'So it's "Come back all is forgiven" – the last six years of rancour are going to be swept under the carpet, just like that?' demands Alison with more than a hint of disbelief.

'More or less,' I admit carefully.

Truthfully, I have niggling doubts about the arrangement too but I so want to believe it might work. Me in Italy, at last! Roberto has made a large number of phone calls to his mother in the past week; every one of which has been very Latino and impassioned. There have been tears, yelling, reproaches, apologies and eventually laughter. Roberto assures me that Raffaella is ready to take back her prodigal son and to meet her stranger daughter-in-law. I'm sure it's all going to be fine. Wonderful.

'I've always, always wanted to live in Italy,' I gush.

'I know that was your motivation for marrying Roberto in the first place,' she replies with the horrendous, shocking frankness of a best friend who has always known everything and known it forever.

'That wasn't the only reason I married Roberto. You make it sound like I'd have married *any* Italian,' I mumble huffily.

'I didn't mean that. I know you couldn't keep your hands off one another; the attraction was obvious and instant. I'm just saying that dreaming about living in Italy might be quite a different thing from actually living there in his mother's house. This move is a big thing. You've only ever been to Italy once – when you were a teenager.'

'Hmmm. Best holiday I ever had,' I say with as wide a grin as I can muster.

I silently sip on my cocktail. Clearly, we both think moving to Italy might have its challenges. I'm trying to ignore as much, Alison seems hellbent on confronting the possibility. Unlike me, Alison insists on facts, plans and detail. She is the ultimate girl-scout and likes to always be prepared. I prefer to view life as one big adventure, full of surprises uncurling out in front of me. I hope Alison will start to talk about what she received for Christmas.

'So what is Roberto's family business?' she asks.

'They are in the wine trade.'

'Really.' Alison is impressed. 'I never heard Roberto mention that. He doesn't even drink much or show much of an interest in wine beyond the price tag, so I'm surprised. How exciting.'

'Isn't it?'

I hope Alison doesn't ask me too much about the business. Frankly, I'm not that up on it at all. We've never discussed the business beyond the very first time when he told me his family were in the wine trade. Roberto suggested going back to Italy because at least he'd have work there. He mentioned that I could help out in the bar, so his family must have one of those bars on the vineyard where tourists can taste the produce. I imagine it's very quaint. I've already chosen a whole new peasant girl wardrobe for my new career.

I look up and see that Alison's face is contorted with worry.

'I thought you'd be pleased,' I say huffily. 'After all, it was you who said that something had to change in my life. You as good as said Roberto and I were in a rut. When he was made redundant we were forced to have a number of different conversations and it was clear that he had a series of things that he was dissatisfied with here in London. This is a great solution.'

'Well, it's fantastic that you two are talking about the big things *at last*.' She pauses, waiting for me to respond, but I ignore her heavy emphasis.

'I'm looking forward to seeing Paolina again,' I say cheerily. 'I think we might become really good friends.'

Roberto's sister Paolina has visited us on two or three occasions. She's extremely graceful and polite. Truthfully, she was rather over-keen on sightseeing for my liking. She wanted to visit every museum and gallery in London. I was happy enough to tramp for miles around the shops but after that I introduced her to my parents. Her passion for depressing old churches and willingness to sit through deathly boring recitals meant that they were more than glad to entertain her. They reported back that they were utterly impressed with her. I couldn't help but wonder if she was the daughter they wished they'd had.

Paolina is exquisite to look at. She has the tiniest limbs I've ever seen. She's so delicate that whenever I stand next to her my average size body seems to take on elephantine proportions, which leaves two options, eat less or stand at the other side of the room. I opted to stand at the other side of the room during her visit. Roberto told me she loves food and eats whatever she wants. It would have been hard not to hate her until I discovered that this was absolutely not the case, just the kind of thing a devoted but rather unobservant brother might believe. If Paolina has a ferocious appetite she manages to effectively subdue it; she rations herself to portions fit for Thumbelina. Honestly, she can make an olive last ten to fifteen minutes. Natural skinny girls appal me. Starving to be thin is not for me. I think it's a ludicrous way to live, but at least if a skinny girl is suffering to be thin I sort of give her grudging respect and recognize some sort of justice in there somewhere. If Paolina had been naturally thin I doubt our relationship would have had a future; as it is she and I get along well enough. And well enough isn't such a giant leap from best friends, is it? We're sisters – well, almost. I imagine we'll become inseparable within days.

And I have great hopes for my relationship with Raffaella too. After all, *I've* never rowed with her. I've never even spoken to her. She can't dislike *me*. Roberto never expected the bad feelings to linger for so long. When we first married he used to insist that things would smooth over as soon as we had children; new babies are very bonding. So of course things never smoothed over. But we're going to mend bridges. I'm not daunted. I'm going on a charm offensive. Besides, I'm pretty sure that I will be presenting her with her first grandchild within the year and then everyone will be smiling.

My new-found confidence comes from another article I read on that website – the one with the curvy, smiley lady sitting in the forest. It said that the natural approach to fertility is and has always been enormously successful. And that's largely because fertility is *multi-factorial*, meaning that there are many, many elements that can be at the root of fertility problems.

The article went on to say that a study conducted by the University of Surrey showed that couples with a previous history of fertility problems who made changes in their lifestyle, paid attention to their diet and took nutritional supplements had an 80 per cent success rate. Given that the success rate for assisted conception is around 20 per cent, that's a cheering statistic. Obviously it's worth considering.

Duh. Why didn't I think of it before? We've been careful about our diet and I've taken the (endless) relevant supplements but we've never addressed the other bit; the big bit – a change in lifestyle. Everyone knows sun is good for growing things. Why not for growing babies? As soon as I read the article I knew that moving to Italy was *exactly* what Roberto and I needed. We don't get enough sun here in London. Even over the last couple of years, when we've had global-warming-enhanced summers, I still can't claim to have developed an actual tan.

Our flat boasts a London backyard but only the very cockiest estate agent would have the balls to describe it as a garden. When I sunbathe there I am less than a foot away from our Sky dish and three foot from the neighbour's Sky dish. There's a telephone pylon practically sitting on my lap. There's no grass, just a few dried-up plants in cracked pots. The only greenery is the mould climbing up and out of the rubbish bin. It's not a place conducive to long spells of sunbathing.

Many of the articles I've read on fertility suggest that fresh air (the old-fashioned stuff) – for about six hours a day – might help in some way, so I try to get fresh air as often as I can. We eat outside whenever it's not snowing or raining. This can also be attributed to the fact that we haven't space for a dining table inside our flat and as Roberto is Italian he really cannot bring himself to eat his supper from a tray in front of the TV. We do have a small but unbelievably heavy, square wooden garden table and four clunky chairs. The set was once 'the thing' from Habitat and cost a couple of weeks' wages. But now it's impossible to have a meal without getting a splinter; apparently we should have rubbed teak oil or something into the wood every six weeks or so. We should dump the table, it's useless. Maybe it's a good thing we don't have a child. It would probably die through lack of regular varnishing and a waterproof covering in the winter.

There are parks in London; beautiful ones. But the vast majority of the seven million Londoners have equal or less personal space than us, and so on hot days London parks are reminiscent of very industrious ant colonies. Except none of the ants are working together; instead they are all prepared to go to war for an extra inch of space for their picnic rug.

My conclusion is that London equals no sun, no fresh air and no space. Add to that poor wages, long working hours and hectic commutes and it's little wonder I haven't conceived. I push to the back of my mind the fact that wherever I turn in London I bump into a pregnant woman, proving that, whatever stresses there may be involved in living in a vast Mediapolis, it clearly doesn't annihilate everyone's fertility.

'Won't you miss your flat?' asks Alison.

'We're not selling, just letting it out.'

But no, I won't miss it. We've lived in the flat for six years – that amounts to seventy-two opportunities to have a family and I've botched every one of them. The place is crammed with the ghosts of what might have been. Besides, in Chiswick the GapKids is almost next door to the smart convenience store which is open twenty-four hours a day. So at midnight, when I am obsessing about my lack of children and desperately need to be in possession of chocolate or alcopops, I make a mad dash for the store and am brought face to face with cutesy displays of dinky socks and T-shirts with charming motifs. It's a form of torture. I've often thought of writing to the council to try to get Gap's lease revoked. I could use my mental stability for grounds of objection or something. Couldn't they relocate to the other end of the high street, at least until I conceive?

'So you are sure you're ready to leave London?' Alison probes. 'The nightlife, the fab restaurants, the shops?'

'I'll miss you, but London is so busy and crazy. I no longer belong here.'

The only people who belong less than I do are mothers with kids and pushchairs. I see them struggle up and down the stairs at Tube stations. I've heard the impatient tuts as a mother pulls out her breast in a smart restaurant and starts feeding her hungry baby. The skinny people aren't grateful for the hush; they are offended by the most natural thing in the world. London is an accepting melting-pot, rightly tolerant of any religion, race or sexual proclivity but intolerant of motherhood. Perhaps my body can sense the city's reluctance to embrace.

I take a deep breath and grin broadly. None of this is going to be a problem any more. Everyone knows that

Italians love kids. There will be an abundance of wide open spaces, fresh air and sun. I'll probably be pregnant before we get through passport control.

9

Veganze is an ancient centre of grape cultivation in the province of Vicenza, in the Veneto. I am a bit confused as to exactly what that means geographically; a village inside a county, inside a region – I guess. I'm finding Italian geography a bit tricky, what with its numerous provinces and regions and names of cities that are inconveniently similar to names of other towns that just happen to be right next door. However, I have repeated the phrase, 'Veganze is an ancient centre of grape cultivation in the province of Vicenza, in the Veneto' often enough in the past few weeks to at least give the impression of authority and knowledge.

Throughout the crazily busy last few weeks, while I've been packing, sorting and discarding my worldly belongings, cleaning, advertising and renting our flat, browsing and buying a new wardrobe, and planning, catering and throwing a tremendous leaving party, I have found a little bit of time to read up on Veganze.

I don't want to appear totally ignorant on arrival.

I have bought several huge fat guidebooks about Italy. But I was disappointed to discover only one of them mentions Veganze, which suggests Roberto's home town is more of a home village. None of the designer brands have flagship stores or even factory outlets in Veganze.

Then again I ought to be thankful there are no galleries or museums. It saves me the effort of feigning interest in them.

The guidebook informs me that the finest wines of the area have been sent to the market in Veganze for centuries, to be shipped from there to many parts of the country. In the second half of the nineteenth century, the vineyards of the region were practically destroyed by phylloxera (I'm not exactly sure what that is but it sounds awful – definitely worse than a heavy cold). Apparently, phylloxera made its first appearance in Italy precisely at Veganze. I hope it is long gone and I hope it's a disease that's restricted to grapes and not something that can in *any way* effect fertility in people. I make a mental note to look up phylloxera next time I'm on the web. They must at least have an internet café in Veganze.

I continue reading and discover that when the vineyards were replanted, the Pinot Bianco and Nero, Cabernet Franc and Cabernet Sauvignon varieties were introduced. And that step provided local growers great and immediate satisfaction. I imagine the local growers rolling around drunk and I smile to myself.

'What is our business?' I ask, turning to Roberto. 'Pinot Bianco, Pinot Nero, Cabernet Franc or Cabernet Sauvignon?'

Roberto is listening to his iPod and totally engrossed in the lyrics of some Arctic Monkeys track. Song lyrics mystify him. For years he thought Oasis were singing about being chained to a mirror and roller blades rather than razor blades, in 'What's the Story Morning Glory'. I thought his mistake was cute and never had the heart to correct him. When he answered a pub quiz question incorrectly as a result, he was furious with me. We've both been so frantic preparing for this short flight (which is also the longest journey of my life), we've barely had a chance to talk about the actual logistics of how we'll live our lives once we reach Veganze. I want to ask a few questions before we touch down.

Roberto accepts water from the air steward and then removes his headphones. I repeat the question. This time I don't have to look at the guidebook as I've already memorized the names of the wines.

'We sell them all.'

'Really! My God, our business must be enormous.' I like saying 'our business' – although technically I have no equity in the vineyard, I *am* family and therefore, as it's a family business, I feel entitled to describe it this way.

'No, quite small really,' says Roberto.

I'm confused; how can a *small* vineyard grow enough grapes to produce four different types of wine? I'm no expert but don't all those wines require various grapes which presumably require different types of soil? Isn't that the idea; chalky, peaty or er . . . muddy soils all produce different types of grape?

'So what grape, exactly, do we grow?' I ask.

It is Roberto's turn to look confused. 'Grape? We don't grow any grapes.'

'We buy them? I can't see how this works at all. I mean don't we need enormous amounts to produce all those wines?'

'Sorry?' Roberto is staring at me as he does when I try to explain the plot of *EastEnders* – or the point of *EastEnders*, come to that. He thinks I should invest thirty minutes, four times a week, in real people rather than watching soaps.

'Look, just start from the beginning and talk me right through the process. I clearly have no idea how vineyards operate or how wine is produced.'

'Vineyard? We don't own a vineyard.' Roberto looks shocked.

'We run one, though?' I ask uncertainly. I think I already know the answer.

'No.'

'But you said your family were in the wine business.'

'We have a bar. My mamma runs a bar. We own that.'

I flop back against my headrest and try to digest this information. A bar. A bar! I've worked in countless bars in London. The work is hard, smelly and relentless. I thought I'd left all that behind me.

'When we met you said your family were in the wine trade.'

'They are.'

'And I assumed you meant they had a vineyard. You didn't correct me.'

'Probably not then, I was trying to impress you.' Roberto leans towards me and kisses the end of my nose; he grins at me as though I am the most amusing creature on earth. I don't feel amusing, I feel stupid.

'But I bought a long white linen gypsy dress,' I stutter. I don't add that I spent a bomb on it. 'It's not suitable for bar work.'

'Or indeed vineyard work, I imagine,' he says pleasantly. 'I said that you would work in the bar. You agreed.'

Yes, I did, didn't I? I am furious with myself for not taking a greater interest and probing further into the exact nature of Roberto's family business. On the couple of occasions that Paolina has visited us I have heard them talk about customers, suppliers, rent. I thought he meant rich American tourists buying cases of European wine to lay down, not backpackers who were thirsty to neck a bottle of beer. It's not always easy to keep track of their conversations; they mostly talk in Italian when they are together, even if I am there.

Roberto sees that I am crestfallen. 'Don't look so sad. You will be amazing in the bar. All your experience will be invaluable. We will work side by side. It will be a great challenge. Lots of work but lots of fun.'

Roberto quickly kisses me with affection, shakes his head and then starts to chuckle to himself. I can't see what's so funny.

IO

Italy smells just as I remembered it: delicious. Even in the airport there is a vivid aroma of strong coffee sweetened to treacle. Beautiful, slight women glide past me, leaving behind the scent of clean hair, clean bodies, clean clothes and the latest designer perfume. The young men also smell delicious and I swivel my head to follow their scent, which twice almost causes me to trip up over someone's suitcase.

One or two of the older men smell of bitter, stale sweat, which practically makes my eyes water, I'd forgotten that.

I fight my way through the cigarette fog, which is strange to me now that smoking is prohibited in Britain's public places. I'm normally apathetic about anything political but I did sign a petition to get smoking banned. The smoke crackles in my throat, no matter how much water I drink. I want to like everything but the smoke is annoying.

Roberto has hired a car. We plan to buy one as soon as we can, although I'm nervous about driving on the right-hand side of the road. By the time we drive from Verona to Veganze I'm nervous about driving at all. I'd forgotten how fast and aggressively everyone drives here. Every car wears a bang or a scratch almost like a badge of honour. I wonder if Roberto took out the extra insurance to waive the excess. Plus, the roads are pockmarked with potholes so I'm sure we are going to burst a tyre. Still, I admire the Italians who are having too good a time to waste it digging up roads. In Britain I sometimes think we do little else other than dig up roads. With relief I note that some things *have* changed. Everyone now, very sensibly, wears a helmet while driving a scooter or motorbike. I approve. I remember when I visited as a teenager no one would risk messing up their haircut by wearing a helmet, so a sickening number of floral tributes and elaborate shrines littered the roadside.

I make an effort to turn my thoughts away from such grimness and concentrate instead on the scenes that are flashing past outside.

'The countryside looks glorious, hey?' asks Roberto with a wide and relaxed beam. I haven't seen him smile in such an open way for a long time, so I nod enthusiastically. It's a lot colder than I expected. I'm already regretting my ruthless pruning of my winter wardrobe and my insistence that I'd only need a light mac. Secretly I'm longing for my thick winter coat, which I left behind with Alison. I daren't grumble to Roberto because he said I was being stupid giving all my winter clothes to friends and the charity shop. He kept telling me that it was just as cold in north Italy in the winter as it was in the UK. I'd sort of thought that he must be mistaken or joking. After all, Italy is hot, isn't it? OK, not all year round, like in Africa, but I was certainly expecting it to be a few degrees warmer than Blighty. My memories of the place are all bathed in orange sunlight.

Right now there's snow on the mountains and the fields are waterlogged. But the light in Italy is always beautiful. The pale winter sun valiantly shines, offering if not warmth then at least a beautiful pink hue. I watch as the sun begins to set behind the mountains and amber rays gently slip and seep on to the fields as they have done for thousands and thousands of years. Somehow everything seems older in Italy, which is ridiculous. I'm aware that the sun has set on land masses that are recognized as Britain for the same length of time as the sun has set on Italy; however, there is something at once timeless and dignified about the air here.

We arrive at Veganze at about seven. It's pitch black but with the help of street- and head-lights I stare at the streets that now belong to me. Roberto excitedly gives me a running commentary on the places of interest.

'Veganze's central focus, somewhat atypically, is a T-junction rather than a square, although it's still referred to as a piazza.'

I want to show my enthusiasm but most of the buildings are functional rather than beautiful. I fall with relief on the only exception. 'That's impressive.' I point to a grand, creamy-custard-coloured church that is flanked by an enormous tower.

'The tower is over a hundred metres high and over a century old,' says Roberto proudly.

I nod, silently committing the facts to memory. I can already imagine giving my parents this guided tour when they come to visit me. I'd like to impress them with a bit of local knowledge.

The streets are cobbled, and while they're nominally pedestrianized I watch cars drive and park right outside the bars where people are taking drinks and eating cakes. I mildly resent the cars as they somewhat break the idyll, but no one else seems put out. The shops are just closing. Owners rattle large bundles of keys while customers wave their goodbyes and then scuttle home to the warmth. I quickly total up the facilities the town offers. There's a chemist, a shop that sells all manner of plastic (toys, deckchairs, buckets and mops), a shirt shop, a bakery, a hairdresser's. Hmm, I was hoping for more. There are also three banks and at least four bars.

'Which is our bar?' I ask Roberto.

'It is not on the square.'

'Oh.'

'We passed it driving in, but not to worry, we will see it soon enough.'

I'm nervous that he didn't point it out to me; is it a wreck? I push the thought away and concentrate on the innumerable mysterious shuttered buildings. I hope they are shops.

'The streets are emptier than I expected,' I comment.

'But then it is bitterly cold and it's after *passeggiata* and yet too early for the teenagers to hang out,' reasons Roberto.

I can imagine the teenagers, now boisterous but harmless, leaning on their mopeds. There are a couple of resilient old guys chatting happily outside one of the bars and a young family, the mother (heavily pregnant) pushing the empty stroller as her husband stays close to their giddy toddler who is rushing ahead chasing pigeons. It's frustrating that the place is practically deserted but it's adding insult to injury that the only woman in sight is pregnant. I shudder.

'I said you'd be cold,' tuts Roberto.

I don't want to give him the opportunity to say I told you so and so inadvisably I rush to explain the true cause of the shudder. 'I was just looking at that family.'

Roberto's gaze follows the direction I am pointing in.

'Elizabeth.' He sounds weary.

'What? I'm not sad. It might be a good omen. Mightn't it?'

Roberto doesn't reply but instead says, 'That one is Mamma's home.'

He points to a building that is unremarkable in every way. It's painted a shadowy grey colour, rather than rich terracotta or warm yellow like many of the other buildings scattered about. It looks neither well kept nor dilapidated. There are no plants or hanging baskets decorating the sills or balcony but then there's no peeling paint either. The large, rectangular shutters are clamped down and for reasons I can't quite explain they put me in mind of a toddler refusing food. There is a modern bell and intercom next to the door; I had imagined a large brass knocker. As Roberto's finger stretches towards the buzzer the door flings open.

'*Mio figlio, mio figlio!*'

I I

It crosses my mind that I have never actually been inside an Italian home before, but still, I know exactly what to expect. I'm thinking high ceilings, marble floors, stylish arrangement of furniture, a warm, large kitchen with a pan of pasta on the stove and a bowl of fruit on the table. Raffaella's house does not disappoint, but there are elements that are unanticipated. The ceilings are high and the floor in the hall is marble, but both facts appear to be effectively disguised by a scattering of dusty, mismatched rugs on the floor and by a hideous brown flowered wallpaper which is peeling at the skirting board. With a lot of excited fuss, jubilant shouting, waving of arms and kissing we are ushered into the living room, which at first glance appears extremely small. After a while I realize it is in fact a reasonably big room – it's simply packed with dark, heavy furniture which makes it feel as though the walls are closing in. In fact, there's so much furniture that it's quite difficult for us all to squeeze into the room. I hang back a little, allowing Raffaella, Paolina and the old grandpa to welcome Roberto.

There's a huge dining table with eight chairs stood against one wall but it's clear that this dining table does not get used. It's pushed close to the wall so that three of the seats cannot be accessed. It's made of a deep mahogany wood that is polished to resemble an icy lake. I'd be terrified to put crockery or cutlery on to the gleaming surface for fear of scratching. There are two leather arm-chairs that are heavily stuffed and a small wooden two-seat settee which looks uncomfortable as the only padding is a thin, embroidered rectangular cushion. I note that home crafts seem to be alive and well in Veganze – besides the embroidered cushions, traycloths and table runner, it looks as though the room is suffering from a terrible case of measles – there are crocheted head- and arm-rests on the chairs and a plethora of crocheted place and drink mats dotted all over the place.

There's an enormous dresser groaning under the weight of beautiful earthenware. I quickly count that it's a set for at least twelve. There are dinner plates, pasta plates, soup dishes, side plates, dessert bowls, tea cups and saucers, espresso cups and saucers. I smile to myself imagining the hours Mamma-in-law and I will spend together in the kitchen preparing wonderful dishes for friends and family that we'll serve from the beautiful hand-painted bowls. I've (repeatedly) heard from Roberto that Raffaella is a great cook; I'm not a great cook but I'm determined to learn. I wonder if she has any secret family recipes that she'll pass on to me and whether crochet is hard to pick up. Pictures and photos are squeezed into every inch of available wall space. The pictures are mostly slightly creepy sketches of birds and fish, but I'm keen to browse and take a better look at the sepia photos. I consider that there will be plenty of time for that. Raffaella has finally released Roberto from her wide arms and I see my moment. Roberto sees it too.

'Mamma, this is my wife, Elizabeth,' he says in Italian. His voice is proud and confident.

I step forward, squeeze in among them, and move to hug my mother-in-law.

'*Piacere*,' she says stiffly.

Disappointingly, there is nothing about my mother-in-law's face to suggest that she does think our meeting is a pleasure. I put my arms around her and while she does not pull away from my embrace I sense that every fibre in her body is silently resisting it. Immediately embarrassed that I've been too forward, I quickly break away. How silly of me! I've been day-dreaming about an immediate and entire welcome into Roberto's family and I'm expecting too much. Of course Raffaella is a little uncomfortable with me; this meeting is long overdue. I shouldn't have tried to rush things.

Raffaella takes a step back and starts to rattle on again in Italian. It's clear she's offering Roberto something to eat. She keeps pointing towards the hostess trolley which is situated between the comfy chairs and the austere two-seat settee. It's full of fruit and cheeses, olives and other delicious-looking antipasti that I don't know the name of. I'm very hungry; while Roberto is shaking his head and refusing food, I'm staring meaningfully at the focaccia, desperately hoping to be offered a plate. I'm not.

I so want to make a good impression with my new Italian family. I decide that I must seize the moment to energetically recite my parrot-learned expressions. I ask after Raffaella's health and say how happy I am to meet her at last. She stares at me in confusion.

'*Che? Che? Parla Italiano. Parla Italiano.*' She shrugs, puts her hands to her ears and rolls her eyes at Roberto, Paolina and their old grandpa, who is now sitting quietly in one of the over-stuffed chairs.

65

I repeat my comments to him this time, slower and louder. I'm pretty sure I have the pronunciation spot on. For goodness sake, it's just a greeting; I can't have muddled that, can I? Roberto's grandpa offers me a toothless grin in reply but he doesn't look as though he understands much. I'm not sure if that's me or his age. I try for a third time to tell Raffaella that she's looking well. Once again she rolls her eyes and shrugs. Roberto and the senile old grandpa grin affably with her, not understanding my embarrassment. A bucket of icy water sloshes over me. This time I understand Raffaella's point with stunning clarity. There's no language barrier between the two of us. Her gestures manage to insult me and fool the others at the same time; they think she's being funny. I suppose she is, but not in the ha-ha sense. I see at once that she is a woman to be reckoned with and that she'll be expecting me to work hard for her approval.

Paolina seems to understand Raffaella's gesture too and kindly tries to come to my rescue. She translates my questions and Raffaella's responses.

'*Mamma, lei sei*, "*Buonasera. Come sta? Piacere.*" Elizabeth, Mamma says, "What? What? Speak Italian. Speak Italian!"'

Paolina means well but her efforts to translate just add to my embarrassment. Frustrated and cross, I mutter, 'I *am* speaking Italian.' Roberto simply smiles and nods, all the nuances and friction drifting over his head; he pops an olive into his mouth.

Raffaella sits in the second comfy chair and pushes Paolina and Roberto into the wooden two-seat settee; I linger, unsure where to plonk myself. The floor looks dusty and Raffaella has her feet on the footstool, so I drag out a heavy dining room chair and sit in that. For reasons

I can't quite explain – something to do with Raffaella insisting that she doesn't understand my attempts at Italian or maybe the fact that she hasn't even offered me so much as a slice of tomato – I daren't pull the chair to join the semicircle of chat but just move it enough so I can squeeze into the seat. Roberto glances my way and mouths, 'You OK?'

I don't want to make a fuss so I vigorously nod and grin like a mad Cheshire cat. He beams at me, easily reassured.

I see what has happened here. Raffaella has totally forgiven her son his six-year silence. She's embraced him fully and firmly. But at the same time she has a need of a target for her resentment and fury. She's been angry for a very long time and that anger has not vanished in an instant. No, she's found a new vessel into which she can pour her umbrage. Me.

I spend an uncomfortable evening trying to follow the conversation but I fail miserably. Trying to follow a conversation in a language I don't speak reminds me of the occasions when I'm the only sober person at a party of drunks, or worse, the only drunk with a bunch of teetotallers. I do recognize the words 'my family', which Raffaella repeats with greater and greater enthusiasm as the night progresses and the grappa is sunk, but pretty much everything else escapes me. It soon becomes clear that when Raffaella is talking to Roberto she seems to have only two modes of communication: garrulous and very garrulous. Her soliloquies, directed towards him, are punctuated with grandiose hand gestures and hugs. He accepts her affection and noise with a resigned shyness that's quite touching. I only wish I could understand what she was saying or that some of her affection was directed my way. Still, I can't expect miracles. At least it's good news that the two of them are getting on so well.

After about an hour Paolina brings me a plate of food and hangs around to chat while I munch.

'Mamma is so pleased Roberto has come home,' she says.

'I can see that.'

'And you too, of course,' she adds, colouring slightly. Neither of us is really convinced, but it's pleasant of Paolina to pretend I am at all important to the family. 'You'll have more time with Mamma another day,' she says apologetically.

'Naturally she's excited to see her son after such a long time. We'll become friends soon enough; I suppose these things can't be instantaneous,' I reply cheerfully. I'm hoping to convince the two of us.

Paolina quickly nods. 'They are talking business. The bar is in quite a bit of trouble,' she adds gravely.

'Is it?' I'm munching the most delicious cheese, otherwise I might be more alarmed to hear this.

'We don't make much money. Mamma is too old to run a bar that will attract the young crowd. You with your bar experience and Roberto with his advertising ideas and knowledge will make a big difference, I'm sure.'

'Oh yes, probably. This bruschetta is delicious. Did you make it?' I ask.

'No.'

'Your mamma?'

'No, it is bought from shop.'

'Oh.'

Paolina pats my hand, 'Well, don't worry about the bar. I am sure that you can make it work.'

I nod. 'I'm sure we can,' I say with a confident grin.

She pauses and then leans in to hug me. 'It's so nice that you are this positive.' She pulls away and for a moment I think she looks a little concerned, but then she adds, 'I'm tired. I'm going to bed. I probably won't see you in the morning. I leave the house quite early.'

'Where do you work?' I know Paolina is a solicitor but I know little else about her.

'I work in Padova.'

'I know Padova. It was the first Italian city I ever visited,' I gush.

'Really?' Paolina beams. 'Where else have you visited in Italy?'

'Erm, that's it.'

'Oh.' The conversation is bunged up by this confession.

After a couple of moments I think to ask. 'Is Padova a long commute?'

'It's about fifty-five kilometres away. I drive. It takes about forty minutes if the traffic is good. I work quite long hours so I really should be getting to bed. Good night and good luck tomorrow.'

So she's not concerned then, just tired. There's nothing to worry about.

I2

At midnight Roberto turns to me and gives me a weary smile.

'Mamma has been talking about the bar and some of our challenges.'

'Yes, Paolina said so.'

I want to sound bright and interested but I'm knackered and just need my bed, so I don't prolong the conversation by asking exactly what those challenges are; we can talk about it in the morning. *Domani domani* has always been an Italian philosophy which I respect. Roberto asks me if I'll give him a hand bringing the suitcases in from the car. Raffaella watches as we struggle to drag the suitcases into the house; then she kisses Roberto on both cheeks and turns to go up the stairs.

'*Ciao*,' I call after her, rather lamely.

'*Buona notte*,' she replies formally.

'I don't think I made a particularly good impression,' I whisper to Roberto. I pull a face and he in return pulls me into a hug.

'I thought you were very polite. It was kind that you allow Mamma and me to catch up with our news; very thoughtful. I'm sure Mamma think so too.'

'I think she just assumes I'm dull and haven't anything to say for myself.'

'Impossible. When she gets to know you better she'll love you, almost as much as I do.' He smiles at me and his smile manages to massage away some of my insecurities. He squeezes me into a tight, long bear-hug but it doesn't last quite long enough for me, because when he pulls away he says, 'I'm afraid Mamma has not had time to arrange the bedrooms. Tonight you will sleep on a mattress in Paolina's bedroom and I am to sleep on the couch in Grandpa's room.'

'Oh no,' I groan. I just want to hold him tonight, all night. I know I should be feeling on top of the world, I'm finally here in Italy, but oddly I feel just the tiniest bit nervous, a little out of my depth. Holding him would help.

'I know, a pain, isn't it?'

'I don't understand. Isn't there a spare room for us to stay in together?'

'There is room but Mamma has not been able to get it ready yet. It's full of junk and needs to be cleared.'

'Your mum has known we were coming for a couple of weeks now.'

'She's been busy with our other preparation. The cooking for example.'

I haven't the heart to tell him the antipasti was shop-bought. It seems petty to mention it and we are both so tired we might start to bitch at one another. I just need to get to bed – or at least I need to get to the mattress on Paolina's floor.

My restraint is rewarded as Roberto kisses me for a long, lingering time. It's cosy and comforting. I don't know how I'll sleep without the warmth of his body. The house is freezing the moment you move away from the fire.

'We'll make plans for the bedrooms tomorrow or

at least as soon as possible,' he promises, and then he kisses the top of my head. 'Now go upstairs and get some sleep.' He beams at me. 'Just think, Elizabeth, we are here in the Italy of your dreams. Can you believe that?'

No, I can't quite believe it, but we are indeed in Italy.

I 3

16 January

When I wake up it takes a moment for me to become orientated and remember where I am. Paolina's bed is empty; presumably she's already left for work. I hope she doesn't work late tonight; I feel I need her around, as she's the only family member who has said more than two words to me so far. I stretch and rub my arms and legs in an effort to keep warm and to nudge out the cramp; that certainly wasn't the most comfortable night's sleep I've ever had.

There's a tap at the door.

'Roberto,' I squeal – I'm delighted to see him. I pull him towards me and although he's fully clothed I try to edge my fingers under his jumper and run my hands across his back. 'Sleeping separately and sneaking around the house first thing in the morning like a teenager is quite a turn on,' I giggle.

I lead him towards the bed and ease him on top of me. We start to kiss and Roberto's hand is wiggling up my thigh when suddenly he pulls away from me. He sniffs the sheets.

'Not on Paolina's bed. It smells of her. I feel weird,' he says.

'Point taken. How about the mattress?'

We fall on to the mattress and Roberto continues to

kiss me for a minute but then reluctantly disengages. 'I wish we had time but we don't. Come on, you need to get dressed. We have a busy day. Plus Mamma has made breakfast. It's disrespectful to make her wait.'

Looks like it's me who will have to wait then.

I cautiously feel my way around the house. It's all pretty daunting. The bathroom is ancient and it's clear that it's not even on nodding terms with Mr Muscle or any other cleaning product. To think the Italians were the people who were responsible for the introduction of hot and cold running water, steam baths and early lavs. This one looks as though it hasn't been cleaned since Caesar was putting his royal bum on the throne. Of course, some of my friends have dirty bathrooms back home but this is Italy, I wasn't expecting it. The floorboards squeak on the landing and on the stairs. The place seems big but I haven't got the nerve to look behind all the doors that are slammed shut. The whole place is draughty. I remind myself how much I always hated the wall-to-wall carpets, central heating and starched nets that are a feature of my own family home. Haven't I always wanted charm and character from the place where I lived? I suppose I just hadn't realized how much dust and grime accompanied charm and character. Still, it hardly matters, it's not as though Roberto and I are going to stay here forever. We'll just be staying with Raffaella until we can find our own place to rent. Then we can have the towering ceilings and marble floors but we'll have more stylish duvet covers.

I am last down to breakfast, which takes place in a dining room where there's another equally huge mahogany table. I'm relieved to see it's protected by a cloth; at least I won't scratch it. That said, I've never been keen on tablecloths; stems of glasses always seem to become entangled, leading to spills.

Raffaella drops a heavy plate of fatty meats in front of me. Irrationally, I think of feeding my uncle's Alsatian dog.

'Actually, I'm vegetarian, sorry. I eat fish – at a push – but not meat.'

I look beseechingly at Roberto, waiting for him to translate. He's already eaten his breakfast and is drumming his fingers on the cloth waiting for me to be done too. He briefly delivers a translation; I hope he injected the nuance of my 'sorry'. I really am, very much so.

Raffaella stares at me horrified; she looks as though I have just confessed to urinating in the urn holding her great-aunt's ashes. She says something in reply, rushes towards me and pinches my cheeks as though I'm a baby in a pram. Roberto grins and then translates.

'Mamma says she thought you were a little pale last night and that she was worried about you. Maybe you are anaemic.'

'Well, that's sweet but tell her not to worry, I take an iron supplement and so there's no cause for concern. Vegetarianism is very healthy if properly managed.'

Roberto patiently translates for me. His mother throws her hands in the air and turns to me. She shakes her head sadly.

'What did she say?'

'She said that there is no such thing as a vegetarian in Italy,' says Roberto.

'I haven't touched meat since I was nineteen, Roberto. I'm not going to eat this. Not even to ingratiate myself with your mother.'

Roberto shrugs, 'No problem.'

I look around the table. There's some bread and honey. I reach for it and push the plate of dead cow and pig to one side.

I eat in silence.

It's a cold and grey morning, but even so as I close the door on the house I feel grateful to be scurrying to the bar. I'm sure that it's just teething trouble but I can't help but think that there is definite tension between Raffaella and me. I don't know what I've done wrong but I must fix it as soon as possible. I silently fret for about two minutes and then I blurt.

'Do you think your mother was upset about the vegetarianism?'

Roberto has much longer strides than I have and I'm dashing to keep pace with him so my question comes out a little breathy and desperate as a result; shame, I wanted to try for casual and gently concerned.

'It's no problem, don't worry about it. Being a vegetarian is a little unusual in Italy, especially in my mother's generation, but certainly not unheard of. I'm sure tomorrow she will make you some delicious eggs for breakfast; her omelettes are sublime.' He pulls me close to him.

Happy to accept his comfort, I change the subject. 'I'm so excited at the thought of seeing the bar.'

'Me too. But . . .'

'What?'

'Nothing.'

'Tell me.'

'Well, I'm just with worry for the things Paolina said.'

'I'm sure she's exaggerating,' I say with an encouraging smile.

It turns out that Paolina wasn't exaggerating. The bar is a disappointment. Besides the fact that it's not a vineyard, it is still some way from anything I might have hoped for. As Paolina hinted last night, it is not a thriving hub full of beautiful young Italians, decked in designer clothes, lounging on stylish stools. It is not even a quaintly old-fashioned haunt, stuffed with rustic charm and several generations of buoyant families. It's simply old, tatty and neglected. The air in the bar is stale and has all the allure of a middle-aged lady of the night.

We hurry to the bar but when we arrive we're greeted with such stillness that Roberto seems to slump a fraction and I hear him sigh quietly. Other than a couple of crusty friends of Raffaella's, the place is empty. I squeeze his hand in order to offer some support. It seems to do the trick; Roberto pulls on a mask. He cheerfully greets the old fellas, taking the time to warmly shake hands with them and chat for quite some minutes. Then he introduces me.

'*Bella, bella*,' they say with appreciative smiles, even though they are grandfathers; I love the fact that Italians are eternal flirts. After Roberto's offered each a drink on the house he grins at me and then says, 'OK, let's get this show started. Mamma said the books are kept in a back room.'

14

Because the bar is in financial trouble, Roberto's immediate and full attention is required to fire-fight. He spends ten days poring over the accounts with Paolina while I clear junk out of spare rooms and scrub floorboards. My work isn't glamorous but I enjoy feeling useful. I reason that after a week or so of this frantic activity Roberto and I will have time to take stock, discuss our future, sight-see, make love and perhaps even hunt for our own apartment. We have plenty of time ahead of us. The work is undeniably hard but there's a real buzz to be had from working alongside Roberto, building a family business. I get great pleasure from rehearsing in my head the stories I will one day tell our grandchildren.

'Your grandpa was always good with numbers and a real ideas man. I was more of a behind-the-scenes contributor but my sparkling windows were the talk of the town,' I'll say. The grandkids will roll their eyes because it won't be the first time I've told them this tale. Honing fantasies such as these make the days fly by.

Roberto hunts me out when I'm clearing out the attic.

'Hey *bambina*, I've brought you hot chocolate.'

'Thanks, I'm freezing.' I stand up, toss the scrubbing brush into the bucket and peel off my rubber gloves.

'Nice look,' says Roberto with a playful grin and nod towards the discarded rubber gloves.

'Paolina left them on my bed last night.'

'Thoughtful gift.'

'It was actually, look at my hands.' I hold them up for inspection; they have started to crack as they are constantly dipped in and out of soapy water; Paolina must have noticed.

'You and Paolina are getting on well.' I'm not sure if Roberto is asking a question or making a statement.

'Yes, when I see her. We've only spent minutes together, even though we are sharing a room. She works such long hours.' Roberto gives me a quizzical look. 'What?' I ask.

'You think she works long hours?'

'Yes. She said so.'

'I think it is a man.'

'Do you?' I'm suddenly curious, I adore a romance. Roberto, being male, is less interested in other people's love lives so he doesn't bother to pursue the thought. I don't dwell either; instead I turn my attention back to our own love life. 'I'm hoping to have this attic cleared by tonight then we can bring our mattress up here. We'll sort out a bed at the weekend.'

The attic is not a hideous black hole in the roof affair. Now I've cleared out most of the boxes and old furniture I've discovered a really lovely room with wooden floors and two skylights. I can't wait to be sleeping with Roberto again. I miss his night-time warmth.

'Actually Elizabeth, my darling, we won't be sleeping in this room.'

'We won't?' A flicker of excitement trembles inside my belly. I wonder if Roberto is going to announce that he's already found us our own place to live.

'No, Mamma will sleep in here. We will sleep in Mamma's room.'

'Oh.' The flicker is well and truly doused. I rub my back, which aches with stretching to scrub, and I consider what to say next.

'Mamma thinks the master bedroom is the most fitting for us as a married couple. She told me that the man of the Risso family has been sleeping in that bed and that room for four generations.'

Ugh, the hygiene issues which that piece of family history brings to my mind!

'That's really kind of her, but it seems daft for her to move all her clothes out of the wardrobes,' I say carefully.

'I said the same to Mamma too and she agrees, so she will leave her clothes in the wardrobe.'

'But then where are our clothes to go?'

'We'll manage.'

'Won't she miss the balcony?' I'm clutching at straws. I've put my back into cleaning this room, I've become quite attached to it; I've already started to imagine Roberto and I making love under a canopy of white cotton. I've been wondering where I'll source a four-poster bed.

'She never uses the balcony and nor must you. Mamma says it's too high, too old. A death cage, really.'

'A death trap,' I correct. 'Well, if we can't use the balcony and have no wardrobe space, what are the advantages to the master room? This attic is far nicer.'

Roberto looks pained. 'Why are you talking about advantages? Mamma is doing a good thing. She wants the tradition of our family to continue. You must understand that.'

'Well, yes, of course.' I feel guilty and ungrateful. 'It's very kind of her to offer up the master room but honestly I'd prefer moving up to the attic. I rather like the idea of us being as far away as possible from the rest of the family.'

'Why? What is wrong with them?' Roberto asks and I can hear the hurt in his voice. My guilt instantly turns to misery as I realize that I've offended him.

'There's nothing wrong with them,' I say quickly and I lean in to give him a reassuring caress on the arm. 'I just think we need some privacy.'

'Why?'

'Baby-making for one,' I grin. Concern flicks into Roberto's eyes. I know he gets tense when I mention baby-making, he thinks I think about it too much. I think he doesn't think about it enough, but we both think it is best not to draw attention to this discrepancy in perspective.

'We'll have to make love with much quietness,' says Roberto. 'We could practise now.' He grins cheekily, then puts his hand flat on my breast and starts to massage my nipple with his thumb. I make a quick calculation. I'm days away from my most fertile time of the month. There is a theory that sex just before the best time weakens the sperm and therefore makes the best time more of a second best time. I can't risk it. I move his hand off my boob.

'I'd love to but I have so much to get on with. We want this room looking nice for your mamma, don't we?'

Roberto looks a bit disappointed but shrugs. 'I guess you are right. I have much to do too.'

It's true that while I've cleared, cleaned and sorted, Roberto has run around like a mad March hare. He calls on old friends and neighbours and drums up custom by simply appealing to their curiosity. People have begun to trickle into the bar because they want to see me; I'm a low-grade circus freak – everyone is curious about the English girl Roberto married. The few patrons we have are always extremely polite and gracious with me, although I'm longing for a more robust connection than a recommendation for what I should eat. The women comment on my hair and skin and while they are always generous with their compliments I can't wait until we are swapping gossip and confidences. The men beam and tell Roberto he has done well.

Sadly, whatever pleasantries are being swapped are aborted when these new acquaintances ask the inevitable question – how many *bambini* do we have? As in England, they are stumped when we say none. I guess some things are universal – like disappointment for example. Still, I'm sure neither I, nor these kind enquiring folk, will be disappointed for much longer. I can barely imagine the excitement there'll be when I do finally announce a pregnancy.

I am thrilled when it becomes clear that many customers are coming back for more than one visit and that isn't down to curiosity about me, it's due to Roberto. It turns out that Roberto is a natural landlord. He's gregarious, authoritative and amusing. It is fun to watch him greet and entertain. I feel distinctly proud of him. Seeing him so excited by this project makes it easier for me to put my hands into pail after pail of hot soapy water.

A mixture of guilt at having turned down his amorous

82

advances and pride at his professional advances prompts me to suggest, 'Listen, I have a great idea. How about we have a night off tonight and we go to a *ristorante*? Your mamma has had to do so much cooking since we arrived; it will be a break for her.'

'That is very thoughtful, Elizabeth. Mamma doesn't get out much. She will love a dinner in a *ristorante*.'

Bugger, I'd meant that Roberto and I should go out alone and Raffaella would get a night off from cooking for us. I wasn't planning on taking her along. I wanted Roberto to myself. Still, my own fault, I should have been more explicit. Now, if I say I don't want to include Raffaella, I'll look mean.

'Grandpa should come too,' says Roberto. 'We can't leave him alone to eat.'

'Of course,' I say with an enthusiasm I wish I felt. 'And Paolina. My treat.'

15

Paolina says she's really, really sorry but she can't come out with us tonight, she has an important case starting tomorrow and her boss is insisting that she runs through the facts of the case one more time. She sounds disappointed to be missing out; I'm devastated. I was depending on her to keep the conversation lively. But on the other hand, Raffaella and Grandpa accept with more keenness than I was expecting, which is cheering – I suppose. I really want to believe that Raffaella and I have a chance to draw a line under any issues that might be brewing and become close.

Raffaella suggests a *ristorante* in Marostica and naturally I agree to her suggestion. When we arrive I'm surprised that it's rather more formal than I was expecting and significantly more expensive than I've budgeted for. But I remind myself that this is our first family meal out together and no expense should be spared, plus the white tablecloths and gleaming silverware are very impressive.

We are shown to our table but Raffaella is concerned that Grandpa is in a draught and so we move seats. Then Raffaella doesn't like that table because she is sitting under a speaker and says it hampers her chance of understanding me, even though the tunes being piped out are low-key and at a sensible volume, so we move to a third table where I find I'm facing the bathrooms. This is a pet hate of mine in restaurants, but I can't stand the idea of us all moving yet again; I'm worried that the waiters will spit in our soup.

Having recovered from the shock of the formality and cost of the restaurant, I now give into the experience and find it's wonderful. The waiters are attentive and cordial and show no signs of impatience with us for playing musical chairs. They offer us aperitifs on the house and small dishes arrive even before we've ordered. When we do get to look at the menu two waiters spend a serious amount of time discussing our choices with us and no query is too silly and no request is dismissed. Food is a serious business here.

Raffaella asks how fresh is the meat that she's considering ordering, so the chef comes out of the kitchen carrying the bloody cut; it's veal I think. The sight is enough to put me off my food (and that's quite something), but Raffaella is satisfied. We order a selection of antipasti to share and I order *pomodori farciti di magro* (meatless stuffed tomatoes) and a fresh green salad for my main. I'm salivating at the thought of the juicy, home-grown tomatoes. The antipasti is delicious, although I find I'm a little squeamish about sharing food from the same plate as Grandpa and Raffaella.

The old grandpa says little at most times and nothing during meals. In my mind he is ancient and frail and I am somewhat disconcerted when I calculate he's eighty-four, only a few years older than my father. He comes to the table and wraps himself in an enormous napkin, so big it gives the impression that he has slipped into bed and has pulled up a sheet, and then he methodically sets to on the monumentous matter of eating. He's a loud and appreciative eater but the sounds of gnawing, chomping and swallowing are a symphony that I simply can't welcome. With every slurp and burp my stomach churns. My mamma-in-law, on the other hand, congratulates her father as though he's a child whenever he takes a bite. She also enjoys her food so much that she has a habit of repeatedly licking her fingers and then touching everything, even the stuff she doesn't want to eat. Roberto doesn't seem squeamish about their manners; I remind myself they are family but can't help thinking flu bugs.

When Roberto is in the loo Raffaella calls over the waiter and speaks to him in quick, almost liquid Italian. The waiter nods approvingly, crosses out something on his notepad and writes something different. I wonder what else she's ordering and how much it will cost. I don't want to be mean, but we haven't discussed my wages at the bar yet; anything I spend here comes from my UK savings account.

When our dishes arrive I am surprised that I'm given *pollo alla cacciatora.*

'Oh dear, they've mixed the dishes,' I say to Roberto. I call out to the waiter, '*Mi dispiace* but I ordered *pomodori farciti di magro.*'

The waiter holds his hands wide and then brings the tips of his fingers on both hands together and shakes them up and down; he looks as though he's pleading with me. He says something to Roberto.

'Mamma ordered the *pollo alla cacciatora* for you,' translates Roberto. 'She was concerned that the dish you ordered was small and that you'd be hungry.'

'But this has chicken in it.'

Roberto looks surprised. 'Oh, of course. Sorry, Elizabeth.' He hesitantly holds his fork over his dish; clearly he's itching to start his but now doesn't think he can. I feel such a nuisance but it's not my fault; Raffaella changed the order.

Raffaella says something in Italian. Roberto translates, 'She's so sorry, she did not understand you don't eat chicken as well as meat.' Raffaella does look horrified; she is beating her chest with her hand and rocking backwards and forwards on her chair.

Roberto grabs her hand and squeezes it tightly. 'Don't worry, Mamma, it is nothing.'

She smiles back at him and for a moment looks like a gentle, dear lady. Then she turns to me and instantly all her softness vanishes. She looks cross and her tone is antagonistic when she pushes the breadsticks my way. '*Finire di mangiare.*' Eat up. 'Eat Roberto's food.'

'His is pheasant,' I argue.

'Is pheasant meat to you? I don't understand the vegetarianism,' she says in whispered angry Italian.

I look to Roberto to see if he's clocked her face or tone but he's busy re-tucking a napkin into Grandpa's shirt and doesn't notice.

I try to remain patient. It is just about possible that Raffaella made a genuine mistake when she ordered me a meat dish but I don't think so. I think she understands way more than she lets on. Since we've arrived she's maintained that she doesn't understand my pronunciation, however hard I try. Apparently she doesn't even understand me when I say no, which gives her the opportunity to serve me more food when I say I have had enough – '*Basta, grazie.*' She ignores my requests for seconds if something is truly delicious and I have a hunger and she's pretending to have understood that I don't like wine, so she never offers me a glass at dinner. I consider that Mamma-in-law has chosen a clever weapon of war: food. As I'm invariably hungry I'm becoming listless and short-tempered just when I need energy and patience the most.

Roberto re-orders my tomatoes and tells the waiter that the mistake is entirely ours so we'll pay for both dishes. The waiter eventually returns with my food but the others have finished their meals by this time, so I eat in a hurried and uncomfortable silence.

Raffaella orders dessert and coffee, then a second bottle of wine and liqueurs. When the bill comes she makes an enormous fuss over Roberto's generosity.

'No, no, Mamma. It is Elizabeth you should thank. It was her idea and it is her treat.'

Raffaella looks my way and smiles. I notice the smile doesn't manage to climb to her eyes.

'You must have big money in bank in London. Big job in London,' she says.

'No big job. Two jobs. I was a barmaid and a waitress,' I reply in what is undoubtedly poor Italian.

Raffaella laughs and says something else in the fast Italian that I can't catch. Roberto shakes his head but he doesn't look cross, more indulgent. I translate that he's saying Raffaella must not tease so much.

'What?' I ask.

Still smiling, he says, 'Mamma could not believe you had experience as a barmaid.'

In London I was considered a good barmaid, popular and efficient, and my waitressing work was second to none. I never used notebooks to list specials or to take orders. I prided myself on remembering who ordered what, and even with large parties that changed seats I rarely laid the food in front of the wrong person. Here, I'm embarrassed to admit I behave like an imbecile. I'm unfamiliar with the beer brands and the liqueurs. I barely understand the language and even with a crash course, 100 per cent immersion, I can't understand what clients want to order, let alone chatter or banter with them. The day that I will be able to do so seems a long, long way off. Raffaella has no doubt noticed every mistake I've made. I blush furiously but pretend not to understand her meaning; instead I try to bring the conversation back to money. I've been intending to ask what I'll get paid here; now is as good a time as any. I'm not expecting to be paid for clearing and cleaning but I think the bar work does demand a fair wage.

'Well, I'm happy to treat you all to a meal because I'll be getting my first wage pack soon. I've been working behind the bar for over a week now. Do you pay weekly or monthly?'

Roberto starts to play with the spoon on his coffee saucer. 'Ah, yes, Mamma and I were talking about your wage and in fact we thought it was an insult to give you one.'

'What? I don't understand.'

'Well, Mamma pointed out that it is a family business and we are all working for a greater good. If we pay you, you are just like the other staff and you are not that.' Roberto meets my eye and I know that he's a little uncomfortable with this decision, but then why is he backing it? Is the bar so profitless?

'But you get paid,' I point out.

'Exactly,' Roberto smiles, but I wasn't trying to prove

his argument. 'And we have food and a home. What do you need money for?'

'Stuff,' I splutter.

'What stuff?'

'Clothes, make-up, music, books.'

'But you have lots of clothes.'

I hope to God it was my imagination but it seemed as though when he said this there was a slight sneer around his mouth, a diluted form of the look I have seen Raffaella wear. Surely not.

'We haven't got wardrobe space for a quarter of the clothes you've brought with you, despite your charity shop dump,' he adds.

True, nearly everything I own is still in my suitcases, which lie on the floor swallowing up Paolina's bedroom. That's why it's important that Raffaella takes her ancient clothes out of the wardrobes and makes some room. Even Bruno's clothes are still hanging there.

'You can use our savings account from England if you see anything you want that is special. That is fair, because I'm also to use that for the bar refurbishment.'

'What happens when the account dries up? Our savings aren't vast.'

'I'll give you an allowance from my earnings.'

I realize that while Roberto's tone has remained perfectly calm and civilized, we are having a row. I mostly realize this because Raffaella looks delighted; her eyes bounce from one to the other of us, as though she is watching a Wimbledon final. I'm so shocked that my mother-in-law is happy enough for me to roll up my sleeves and join the staff but she has no intention of paying me for my trouble that I find I'm struggling to articulate why I feel her, *their*, decision is wrong. Roberto's argument sounds reasonable but somehow it doesn't feel it.

'I don't want to row about this with you,' I say.

'Well, don't then,' replies Roberto, and he leans in to kiss me square on the lips, silencing me.

16

30 January

Alison has called me every two or three days since I
arrived and I've done the strangest thing: when the phone
rings I invariably let it go through to voice-mail. I then
listen to her messages and send her a text in reply. Yup,
I'm guilty of screening my best friend's calls. Why? Because a devastating awkwardness has developed between
us – for the first time since we met I think it's going to
be difficult to be totally honest with her. I mean, how
am I going to explain that the romantic, profit-making
vineyard of my dreams is in fact a scruffy, ready-to-go-bust
bar? I have to confront this dilemma, yet again, when my
phone shudders in my pocket and I see her name on the
screen. I briefly consider a lifetime of avoiding Alison's
calls but the thought is unbearable. Two weeks has been
long enough. I pick up.

'Hi,' says Alison. She sounds relieved to have caught
me, but hearing her voice makes me feel guilty, shy and
nervous all at once. 'Finally! Oh my God, I get to speak
to you! So, what's it like? Are you working hard? A
vineyard. I just can't imagine it.' Which makes two of us.
'Start from the very beginning, tell me every detail of your
working day,' she insists.

Alison is normally calm and considered. The fact that
her excitement is verging on hysteria in this particular

case disconcerts me horribly. For a moment I seriously wonder whether there is the slightest possibility that I don't have to confess to my mistake but I know I'll be discovered sooner or later – besides the fact I can't furnish her with details of my working day in a vineyard (even I haven't got *that* much imagination), at some point she'll come and visit me and then I'll be stuffed.

'The family business isn't a vineyard. When Roberto said they were in the wine trade it turns out that he meant his family own a small bar.' I utter my confession in a hurry but it's no less painful.

'What?'

'It's an easy mistake to make,' I insist.

'No, it isn't. Why didn't you know that?' she asks with astonishment. 'How could you have got that so wrong? My God, you are a bloody idiot at times.'

Alison follows up her insult with a spurt of laughter. She cannot hide her amusement. She doesn't much try. I know for a fact that she is going to exercise her prerogative, as best friend, to take the mick out of me mercilessly and forever.

I keep a stony, dignified silence; whatever I say will only make her tease me more. She'll lose interest sooner rather than later – maybe when I'm sixty or something.

Once she realizes I'm unprepared to comment further she says, 'Err, right, well, how's everything else going? How are you finding Italy? You are in Italy, aren't you? You haven't muddled it up and discovered that Roberto is Albanian after all?'

'Ha ha, very funny. Italy is wonderful, thank you.'

'Lives up to your expectations, does it?' she asks.

'It's much colder than I imagined but yes, pretty much.'

'Marvellous! A miracle actually, as your expectations were very high.'

I start to wax lyrical about the aspects of Italy that have delighted me. 'The food is delicious and the people are wonderfully sociable. I love the way Italians enjoy time. When they order a drink they don't guzzle it with one eye on the clock, mindful of happy hour limits. Instead they take time to chat to their server, choose a table, and maybe have a nibble with their drink. They seem to have a deeper understanding of civilization and civility.'

'So what's this bar like then?' Alison cuts in.

'Pretty grubby at the moment but Roberto and I have great plans for it.'

'Rustic charm?'

'No, I'm thinking über-chic.'

'How's business?'

'We've some challenges. There is a market. There are six bars in Veganze, four in the square and two just a stone's throw away, including ours; so I can't see any of us ever becoming millionaires, but the other bars always seem pretty busy, even though Veganze only has a population of eight thousand people. I can't work that out. Over half the population must be minors or very elderly and Italians are not heavy drinkers, yet there's always someone to serve. We just need to attract a more constant flow of customers.'

'Are you listening to that CD I bought you?' she asks.

'Yes.'

In fact, no. 'Learn conversational Italian in three weeks; one hour's work a day' has not been out of its box yet. I never seem to have one hour to devote to learning the language. I suppose I could have listened when I was cleaning and sorting but I prefer being inside my own head and thinking about plump-thighed *bambini* with thick, dark, curly hair – that's such a pleasant way to pass time.

'How are you getting along with your mother-in-law?'

I sigh and wonder how much I ought to confess. I've replayed the events of our dinner out over and over again in my head. Did I imagine the extent of Raffaella's awkwardness? Roberto came home from the meal and waxed lyrical about how wonderful it had been to be out with his wife and his family, and how marvellously everyone had got on, and how sensational the food was. I'll give him that – the food was good. It was almost as though he'd attended a separate dinner from the one I was at. I'm really confused.

'We're not what you'd describe as bosom buddies yet,' I admit. 'But as you said, I had high expectations. It will take a bit of time for us to get to the place I want us to be. Since we've arrived most of her attention has been focused on Roberto, but that's to be expected.'

'Did she like the presents you brought?' Alison asks.

Alison had been with me for most of my expeditions into the shops of west and central London. I can't bring myself to tell her that the pretty packages remain unopened. They are casually discarded on the large dark wood dresser in the living room. Every time I spot them I feel sorry for the painstakingly selected toiletries, the silk scarf, the scented candles and the fancy chocolates that expected, not unreasonably, to be loved. At night I imagine them languishing and feeling useless, a little like my ovaries must feel.

'Mmm,' I mumble, not committing. I need to change

the subject. 'So, tell me about the big date, wasn't that this week?'

'Last night, actually.'

Before Christmas Alison had met a girl at book group, and after swapping views on Ivo Andrić and other fiercely intellectual authors they finally admitted to having the hots for each other. This date with Fiona had been set up weeks ago because, like Alison, Fiona has an amazing career and fabulous social life and it's taken a while for them to find a mutually convenient date. Alison has been quietly excited about this date, as she rarely meets anyone who catches her imagination.

She talks me through the evening, blow by blow; it clearly went really well. In summary, they went to the theatre and then on for a curry afterwards; there was no tongue action but she is meeting Fiona again, tonight.

'Tonight? Wow. You're breaking your own rule. Seeing her the very next night.'

'Well, I haven't got you to waste my time with,' she says affectionately. 'I guess I couldn't think of anything better to do.' I have a feeling she's trying to play down her excitement.

'Listen, Alison, I don't want to seem rude but I was right in the middle of painting a wall when you rang and I need to get it finished within the hour as I'm working a shift tonight.' Actually, the truth is that when Alison mentioned wasting time I made a quick calculation and realized what the date is. I need to find Roberto at once. 'Have fun tonight,' I garble.

'I will. I promise,' she giggles.

17

I consider whether it's worth taking the time to change into something more alluring than my paint-splattered gear before I seduce Roberto but I can't summon the energy. Paint-splashed dungarees and no make-up is a different look, but they say a change is as good as a rest. He's sitting at the bar poring over the bar's accounts *again*. Before I interrupt him I take the time to make him a strong espresso – his favourite.

I gently place a coffee down in front of him and wrap my arms around him, smudging my breasts into his back.

'You really are doing a sensational job,' I whisper into his ear. 'This place is looking better already and I'm not the only one who says so, I've heard customers make the same comments. *And* I'm quite the scrubber, even if I say so myself,' I joke.

Roberto either doesn't get or doesn't hear the joke. I guess he has so much on his mind he hasn't got time to think about my double entendre.

'I have a vision to restore Bruno's to the thriving hub that it was in my father's heyday,' says Roberto.

I smile to myself at his verbose declaration. I suppose he's becoming a little more flamboyant and sentimental because he's back in his Italian family home. Going home always does strange things to people. Whenever I go home I find myself drinking Bailey's and pretending to like watching repeats of *Some Mothers Do 'Ave 'Em* on

Sky. His statement sounds like something a movie hero following a script might say. Occasionally, since we've arrived in Italy, I get this strange feeling that I'm somehow disconnected from reality; I think it's something to do with not having a deep understanding of the language. I often feel like I'm in a movie or something. I'm not exactly the leading lady (although I am married to the leading man), I'm more of an extra.

'You mean we really have no choice but to shape this place up if we are hoping to eat?' I say with a smile.

'More than the money, it is about pride too. My vision will require lots of commitment and hard work,' adds Roberto. I resist looking around for his autocue and smile indulgently. 'Are you with me?' he demands, rather surprisingly.

I like seeing him this fired up. I admit the advertising agency hadn't pushed his buttons for quite some time. I'm keen for a family business too, but mostly I'm keen for a family, so everyone needs to take a break now and again – a break that coincides with the green light marked on my fertility calendar. I kiss him. I lean closer in to him and then, in a not too cleverly thought-out move, I sort of hoist myself up on to the bar stool next to him and push my body up against his. I feel my nipples hardening, I hope he can.

'I know you are busy, my darling, and I support you wholeheartedly. We can come back later if you like, together. But I really think we should go home now. The siesta is a tradition in Italy, isn't it? I know you love a tradition.'

'Is it a good time?'

Roberto sounds a little tired but I try to ignore that.

He pulls away from me and checks the date on his watch. He sighs ever so quietly as I nod. I feel a bit guilty as I realize that we rarely spontaneously make love any more. Or even have sex. We try for a baby. Maybe I should have let him take me in the attic the other day.

Roberto obligingly puts down his pen and the accounts book. 'I need Paolina to look at these numbers again anyway. I can't make much sense of them. Come on, my darling.' We walk back to Raffaella's hand-in-hand but in silence.

The baby-trying takes an efficient ten minutes. There's no point in prolonging it, as I know Roberto is bushed. I've long since stopped thinking that my orgasm is an essential part of our sex act; that would be rather indulgent. When it's over I lie on my back with my head at the toe end of the bed and my legs in the air, resting against the headboard.

'What are you doing?' asks Roberto curiously. 'You look as though you are practising yoga.'

I beam at him, as I'm appreciative that he's made the effort this afternoon. 'I'm just giving the sperm its best chance. I've just read about this.'

For a moment Roberto is silent. I see irritation flash across his face. I should have known he'd take it the wrong way and been a little more careful. I think I'm sometimes rather less sensitive than I should be, but maybe he's rather more sensitive than he should be. 'You think I produce inadequate sperm?' he asks sorrowfully.

'No,' I reply calmly.

'Good. Because I don't make inadequate sperm. We had the test. We know my sperm is fine.' Now his tone is defiant.

'As are my eggs,' I add. I don't want to be arsy but I know I am being a little bit so. I suppose I'm tired as well. Too much scrubbing.

'In fact,' says Roberto crossly.

He snaps back the sheets and bounces out of bed. He stands with his back to me and stares at the ceiling. I can almost touch the steaming fury that he's emitting. Oh bugger, where did this row come from? I'd been really happy that he'd agreed to leave his work and do the deed; I hadn't intended for us to row. I try to comfort him.

'Look, you have great sperm. I have great eggs. They just don't like each other. It's no one's fault, it's just the way it is. So please don't go all Italian stallion on me.'

'Don't accuse me of being mistakenly macho,' he barks.

I had done just that but I hadn't meant to; besides, who would have thought he'd notice? Often the language barriers protect us from registering the unnecessary but irresistible digs that pass between married couples from time to time. We both fall silent for a moment. I want to put my arms around him and cheer him up but I have to keep my legs in the air for at least a quarter of an hour. Roberto gets dressed and leaves the room. I wait the allotted fifteen minutes before I follow him. I find him in the bar with Raffaella. They are serving and the moment to explain myself has passed. Damn. I feel such a horror. I roll up my sleeves and resign myself to a long night.

18

14 February

I prise back the enormous shutters with some effort and look out of the window. Hurrah, it's not raining. It's rained pretty much non-stop since we arrived here, which, I have to confess, has been a big shock to me. I hadn't expected rain. Although it still feels chilly, today the sky is a vivid, exciting blue and it's beckoning me out to play. I take a deep breath and try to absorb as much of Italy as I can squeeze into my lungs.

As I reach for my robe I discover a small blue tube of three Bacci chocolates lying on the dressing table. They are the type of chocolates you can find in any bar or supermarket in Italy and so in some ways unremarkable, but they cause me to squeal with delight. *Bacci* means kisses in Italian. Roberto has left me kisses and they are all the more thoughtful because of the time in my cycle.

The week before my period is often a tricky time for Roberto and me. We don't row but we warily prowl around one another with our opposing viewpoints. I love this time of the month, when maybe everything is possible. Maybe I am pregnant and maybe my body is finally cooperating. Often I begin to feel the symptoms of pregnancy: my breasts become tender, my stomach swells to a rumour-making size and I feel overwhelmed by an extraordinary tiredness. I like to revel in these symptoms and enjoy the inconvenience with a masochistic pleasure as I anticipate the little blue line indicating a positive life, on the stick of the pregnancy kit.

Roberto hates this time, as after seven or eight false alarms he accepts I simply suffer from PMT – the symptoms being cruelly similar to pregnancy.

How thoughtful of him to know that this is such an important week for us, perhaps our most important for years. After our first full month in Italy is he thinking what I'm thinking? Maybe baby.

I dash to the bathroom, shower and dress in record time. I haven't got a plan as to exactly what I should do with myself today but I'm certain that I don't want to spend my first dry day in Italy poking at grunge behind the kitchen sink or flinging out old boxes of moth-eaten bric-a-brac. I'm having a day off.

When I wander downstairs I find Raffaella has already cleared away breakfast and Roberto has left for work. I go into the kitchen and find her sitting at the table, peeling potatoes.

In Italian I say, 'Good morning.'

'Morning.'

'I am sorry I missed breakfast.'

She shrugs but doesn't appear irritated, 'There is a plate in fridge.'

Sure enough there is a huge plate in the fridge – of salami.

'Do you mind if I use the eggs?' I continue in Italian.

She tuts and violently shakes her head with what I think to be disproportionate alarm. 'No eggs, no eggs. Eggs for pasta-making.'

There are twelve eggs, which seems to be enough to

go round, but I don't say as much; I have no idea how many eggs are required for fresh pasta. I glance around the kitchen and spot a heaving fruit bowl. Fresh fruit, an ideal breakfast for a tiny embryo!

'No problem, I'll just have fruit.' As I stretch towards the bowl Raffaella's arm darts out of nowhere and she deftly snatches it from me.

'Breakfast, seven to eight in my house,' she says curtly. I doubt this, because yesterday I was up at seven and she didn't serve until eight fifteen, which is exactly what time it is now. She holds the bowl of fruit close to her body and I almost laugh. This situation is comical. I count to ten. I might be pregnant. I might be pregnant.

That thought gives me the strength to smile, with a studied lightness I don't feel.

'No problem, I'll pick up a brioche in the piazza. I'm having a day off work today.' I don't know why I feel I need to tell her. I've worked every day since we got here. I'm not even being paid.

Raffaella says something in Italian. I think she says, '*Pigra.*'

I'm not certain but I think *pigra* means lazy. I could be wrong, so I don't know how to respond. Lord, how do I respond if I'm right? I stand for a moment, unsure as to what to do with myself next. Pathetically, I decide there is nothing I can do and I sneak out of the door. Despite having an empty stomach I have a heavy feeling.

19

Even before I reach the end of the street I've dialled Alison's number.

'Hi, this is a nice surprise. How goes it?'

I decide to confess all, isn't that why I called her? 'Not well. Frankly, my high-grade charm offensive towards my mother-in-law is not working. It's becoming clear that my ambition of developing a warm, intimate relationship with her is going to be so much more than an uphill struggle, it's going to be a one-girl trek to the top of Everest without so much as a bar of Kendal mint cake for sustenance.'

Alison laughs at my image but then more seriously adds, 'I knew you were holding something back last week; if you could have described your mother-in-law as a doll, you would have. Go on, spill.'

'For reasons which I don't at present totally under-stand, Raffaella sees me as the enemy, and while she fights with stealth, she fights relentlessly and aggressively.'

'But why would she dislike you?'

'I don't know; you hear it all the time, don't you, mothers being jealous of their sons' wives.'

'I suppose.'

'Maybe she blames me for all those years that they didn't talk.'

'That's unreasonable – they'd already fallen out before he met you.'

'I know, but love can be unreasonable. Who knows

what's going on in her mind? All I know is that we didn't get off to a very good start and things have got progressively worse ever since.'

I think back to the excruciatingly embarrassing night of our arrival. It takes quite some humour and guts, but I describe the scene to Alison and I tell her about Raffaella changing my order at the restaurant the other week and her denying me a bite this morning. I'm hoping she'll laugh and tell me not to worry. I want her to buoy me up and say hiccups are to be expected. Which they are, I know that. But she stays quiet, suggesting that she too thinks I'm up against more than a hiccup.

'I think she hates me,' I conclude.

'Really?'

'Yes.'

'You don't think you are being a tiny bit melodramatic?'

'Do you?'

'I don't know, I'm not there. What does Roberto think?'

'He doesn't see any of it.' I sigh my exasperation.

'You sound irritated with him. Are you irritated with him?'

'No. Not him.'

I know it's not his fault that the family business is a time-intensive, profitless bar rather than a wealthy beatific vineyard, and it's not his fault his mother is a battleaxe, and he can't be blamed that it's cold and I don't know the language, so I'm struggling to make conversation, let alone friends. I know none of this is his fault but –

'Are you pre-menstrual?' Alison is the only person in the world who would dare ask me this question and even then it would only be over a phone line.

'Good God, I really, really hope not.'

Falling pregnant is the only thing that will make me happy. Falling pregnant would undoubtedly win Raffaella over, and even if it didn't I'd be immune to her digs then. I'd be protected – I'd live in a big bag of bliss.

I wonder if Raffaella wants a grandchild almost as much as I want a baby. Maybe that's why she dislikes me, because I've failed to produce one for her. Suddenly, I almost understand why she wouldn't open the gifts I brought her from England. I can respect her disdain; all she wants from me is her son's child. The thought almost floors me as it stands big and proud; a reasonable conclusion, an unequivocal truth. Everything will be OK if I'm pregnant.

If.

'Cheer me up,' I wail.

Alison is silent for a second and then says, 'Fiona and I are getting along brilliantly. I'm seeing her tonight, actually, which is quite special.' I can't think why tonight might be 'quite special'. Alison's birthday is November. I suppose it might be Fiona's birthday? I don't care enough to enquire. 'In fact, speaking of which, I'm really sorry to cut you short but I have to go. I have a lunchtime appointment to have my bikini line waxed.'

As she hangs up I feel a powerful wave of dreary spirits slosh over me. Talking to her was supposed to cheer me up but it's left me feeling homesick. I can't help but think it would be fun to spend time sitting in Alison's flat watching her paint her nails and choose her outfit for her big date, more fun than struggling to take orders in the bar. I decide I need a cup of coffee – it will cheer me up, or at the very least warm me up.

That will have to do.

20

As I sit eking out my cup of coffee I have time to notice that lots of people ride bikes here (both push and motor), but there are also cars and complicated parking restrictions – like at home. Veganze is old and quaint but it resists cliché. I tell myself it's unreasonable to feel cheated that it isn't quite as I imagined. At exactly midday I notice the local village misfit shuffle into the square. I wonder why he's so late today. I've seen him every morning as I head to work; he is out in all weathers. He shuffles up to me and asks me for a cigarette, as he has done every day, whenever I've sat to enjoy a coffee. The fact that every time he's asked I have told him that I don't smoke has not deterred him from asking again.

I've tried '*Io no fumo*' and '*Io fumo no*', and the more straightforward '*No fumo*', because I'm not sure which is correct. One of them must be, yet he still doesn't seem to understand. After a few meetings I began to realize this isn't a language barrier; the guy is ill. I'm unsure if he's suffering from something like Alzheimer's or if he has always been this way, I'm no doctor.

Forgetful Man is probably in his late sixties. I have no idea who he lives with, but someone must take care of him because he is always well dressed and clean. British misfits never look dapper. I imagine a mamma, aged about ninety, laboriously and lovingly pressing his shirts every morning. I watch as he walks endless routes around the town, stopping at each bar on every lap. Today, because it's dry, he does not go inside any of the establishments, he's more interested in the people occupying the outdoor seats. His routine is to pull up a seat, sit, pause for a minute, then stand and approach the customers; he works in a clockwise direction, relentlessly trying to bum a cigarette. Some customers sitting for an hour or more can be approached four or even six times. Each time he greets us as though he has never set eyes on any one of us before, and maybe he hasn't.

I watch this endless drudge with fascination. I've always hated smoking and never so much as taken a drag, but, for the first time in my life, I wish I had a cigarette in my bag so I'd be able to hand it over. His pathetic shuffling, and the wary look in his eyes, saddens me. Even though his shirts are pressed, he is still an outsider, I empathize.

I notice that the reactions he stirs in others vary from embarrassment to irritation. He is never treated rudely or aggressively, but then neither does he find compassion. Younger people are often wary and uncomfortable around him, the older locals are anaesthetized to him. Forgetful Man must have pushed himself into their presence thousands of times over the years. He's part of the scenery; like a fountain or a statue.

Today, as usual, I shake my head. I've considered buying him a packet of cigarettes but wonder whether I should encourage such an unhealthy habit. His shoulders drop a fraction and he shuffles on. He picks up a discarded butt from the street and lights it, then sucks on the stub as though his very life depends on it, when in fact the opposite is true. In all the time I've watched him, I've never seen him receive a cigarette, so I take note when the next guy he asks, the guy sitting behind me, says, 'Sure buddy,' and pulls out a fresh packet of ciggies.

I realize I'm staring and try to quickly flick my expression from nosy to smiley as Cigarette Guy lights Forgetful Man's smoke.

'Glad the rain has stopped, it's a beautiful day,' says Cigarette Guy.

'Yes,' I smile. 'Is that an American accent?'

'Yup.'

Forgetful Man has shuffled on now. He showed no more or less appreciation to Cigarette Guy, who did furnish him with a cigarette, than he does to everyone who refuses. I watch him disappear around the corner. I expect I'll see him again in ten minutes or so.

'Are you a tourist?' I realize that my question might seem a little brutal, but I'm all out of small talk. Speaking in pidgin Italian means I've lost the gift of the gab.

'No, I live here in Veganze.'

'I haven't seen you before.' I hit the wrong tone and my comment sounds suspicious. Who am I? Neighbourhood watch chairman?

Cigarette Guy does not take offence. He grins. His is a wide, generous smile.

'I'm a teacher at the language school in Bassano del Grappa. Normally I'm teaching right now, but it's half-term so I get to loaf around instead.'

'I see. It's just that I know most faces.' He's handsome. I'm sure I'd have remembered him if I'd seen him, even if he is handsome in a blond way. I manage to keep this gem to myself, proving I haven't entirely lost sight of all social norms. Instead I comment, 'My husband's family own the bar on the corner of via Mazzini, so I thought I knew most locals by sight at least. Obviously not.'

'Your husband's family own Bruno's?'

'Yes.' I feel slightly embarrassed by this. Bruno's is not what you'd call a cool haunt and this guy looks as though he only visits very trendy places. I remind myself I'm not a teenager and my response is ridiculous. What do I care if I impress this stranger or not? 'I guess it's not your sort of place as it stands.' I hazard, 'But we are doing a refit, you should check it out.'

When did the phrase 'check it out' creep into my vocab? I have no idea why I've started to talk in American speak. Or worse, in what I perceive to be American speak – terms gleaned from the movies I watch, no doubt wildly inaccurate.

'Yeah, I will. I haven't been going out much in Veganze recently. My girlfriend lives in Bassano del Grappa too. So since Christmas I've been spending most of my time over there. Made sense since I work there.'

It's great that he has a girlfriend and I have a husband and we both just got those facts out there early on in the conversation. I always find that sort of thing tricky when I'm talking to attractive men. He's not my type but he won't know that. All he'll know is that he is attractive, and the problem with attractive men is that they are always *so* vain and they tend to think they are way beyond attractive and are, in fact, irresistible.

Roberto is a bit vain, it comes with the territory. He often gets chatting to some girl or other (say in a queue or at work) and then says to me, 'She is hot for me.' It always makes me laugh. Truth is, maybe the girl might fancy him *a bit*, he is fanciable, but really! Men! They should know we can chat without having the hots. We do think of other things too. Like babies and food. Anyway, I'm glad that this American guy and I just got our non-single status out there to save any confusion. It's not the kind of thing you can ask, because if you do ask a guy if he has a wife or a serious girlfriend, they always think you are fishing for them and the truth might be the opposite. You might be just trying to establish that they are safe to talk to, without the risk of gossip or messy misunderstandings. And I'm not in the slightest bit disappointed that he has a serious girlfriend, with whom he spends practically every night. Why should I be?

'But we've split up now, so maybe you'll see more of me around here from now on.' And I'm not delighted to hear that either.

I'm not.

Really.

2 1

The reason I say the American is not my type is as follows. Roberto is my type. Full stop. He's my husband. End of story.

But honestly? That should read: Roberto is my type; semi-colon. Because everyone knows that when you get married you don't suddenly become blind, deaf and mute. Yet Roberto and I have a healthy attitude towards such stuff. We acknowledge that there are other attractive people out there but we know that acting on an attraction, in *any way*, would result in a very slow and painful death. Trust me, if Roberto was unfaithful, I would consider a bitter and costly divorce, shredded clothes and cress seeds sown into the carpet as an under-reaction.

Still, I'm deadly serious that the American guy is not my type. For a start he's not Italian, he's American, and for a second he's got green eyes and light brown (almost blond) hair. I've only ever been attracted to men with dark hair and chocolate-coloured eyes. The American guy is taller and bulkier than the men I generally go for. Italians are lean and lithe and I like that. He's not fat but he's big. His forearms are about as wide as my thighs, he clearly works out and I can't stand all that nonsense. Men are vain even if they look like pigs; men who visit the gym regularly to pump iron and know more than women do about the calorie content of a BLT sandwich are off-the-scale losers.

In my opinion.

The American guy paid for his coffee and left almost immediately after our chat. I notice he left a cigarette on the table which Forgetful Man duly collected within five minutes.

Oddly, despite believing that the American guy is an off-the-scale loser, I find my thoughts drifting to him all day and I can't concentrate on my novel (even though the plot is good) or my lunch (even though the pasta sauce is sublime). I'm not being weird or inappropriate – it's just that I think it would be nice to have someone to chat to in English. That's all.

I thoroughly enjoy my day off. I spend it mooching around Veganze's streets and then lying in my room snoozing. The constant early mornings and late nights have built up quite a sleep debt. I set the alarm so I don't sleep through supper; without being expressly told, I'm sure the consequences of such an act would be gruesome.

I'd sent Roberto a text to say I fancied a day off and he was totally cool with that. Raffaella clearly isn't as relaxed. The minute I walk into dinner she starts to fuss about the *entire* family having to get to the bar to watch the staff and therefore insisting that there isn't time for a leisurely meal. It's no great loss. Roberto is often very agitated and anxious to get back to business, and seems to find the multiple courses gruelling rather than a delight. He sometimes eats speedily and silently ruminates. Or he spends the entire meal talking about work – the problems, his plans, past mistakes, future goals – I've started to tune out a little bit when he chats about the bar. I am interested but I find myself drifting and thinking about stuff like our baby's first Christmas. Can you imagine how much fun

Christmas will be once we have children! Sadly, Paolina is often physically absent or at least mentally distracted too. They work her very hard at the solicitor's firm.

I have no idea why Raffaella has a bee in her bonnet that the staff cannot be trusted on their own this particular Tuesday evening. We have a pool of three part-timers; all girls in their twenties, all exhaustingly beautiful and magnetic. They seem entirely trustworthy and capable and have managed on their own until about 9 p.m. on nearly every weekday since I arrived here. It's funny, I never see Roberto draft anything as prosaic as a rota but somehow Laurana, Gina and Alexandra all seem to drift in and out of the bar exactly as and when we need their help. Each one of them seems to understand the rhythm of the bar better than I do.

When we arrive at the bar it's notably busier than usual.

'Wow, this is encouraging for a Tuesday night. What's the buzz?' I yell at Roberto over the noisy crowd.

'It's Valentine's night; it's bound to be busy everywhere. That's why Mamma wanted us both here. She knows that Italians make a fuss on Valentine's night.'

But not my Italian, it appears.

How could I have forgotten? I knew today was the fourteenth because I'm so familiar with my cycle and of course I know it's February but somehow the two facts didn't add up to equal Valentine's day. How is that possible? I am the last of the great romantics. At least, I always have been. I'm out of my usual routine. I have lost track of days before now, when I've been on holiday; I suppose being here is a bit like being on holiday, but without the sun and the fun – just with the bit about losing track of the days.

Two thoughts hit me simultaneously. One: oh-my-God Alison has a Valentine date – unprecedented. Two: oh-my-God I haven't got a Valentine date – unprecedented. I mean, every year since Roberto and I met he has made such a big deal out of Valentine's day and today he hasn't so much as uttered a word of endearment.

I glance around the bar and try to locate a bouquet of flowers stashed in the corner waiting to be claimed by me, but no such luck. There are countless bouquets of flowers, but they are all being closely guarded by their lucky recipients. It appears every girl in the joint is wearing new jewellery or nursing a box of chocs the size of a swimming pool.

Roberto has already scuttled to the kitchen to check stock, or staff, or something. I chase after him.

'I'd forgotten that it is Valentine's day,' I announce.

'No problem, I wasn't expecting a gift,' says Roberto with a relaxed beam.

I'm stumped. His reasonable demeanour in the face of my non-gift rather trivializes my fury in the face of his non-gift.

'We haven't celebrated,' I point out.

'Didn't you find the Bacci?'

'I thought they were for –' I don't finish the sentence. The tiny tube of chocolates seemed a thoughtful 'anticipating baby-news' gift but they are a lousy Valentine's gift. We sell them in the bar.

'And you had the day off,' he adds.

'But *we* haven't celebrated.'

'We're busy.' He waves in the direction of the bar.

'Too busy to say happy Valentine's day?' I ask crossly. Roberto walks towards me and takes both my hands in his. He brings them to his lips and kisses my knuckles. He keeps his huge, brown eyes locked on me throughout.

'It's not a problem. Not to me or to you. I'm not worried that you forgot altogether it was Valentine's day.'

'I'm worried,' I whine. I try to pull my hands out of his grasp but he holds them firmly.

'I'm not, so forget it.'

Roberto suddenly drops my hands, bends to pick up a crate of red wine and sweeps past me, back into the bar. I put my head in my hands and try to think clearly. I'm not sure what is distressing me the most, his tiny unimpressive gift or me forgetting altogether. I am an eternal romantic, how could this day have slipped out of my consciousness? Valentine's day is always such a big deal for us. One year Roberto bought me eight bouquets of flowers and had them delivered on the hour, every hour, to the restaurant where I was waitressing. Another year he flew us to New York and we ate oysters in a rooftop restaurant, although we couldn't really afford to do so. Everyone, even Alison, had to admit that the advantages of dating an Italian were transparent when it came to Valentine's day. This year – the Italian equivalent of a bunch of carnations bought from a garage.

I pause for thought. We've been married six, nearly seven years. Is this it? The fatal seven-year itch. Are my years of being romanced over? I feel tears pinch my nose and I want to howl. I scrabble around in my handbag and dig out a tissue.

Suddenly I feel a light touch on my arm.

'Oh, hi, Paolina,' I say with little enthusiasm.

'Join me for a drink?' she asks.

I shouldn't, I'm supposed to be here to help, but sod

the bar and sod Roberto, it's Valentine's day and the very least I deserve is a glass of wine. I sniff and nod. Paolina pulls a bottle of red off the shelf. I notice that she picks a very expensive one. I follow her as she weaves her way towards a table in the middle of the bar. I'd have preferred to hide away in a corner but all the cosy seats are occupied by loving, amorous couples. Paolina pours the wine into two glasses and then takes a sip.

'Happy Valentine's day,' she mutters.

'Yeah, right.' I think I'm in serious danger of betraying my raving disappointment at her brother, so I dig deep and manage to muster a polite enquiry. 'No date?'

'No date,' she confirms.

I wouldn't normally draw attention to the dateless status of any woman, particularly on Valentine's night, but Paolina is beautiful, clever, elegant, slim, etc., etc. I'm pretty certain that if she hasn't got a date tonight it's because she doesn't want one. I bet Paolina thinks the whole Valentine's day thing is just stupid. She's probably one of those women who complain that it's all a marketing ploy for the naïve, and I bet she actually means it. I can't imagine Paolina ever feeling resentment and disappointment because someone downgraded the romance of the day to three chocolates in a tube. Yes, it must be lovely to be cool, calm and collected; totally in control of your own destiny and happiness.

I bet if I was a mother I wouldn't care if Roberto had forgotten Valentine's day.

'Sorry I haven't been around much since you arrived here. I've been meaning for us to have time together,' says Paolina, proving she isn't even thinking of Valentine's day. 'How are you settling?'

'Oh, fine.' I'm not sure I sound that convincing. 'I'm glad it was dry today. There's nothing to do when it rains in Veganze. There are no shops large enough to hide in. No cinema to disappear into for an hour or so. The Brits do rain very well. We have central heating and lots of indoor, on-couch activities. Fitted carpets are no longer a mystery to me.'

I pause, as I consider I sound very rude. But it's a fact that Raffaella's house is perpetually cold. The marble floors that I long dreamt of are icy, I hadn't expected that.

'The rain runs in rivers through the streets, splashing over my trainers and making my feet dirty. I brought four pairs of flip-flops with me but seriously regret my lack of boots,' I add.

Paolina looks at me as though I'm slightly slow. She abandons the pretence that this conversation is about anything other than Valentine's day and asks, 'What's the matter? Didn't you like the flowers?'

'There were no flowers,' I reply grumpily. 'He gave me a tiny packet of Bacci. Three in a tube. Not even a box.'

'But –' she looks confused – 'I saw Roberto buy them. A huge bunch of red roses. At least thirty, forty stems. They made me quite nauseous with jealousy.'

'Really!' Excitement floods through my body. I beam at her.

'Yes, this morning.'

'The pig! Roberto is pretending to have forgotten all about Valentine's day.'

I don't mean the pig bit. Thirty or forty stems! I mean, he's a prince. I feel dizzy with relief. I grin at Paolina and she generously throws back a beam. I don't dwell on her comment that she feels nauseous with jealousy; I'm sure she didn't really mean it. I bet he's going to present me with the flowers tonight. Maybe he's going to lay the stems across our bed; now that would be romantic. The chocolates were a ruse. I knock back my glass of wine and then excuse myself.

'I'd better get back to work. I have to do my bit tonight. Thirty or forty stems – how extravagant.'

I dash away, leaving Paolina to finish the bottle on her own. I'm sure she can't mind. I bet she only asked me to join her in the first place to be polite.

22

I work the rest of the shift with a notable enthusiasm that surprises Roberto. As he's cashing up he pulls me towards him and gives me a hug. I drift into a fantasy about making love on a bed strewn with thirty or forty stems of roses.

'Thanks for not getting in huff because I get you just an economical Valentine's gift,' he says. 'I'm really sorry. I'll make it up to you.'

Nice touch. I nearly giggle. I resist an urge to poke him in the ribs and force him to admit that there's a huge bouquet stashed somewhere. I might as well go along with the surprise now.

'I'm going to head off to bed, don't be long,' I say, and I wink in a not too subtle way.

The roses are not strewn across our bed but that's OK, he'll be able to present them to me. It's not that I'm so shallow that my happiness can be bought with a bunch of flowers, it's more that disappointment and panic can be kept at bay by a bunch of flowers. My happiness would be secured with a Moses basket tucked in the corner of the room. I quickly tug off my smoky clothes and root through my suitcases until I unearth sexy matching bra and knickers. I check my legs, which are, luckily, fairly fuzz-free, and then I throw myself across the bed. For one Moses basket, step this way.

Only ten minutes later I hear Roberto's footsteps on

the stairs. He says goodnight to his mother and sister as I arrange myself into a welcoming 'tadaaar' pose; stomach in, boobs and booty out.

Roberto strides into the room. He's carrying a bottle of champagne and two glasses.

'Happy Valentine's day,' he smiles. 'Better late than never. Nice bra.' He puts the bottle and glasses on the bedside and then crawls on top of me. For once he doesn't fuss about taking off his shoes and clothes. The moment has been lost so often as I've waited for him to fold and put away. Roberto starts to kiss me. Between kisses he murmurs that he's sorry and he'll make it up to me. His kisses are familiar and wonderful but I gently push him off.

'OK, a joke's a joke, give me the roses now. They'll need to go in water.'

'What roses?'

'The ones Paolina saw you buy this morning. Stop messing around or else they'll droop and then I won't shag you,' I say with a grin.

For a moment Roberto looks disorientated; finally he says, 'Oh, those roses. They weren't for you.'

'What? Well, who were they for?' I ask, stunned.

'Mamma.'

'Your mother!' I push him off me and scramble into an upright position. I grab my robe, not a sign of my modesty but a clue that I'm about to kill him and I think it's more fitting to be dressed for that.

'She finds Valentine's day sad. She's a widow. I wanted to make her happy.'

'She been a widow for nearly two decades,' I point out.

'I just wanted to do a nice thing.'

Roberto has moved to the edge of the bed and he has his back to me. I consider his excuse. Does being the most thoughtful and loving son on the planet make up for being a useless, crap husband?

'So why didn't you do a nice thing for me?' I demand.

'I didn't think of –'

'Me.' I finish the sentence with an honesty that Roberto might not have managed. He blushes. 'You bought forty roses for your mother and a cheap packet of sweets for me. You are weird.' I spit angrily.

I sink the glass of champagne he's poured. It's warm. We must have sold all the chilled stuff to couples who had planned to celebrate. The bubbles scorch my throat as though announcing they were an afterthought.

'It's not weird to love your mamma,' he says.

'Yes it is. Sort of. Well, no, not to love her but to buy her a better Valentine's gift than the one you get your wife. That's weird!'

I'm probably yelling because Roberto is looking nervously towards the door and he keeps trying to put his fingers on my lips to silence me. I impatiently brush him away.

'I'm fed up here, Roberto. You seem to think we are playing happy families but we are not. You shouldn't be thinking of your mother before me. I think it's a consequence of us living in her house. It's all mixed up. We should get our own place.'

Suddenly, after only a pathetic couple of minutes of grovelling, his mood changes; he gives up trying to console me and turns angry. What is going on? Shouldn't he have to plead and beg for hours?

'This is Italy. We do things different here. It is not

weird to buy Mamma some flowers. This is Italy. Here we care for our parents.'

He says Italy with all the pride and ferocity that a Roman Caesar would have used. I want to remind him that it's now a country with too many pensioners and a fucked political system but I stay silent. He's right, we are in Italy. Maybe I am missing something or making something of nothing. I don't know.

Confused, I turn off my bedside light. Roberto sighs and then climbs into bed next to me. He tries to hold me but I bat his hand away; I do not feel in the least bit randy. I don't care if the warm champagne goes flat.

'I truly am sorry. Tomorrow I will get you flowers. We'll go out for dinner,' he whispers.

'Forget it,' I mutter huffily. 'But just don't let me catch sight of Raffaella's roses or else I won't be responsible for my actions.' I quietly steam as I imagine force-feeding the roses to Roberto, thorns and all.

'No, you won't see them,' he promises.

23

I wake up in the middle of the night, a familiar stickiness between my legs. Weeping, I shuffle to the bathroom, clean up, dig out Tampax and then return to bed.

I find I've disturbed Roberto; he's sitting bolt upright with the bedside light on. He doesn't say a word because he's said every one there is to say over the years. He holds out his arms, and despite being fed up about the roses I sink into him and cry quietly. My tears trickle on to his chest. The roses are nothing. Valentine's day is nothing. It's all nothing without a baby.

We stay like this for just a few minutes. My tears, like his words, dry up quicker than they used to.

'I didn't realize you were hoping for so much this month,' he says as he smooths my hair.

'How do you mean?'

'Well, I noticed that you not pack the thermometer or the ovulation kits when you came to Italy. I thought you were –'

'What? Accepting it?' I pull away from him so that I can look at his face.

'Not that, just –' Roberto lets his sentence trail away again. We rarely have the energy or will to finish conversations of this nature. A lot gets left unsaid.

'I might not have packed the kits but I'm still keeping an eye on the calendar.' In fact I have been keeping my eye so firmly on my cycle I failed to note that February the fourteenth was anything other than the day I might or might not have a period. Is that healthy? I push the thought aside. 'OK, so the legs in the air didn't do the trick.' I reach for a hanky and blow my nose. 'We have to be brave. It's disappointing, there's no denying it, but my disappointment isn't gut-wrenching like it was month after month, year after year in England. I know things will work out here.' I briefly fling my arms around Roberto. 'I am sure with a blind faith that in Italy, the country of Romance, we *will* conceive without undue effort or intervention.'

'That is illogical,' he says quietly.

'No, no, it's not.' I insist. 'True love *will* prevail. The sun is bound to help, once it starts to shine. I read that. It was always unlikely that we'd get lucky straight away; house moves are stressful – everyone knows that – besides, we didn't actually have that much sex. The move, the initial peculiar bedroom arrangements, the funny hours at the bar – everything worked against us. There is no point looking back, we have to look forward.'

What else can we do?

24

6 March

In this past week the weather has taken a distinct turn for the better, as though spring has sprung. The mornings are bright and crisp, rather than gloomy and sodden; occasionally the sun makes a brief appearance. Bright beams splatter on to the cobbled pavements and glint cheerfully, promising that the summer I'd imagined is just round the corner

By March my days have started to fall into a routine. My days are full, although not full of lengthy mealtimes and coffee-drinking in the piazza. I work two shifts in the bar (10 a.m. to 3 p.m. and 7 p.m. until 2 a.m.) six days a week. The seventy-two-hour week is longer than the week I worked in the UK, and I'm privately concerned that the long hours are detrimental to my plan to relax and conceive. I tried to discuss as much with Roberto but he just said that the family business is a real concern and, as yet, the pregnancy isn't. I didn't speak to him for two days following this tactless comment, although I'm not sure he was aware that I was cross, he's so busy. He works even longer hours than I do, refusing to relax, even during the siesta. At first I was delighted to discover that the afternoon nap is still cherished. I'd assumed that would give Roberto and me the opportunity to slink back to bed, if the mood took us (and I was going to ensure it would, when necessary). Or – at the very least – that we'd be free to go for a drive and see more of the region. It hasn't really panned out that way. Roberto is so busy, he uses the siesta to visit suppliers and I read novels or baby books.

This morning, like every other morning, Roberto and I get up at quarter to seven and are showered, dressed and seated at the dining room table for breakfast by seven thirty. As usual, Raffaella places a plate of cold meats on the table and as usual, I ignore it and reach for the bread and honey.

When we leave the dining room I dig Roberto in the ribs.

'You are going to have to say something about her ongoing campaign to get me to eat meat,' I say with some exasperation.

'I know it's crazy. I will say something. I keep meaning to. I have so much on my mind. I forget all about your problem until every mealtime. Come on, let's walk into the piazza and I'll buy you a coffee and a brioche.'

I slip my hand in his as we amble the very short distance into the town square. On the jaunt Roberto buys a newspaper and says hello to the folks he knows. I wave and smile shyly in their direction; the younger ones shout '*Ciao*', the older ones touch their hats in response, but our conversations can go no further.

'You must try to learn our language,' Roberto says, not for the first time.

'I know.'

'You have to be brave and just risk to say something; it doesn't matter if your pronunciation is not perfect.'

It mattered to Raffaella. I keep this point to myself. 'How did you learn English?'

'A little at school, and then mostly on the spot, in England.'

'With a tutor?'

'No. I managed by focusing. You have to concentrate, Elizabeth. You have to be aware of the conversations around you and immerse yourself. I know it is not easy, especially for a day-dreamer,' he adds, not unkindly.

We always take our morning coffee at someone else's bar. Roberto sees this as an opportunity to informally analyse the competition, I see it as time off when I can choose between people-watching (no language skills required) or thinking about baby names (my current favourites are Louisa for a girl and it's still Matthew for a boy). Roberto doesn't have a view on the name Louisa. I'm not sure if he likes it more or less than Lottie, which has been my favourite for a year; he won't say, although I've asked him twice.

Roberto goes inside to order the coffees (his is an espresso, mine's a cappuccino) and my gaze falls on to the small, already familiar gangs of chatty characters who prefer to take their coffee outside the bars; they did so even in chilly February and now they bathe like fat seals in the weak spring sunlight. It's clear that not only do they enjoy the fresh air but they also have an insatiable curiosity about the comings and goings in Veganze's piazza. Old men sit in convivial silences and watch with interest the progress of audacious pigeons pecking their way through the street. Old women sit in sociable gangs and watch young lovers do the same thing. These oldies behave exactly as I imagined Continental pensioners to behave; they are the epitome of faded elegance. I adore being near them.

Roberto puts a cappuccino on the table but does not sit down.

'Where's yours?' I ask.

'I can't take coffee with you today. I have to be in the bar right away.'

'Why?'

'I must be there to receive an order.'

'I thought you did that yesterday.'

'No, yesterday was an early start because I had need to talk to Antonella, the cleaner. You say she is skiver and I have to have a talk with her about her hours. You not remember?'

The cleaner is such a skiver. She's an ancient old friend of Raffaella's and I'm unsure why we bother keeping her on the books at all, as she calls in sick at least once a week and even when she is around she's next to useless. I suggested we fired her and hired someone more responsible and effective, but Raffaella wouldn't hear of it and ranted to me about the importance of loyalty to old friends; she insisted we could cover for Antonella. Lately, I've begun to suspect that this is just one more of Raffaella's assaults. I am the only one who ever does any 'covering' for the cleaner; I spend half my life in rubber gloves.

'Oh, yes, so you did.' Actually, I had forgotten. 'How did that go?'

'Fine.'

I do try and concentrate on every issue involving the bar but because Roberto is continually rushing around it's difficult to keep track.

'I'll be in the bar by ten or ten thirty, latest,' I tell him.

He nods briefly and kisses me on the forehead before dashing off, at an almost comical speed, towards Bruno's.

I breathe a sigh of relief. As the mornings have brightened and the novelty of scrubbing clean or even serving in the bar has begun to wear off, I've been less inclined to arrive in for 10 a.m. sharp. My cappuccino-drinking in the square occasionally drags on till eleven; yesterday I only managed to lug myself there by noon. Roberto hasn't mentioned my tardiness. Maybe it's another thing he's failed to notice. I can't decide if that's infuriating or a relief. I mean, it's great that he's not grumbling that I need to spend every working minute in the bar, but on the other hand a girl likes to think she's indispensable.

As I sip the delightfully frothy cappuccino I glance around the piazza hoping to spot the American guy who gave the fag to Forgetful Man. I've found myself doing that a lot. Odd, because it's not that I have anything particular to say to him, or anything particular in common with him, come to that. He's nothing to me. I'm nothing to him. OK, so we are two non-Italians living in a small town, I suppose we have that in common, but that's all. While I have found myself thinking about him quite a lot, I don't imagine he's ever given me another thought.

And quite right too. I'm a married woman.

It would be nice to have a chat though, in my mother tongue.

I've noticed that Forgetful Man still makes his appearance regularly but there's never any sign of his cigarette-benefactor. Every time I don't see him I feel a sting of disappointment spike me, which is really peculiar. It's not as though we even suggested meeting up here again; we didn't make any plans or suggest any firm dates. He hasn't actually let me down by not being about but –

But I had thought he might drop into the bar. He did

say he might do that. And because he said he might I've found that when I am working, every time the door of the bar creaks open my eyes shoot to it. But he hasn't stopped by, and it's only when we are cashing up that I sigh and admit to myself how much I want him to. I realize that he's probably made up with his girlfriend by now and spending his time in Bassano del Grappa again. Well, good for him. That's nice. Another healthy, happy relationship. That's what I like to hear of. Alison and Fiona. The American guy and his beautiful Italian girlfriend. Roberto and me. Lovely.

'Hi.' I look up and am face to face with the American guy. Irrationally I believe he's been reading my thoughts, and I nearly scald myself as I jump a foot into the air with shock and embarrassment. 'Sorry, I didn't mean to startle you,' he says with a wide, lazy grin that somehow communicates that he's very used to startling women. 'Can I join you?'

I consider that perhaps I ought to say no. Perhaps I ought to point out that I've just drained my coffee and now must be scurrying back to the bar to support my husband as he regenerates our family business; instead I nod mutely, unable to find my tongue.

'Are you on your way to work?' he asks.

I nod again and mutter, 'You?'

'Yup, bit of a late start for me today. Normally I'm at school by now.'

'Roberto, my husband, is already at Bruno's.' I'm not quite sure why I feel I have to keep mentioning Roberto in front of this man, but I do. 'I find it hard to pull myself away from the piazza though,' I add with a wistful and appreciative glance around.

'I love it here too. I often spend my siesta lolling about in the piazza.'

'Not this one,' I state, 'I've looked for you.' Inwardly I squirm. What possessed me to admit that? I clamp my mouth shut and vow never to utter another word until my deathbed.

'I mean the piazza in Bassano del Grappa.' He stares at me with a peculiar mix of curiosity and challenge. It's uncomfortable under his gaze, a little like being in too hot sunlight.

'I prefer the mornings. The afternoons are too quiet for me,' I say.

I want to explain my preference for busy, hopeful mornings to the American, without hinting at my exasperation at my husband's demanding timetable.

When the shutters are open all manner of excitement is promised: pretty frilly knickers, glittering glassware and jewellery, gorgeous cakes and a rainbow choice of ice-cream flavours all lie in front of me. Tent-like frocks designed for mammas and scanty swimwear, designed for vixens, dress the same windows, proudly demonstrating that Italy is a place of contradictions.

'Mornings here are chaotic, cluttered and vivacious. But at three o'clock when the shutters on the shop windows are systematically slammed closed, curiosity is defied and possibility, glamour and vibrancy seem to vanish.'

'Are you saying that the shutters are a pertinent metaphor of your experiences in Italy to date?' asks the American guy, with unexpected insight that rattles me.

I fidget on my seat. Yes, when the shutters close I am left wondering if, all along, I imagined the possibility, glamour and vibrancy, but I hadn't realized as much until he articulated it.

'I think I'm just confessing to being a shopaholic,' I joke. 'I better get going now. Roberto will be wondering what's keeping me.'

I quickly stand up, scraping my heavy metal chair along the cobbles; the uncomfortable clanking sound reverberates around the piazza, announcing my hurried and clumsy exit.

'It's been good talking to you. Do you think –'

'Lovely to chat to you too,' I say and then I scuttle away from the American before he has the chance to finish his sentence.

He might have been about to ask did I think espresso was a preferable drink to latte, or did I think celebrating so many saints' days was a good custom, or did I think we should carry on talking another time, maybe have a drink. Something wouldn't allow me to stay to find out, especially since a big part of me wanted it to be the latter.

25

Curled up in bed it occurs to me that I have to have sex with Roberto tonight, even though it is not an especially good time in my cycle. Really, what is this nonsense about wanting some American stranger to chat to me? It's not like I'm *that* desperate for conversation. Or if it is, Roberto is the one that I should be turning to, not some not-my-type American guy.

'How were the takings tonight?' I ask, but I don't care. I ask because Roberto cares and I want to sweeten his mood. He's clearly exhausted again tonight, after another long day in the bar.

'Good. Generally this month is very up on March last year.'

'Your mamma will be pleased.'

'We should all be pleased. Mamma thinks the increase in trade is because the weather is more better. I'm hoping it's because the changes I make in the bar have started to have impression and therefore will last whatever the season. You know, things like the new decks and decent sound system. What do you think?'

I'm not especially interested either way. All I know is that the loud music hampers my already pathetic chance of correctly understanding the customers' orders so the evenings are extremely frustrating and tiring. Tonight I gave one customer cheese when he'd asked for ham, and another eggs when she'd wanted sparkling wine. I struggle to get pecorino and prosciutto the right way round and *uovo* sounds a little like Lambrusco if you only catch the end of the order.

'I'm not sure.' I stifle a yawn. 'I do know that Bruno's has a terrific selection of ice-creams. I've sampled every one of the twenty-eight flavours.' Last week I read that eating ice-cream increases chances of conceiving. 'And there's a constant dribble of customers who want to do the same – maybe it's the ice-cream sales that are pushing up the profits.'

'Our ice-cream is known. In the summer we have to hire extra staff just to serve cones. Mamma has said that this year you can do that job.'

'Right.' I can't think of an appropriate response. I don't want to admit to being bored or fed up, least of all patronized, and I do want us to have sex tonight, so I add, 'It's nice to be needed.'

I've found it useful to remind myself of this when I'm asked to clean loos or work on a Sunday. It's in everyone's best interests to accentuate the positive.

Roberto carefully takes off his clothes and gently lowers them into the wash basket with a tenderness most men reserve for handling their newborn infants.

I have to admit that there is at least one perk attached to living with his mother; I am no longer responsible for retrieving his shirts, trousers, pants, etc. from the wash basket, washing them, pressing them and returning them to his cupboard in pristine condition. I've never got the hang of folding his T-shirts exactly the way he likes them. I once asked Alison to practise with me but she said I ought to tell Roberto to stuff his T-shirts where the sun don't shine or at least tell him to do his own washing.

She didn't understand that I actually enjoyed the challenge of looking after Roberto's laundry and reaching a standard that makes him happy, the way his mother did. Or, at least, I initially enjoyed the challenge, but when it became clear that I was never going to achieve that standard, the whole washing thing became a nightmare and I was sorely tempted to follow Alison's advice.

To be fair, now I have seen Raffaella's ironing I'm forced to acknowledge it is second to none. Roberto's shirts are returned to him looking as though she buys them fresh every morning. I do my own washing and have found nothing really *needs* an iron.

Roberto pulls on pyjama bottoms and slips between the sheets.

'Why have you started to wear pyjamas?' I ask. 'It's getting warmer, not cooler.' Roberto and I have always slept naked, ever since we met. The pyjamas are white and made from linen, so they do look good against his permanently tanned torso, but even so I don't like fabric coming between us. I miss the feel of his skin when we snuggle at night.

'We are in my mamma's house.' He turns off the bed-side light. 'Goodnight.'

I stare into the blackness. It takes a moment for my eyes to adjust. Once I can see the outline of the enormous mahogany dressing table I reply.

'But we dress before we go down to breakfast and she sleeps on a different floor, so she's not likely to get a glimpse of your tackle if you make a dash to the bathroom in the middle of the night.'

'But what if she ever came into our room? Many of her clothes are still stored in here.'

The idea is so disturbing that I lose the trail of my thoughts and find I can't argue effectively.

'By the way, I don't like Mamma sleeping in the attic rooms. I'm going to make Paolina swap. I don't think Mamma can handle the stairs.'

I freeze with horror at the very thought. Paolina is often out until quite late, but even so, I'm aware that she sleeps about two feet away from us and all that separates us is a wall. If Paolina moves into the attic and Raffaella moves into the bedroom next door, I might as well take religious orders because there is no way on God's earth that I could orgasm knowing Raffaella could be listening. Besides, *I* like the attic room. Why can't Raffaella move back into this room; why does she insist on disrupting everybody?

'We'd never shag again if your mother was in Paolina's room. It's bad enough now, Paolina's proximity has quite an inhibiting effect,' I say.

'Paolina can't hear a thing. The walls are thick.' Roberto yawns.

'How can you be sure?'

'Well, even if she can, Mamma is deaf and would hear nothing,' he mumbles.

'Your mother is not deaf, her hearing is selective.' And I have a definite feeling she would elect to hear our lovemaking, assuming there ever was any to hear, that is.

'You are not rational. In London the flat was tiny and the walls so thin that our Chiswick neighbours must have heard every mattress squeak.' He yawns again, somewhat pointedly, I feel.

'Maybe, but I wasn't related to those guys,' I mutter.

We lived in the same flat in Chiswick for several years

and rarely passed the neighbours on the stairs, let alone found ourselves passing the coffee at breakfast. I decide this isn't the best moment to discuss the sleeping arrangements with Roberto. He's tired and therefore defensive. However, as Paolina is out tonight, we should take advantage. I need him to slip out of those pyjamas and slip into something more comfortable instead. Me, for example.

Slowly, I snake my arms around Roberto's body. I love the feel of him. There's nothing I like more than trailing my hands over his warm chest – except perhaps moving my hands a little southwards. I start to gently kiss and caress him.

Roberto's breathing doesn't quicken, nor does he stiffen. He's asleep. I flop on to my back and breathe out, deeply. I try to expel the disappointment from my body. If it harbours there until morning we are bound to be snappy over the breakfast table. That won't do at all. I can't afford to waste another month.

I lie on my back and stare into blackness. I'm restless and don't think I'll ever fall asleep. I try to think about some of the ideas for the bar that Roberto has shared with me today. Something about new chandeliers and a live impromptu DJ session once a month, but my mind won't stay on the subject. Before I know it, I'm thinking about the American guy. I wonder what his favourite ice-cream flavour is. I wonder if he'd come to the DJ sessions? I wonder what he's doing right now and who with? I wonder if he's asleep and if so, who with?

Aaghh. Where did that thought come from? I start to mutter Louisa, Matthew, Louisa, Matthew, and hope this mantra will send me off.

26

7 March

This morning I made Roberto feel guilty about his exhaustion last night, so we managed a quick session before breakfast. It wasn't a full-on pash-sesh, it did have a whiff of duty about it, but I don't care. That sort of thing makes no difference to the end result. Raffaella didn't comment that we were both late for breakfast and Paolina simply waved as she gulped back a coffee and rushed for the door.

'That girl is always rushing,' says Raffaella. Actually, I translated that she had said, 'That girl is a speed,' but that seems unlikely.

Paolina didn't get home until the early hours last night, I heard her come in; sadly, even the chant 'Louisa and Matthew' could not send me to sleep. I thought Italians were meant to be relaxed and only English people worked bloody silly hours and stayed chained to their desk for eighteen hours a day.

'She works hard,' I say with a smile.

Raffaella nods and says, '*Sì.*'

It's a very articulate '*Sì*', and somehow I believe she's really said, 'Yes, and she shouldn't be a career woman, how will she find a husband? She needs to put more energy into doing that. Unlike you. You have a husband, so now all you should do is work hard but instead you are lazy and come to breakfast late.' But that could just be my imagination.

There's this picture of Roberto's mother and father on their wedding day, which hangs in the dining room. Increasingly, throughout mealtimes, I have found myself drawn to looking at it for long periods of time. The more I stare at the photo the more mysterious it seems.

I'm told that the picture is thirty-seven years old and I discover Raffaella and Bruno married when they were twenty-three and twenty-six respectively. This, in itself, is a bit of a surprise, as the smiling stars of the pic look even younger than that – little more than a couple of kids; besides, the Raffaella I know is about one hundred and ten so the maths doesn't add up. Roberto once told me that Raffaella and Bruno used to win dancing competitions; they were quite well known throughout the region. I'd always found this as hard to believe as believing in the tooth fairy, until I saw the wedding photo. *This* Raffaella I can imagine gliding across a dance floor in someone's arms.

I stare at this picture and try to understand how this delightful girl became the woman I know as my mother-in-law.

I can see from the picture that there is a lot of Roberto's father in Roberto. They're both tall and broad-shouldered. Bruno's eyes also twinkled and his grin was as confident and relaxed. I wish Bruno was still alive; I like to think he'd have been my friend and ally. And I sure could do with one of those.

From the wedding picture, it's also possible to see that while Roberto looks like his father, Paolina (rather neatly) takes after her mother (although only physically, thank the lord). The photo is proof that Paolina inherited her graceful limbs and tiny pinched waist from Raffaella – who would have thought it? Her exotic almond-shaped eyes are her mother's too. Raffaella now has large bags under her eyes. Bags so full that her former, pleasantly mystifying eyes are reduced to ugly black currants. At first my heart swelled with sympathy. Given that she's a widow, I wondered whether the bags were a result of struggle and pain, but then I realized that they are because of the wine; it transpires that she likes a glass or two.

I wonder if Paolina's boyfriends look at her mother with total horror. I've heard it said that you marry the daughter but the mother is your wife. The dancing girl has been swallowed by the indolent woman who sits in the kitchen all morning, in the parlour all afternoon and in the bar all evening. Thinking about it, Paolina has yet to bring a boyfriend to the bar. Maybe she's scared her mother will frighten them off – not an unreasonable thought.

I'd like to defy stereotype and reveal that my mother-in-law is a slim, colourfully dressed suffragette, but sadly, I can't. She's what polite people might describe as rotund or fleshy (read fat). Under her floral aprons she wears nothing other than black sweaters that she repeatedly yanks down over her large belly to meet her black skirt. Her tights are American Tan and I have to wonder who her supplier is, I didn't think they were still produced. Bride Raffaella had coal-black hair running like a waterfall down her back. Now her hair is streaked with white, it's a stark contrast, and she looks as though she is wearing a piano keyboard on her head. Her shoes are the only things that suggest a faint echo of the lovely young woman in the wedding picture. Her shoes are made of the highest-quality leather and they are polished like mirrors so that you can probably see up her skirt. But then you'd have to have some sort of masochistic streak if you wanted to see up her skirt.

As I watch her wade through her breakfast it strikes me that she's the literal opposite to the expression 'no flies on me'. Unlike her children, she is lazy and therefore is often still for extended periods, so flies *do* frequently settle on her. One is crawling up her slack arm right now. I watch with barely disguised disgust as another hides in the folds of her patterned apron. Raffaella seems not to notice the flies, although I can't drag my eyes away from their busy, black backs and hairy legs. For God's sake, it's only March, I didn't think there were flies in March; how did they find her?

Roberto drags me from my thoughts as he dashes around the room leaving behind him startled dust particles. I look up as he's halfway out of the door.

'Where are you going? You've hardly had a bite to eat.'

'I have an appointment. Out of town. I need to be there early, to get back in time for the lunchtime rush.'

'Rush? I know we are a bit busier nowadays but I wouldn't call it a rush,' I say bluntly. I regret the words instantly as Roberto looks disappointed and disgruntled.

'Yes, rush,' he declares staunchly. 'Do you mind being in charge? It will mean going to the bar in time to open up.' He throws me the keys. I catch them quite messily, with two hands and the aid of my right boob. 'Will you manage?'

'Yes, of course. You go ahead.' I'm basking in the light

of new responsibility and forget to ask him where his appointment is or what it is about.

I spread honey on to my bread and chew carefully as I ponder what I should wear today. Raffaella starts to clear up around me. I tell myself she's just being efficient and she's not trying to make me feel uncomfortable but I don't believe my own line of consolation – since she's not noted for her efficiency and I know she's always trying to make me feel uneasy.

Raffaella is muttering something or other, a prayer I think. I catch the names Ana and Maria; grandmother and mother of Jesus Christ – Raffaella's personal favourites. I pay little attention. Things are at a pass whereby whenever my mother-in-law claps eyes on me she draws in her breath as though she can't bear to as much as breathe the same air I do. The effect is that her mouth looks like it has been stapled. When we are alone she makes it clear that she thinks of me as one step away from the devil himself; I swear she clasps her hands together to resist making the sign of the cross to ward off my evilness. We are enemies but we fight with stealth. We camouflage our clawing by grumbling about the domestic necessities that structure our days together.

Raffaella complains to Roberto because I don't go to church, because I can't make fresh pasta, because I fold the tablecloths incorrectly when I am clearing away. I hint that I find it annoying because his mother won't meet my eye when she's talking to me, besides which she talks ridiculously quickly so that I can't understand her and she won't allow me to put a lock on the bathroom door. Privacy appears to be a concept she cannot, or at least will not, acknowledge. Roberto's approach to peacekeeping is to largely ignore our problems. He begs her for understanding, me for patience and both of us for tolerance.

I've given this some thought, and I suspect our rows about housekeeping, food, work and privacy are not the true source of our antipathy towards one another. I fear we are arguing about much bigger issues but we are too ashamed and afraid to argue out the questions that we both want answers to. We are women who both want to know who has the biggest claim to Roberto. Who needs him most? Who does he need most? Who loves him most? Who is the most loved? Jealousy is never pretty, and on this occasion it's fairly frightening, as it's unexpected. I did not expect my mother-in-law to be jealous of me but then I did not expect to be small-minded towards her. I hoped Raffaella would be a comfort, a guide, at the very least a source of some decent cooking tips.

'*Ana-Maria e molto simpatico*,' she tells me. What is she on about? The saints Anne and Mary are very nice? I'm confused. Raffaella stops what she is doing and turns to me; she treats me to a broad but insincere smile. Then in clear, practised English she says, 'He has to be with Ana-Maria today. She grateful.' Then she sighs and looks unbearably sorrowful; after the dramatic pause she adds, 'Ana-Maria is very nice. We all had hope for a marriage with Ana-Maria.'

27

I skip my morning coffee in the square and rush to Bruno's. As I'm my own boss today I can make myself a coffee there. I've never heard of an Ana-Maria.

I chop salad, polish the bar and glasses and take the coffee machine apart so that I can give it a thorough clean before I reassemble it, plus I serve several customers a morning espresso, but all the time the same two questions keep popping into my head, screwing up my ability to enjoy my efficiency. 'Who is Ana-Maria?' and 'Where is Roberto right now?'

At half past eleven I realize I can't exercise restraint for a moment longer. I dig out my mobile and call Alison.

'Hey, how's it going?' she asks the moment she picks up.

I loosen at the sound of Alison's voice, immediately forgetting that I'm a bit miffed off with her too. I suppose my miffed-off-ness is irrational. I spent the first few weeks here avoiding her calls and the last few wondering why she's not ringing as often as she used to. I can't reflect too long on that inconsistency because it would become undeniably transparent that I'm irritatingly irrational.

'Er, fine,' I lie. I've rung her to talk about this Ana-Maria but find I'm not brave enough to instantly launch into the issue.

'Sorry I didn't call last week. I was out with Fiona every night. I kept meaning to but –'

'It's OK. I understand,' I say nobly.

As unfashionable and undesirable as it is, I have to admit that historically I have been one of those girls who neglected her friends whenever a new boyfriend arrived on the scene. I never meant to do so but it sort of happened. I remember when I first met Roberto I didn't crawl out of bed for a month, let alone think of calling Alison. I guess I can cut her some slack now she's met Fiona. It's just a bit unexpected, that's all. Alison has never put a fledgling relationship in front of friendship before. In a perverse way I ought to be pleased she's neglecting me; everyone needs to be overwhelmed by new love at least once in a lifetime.

Of course I'm not an idiot, I knew that coming to Italy would sluice away some of the immediacy and therefore intimacy of our friendship. Obviously, when Alison worked just a short bus ride away from where I lived it was easy to catch up twice a week, minimum, and we spoke on the phone pretty much daily. I just hadn't expected there to be such an enormous gap where our friendship used to be. I thought I'd be living a thrilling new life, and that when I did call Alison and all my other friends and family, I'd have oodles of news and excitement to relay. Let's face it – I was expecting to be announcing the pattering of tiny feet by now.

'How's work?' I ask. Normally Alison is keen to talk about work and I feel a need to get us on familiar footing.

'I'm having a day away from the office today.'

'You're throwing a sickie?' I ask, unable to hide my surprise. Alison has never, ever thrown a sickie. If she's throwing sickies I have to consider the possibility of body-snatchers.

'No, I'm working from home. Fiona is on holiday,' she adds shyly.

'How is Fiona?' I ask graciously.

Alison talks non-stop for about ten minutes, singing every one of Fiona's many great virtues. No, I had no idea she could play the saxophone; that *is* amazing. No, I haven't ever seen *Good Night Good Luck* but if it's Fiona's favourite then I'm sure it must be wonderful. It's just that I prefer colour movies, I even have problems with *The Wizard of Oz* because that movie can't make up its mind. No, I haven't ever seen anyone skim stones so they hop five times minimum *every time*; what an achievement.

'Where's Fiona now?' I ask.

'She's out getting the weekly shop.'

'*Your* weekly shop?'

'Yes, she's so thoughtful. She has a car. You know how I hate dragging bags home on the bus.'

My God, it all sounds very cosy, very established. I haven't even met or vetted this Fiona. Not that she sounds anything other than lovely, it's just that things seem to be moving so fast and I'm not there to be part of any of it.

'I thought you were going to buy online and have the supermarket deliver your groceries because that's greenest. That was your new year's resolution,' I point out, a little tetchily.

'I know. I am going to do that. I just haven't got round to it. I don't seem to have a minute nowadays, although I'm not sure where our time goes. We lost last night just chatting and listening to music. It seemed that one second it was eight p.m., the next it was two in the morning, you know what I mean.'

I do vaguely remember that stage when time flew like

a migrating bird in autumn, but such relaxed and cosy intimacy seems a distant memory for Roberto and me. Odd, because isn't intimacy supposed to increase over the years? I mean that's logical, isn't it? But time stands still when he talks about the bar.

'So how are things going for you?' asks Alison.

I tell her what Raffaella said about this Ana-Maria.

'Who do you think she is?' I ask.

'Well, I could reasonably guess that's she's an ex-girlfriend.'

'But Roberto has never uttered her name.'

'Well, maybe he doesn't think she's important.'

Frankly, Alison doesn't sound that convinced or convincing, but I see a glimmer of hope and I surge towards it. 'That's probably why he's never mentioned her, don't you think?'

'I don't know for certain, obviously. You'll have to ask Roberto.'

'So you think I should talk to him about her?'

'Yes!' Alison sounds exasperated. 'What Raffaella said is clearly worrying you; of course you ought to discuss it with Roberto.'

'I don't want to upset him, especially not in the next day or so.'

'Why especially not in the next day or so?'

'It's a good time of the month. I don't want to waste it rowing.'

I hoped that this comment would sound mature and considered, but I am suddenly hit with the thought that if Roberto is having a flirtation with someone then it might be pathetic and sad to ignore it. I couldn't conceive a baby with a man who is having an affair, could I? No, I couldn't, but it's an academic question because Roberto isn't having an affair. Who said *affair*? A flirtation, maybe. Best not to blow this out of proportion.

I can hear Alison take a deep breath; she sounds exasperated. After a pause she says, 'I think you are going to have to risk that. You need to get to the bottom of this and I can't do that for you.'

'But you think there's a simple explanation?' I ask hopefully.

'Maybe. Look, Elizabeth, I don't know, I'm not the one you should be talking to about this. You have to ask Roberto. Call him now.'

I hang up and then return to cleaning the bar. Alison was the wrong person to call. She's all loved up and people who are loved up are notoriously selfish. I was mad to think she'd be supportive or sympathetic.

'Hi, hoped I'd catch you. How's it going?'

Bugger. Alarm bells fling their way around my head, as I realize I couldn't imagine any voice I'd rather hear interrupt my internal muttering and worrying than this deep, melodious American one. I tell myself that there's nothing odd about that, it's only because he speaks English. If the American guy was an American girl there wouldn't be any alarm bells. I'm being silly.

I'm not sure I believe me.

I look up and am slapped by the intensity of his eyes. Who'd have thought green eyes could have such a punch in the gut effect? I feel a devastating and unprecedented pull internally; starting in my thighs and moving upward, enveloping my belly, chest and throat. What is this? I have encountered sexual attraction before, obviously, but this . . . This is something new. If American Guy was American Girl there wouldn't be this.

I'm suddenly conscious that I dressed in a hurry (and a fury) and didn't even manage to wave the mascara wand anywhere near my eyes. Bugger, I'm wearing my oldest jeans and my hair is tied back in a scruffy (rather than elegant or even casual) pony-tail; I wonder if it is worth-while ironing T-shirts after all.

I give the bar one final rub with my large dusting cloth and then fling it on a shelf, out of sight.

'Not so great if the truth was known,' I splutter without thinking.

'Sorry to hear that.'

'Can I get you a coffee?' I offer.

'I'll take a coke.'

I join him. One thing my years of being a barmaid and a waitress have taught me is the value of chatting to a sympathetic stranger.

'I've been wondering, how long have you lived here?' I ask as I push the coke towards him across the scuffed bar.

'Four years.'

'And how do you manage?' I almost wail.

'How do you mean?'

'Well, didn't you ever feel lonely, alienated, pointless? How did you manage to settle?'

I feel myself sink and shrink a fraction. I'm too weary to wonder why this man makes me feel able to articulate things that I didn't even want to admit were in my subcon-scious. All at once, I realize I don't have enough energy to remind myself how great it is that I'm living my dream by being here in Italy. I gasp, vaguely ashamed that my innermost insecurities are brimming over and lying in a puddle between us. I've completely forgotten my line in barmaid small talk. Bloody hell, I don't even know the guy's name.

As if reading my mind he says, 'Chuck Andrews,' and holds out his enormous paw for me to shake. Is he serious? I must look incredulous because he explains, 'Chuck is a common derivative of Charles in the US.'

'I didn't know that. In the UK it's a sort of old-fashioned term of endearment; strictly limited to use in the communities of the ancient, toothless great-aunts of the north.'

Chuck laughs. 'I didn't know *that*.'

It feels good to hear someone laugh at something I've said. It hasn't happened for a while, yet I consider myself humorous. I'm not a genius or a goddess, I get by in those two departments but I do like to have a laugh and it's only hearing such a genuine and hearty laugh that I realize what's been missing since I arrived in Italy.

'I'm Elizabeth and I'm homesick.'

'Day at a time is the only approach,' says Chuck, immediately getting my reference to AA confessionals. 'I kinda gathered as much yesterday.'

'Well, you were a day ahead of me.'

'That's why I looked in. I thought maybe you needed a buddy.' He slouches forward and rests his upper body on the bar. It should seem intrusive and disrespectful of the correct body space boundaries, but it doesn't, it seems intimate and concerned. Friendly, that's all. 'Tell me.'

Tell me is a direct translation from an Italian expression, '*Di mi*.' Friends use it to mean, 'What's your news?' or 'What's going on?' I've always loved the simplicity and directness of the expression. Roberto used to say '*Di mi*' a lot, but thinking about it he hasn't said it that much recently. I don't think there's much I say that interests him at the moment.

'I love Italy,' I tell Chuck. 'And Italians, they are my favourite people,' I gush. 'I was so looking forward to coming here but it's not quite what I imagined.'

'In what way?'

'Raffaella, my mother-in-law, is a dragon.' I whisper this and look over my shoulder, even though I'm pretty sure that she's safely back at home and not in earshot. Chuck grins and doesn't contradict me, for which I'm grateful. The brief conversations I've had with Roberto's friends have always established that they think Raffaella is the salt of the earth, just because *apparently* she makes a to-die-for lasagne and her tiramisù isn't bad either.

'I thought my sister-in-law and I would become good pals but she's always rushing about and is rarely at home. I don't think I've said more than a sentence at a time to her. And Roberto is very busy too. I don't want to get under his feet or be a worry to him. He has enough on his plate.'

I don't mention Ana-Maria, even though the question of who the hell is she is banging around my head like a pinball. OK, so Chuck has an eye-catching smile and I like the way the blond hairs stand out on his tanned forearms but dare I go that far? I feel vaguely guilty grumbling at all. This is what I always wanted – to live in Italy. This is what I thought would make me happy. I hadn't intended to say so much, but Chuck is one of those people who instantly invite confidences. It's something about the eyes.

'I miss my best friend, Alison, and I miss my family, which is really peculiar because even back in the UK my interaction with them was largely limited to phone calls every Sunday night and I still call them every Sunday night but somehow it's not the same. I can feel the distance between us along the line. I thought that I'd fit right in here. I wanted to be part of a tactile, lively, chatty family. And I was not wrong; Italians do smile and touch each other, they do pat one another's backs and hug each other all the time. They just don't do it to me. They are polite and they shake hands with me but then they dismiss me.'

'What do you expect? Mostly they've known each other since they were babies and they've only known you ten minutes.'

His point is valid but all the more irritating because it's something I can't change.

'You'll make friends in time,' he assures me, kindly. 'Like you said, they are great people. But perhaps you have to be more proactive. You can't just sit still and wait for friends to fall into your lap.' His advice should sound impertinent, but it doesn't; he just sounds concerned. 'How are your Italian lessons coming along?' I blush, embarrassed to admit I'm not actually taking any lessons. Chuck understands my flush. 'You'll need to learn the language. You have to make an effort. You are in Italy. You can't expect everyone to speak English all the time.'

Roberto has said the same thing, pretty much every day since we arrived here. Oddly, hearing this unequivocal truth from Chuck isn't as annoying or condescending. He doesn't sound as though he is accusing me of being lazy or stubborn.

'I know a good tutor,' he says with a smile and a challenging wink.

I bask in the warmth of the idea of Chuck teaching me Italian. I can see it now; the two of us sat in his garden with a bottle of wine and a bowl of fat olives between us, maybe even a textbook too. He takes a pen out of his pocket and jots something down. I assume it's his number.

The paper says 'Signor Castoro' and a local telephone number. 'Oh,' I say with some disappointment.

Chuck is unaware of my day-dream and therefore does not detect any sign of regret.

'Have you heard of him? He's a great teacher. He taught me and it's not easy tutoring a tutor. He's very thorough and demanding.'

Oh fab, my favourite type of teacher, I think miserably. Chuck starts to chat about his job and the best places to visit nearby. He asks me if Roberto and I have visited Verona or Venice yet. I assure him we plan to but things have been too hectic so far. We work weekends and Raffaella isn't keen on us taking the same day off. Chuck comments that this is a shame and says I have to promise myself to 'do Venice' and 'do Verona' in the next month. I snigger when he explains that most tourists can 'do' these great cities in a day.

'You Americans are always in such a hurry. I bet you think you can "do" all of Europe in a month. Surely it's preferable to stay longer in Venice. I'm sure I could spend a day in the Basilica di San Marco, alone,' I say primly.

'Oh yes, longer is preferable,' says Chuck with a benevolent smile. If he's heard my dig at his nation's tick-off-the-sites approach to history and culture, he's choosing to let it pass. His generosity makes me feel a little mean. I'm not sure why I felt the need to push him away but I'm glad he wasn't easily shoved.

'Sorry, I'm not in a great mood, that was a bit rude of me,' I mutter. Chuck shrugs but I regret the awkwardness I've created between us, even if I'm the only one who can feel it. 'Raffaella mentioned something this morning; it's knocked me for six.'

My impulse to give this information as a peace offering, in an effort to re-establish intimacy, is a bit off-centre. I'm not sure there ought to be an intimacy in the first place.

The bar is empty except for an old guy nursing a red wine in the corner. The place should feel huge but I can feel the walls squeeze together, pushing me up against Chuck. Even though we are not physically touching I feel so close to him it's as though we are spooned into one another. What's that about? He waits to see if I want to elaborate. I do. But I don't. If you know what I mean.

'Oh, it's probably something and nothing,' I say with forced breeziness. 'Can I get you another drink?'

'No, I'd love to but I need to get on. I have to be in Bassano del Grappa in an hour. How much for the coke?'

I'd like to say it was on the house but I haven't got that sort of authority so I take his money with reluctance. I draw out the process of counting out his change; I don't want him to leave the bar. I have a feeling that from the moment he leaves I'll find myself thinking about when I'll see him again.

Bugger, I'd better go and polish tables or something.

28

Five minutes after Chuck says his goodbyes, Roberto calls to say he'll be later than he originally expected.

'I have already called Laurana and she is going to come and help you with the lunchtime rush.'

I like Laurana, she's a great cook and she works the hardest out of the three girls on the staff. To date we have done little other than smile manically at one another but I feel she is kind and I promise myself to try to talk to her a little more this afternoon. Chuck would be impressed.

'Right, thanks. That's thoughtful.'

'You OK?' asks Roberto.

'Yes.' Well, no, not really. The question of 'Who the hell is Ana-Maria' burns on my tongue but I don't want to have the discussion over the phone. I do want to ask him exactly where he is and what is the nature of the appointment that is tearing him away from the bar, but before I can do so he says '*Ciao*' and hangs up.

I vow not to worry. Ana-Maria is probably some childhood friend Roberto hasn't seen for twenty years. Raffaella is no doubt just stirring. Even if Roberto is with her right now as Raffaella said, and even if she is an ex-girlfriend as Alison assumed, that doesn't have to spell catastrophe. I'll be able to ask him all about it at teatime; he's bound to be home by then. If this Ana-Maria was a serious part of his past I'd know about her. Wouldn't I? Obviously. Yes.

Laurana and I handle the lunchtime shift easily between us. We manage to converse, if not chat, on and off, throughout the afternoon. Laurana studied English at school for a couple of years and we joke that having the correct vocab to ask, 'Which way is it to the vet's?' and to say 'This is a pencil' doesn't come in particularly useful when trying to get to know one another. We resort to reading the Italian *Heat* equivalent together. We point at the pictures of the stars and make observations such as '*Bella*' and '*Molto* sexy' which spins us both into fits of giggles. I'm pleased to report that, like me, she thinks Drew Barrymore is probably a great best friend to have and that Dr Jack from *Lost* is to-die-for-gorgeous. It's surprising how absorbing it can be discussing which C-lister has or hasn't had plastic surgery.

There's a constant dribble of customers and we forget to close the bar for a siesta break. I promise Laurana we'll pay her overtime but she's gracious about keeping me company and insists it's not important.

'I enjoy the talk with you,' she says with a beam. I beam back at her full of hope that Chuck has it spot on, I will make friends in Italy as I've always dreamed – it just might take a bit of time.

I don't get a chance to bask in the embryonic friendship for too long because soon after seven o'clock customers start to pour in through the door and we are rushed off our feet. Raffaella joins us, but as I've had such fun with Laurana I don't allow her sourpuss face to upset me, instead I busy myself clearing tables and washing up and I leave it to her to lord it over the bar. Part-way through the evening I notice that Gina and Alexandra, our student bar staff, have arrived to help, as the place is suddenly and unusually packed; I assume Raffaella has called them.

At ten Paolina arrives at the bar. She doesn't start to serve; she just helps herself to a whisky on the rocks and then plonks down on a chair in the corner. As a rule Italian women don't drink much and I've only ever seen Paolina imbibe a modest glass of wine with dinner, except on Valentine's day, when she was drinking on her own – then she downed almost a bottle. I suddenly feel concern, as I wonder what's brought on the whisky-drinking. I think of Chuck's advice that I have to be proactive and initiate friendships, so when Raffaella's back is turned I quickly pour a whisky for myself and then I weave through the crowds towards my sister-in-law.

'This really is the busiest I've ever seen the bar,' I comment. She doesn't acknowledge my conversation starter, so I try for something more direct. 'Can I join you?' I have to shout over the chatter and laughter. Paolina, by contrast, seems to be in a pool of gloomy silence.

'Be my guest,' she says coolly.

'Cheers.' I slide into the seat next to her and clink my glass with hers

'*Salute*,' she says with all the enthusiasm of someone who has just heard their pet dog died.

'What's up?'

Paolina reaches for her handbag, retrieves a compact mirror and a lipstick. She reapplies the lippy and pinches her cheeks in an attempt to resurrect some colour. She then scrabbles around until she finds her cigarettes and lighter. Only after she's taken a long hard drag does she say, 'Nothing.'

I'd be more convinced if she didn't look as though she'd been crying and if she wasn't chewing her thumbnail whenever her fag was resting in the ashtray. I continue to stare at her and finally she concedes.

'Work stuff, hard day. Nothing really. It will all be better in the morning.'

I consider whether to pretend to believe her. Then I consider that she's the nearest thing I have to a sister.

'Something is obviously wrong?'

'I have split up with my boyfriend, if you must know,' she says. Her tone is a mix between snippy and wounded.

'I'm sorry.' I hesitate. 'I didn't even realize you had a boyfriend. Was it a new relationship? They can still hurt. If you thought he was special and then –'

'We'd been together five years.'

'Five years?' I'm stunned. 'How come I haven't met him?'

I didn't even know about him. I'm torn between doubting her, accusing her of having a very active imagination and saying this boyfriend is a figment of it, or accepting that there is a boyfriend and my not knowing about him is more evidence of my lack of intimacy with the people I call family. Who is Ana-Maria? How many more secrets? Why do I have the feeling that I'm trying to go up a down escalator? I'm unsure of my footing and seem to be making no progress.

'He's married. I couldn't introduce him to anyone,' says Paolina by way of explanation.

'You are a mistress?' I ask with a gasp. I'm unable to keep the surprise from my voice. I wonder if she can hear my outrage too.

'Yes, or rather I was.' She takes another gulp of whisky, which pretty much drains the glass.

I don't approve of affairs. For one thing, people always

get hurt in situations like these. Well, obviously. Look, she's crying into her whisky. My telling her it will end in tears could only be seen as the wisdom of hindsight rather than anything astute or profound. But, besides that, I don't approve because marriage is marriage. Paolina is gorgeous and intelligent and funny. Not right now, maybe. Right now, she looks horrendous and is being especially un-funny but under normal circumstances she's a catch. Couldn't she have dated a single man? I swallow my indignation and try to ascertain the facts.

'Did you know he was married when it started?'

'Yes.'

'My God.'

'What? You thought Londoners had the market on extra-marital affairs?' Paolina signals to Alexandra and asks her to bring over another glass of whisky. 'Actually, bring the bottle,' she instructs. Raffaella will go crazy when it comes to stock-take but I get the feeling this isn't the moment to say so. Paolina turns back to me. 'Did you think Italians weren't sophisticated enough for any kind of sexual misconduct? Did you think we all married our childhood sweethearts and lived happily ever after making *arrabbiata* sauce?'

Her sarcasm stings, but I suppose I did think exactly this so I decide to leave her remark uncommented upon.

To think I felt sorry for her for working long hours. Now all those late nights take on a more sinister hue.

'I'm very sorry but maybe it's for the best. Does he have kids?'

'One.' I gasp, not able to hide my shock. Paolina turns to me and demands angrily, 'Where is it you live, Elizabeth? Because it's not the real world. Do you live on your own little fantasy island, you deal in black and white only and people only behave as you suppose they ought to? You are so naïve.'

'I'm not. I was a barmaid in London for years. I've seen stuff you could only imagine. It's just that I thought Italians were big into their families and I'm surprised to hear a father would have an affair for five years.'

'Even your stereotypes are underdeveloped,' laughs Paolina, bitterly. She's being very rude but she is drunk – I've heard much worse when people have had one or two too many so I can let it go. 'Where did you do your research on Italian stereotypes? It's not too rigorous. The mistress is institutionalized here, didn't you know?'

'I've never given it any thought,' I admit, somewhat pathetically. It's not a nice thing to think about.

'Well, she is. You ought to know that.'

I can't decide if Paolina is placing particular and loaded emphasis on the word 'you' or whether she's too drunk to know what she's talking about. What is she talking about?

'Does your mother know?' I ask.

'On one level. Perhaps. I've never had a boyfriend she could meet. I often stay in Padova. She pretends to believe I am still sleeping top and toe with my friend Giuliana. Like we did when we were students with not too much money and we shared a flat and a bedroom without any sexual meaning. But Giuliana never visits home and the truth is I haven't seen her for years. She exists only as a cover for me and my lover. When I am away for the night I am not top and toe in a small apartment. I am in a luxurious hotel, sipping champagne and receiving cunnilingus. But Mamma has never shown interest in how anyone reaches orgasm, least of all me.'

Fair enough, I suppose. I pause and then ask, 'Does Roberto know?'

'Of course.'

I take a deep breath and try to take in everything Paolina has told me. Suddenly, I've been shoved quite firmly into the epicentre of the family that I have longed to be part of. Yet, while I may have been lonely circling around the periphery, I now feel unfit for the burden of being part of this family. I did not expect secrets, disillusionment and broken hearts. But somehow I sense that there is no going back.

'Who is Ana-Maria?' I blurt. I want Paolina to confirm that Ana-Maria was some neighbour's kid and that Raffaella and Ana-Maria's mum used to joke that they'd marry one day but Roberto hasn't seen her since he started to wear long trousers. I wait for the gush of reassurances.

'Who is she?' repeats Paolina carefully. Is there an echo in here or just a sophisticated avoidance technique? Paolina stares at her whisky. Then she looks up at me and holds my gaze. Her deep brown eyes, normally so fast and intelligent, are blurred and confused. 'I like you, Elizabeth.' Drunks are always professing friendship or love – I generally find it rather charming but today I'm nervous. I can sense a great big 'but' coming my way. Whisky and heartache are a lethal combination and rarely bring with them good news.

'Who is she to the family? How does she fit in?' I probe.

Abruptly, Paolina snaps back from the almost cloying

closeness that has been engulfing us. She pulls away, necks her whisky and then says, 'We've known her since she was a small girl. A family friend. Do you want another drink? I'm going to the bar.'

I stare at my glass, which is empty, but I shake my head. All of a sudden the bar is too loud for me. I watch Paolina thread her way through the noise, crowds and smoke and I feel exhausted – mentally and physically. It's been a long day. Although Paolina has confirmed that Ana-Maria is a family friend I don't feel as reassured as I'd hoped to be. An uncomfortable and unwelcome feeling of suspicion, tinged with jealousy, snakes its way up my legs and sends shivers throughout my body.

I'm being irrational, plain stupid. Paolina has just said exactly what I thought she'd say.

Yet there was something about the way she said it that suggested I was hearing just half a story. My feet ache so much it's as if I've run a marathon. Not that I've run a marathon, too much training required, but I bet it feels a bit like this. I check my watch and realize that I've been here for fourteen hours in a row. Roberto still hasn't shown his face. The two facts combined have quite some clout. I don't want to cry but I know I'm close to it. I tell myself it's the smoke stinging my eyes. The bar will be open until at least two in the morning but I know I won't be able to go the distance.

I tell Raffaella I'm tired and that I'm going home. Even she can't accuse me of being lazy today, I've held the fort.

As I crawl between the sheets my phone beeps to let me know I have a text. It's from Roberto. He says he's just arrived at the bar and he's going to stay there until closing time. He tells me not to bother trying to stay awake for him. I don't send a reply. Instead I close my eyes, sure that I'll be asleep in moments.

I do sleep but it's not peaceful. I dream that I'm lost in the maze in Hampton Court (I did once get lost in this maze when I was about six and therefore variations of this dream often plague me). This time I am running through the green shrubbery shouting for Roberto. Suddenly a man with large forearms covered in blond hairs sweeps me over the hedge and puts me safely down in front of an ice-cream van. The ice-cream van is branded '*Ana-Maria, the finest in all of Italy.*'

29

8 March

I wake up grateful not to have to deal with any more dreams. The nightmare I'm living is enough. I roll over and am relieved to see that Roberto is still in bed with me. I didn't want to have missed him because he is dashing to some appointment or other. It's Saturday, and Saturdays are busy in the bar but, even so, I'm hoping to persuade him to take the day off. Maybe Paolina can run things without us or Raffaella can pull her finger out for once; they managed well enough before we arrived, surely they can soldier on for one day? My plan is to persuade Roberto to go to Venice. Everyone knows that Venice is *the* most romantic place in the world. Even before we arrived here I spent hours imagining strolling around the Doge's Palace, the Piazza San Marco and the Accademia. I can see it now: there will be sun on our backs and the sound of cooing pigeons and café orchestras will accompany our stroll; it will be wonderful.

A great setting to grill him about exactly who Ana-Maria is and why he's never mentioned her to me. The bastard.

No, no, wrong attitude. I'm jumping to conclusions. I have to allow Roberto time to tell me who this woman is.

I watch Roberto lying next to me. He is quite delicious to look at. I've always known as much. OK, maybe in the last year or so my appreciation of the aesthetics has taken a back seat compared to my desire to have a baby. But it's not that I don't still appreciate him, I do. Really, I do. I wonder what another woman would think if she came across Roberto for the first time or, worse, for the first time in a long time. I imagine any other woman would notice his olive skin, his lean stomach, his beautiful dark eyes, and she'd appreciate him. It's not a comforting thought.

I kiss his brown shoulder and I resist biting it (and I mean out of frustration, not passion). I vow to go softly, softly. I will not jump to conclusions. I do not need to scream and accuse like a shrill, jealous fishwife.

Roberto blinks and rubs his eyes.

'What time is it?' he asks as he stifles a yawn.

'Nearly nine.'

'Christ, I need to get moving, I should be in the bar.' He sits up, suddenly alert, all signs of sleepiness banished.

'Relax.' I try to gently push him back down to the horizontal. 'You only came to bed after three, you need to rest. In fact I thought we might take the day off. Let's go to Venice. I'm dying to see it.'

Despite my best efforts, Roberto is now out of bed and has yanked off his PJs. He's hopping as he tries to push his leg into his jeans in record time.

'Not today. I was away from the bar all yesterday. I have to be there today.'

Where is that written? 'Paolina could take care of things,' I point out reasonably.

'No. It is my responsibility. Go to Venice with Paolina if you must go.' He pulls a T-shirt over his head and mutters, 'Neither of you are much help, anyway.'

How unfair. I'm pretty sure he wanted me to hear that. Why is he in such a mood? Aren't I supposed to be the one with the grievance? Guilty conscience? I push the thought aside the moment it blunders into my head. No, Roberto has nothing to feel guilty about, I'm sure. Well, almost sure. I stick to the matter in hand.

'Excuse me, I ran the place on my own yesterday. I did a fourteen-hour shift.'

'Yes, yes, I'm grateful you kept things ticking over.'

'It was very busy. We did not tick over. You did the cash-up – you must know that from the takings,' I defend hotly.

'I know you had customers yesterday but I understand that you needed three staff to help you. Do you know how much that costs? Plus even poor Mamma had to lend her hand. She really is too much old, Elizabeth. We should be protecting her from the strains of the bar.'

'I didn't call in the extra staff. You called Laurana and Raffaella must have called Gina and Alexandra.'

'She thought it was necessary.' Roberto turns to me and pecks me on the forehead. It's a dry, placatory kiss; it lacks depth or any sort of understanding. If I had to label this kiss I'd call it patronizing – a novel breed of kiss for me – well, no one can say we don't try new things.

'I know you are doing your best, Elizabeth, but I can't just take off on a Saturday, without notice and without planning. It's our busiest day. I have a business to run.' He has a bar to run, not a multinational conglomerate, but I bite my tongue. 'You don't need to come in today though. You take a day off if you want. My friends are coming to see me in the bar this morning, I won't be lonely.' Then, as an afterthought, 'Actually, you would be bored. It's best you go off for the day.'

He doesn't want me around. The thought slams into me like a high-speed heavy goods vehicle. I thought I wasn't gelling with his friends because I hadn't learnt the language sufficiently; what if the root of the issue is that he doesn't want to give me the opportunity to meet his friends?

'Who is coming into the bar today?' I ask through gritted teeth.

'Just friends.'

'Do I know them?'

'I don't think so.'

'Who is Ana-Maria?'

And there it is. Her name is now between us even though I had vowed to keep it to myself, at least until we were somewhere more suitable than our bedroom. I've poured her name across our bed and it's as real as a flashing neon sign in flamingo pink. What was I thinking? It would have been so much more dignified to have subdued my suspicions and persuaded him to have a fun day in Venice instead. Perhaps we could have gone to Santa Maria Gloriosa dei Frari, to see Titian's gloriously uplifting *Assumption* altar painting. Chuck said it is arguably one of Venice's most sublime religious treasure troves.

And *then* I could have screamed, 'Who is Ana-Maria?'

For a moment I wonder whether I have imagined my distrustful question because Roberto remains stonily silent. He is sitting on the edge of the bed; he turns away from me and concentrates on putting on his socks. I can't believe he's going to get fully dressed just to walk to the bathroom to take a shower. Maybe he didn't hear me.

Maybe I whispered my enquiry in my head. Or maybe he just doesn't want to answer me.

'So, who is she?'

'A friend.'

'What sort of friend? An old girlfriend?'

'I dated her for a while,' he says with a reluctant, sorrowful shrug. He stands up and walks to the dressing table. I file his look and decide to re-examine it later. Exactly why is he sorrowful? Because I have called him on this or because they split in the first place? I inwardly gasp at the hideousness of that thought. As Roberto sits down again he looks in the mirror and pretends to be studying his own reflection, but his eyes stare past his sculptured cheekbones and are covertly watching me. He's gauging my reaction and by doing so he's admitting that a reaction is possible. Necessary? Justified?

'How long did you go out with her for?'

'I forget. A year. Or two.'

'Which was it?'

'Three and a half.'

Three and a half years and I have never heard her name. She must have really hurt him. I swallow this information like the water in a deep well swallows a stone. It looks as though it's vanished but ripples are springing in every direction.

'Were you with her yesterday?' I ask. I'm trying to make my question sound casual but my voice betrays me by wobbling. I plaster a broad, enquiring smile on to my face. I hope it convinces him and props me up.

'Yes. She is moving back into town. She has been away at university. I was helping her with her things.'

Italians take a lot longer to get their degrees than we

do in Britain. Often they study on a part-time basis for years, as they work at the same time to pay tuition fees. So the fact that she's just finished her degree does not mean that she's a child – although it does mean she's bright and dedicated.

'Oh, where did she study?' Am I convincing him that I'm merely interested or does he know I am drowning in a filthy puddle of insecurity and jealousy?

'Verona.'

'You drove to Verona yesterday?' I lose my battle for a feigned indifference; a child could hear the indignation in my voice.

'Yes. Twice, in fact. She had so much baggage I had to make two round trips.'

Over four hours' driving. I can taste my resentment. 'I could have come with you. I'd like to have seen Verona,' I say testily. Which he knew; I've begged him to take the trip but he's always too busy. I seethe.

'There was not enough room in the car.'

'And I'd have liked to meet your friend.'

It takes every ounce of dignity I have for me to say that. I dig deep into my reserves. Of course, what I really mean is that I *need* to see her. I have to weigh her up, judge her; I might have to criticize her or be comforted by the fact that she hasn't aged well, maybe she's carrying a bit too much weight or is prematurely balding – is that too much to hope? Obviously, it's of paramount importance that I decide whether she's a threat or not, ASAP.

'You can meet her today. She said she would pop into the bar.'

I see. I get out of bed and walk to where Roberto is

sitting at the dressing table. I put my arms around his neck in a subconscious gesture that psychologists would probably identify as territorial. I consider squeezing really tightly, ripping the life out of the rat, right now, but I realize that would be a little premature – some might say an over-reaction. What has my husband done wrong? Nothing. He helped out an old friend. Why shouldn't he? He wouldn't be the man I love if he didn't have such a generous nature. It's Raffaella's comment that is nibbling at my self-esteem.

'Ana-Maria's the girl your mother wanted you to marry, isn't she?' I ask.

Roberto stares right at me, albeit through the mirror. 'Possibly. But you are the girl *I* married.'

He did! He did and that means something. My God, that means everything. Why am I torturing myself like this? Why am I allowing Raffaella's poisonous little jibes to affect my marriage? Roberto is a good husband. He works hard. Very hard for our family business. So hard that he virtually forgets Valentine's day.

I shudder – not a helpful thought. It's difficult to know what to believe. I can't face asking any more questions on the subject of Ana-Maria just now, I need to digest what I already know. Instead I change my focus.

'Paolina was very upset last night. She's broken up with her boyfriend.' Roberto doesn't comment. I push on. 'Why didn't you tell me your sister had a married lover?'

'I hinted. I thought you'd have guessed. She never brings boys here. She stays out many nights. She's good-looking, I suppose, for a sister. If she was a friend of yours in London, you would have made guess.'

'Are you saying I'm patronizing towards Italians?'

'Not patronizing. It's just you do have rose-coloured sunglasses to see us. Maybe you only see what you want.'

I heard more or less the same from Paolina yesterday so I feel unsettled and defenceless.

'Do you think I'm naïve?' I ask.

'There are worse things to be than innocent, Elizabeth.' Then he turns and lowers me back on to the bed, only pausing to drag his T-shirt over his head in one, quick, fluid movement.

'Maybe we can be a little late this morning,' he mumbles into my ear.

30

Paolina said she could manage the bar on her own. She seemed lack-lustre – hungover and heartbroken. I felt a touch mean that she was being lumbered on a Saturday but as she said herself, she had nothing better to do today. Besides, I was so thrilled that Roberto (in the glow of post-coital activity) had agreed to take the day off (our first day alone together since we'd arrived here!) that I didn't want to ruin things; I accepted her word when she said she was OK.

· 'Will we park the car and then get a water taxi?' I ask Roberto.

I am already sitting in the car and waiting for him. He is carefully checking oil and water, tyre pressure and that sort of thing. I've always found his slightly boy-scout always-be-prepared approach to life vaguely dull and quite at odds with my image of fiery, impetuous Italians, although I admit he's often got me out of a hole because he does think about things such as having enough pound coins for the meters when we drive into central London, or carrying a foldaway umbrella in his laptop bag.

I'm staring at the guidebook and already imagining us stepping on to a beautiful mahogany boat, slipping through the sea, the sun shining down and everything glittering. There'll be a breeze lifting my hair and –

'No, it is too expensive. We'll drive and park in the

Tronchetto car park, it's only eighteen euros a day. Besides, Ana-Maria gets seasick on the ocean.'

It takes me a moment. 'Ana-Maria does? What has she to do with our plans?'

'Well, you said you wanted to meet her and it is her first day back in Veganze. She thought we would meet in the bar; I could not let her down so I invited her to join us. She is delighted.'

I bet she is.

The glow of my orgasm, which Roberto had gently and carefully pulled out of me, still sits like a rich secret between my legs. It's almost impossible to be angry with him. Almost. I sigh and resign myself to the fact that we are not going to have a romantic day for two. Still, the fact that he's so keen to introduce us must mean that their relationship is totally innocent. We might even become friends.

'Have you invited her boyfriend too?' I'm not hopeful there is one but it's worth a shot.

'She hasn't got a boyfriend at the moment.'

'Shame. For her I mean.' And me. 'Can she speak English?' I ask. I don't fancy a day struggling with verbs and flicking through my phrase book.

'Oh yes. She's fluent. She's an extremely brilliant linguist.'

'That's nice. Did she study languages at university?'

'No. Her English and French are self-taught. Hobbies almost. She read politics and economics. She graduated with the most distinguished honour available.'

I love her already.

We drive to Ana-Maria's house although it turns out that she only lives a few minutes from the bar. Roberto leaves me in the car and goes to collect her on his own.

I hear the family's laughter and salutations as he enters (he goes around the back door and does not knock but walks straight in). Then the house swallows him for at least fifteen minutes. I wait impatiently. I sit on my hands so that I don't stretch across the driving seat and hoot on the horn. I know Italians aren't famed for their punctuality and I've got used to the fact that whenever a group of Italian mates are making plans for the evening a debate can be batted back and forth for several hours, but really! It's simply rude to leave me sitting here.

Be patient, be patient, be reasonable, be reasonable, I repeat to myself. Eventually I hear the back door bang, a woman's chatter and Roberto's laughter; Ana-Maria and Roberto emerge.

She's breathtaking. Held from the lower back, she's ramrod straight and her stance suggests that she is confident and able in all matters vegetable, animal or mineral. I can see that her legs are muscled and defined, yet, disconcertingly, she seems to glide rather than walk, moving as though she's liquid below her waist. I imagine she's very good in bed. Her silky black hair is tied neatly in a jaunty pony-tail but she doesn't appear in the least austere; I imagine her loosening her hair and allowing it to fall in mesmerizing cascades around her shoulders. Her smile is generous, her skin is flawless. She is a vision of loveliness and therefore my worst nightmare. I stare at her as though I am in love with her myself. I fight an urge to wind down the window and beg her to be my friend. If she is my friend, she won't hurt me. Right? I want her to like me and I almost fall out of the car as I scramble to be introduced. Her hand is cool and tiny but her handshake is firm. She beams, and if she hates me for marrying her ex, I can't detect it.

31

'The best approach is from the west end of the piazza. Ideally we should have arrived early, before the queues built up – as it is we'll have to be prepared to wait but it will be worth it.'

Ana-Maria is talking about our seeing the Basilica di San Marco but I've found she's equally enthusiastic, knowledgeable and strident about pretty much everything. Her comprehension of all things agricultural, architectural and geographical was verified on our journey here. I wonder where she gets the energy to be so interested in so many things?

'There's a fixed route around the interior of the basilica. You'll have to allow your eyes to become accustomed to the low light levels, and take your time; it is an overwhelming building,' she says.

I try to smile and respond positively to her high-intensity keenness but I'm beginning to run out of cheery 'ohs' and 'ahs'.

On the journey here I sat in the back of the car, like some kid, and Ana-Maria sat in the front because she's a 'splendid map reader' – Roberto's words – and so that I could see clearly the places of interest she pointed out; Ana-Maria has an 'astounding knowledge of local history' – her words. She also has a really grating know-it-all attitude – my words.

Ana-Maria and Roberto have, of course, visited Venice

on hundreds of occasions (many times together, I soon come to realize). Neither of them can remember the wonder and surprise of discovering the city's awesome delights for the first time. I'm alone in that. They both see Venice as a rather charming backdrop in front of which they can showcase their knowledge of culture and history.

Ana-Maria approaches sightseeing with Mary Poppins precision and she has a strategy of discovery that I'm simply too feeble to brook. I am raced through the baroque backstreets and not permitted to stand outside churches as I'm dashed across umpteen pretty bridges until we reach the Piazza San Marco. This is where she wants us to start our day. I'd rather expected that this would be where we'd finish, and only then after a fair amount of ambling, sauntering, mooching and wandering. I accept that the Loggia offers a splendid vantage point from which to view the piazza, I just hadn't expected that I'd be timed as I climbed up the stairs from the atrium to the gallery. I point out the lines of washing flapping in the breeze that look like bunting hanging in the shabby streets, but Ana-Maria does not understand that I find these sights charming, instead she's mildly offended as she thinks I'm saying Venice is dilapidated and unkempt. She primly tells me how much energy British households waste on running driers. I forget exactly how much it is but it's a lot. I tell her I agree and that preserving the environment is of paramount importance but she's moved on.

'The Sant'Alipio doorway is one of five leading to the atrium but it's the only door with the original thirteenth-century mosaic,' she informs me.

The thousands of square feet of mosaics, illustrating Bible stories, glitter in the darkness. They're illuminated by slanting shafts of sunlight and they're breathtaking but we've been in Venice for two hours now and no one has suggested buying an ice-cream, let alone a mooch around the shops.

We stare at four bronze horses with reverence. I take a series of photos but feel a bit foolish when Ana-Maria points out that the ones I've been admiring with gusto are in fact replicas; the originals are inside the museum in the basilica. What sort of joke is that? What's the point of having two sets of famous bronze horses? I doubt I have the energy to reiterate my comments on the beauty of the powerfully evocative statues and I finally insist that I stay outside to catch some rays. I leave Ana-Maria and Roberto to light candles and marvel at the opulent gold and silver altarpiece below which the remains of St Mark lie.

As I lick my ice-cream (one scoop of caramel crunch and another of strawberry – I couldn't decide) I face the fact that no doubt I appear to be an ignorant heathen next to Ana-Maria and I must be a disappointment to Roberto. But I just could not muster one more zestful 'Splendid' at another much-revered twelfth-century Byzantine icon or a final 'Wow' at some fabulous façade. It's like being on holiday with my parents.

When Ana-Maria and Roberto emerge from the basilica they are laughing with one another. Their laughs are vigorous and infectious. I watch tourists swivel their heads in order to look at the joyful pair and I can sense the approval they generate. They look beautiful together. Their darkness and neatness match. I bet people watching them are thinking what a great couple they make. Realizing as much makes it hard to swallow my last bite of cornet; I toss it into a nearby bin. I feel distinctly sick. Is it the large ice-cream or them being a perfect twin set that's making me feel off? I slither in between (not easy, as they seem to be stood unnecessarily close to one another) and slip my arm around Roberto. He looks at me in a way that suggests he doesn't recognize me; a nanosecond later I see guilt in his eyes.

'Let's get an ice-cream,' he suggests. 'Elizabeth *does* appreciate Italian ice-cream.'

While I'm sure he wants to be kind to me, I feel that the comment suggests I'm too silly to appreciate anything else Italian, not true! Or that I'm a heifer. I concede that this might soon become the case because I don't bother to tell him that I've just finished an enormous cone or that I'm fighting nausea, instead I direct him towards a different vendor and I have another double scoop; one of chocolate and another of kiwi. Ana-Maria has a modest one scoop of vanilla; even so, she fails to finish it.

We amble along the waters of St Mark's Basin. I dawdle and make jokes about overly confident pigeons. Ana-Maria makes observations such as, 'The basin is like a natural mirror, as though God wanted to reflect the majesty and splendour of the Basilica of San Giorgio Maggiore, don't you think?'

I think God's part was done long before the architects of the basilica became involved but I hold my tongue. I try to concentrate on the sweetness of the ice-cream but it's offering little comfort. I just feel cold.

32

'What's she like then?' asks Alison.

'Perfect. I have no idea why he didn't marry her,' I admit with a sigh.

'I thought you said she was a bit strident.'

'She was focused and interested in things. He likes that. He once said that I wasn't interested in anything other than having a baby.'

Alison's silence suggests she agrees with my husband but she's too loyal to say so. She knows I've been through enough today. All I need now is someone to listen to me.

'She's beautiful, gracious, fun, educated. She loves and is loved by his entire family and her family adore Roberto too.'

'How do you know that?'

'Well, besides the fact that on pick up and drop off I was left in the car for an aeon while he chatted to her mamma and papa –'

'How rude.'

'I know. Besides that, it turns out that Ana-Maria has a cousin who owns a restaurant in Venice; we ate there today. Her cousins treated Roberto as though he was some conquering Caesar, returning with ships full of gold and concubines and a couple of new countries stuffed in his back pocket.'

Alison giggles. I'm glad I can make her laugh about the

situation; maybe she won't suspect just how humiliating and miserable my afternoon was. I have to admit, at first I was pleased to hear that Ana-Maria knew of a decent restaurant. We didn't even discuss lunch until two thirty, and by the time I swallowed my first bite it was almost four; I'd have eaten anywhere. She dragged us down a labyrinth maze of narrow streets and I did feel a tiny bit smug as we hastened past the pizzerias jammed with tourists paying over the odds for below-par pizza. Momentarily I felt like an insider, exactly what I've been longing to be since I arrived here.

Their family-run restaurant looked over a tiny canal; the balconies were decked with flowers and the tablecloths were crisp and white. It was gorgeous. Ana-Maria's cousins accepted my vegetarianism with little more than a curt nod. They brought me vegetarian dishes that were cooked with style and imagination. They married pumpkin, courgette and fennel with a huge array of cheeses. It was delicious. But, other than repeatedly enquiring whether my food was '*Bene?*' (said with a presumptive nod), I was ignored.

I can't blame them. Why should I expect them to speak English? But it was hard watching them pull out old photo albums rammed full of pictures of Ana-Maria and Roberto, as babies, kids, teenagers, lovers.

'It clearly wasn't a tempestuous break-up,' I comment to Alison, 'as everyone still gets on with one another very well indeed.' I know that Alison doesn't approve of tempestuous break-ups. She doesn't like drama or incivility, but I'd prefer it if they couldn't stand to share the same town, let alone the same plate of pasta.

'That shows there's no romantic feeling left between

them,' says Alison. 'You've nothing to worry about, they are just friends.'

'But she's so gorgeous,' I wail.

'Oh, but all that perfection can become tedious.' I grin because I can't resist my best friend's attempts to cheer me up. 'It's unlikely to come without a price. I bet she's the kind of girl who spends hours and hours grooming, plucking and pruning.'

'Roberto likes that.'

It's true that Roberto does appreciate a 'woman who makes an effort'. I am not one of those women. For years I over-relied on my youth, which pretty much passes as beauty even if you are only just OK-ish. In the last year or so I have noticed that my flesh has a sort of saggy or spongy quality to it, which is not so great. Hangovers are worn for longer and mostly in big bags around the eyes. My laughter-lines are looking a little less characterful and a little more awful as every day passes. In my day-to-day living I fail miserably at making an effort. I'm chaotic, my face is nude of make-up, I only shave my legs three times a year and I try to leave my hair-cut for as long as humanly possible because I don't like having to make a decision about exactly what style I want. My clothes are generally fashionable, as I love the Mecca that is Zara, but I'm not so hot about sewing on loose buttons, ironing or even removing price tags, so the impression I create is not what anyone could call polished.

I suppose trying for a baby has taken its toll even on everyday grooming. You have to feel good to want to look good and if you look good, you usually feel good; sadly, that's a virtuous circle that I haven't gotten on board yet. Shall we say there's room for improvement?

'When are you coming to visit me? Have you booked your tickets?' I ask Alison. I feel in need of moral support.

'Fiona and I thought we might come at the end of July. It depends if she can get holiday.'

My heart plummets. I'm pleased that Alison and Fiona are sure enough of one another that they are making plans for months ahead. I know Alison is dying to show off her new girlfriend, but I can see that my best friend and her lesbian lover coming to visit will cause problems. What will Raffaella think? Besides, I was rather keen to have Alison to myself for a spell. I swallow my wail of indignation and say, 'Well, don't leave it too late. The seats on the flights will get booked up.'

'OK, I'm on it. Any other news?'

'I met an American teacher.'

'A crusty old academic, just what you need in a friend,' says Alison lightly. I have no idea what made her jump to the conclusion that Chuck was crusty or old. And I have no idea why I don't point out that he is actually a cute young hotty.

'He gave me the number of an Italian tutor.'

'And?'

'I called him. My first lesson's on Thursday morning, before the bar opens.'

'Good for you! Well done,' says Alison, as though she is encouraging a highly strung, inbred puppy.

I'm not sure why I called Signor Castoro in the end. Maybe it was because I found it exhausting when Ana-Maria and Roberto drifted back into Italian as we drove home from Venice. Bushed from the day's sightseeing, I had no energy to struggle to keep up with the conversation. I have no idea what was so hilarious that they both

183

laughed until they gripped their sides. Nor do I know what was said that made Ana-Maria tearful; she had to look away to stop Roberto noticing her brimming eyes. I think it would be in my best interests to keep up with Roberto and Ana-Maria's conversations, and while I can't expect Signor Castoro to teach me more than greetings and introductions on Thursday, everyone has to start somewhere.

There's another thing. Maybe learning Italian has less to do with Roberto and Ana-Maria, maybe I just didn't want to have to face Chuck and admit that I'd done nothing about learning the language of the country I'm living in. He's fluent and I seem idle by comparison. That is, if I do ever see Chuck again. And while there's no reason why I should see him again, or even why I should *want* to see him again, if I do it will be nice to tell him I'm taking lessons.

That's all.

33

13 March

As I walk back to Bruno's after my first ever Italian lesson, I breathe in the surprisingly warm March air that cradles the town right now and smile to myself. I feel certain this month that I'm pregnant.

I put my hand on my stomach; it's never what anyone would call flat but is it actually rounded? I think about my boobs – more or less sensitive than usual? I can't honestly detect a difference but within a day or two I'll know. The possibility makes me grin helplessly for my entire walk back to Bruno's. One of my most finely tuned day-dreams is the one where I announce my pregnancy to Roberto. Oh my God, that will be the most special day imaginable.

By the time I arrive at the bar I have worked myself up to such a state of excitement that I have to bite my tongue to stop me flinging back the doors and scream-ing, *Who's the Daddy?*

'Wow, that's some big smile,' says Laurana the moment she claps eyes on me. I giggle and scrabble around for a feasible excuse. I can't admit that something in the air tells me I'm pregnant.

'I've just had my first lesson with Signor Castoro,' I offer.

'Clearly, you enjoy. You are full with excitement.'

Actually I did enjoy my lesson. I surprised myself. It

turns out that I know much more than I thought. Signor Castoro explained that of course I must have absorbed a little of the language while being married to Roberto for so long, it's only natural. Although obviously I still have quite some way to go before I'll impress Raffaella or be totally confident with the customers.

'I can't wait to tell Roberto how it went.' I pull out of my bag a textbook that Signor Castoro has lent me and shyly show it to her. She offers up a huge smile which rests like a pat on my back. 'Where is he?'

'Roberto got called away. We are running the bar together again today.'

I reckon we must have done a pretty good job the other Friday because in the past six days Laurana and I have been left to our own devices three times. I must fail to hide my disappointment that Roberto isn't here, because Laurana comments, 'Hey, Roberto must be at something vital or he'd be in the bar, right? The bar is his life.'

I nod and smile, because I know she's trying to comfort me, although hearing that the bar is generally considered his life doesn't actually do that.

'It's not his fault. He didn't know I had anything special to tell him. I haven't mentioned the lessons.'

'Ah, you want to surprise him,' shrieks Laurana with excitement.

'Sort of.'

Truth is, ever since our day off to visit Venice Roberto has worked unimaginably long hours. I don't understand, it's not like he's in an office and needs to catch up because he took holiday. The customers he missed that day have been served now. We are becoming a little like ships passing in the night and I haven't got round to telling him about the lessons. I'm sure he's going to be pleased and proud of me but he's bound to ask who gave me the contact, and while I have no reason not to talk about Chuck, I find I haven't mentioned him.

Laurana puts down my textbooks. 'Bravo! Now you must be a good student and practise as much as possible. I speak only to you Italian.'

'Don't do that, we were getting on so well,' I joke.

'I no hear you. In only Italian,' she says, throwing her arms in the air. In Italian she tells me she's going to start preparing the salads for lunch. I stay in the bar and try to memorize the verbs 'to be', 'to do' and 'to have'.

'Wow, I'm impressed,' Chuck appears out of nowhere, and before I get a chance to so much as yank my hair behind my ears, he's right by my side. My insides slither about uncontrollably. 'What you studying?'

'Verbs.'

'Signor Castoro said you were at his place bright and early this morning.'

'Are you checking up on me?' I ask with a grin and a blush. Would it be so bad if he was?

'I've just bumped into him in the piazza. We took an espresso together. You know what this place is like; nothing stays a secret for more than five minutes.' I really must tell Roberto about the lessons tonight. 'Signor Castoro says you are a *gran piacere* as a pupil.'

'A great like?' I check, hesitantly.

'Yup, a great like. A delight, actually.'

'Oh, yes, it would be that.' I'm a bit embarrassed with my inadequate translation.

'It will come to you in no time. Signor Castoro says you made a promising start.'

'That's because he hasn't had to decode my hand-writing yet. I bet he's not so keen on me after that,' I joke.

'Did you enjoy your lesson?'

'Yes, surprisingly I did. Very much. Signor Castoro is very patient. Thanks for the recommendation.'

'My pleasure.'

I force myself to look at Chuck now. So far, throughout the conversation I've managed to remain ridiculously interested in the bar top. Stupidly, I feel girlish and shy. His toned bulk is intimidating. I wonder what he feels like to touch. In an effort to deny that I've even had this thought I force myself to meet his eyes. I mean he's not *that* attractive, is he? He can't be. Bang. His sincere gaze hits me in the throat, gut and knickers simultaneously. Oh hell. He *is* that attractive. Quickly I pick up a duster and start to polish the already gleaming bar. Damn my hormones. I concentrate on the fact that he says things like 'We need to share' and 'Have a nice day' – not that I've ever heard him say either of these things but Americans do say those things, don't they? And they don't mean them necessarily. They are a nation of really glib people, aren't they? And therefore I mustn't take anything he says too seriously.

But.

Well, he does look sincere. And he's always been sincere. In truth, I haven't noticed anything at all that's glib about him.

'So what have you been getting up to since I was last in here?' he asks. Mercifully, he looks around the bar and stops staring at me. I guess my rabbit-in-the-headlights act was embarrassing him too.

I search my mind for interesting things I've done with my time.

'We went to Venice.'

'Wow, great, man. Did you love it?'

'Yes, I love Venice,' I reply truthfully and carefully.

'I wish I'd been with you.'

I know his comment is nothing more than a reflection for his enthusiasm for Venice but I can't help wishing he'd come with us too, if only to even up the numbers. Hey, that's a thought – maybe I can introduce him to Ana-Maria.

'Do you know Ana-Maria Provero?' I ask.

'Yes, I know the whole family.'

'She's very pretty, don't you think?'

'A little too polished for my liking,' says Chuck with a shrug. 'Between you and me, I have her down as seriously high maintenance. Hey, but it's good that you are thinking of me,' he says with a playful wink.

I squirm now that he's seen through my clumsy attempt at matchmaking. The odd thing is I should be disappointed. It would be an ideal solution if Ana-Maria got herself a boyfriend and fell in love. New love is always more distracting than old love, at least that's my experience, and yet I'm secretly chuffed to hear that Chuck isn't into her.

'Look at you, girl – sightseeing, taking Italian lessons; you'll banish that homesickness in a flash. Way to go. I think this calls for a celebration.'

'Do you want a drink?'

'Yes, but not now – tonight and not here. I'll take you to a bar in Marostica. It's called Perche No? Which means –'

'Why Not.'

'Yes. So, why not? My friend runs it. You'll love the vibe. Roberto is invited as well, of course,' he adds.

'We can't both bunk off. We have this place to run.'

'Well, just you then.'

I hesitate. Officially it is my night off anyway and I really don't fancy a night in with just Roberto's grandpa for company. In England I have a number of guy friends and Roberto never had any problem with me seeing them alone. Why should he? He trusts me. And so he should. I am very trustworthy. So.

'OK,' I agree before I over-analyse the situation.

'Great. Don't dress up, it's very casual. I'll pick you up at say eight? Here?'

'No. I'll wait for you at the clock tower. If I come in here I'll get dragged behind the bar.' It's not even a teeny white lie. I would be dragged behind the bar. But it's also not the 'whole truth and nothing but the truth'. I'm unsure as to whether Raffaella would approve of my friendship with Chuck – however platonic. There's no point in rocking the boat, especially as this particular boat already has one or two major leaks to worry about.

'OK,' he agrees.

'OK,' I confirm.

I am fizzing with excitement. I pick up the duster again. It's best I don't think about it any more, or maybe I should think about it a great deal. I opt for the former and go into the kitchen to help Laurana with the salads. I probably should give serious thought to this unprecedented attraction, but after the salads, I have verbs to practise.

34

When Chuck pulls up next to the clock tower at exactly 8 p.m., I thank God for American punctuality. Roberto is always a minimum of half an hour late, sometimes up to two hours. I don't think I could have borne waiting for Chuck a minute longer than necessary. It's not that I am totally desperate and dying to see him or anything (although I have been looking forward to it, I admit); it's more a question of not wanting to be spotted by anyone.

I had planned to tell Roberto who I was going out with tonight, only the moment never arose as we continue to operate like passing ships. I finished the afternoon shift and went to find him on the offchance we could spend the siesta hours together. He wasn't in the study doing the accounts as I expected, so I called him on his mobile.

'Where are you?'

'Out.'

'Well, I realize that, where out?' I asked.

'I'm with a supplier. Why all the questions?' he asked tetchily, making it clear that he didn't want to be interrupted. I managed to tell him about my Italian lesson with Signor Castoro.

'That is wonderful. Well done. Castoro is a magnificent tutor. He helped me through my school exams in literature when I was a kid.'

'Really? You know him?' I wonder why Roberto never

mentioned me having a tutor in all the times he nagged me to learn the language.

'He was a friend of Papa's.'

I like knowing that about Signor Castoro. I can see that he might well be the pal of the smiley Bruno in the wedding photo. I like having a context for people and knowing something about their roots and histories. I hadn't realized how much that mattered until I left the UK. It used to annoy me that whenever my parents started a conversation they'd begin with a sentence such as, 'You know Mr Blar Blar; he had a daughter Tom's age.' I'd shake my head. 'His wife used to knit for you when you were a baby,' they'd continue, but I'd be none the wiser. Usually their conversations would culminate in something unspectacular such as, 'Well, I saw him at the greengrocer's. He was asking after you.'

Suddenly I realized that someone being interested in me is the nicest thing in the world. I thought of Chuck asking Signor Castoro about me and I brightened.

'I'm going out tonight, Roberto. There's a bar called Perche No? in Marostica. Do you know it?'

'Yes, I've heard of it. Keep your eyes open and see if they are doing anything we're not. It's good to keep a watch on the competition. Have fun,' he said and abruptly rang off. It was clear I was tearing him away from something vital. He forgot to ask me who I was going with and because he forgot to ask I didn't think I had to tell him.

I appreciated Chuck telling me not to dress up and that the bar was very casual, otherwise I'd have been in serious danger of spending absolutely hours deciding what to wear. As it was I only had to try on nine outfits.

I settle for Diesel jeans and a beige vest top with a reasonable amount of glittering bits. I know he said the gig was casual but the Italians dress so well that I feel duty bound to dab on a bit of lipstick and dig out my heels. I feel as though I'm the British contestant in the Eurovision Sartorial Contest. Britain has no chance of winning but it's a matter of national pride that we at least enter.

'You look great,' says Chuck the moment he meets me; his casual compliment soothes the blister that I know is already bubbling on my little toe on the right foot. I bought these strappy shoes on the first afternoon I arrived in Italy. Wearing them is a little like balancing on stilts. They are beyond impractical but breathtakingly pretty and as they didn't break the bank I consider them perfect, despite the fact that they don't quite fit. How do other girls do it? This glamour thing takes such effort and commitment.

I worry that by choosing between nine outfits and wearing sexy, painful shoes the evening is taking on a distinct 'first-date feel', which is of course inappropriate when you consider that I've been married for six years. However, I'm immediately put at ease when Chuck starts chatting about his car, his job and his mate's bar. The conversation flows freely and is entirely devoid of tension. Which, if I remember rightly, is not how conversations are conducted on a first date. Other than Roberto (who was a motor-mouth and spent the entire first date talking and kissing), all my first dates have been punctuated with awkward silences and maladroit hints at whether or not the evening promised any action between the sheets.

I tell myself that Chuck is just being a nice guy. He

knows I'm a bit lonely and he's looking out for me as any fellow ex-pat would do.

Oddly, only half of me wants this to be true.

I have always been faithful. And I'm talking about *one hundred per cent* faithful, not a blurred line type of faithful. I'm not the type to have had a quick tongue sandwich with a colleague in the spice cupboard at a Christmas party but then insist that it didn't mean anything because it's Christmas. I do have vague fantasies about unobtainable men from time to time, the ones that date movie stars and appear in gossip mags. But I don't even bother to hone these fantasies. They are not important to me. Roberto has always been the living embodiment of everything I want. He's tall enough, dark, handsome, and Italian. My detailed fantasies are all anchored around a family life.

But.

But Chuck with his lazy drawl and blondness is really stirring me up. Everything I think is inappropriate. Like, I'm impressed with the way he handles a gear stick – duh – and I actually hear myself say, 'Not many Americans can handle a shift stick, where'd you learn that?'

I want to eat my own tongue and would punch myself except that would draw more attention to my moronicness. For goodness sake! Every man I've ever known can change gears and I've never felt the need to compliment anyone on it before! And why did I feel the need to call the gear stick a shift stick? He'll think I'm some sort of weird American-devotee that can name all the states.

Chuck is the epitome of good manners; he smiles and says he had to learn to drive using gears when he moved to Europe. He's used to changing gears now but doesn't get this crap European blokes go on about with regard to 'feeling the road'. I like his honesty.

When we arrive at the bar it is buzzing. Groups of guys and girls spill on to the pavement. They are all shouting and chatting but I know that none of them will be drunk. Amazingly Italians manage to reach a state of uninhibited joyfulness without sinking twelve pints.

The bar is full, smoky and noisy. I look around for something obvious that is responsible for attracting such a substantial crowd. It would be good to have something to report back to Roberto. Unfortunately I can't see anything that is visibly drawing the crowds. There isn't a live band, an Elvis impersonator or a DJ. The food looks nice, but then where doesn't the food look nice in Italy? The bar is full of nothing other than high spirits. I wonder if Roberto can emulate that with Raffaella perpetually sitting in the corner doing a convincing impression of the Grim Reaper's more miserable older sister.

Chuck knows loads of people and even while we weave our way to the bar he's stopped two or three times. He introduces me to everyone and no one comments on my curls or my freckles, nor does anyone recommend something I should eat. They ask where I met Chuck, how long I've been in Italy and how I find living with my mother-in-law. Chuck's mates seem genuinely interested in me. I tell Chuck that I'll get the drinks. I buy mineral water because he's driving and I try not to drink during the last two weeks of my cycle. I find Chuck standing near the retro jukebox.

I wonder whether I ought to tell him that my blister is really nasty now. It's the sort of thing Alison and I do tell one another and I'm desperately trying to pigeonhole my relationship with this gorgeous-looking man as platonic. Mates would be fine.

'Thanks for introducing me to your friends.'

It's always such a generous thing to do. I can't help but wonder why Roberto hasn't made much of an effort to get me to mix with his pals. Shouldn't he have engineered a social occasion to give me a chance to get to know his mates properly?

'Despite my inadequate Italian we managed to cut past the small talk and say something real. That hasn't happened much since I arrived.'

'To be fair, you are only seeing Italians across the bar. I don't suppose you get much chance to say anything beyond, "Here's your order."'

'Not even that, as I get the order wrong so often.'

Chuck grins. 'The women that work in the bar are great though, aren't they?'

I wonder if he fancies one of them. Or all of them?

'Yes, particularly Laurana, we're becoming a bit closer. We chat about soap stars and Hollywood and stuff. Don't you think she's pretty?'

'Yes. A beauty.' Chuck doesn't elaborate and I wished I hadn't asked the question. The teeniest, tiniest spark of jealousy flickers inside me, which is hardly very friendly. I douse it immediately.

'She's single at the moment, maybe you should think about asking her out.'

'Right,' says Chuck, but he's looking at me with amusement rather than with excitement at the prospect.

'That is, if you are still single.'

'I am.'

'Well, perfect then,' I say with a forced enthusiasm.

Chuck grins. 'You are quite the little matchmaker, aren't you?'

'Happily married women often are,' I bluster, embarrassed by my clumsiness. 'We want our friends to have what we have.'

'Well, I'll take it that's a compliment because it means you consider me a friend but I don't think I will ask Laurana out at the moment, if it's all the same to you.'

'Oh, fine,' I say breezily. Crap. Why am I making such a pig's ear out of being his mate? Everything I say sounds dull, pushy or plain weird. My tongue fails to engage my brain again when I add, 'Look, I really need to sit down. I have a blister the size of an egg on my foot. Can we find a table?'

We find a snug little booth tucked at the back of the bar. Clearly the booth has been designed for smoochy couples and for a brief moment I feel really bad about handicapping a budding romance but hell, do my feet hurt.

'I've never seen you smoke since that first day we met in the piazza,' I say to Chuck.

'Correction, you've never seen me smoke. I don't.'

'But you gave the Forgetful Guy cigarettes.'

'I buy them for him. Do you think that's morally wrong?'

'No.' I think it's kind.

'I just sort of feel bad for him, you know? He doesn't seem to have many pleasures in life.' I consider whether I'm another pity case – probably. We fall silent for some moments, then eventually Chuck asks, 'Was Roberto cool with you coming out tonight?'

His question betrays the fact that he must also see that two people of the opposite sex, of a certain age, might attract some notice by coming out alone together.

'Yes. Laurana and Gina are in tonight, he doesn't need me around. He just told me to look out for any edge the competition have here. You might think I'm here just for fun but actually I'm planning on a bit of industrial espionage.'

'I'm glad you are having fun.'

'Yes.' I smile.

'Roberto is really serious about turning Bruno's around, isn't he? Up until you guys arrived it was generally agreed that the place was on its last legs. The decor was dated, the stock limited, the only people that ever went near were Raffaella and Bruno's friends.'

'Most of whom are dead,' I wisecrack.

'I like what Roberto has done with the decor,' adds Chuck.

I briefly consider the possibility that he's gay. On the one hand it would explain a lot (his good manners, his wit, his high level of personal grooming and cleanliness and his willingness to spend time with me – truly, all my best friends are gay). On the other hand I'd be a bit fed up. Why? If he's gay we can openly spend time together without anyone raising so much as an eyebrow and I'd really like to spend time with Chuck because besides all the good manners, wit, high level of personal grooming slash cleanliness stuff, he's the person I feel most comfortable with in all of Italy. I park that thought as it's far too messy to face right now. Isn't my husband supposed to be that person? The memory that Chuck has recently split from his girlfriend flings itself to the front of my mind. One thing at a time. He's not gay.

I think about Chuck's observation. When we arrived Bruno's was very dated. However much I tried to tell myself that it was rustic and charming, I knew it was just ugly and empty. Not that I gave the decor much thought at all in the first week or so. I was too busy, up to my elbows in soapy water; just trying to see the decor through the dust mites was an achievement. Plus I was more than a little taken aback with the whole family business being a shoddy bar, rather than a beatific vineyard, thing.

Thinking about it now, I suppose there have been quite some changes since we arrived. While Roberto hasn't changed anything structurally, he has got rid of the hideous mismatched bar stools. I remember the first time I sat on one it actually cracked. We have funky Kartell transparent ones now. Plus I cleared out a large end room that Raffaella had stored God knows what in, and by doing so we've doubled the space available for punters. He's created enough room for a snug area which he's filled with a squashy leather settee and a low square coffee table. He pulled up the dirty carpets, stained by slopped drinks and muddy shoes, and exposed beautiful wooden floors. Paolina, Laurana and I spent a long weekend scrubbing, sanding and varnishing them. I have been following the revamp of the bar enough to express concern that a fair amount of our personal savings has been spent on fake zebra skin beanbags and bamboo plants.

'Yes, I suppose he's making a good job of it,' I admit.

'It must be amazing having a project like this to work on together,' says Chuck.

I stare at him for some moments. I could politely agree with Chuck – effectively bringing that line of small talk to a close (although raising the need for me to introduce another topic) – and would at least leave him with the impression that all is well on the home front. Or I could just blurt out the truth.

'I'm not much interested in the bar. I wish I could be but I'm just not.' I need to be honest with Chuck. Isn't that the base of all relationships? Friendships, I mean.

'Oh.'

'Exactly. Oh, indeed. It's Raffaella's bar and no matter how many pot plants we introduce or how much we change the interior or even how many hours we slave in there, it's still *her* bar. She's made it very clear I'm not welcome at all, and besides, I didn't think I was coming to Italy to work in bars. I've done that for years in the UK. I thought the family business was a vineyard.'

'What?' asks Chuck. He's clearly dazed and confused.

I take a deep breath and tell him about my mistake. I'm only about a third of a way through my very serious account of the miscommunication when Chuck starts to rock backwards and forwards with hysteria.

'It's not funny!' I insist.

'I think you'll find it is,' he asserts, and all at once I stop seeing the lack of vineyard as a terrible embarrassment and heartrending disappointment and I begin to see the entire mix-up as Chuck must be seeing it. Pretty hilarious.

I start to laugh and I manage to keep laughing even when I'm describing Raffaella's coldness and Roberto's neglect. I even make a joke about the secrecy that has shrouded Ana-Maria. Chuck laughs right along with me but he's not insensitive. He tells me that everyone in

Veganze finds Raffaella scary and he assures me that Roberto is simply busy and is undoubtedly devoted. He dismisses my fears about Ana-Maria with a brief wave of the hand and a comment, 'She's no competition.'

He starts to tell me a little about his world. He's travelled for the last twelve years. He's visited Russia, India and many European countries. He's a crazy risk-taker and never happier than when he's climbing up a mountain or diving into a sea. His ambition is to buy a language school and be his own boss. He's been saving like crazy for four years. He's so attractive that I feel he is out of my orbit and so I don't even try to be attractive for him; I mean, that would be inappropriate anyway, given the circumstances. I am *not* trying to *pull* him. Instead I try to sponge up his knowledge and sit in the warm glow of his confidence; he is confident about himself, life, me, everything in fact. I don't worry about what might be the right thing to say. As a result, everything I say seems to be something he wants to hear. I wish I'd learnt that trick when I was a teenager.

'Tell me more about your family,' he says.

'What more do you want to know?'

'Everything.'

So I tell him everything. I tell him that as a kid I was largely embarrassed by my parents' age and austerity but I add that I've come to respect and understand them more now I'm older. They were always, and still are, old-fashioned but caring.

'I mean truly caring. They wanted me to be safe and healthy like all parents do but they also wanted me to know stuff. You know, about buildings and music and history and important dead people. Largely it went over my head but now I sort of see what they were trying to achieve. They wanted me to understand the enormity of being human. Obviously, I've let them down.'

'How so?'

'Max and Thomas, my brothers, went to prestigious universities; they both got firsts and great careers after that. Max isn't a slimy tabloid journo, which would actually suit me fine, no, he's the sort that's always uncovering injustice and campaigning against it. His byline, Max Gardiner, has graced every quality newspaper imaginable. Honestly, he's terrifying as a guest for lunch on Christmas day. I only understand about thirty per cent of what he talks about. And Thomas pretty much runs the NHS if Mum is to be believed, and she usually can be. They are both so worthwhile. The same can't be said of me.'

'You've achieved other things.'

'Like?'

'You are travelling, seeing a bit of the world. Your parents must be pleased about that.'

'Maybe they would be, if I could tell them a little more about Renaissance art and architecture or the sculptors of Biduino, but when I call every Sunday night I normally limit my conversation to what I've eaten for lunch. I'm living in Italy but I'm still pouring beer.'

'Not everyone has a kick-ass career. It takes people different lengths of time to discover what they want in life. What some call drifting might just be –' he searches for the right word and lands upon – 'exploring the options. Think of it as research?'

'I like that idea. I've never thought of it like that.'

I am tempted to explain that I haven't been drifting or researching a career but that I've always, always known what I wanted from life. I wanted to marry an Italian and then after that I wanted babies. I've been totally, completely, entirely focused on that for years, but to no avail. Would he get it? Before I can decide if I want to reveal this much, Chuck makes a suggestion.

'Have you thought of getting a job outside the bar? Maybe a bit of independence would be a good thing.'

'No, I haven't thought of that.' But maybe he's on to something. It would be worth finding a new job just for the satisfaction of telling Mamma-in-law where to shove her unreasonable and unpaid hours. 'What could I do?'

'I don't know. Work in another bar.'

'It seems a bit disloyal,' I murmur.

'Maybe,' agrees Chuck, understanding the nuances of my family life. 'You could teach English.'

I start to laugh again but this time Chuck doesn't join in.

'You're serious, aren't you?'

'Deadly. I could ask around for you and see if there are any jobs going in any of the language schools. Truly, you can't spit around here without hitting a language school and everyone will want to employ a beautiful English rose with the proper accent.'

I've never thought of myself as an English rose, beautiful or otherwise. I blush and smile and bloody hell, I simper. I try to pull myself together as I point out, 'But I can't speak Italian.'

'Well, you are working on that – besides, you could teach the more advanced full-immersion classes.'

This doesn't sound like total madness. I nod and tell Chuck I'd appreciate him asking around on my behalf; he smiles. Then he makes a trivial comment about something or other, I can't even remember what, but we both dissolve into peals of laughter once again and we don't stop chatting all night, not until Chuck drops me back at Raffaella's at midnight.

35

14 March

Roberto comes in at two and while he's undressing I go to the bathroom with a familiar sinking feeling. This month when I return to our bedroom to root out a new box of Tampax Roberto doesn't take me in his arms. He shrugs and mutters, 'Maybe next time.'

'Yes, there's always next month,' I reply quietly. I manage to say this without weeping; that's what we call progress.

I get back into bed and stare through the darkness at the ceiling. Within minutes Roberto's breathing calms and I know he is asleep. I can't sleep but I can't stay still either. I decide to get up and make myself some warm milk.

I find Paolina in the kitchen. She's surrounded by waves of cigarette smoke.

'Sorry,' she says, making an ineffective but well-meaning attempt to waft the smoke away.

'Oh, don't worry for me,' I mutter.

'I just know that –' she pauses and looks away. I stare at her and the penny drops.

'You know that we are trying for a baby?'

'Yes. I thought the smoke might be a bother to you.'

'I'm not pregnant,' I say, trying to sound strong and factual when in fact I'm sad and fractured. 'I've just got my period. I've come down for some warm milk.'

Paolina waves the bottle of red wine she's nursing. 'I think maybe this is more help.' I smile weakly and nod.

She pours me a large glass and slides it across the table. I take a massive gulp. If I'd known that I wasn't pregnant I'd have drunk with Chuck tonight; that would have been fun. The thought flits into my head and I instantly, violently punch it away. What am I saying? Not being pregnant is devastating. It's everything. How can I possibly think about something so trivial as missing a night's drinking at a time like this?

'How are you, Paolina?' I ask in an attempt to think about something else.

'Oh, you know, alone,' replies Paolina. She shrugs. 'But I brought it on myself, hey? This aloneness. You have no sympathy for me.'

I don't know how to answer. I'm unused to such directness from the Risso family. Roberto communicates through the things he fails to say and Raffaella says the opposite to what she means. Paolina's honesty, while putting me in an uncomfortable position, is a great compliment.

I search around for something that is non-offensive but sincere. 'Maybe it's for the best,' I say and I squeeze her hand.

Her hands are dainty, cool and manicured. I am reminded of the first time I saw the marble statue of Venus in the British Museum. It was some ghastly, dreary trip my parents had dragged me on as a child. They said it was a birthday treat but I was deeply unimpressed and wanted to know what was wrong with the Odeon and Pizza Hut. I was bored stiff and desperate to be set free in the gift shop, where at least I could buy a compensatory pencil case or pin-on badge, but then I saw her: the marble Venus. I was drawn to her pearly skin and mellow curves. I studied this iconic statue that represented womanhood and I did not understand what I was seeing. She seemed podgier than my exacting youngster self imagined female perfection to be, and her nose seemed long and hard, plus she had tiny boobs and yet her pose was interesting. She managed to be both vulnerable and robust at once. I thought that was a fair representation of womanhood. Transfixed for some moments, I felt utterly compelled to trail my finger along the statue. As a pre-teen I was faintly embarrassed by this compulsion and I wondered whereabouts on the statue I should caress. A plump thigh, her stout arms, her gently rounded tummy? In the end I stroked her back, at about waist height, and was amazed that the marble felt at once cool and tender. Sturdy yet delicate. My sister-in-law feels the same.

'Let's hope,' says Paolina with a reclusive smile. 'God moves in mysterious ways, hey? Sometimes we don't know what we really need.'

'Well, right now I need ice-cream,' I say firmly. 'Join me?'

Paolina nods. 'Right now, ice-cream would be wonderful.'

36

18 March

It's Tuesday and I haven't heard a word from Chuck since we went out. I can't pretend not to be a little down in the mouth about this. We had such a laugh on Thursday evening I thought he'd be in touch before now, just to say hi. Still, he has loads of friends here; five days probably doesn't seem an eternity to *him*.

I've worked endless hours in the bar this week. I've done this so that Chuck can easily find me if he wants to and as he hasn't found me – only one conclusion can be drawn. I'm worried about how much that conclusion bothers me. I wish we'd swapped mobile numbers and I could have sent him a text, but he didn't offer his number so I was too shy to offer mine. Roberto interprets my willingness to do double shifts as a new-found interest in the bar and a sort of peace-offering to quell the tensions that have risen between us over the subject of Ana-Maria and our latest disappointment. He's delighted. Strangely, I hardly care that we are not bickering, as all my energy is focused on the entrance of the bar; I will Chuck to make an appearance.

Of course, all I am interested in is whether he has found me a new position or, at the very least, an interview at a language school. Nothing more. Fingers crossed.

This morning Roberto was out somewhere or other,

leaving Gina and me alone in the bar, and the cleaner has called in sick – situation normal. I'm beginning to get the feeling people are taking advantage. So, as the miserable witch Lady Luck would have it, I am cleaning the loos when he arrives.

Gina calls through to me, 'There is someone here to see you.'

Having waited for him all week, I find that I'm no longer expecting him and so when I emerge from the loos, with bucket and mop in hand and wearing rubber gloves, I am startled by his big, blond presence. He looks amazing, I look horrific. Mop and bucket are not the accessories of choice.

'Oh, hi,' I smile, despite my embarrassment. I'm simply pleased to see him.

'Sorry, have I called at a bad time? You're obviously busy,' says Chuck.

He seems considerably more formal than he did on Thursday evening and I begin to think I might have imagined our intimacy. Nascent friendships are tricky at the best of times but between men and women they are usually minefields.

Bruno's, like all watering-holes, looks bizarre in the daylight before the customers arrive to give the place meaning. The zebra skin beanbags and low loungey sofas suddenly look sleazy rather than cool. The entire place has the appearance of a cheesy brothel; I feel like a Madam (one that does her own cleaning) and Chuck looks like a terrified virgin. We stare at one another for a few torturous, silent minutes. It's clear Chuck is at sea and I feel faintly ridiculous – the rubber gloves don't help. The dust particles dance between us, illuminated in the shafts of light that squeeze through the still-shuttered windows. Chuck looks away, which is considerate of him as I have time to struggle with the gloves and fling the bucket and mop to one side.

'I just thought it was a good time to catch you alone, so we can talk about your new career,' he says.

Suddenly the embarrassment between us dissolves, as I'm touched by his consideration and his confidence in my ability to teach; he really thinks I can do it! The relief is enormous. I realize that the idea of teaching has caught my imagination and I'd be crushed if Chuck wasn't serious about his suggestion.

'Good thinking. This is a great time to talk. You're not interrupting anything at all. I was just cleaning the loos. They are the hideous little hole-in-the-floor affairs that perpetually stink. I must tell Roberto we need to install modern ones,' I garble. Then I clamp my mouth shut. 'Sorry, too much information?'

'Not at all. I'm fascinated,' jokes Chuck.

Gina hands Chuck a coke. 'It's on the house,' she says with a smile. How come she has the confidence to offer drinks on the house? I daren't do that and I'm married to the manager and shackled to the owner. I wonder if she fancies him? Not that it's any of my business if she does. But.

I wash my hands and grab a lemonade and then Chuck and I make our way to the squishy leather settee in the corner. I try to put the initial brothel/Madam/virgin scenario out of my head as we sink into our seats.

'I was wondering if I'd ever see you again,' I blurt.

It appears that I'm truly incapable of filtering the thoughts in my brain; they rush out of my mouth –

unchecked – whenever I'm with Chuck. I must try to sound less like a heroine in a black and white movie. I don't think it's a great idea for Chuck to know that he is my only friend and I'm disproportionately dependent on him. 'I just mean that on Thursday I went on a bit about Raffaella and everything, I wondered how boring I'd been.'

'Not at all.'

'I thought I might have scared you away.'

'I've been busy.'

'Right.' Distress lands with a fierce thump in my gut. I feel like I'm being dumped. Which is ridiculous. It's not like I'm his girlfriend. I wonder if he's got a new girl-friend already? Probably, he's gorgeous. Well, if so, I can kiss goodbye to the idea of us developing a friendship. One thing I do know about Italian women is that they don't allow their boyfriends to have unchecked friend-ships with members of the opposite sex. Thinking about Roberto and Ana-Maria, I admit their strategy might be wise.

'I've been busy asking around, trying to find out if there's anywhere that's prepared to take you on without any relevant experience or qualifications.'

'Oh.' I'm delighted that Chuck has been busy with me, even while he's not been *with me*. But then I'm instantly disappointed when I think of his realistic but somewhat depressing description of my job prospects. I can't imagine that he's here to give me good news.

'And?' I ask tentatively.

'Well, it's not straightforward. All the schools con-firmed what I thought, that you do need to take a qualifi-cation in teaching English as a foreign language.'

'Oh, TEFL, yes. A long time ago I considered doing that course.'

'Why didn't you?'

'I never got round to it, I suppose.'

Chuck looks confused. Americans are self-improvers. I am a sloth by comparison.

'Well, you can do it now as a correspondence course. Here.' He passes over a bundle of sheets of information which he's printed off the web, regarding ways in which I can study for this qualification.

'Thanks,' I mutter. Oh bugger. I hate studying. Really, I just wanted to get on with teaching right away. Specifically, I wanted to get out of Bruno's and away from Raffaella. I try to hide my disappointment. Chuck is doing his best, especially considering the material he has to work with. It's not like he's my fairy godmother and can wave a magic wand to turn my rags into couture.

'But the really good news is that there's an opportunity for you to teach a few hours a week straight away.'

'Really?' I almost hug him. Almost.

'Yes, well, more chat than teach, I suppose. I thought you'd be good at that.' Chuck grins at me with encouragement. I think he's gently teasing me but I don't mind in the slightest. 'The situation is as I expected, you can provide something unique just by talking in your mother tongue to pupils. My director is really pleased I found you. She thinks you'll provide quite a professional advantage over the other schools by offering conversational classes to the advanced pupils.'

'*Your* director? I'm going to be working with you?'

'Yes.'

I beam at him; I can't help it. 'And someone's going

to pay me to talk?' I ask with disbelief. It sounds amazing, especially considering that in my current position I'm not even paid for hard and dirty labour.

'Pretty much. And to listen of course.'

'Sounds wonderful.'

'Doesn't it? What do you think Roberto will say?'

'I'm not sure,' I admit.

I feel a little shamefaced that I can't reassure this kind and gorgeous man that my husband will be delighted for me and that he will celebrate my independence and wish me well. The truth is I honestly have no idea how Roberto will react. A couple of months ago when we were still in London I would have been confident that he'd be thrilled in my taking an interest in anything other than baby-making. He'd have been ecstatic that I wanted to gain further qualifications, as he always said I was wasting my brain and marking time in my various waitress and bar jobs. But now that we run his bar his attitude seems to have changed. In Italy Roberto isn't so pro my independence. It's a funny position to be in when you can't gauge the likely reaction of your nearest and dearest.

Chuck clearly senses that there might be an issue, but sensibly decides that it's my issue and doesn't delve any deeper into the subject of Roberto; instead he continues to tell me how he's fixed things to improve my life here in Italy.

'With a bit of management of timetable the director and I think we'll be able to group all your classes into one morning. That way I can give you a lift over to the school and back again, if you like.'

'Of course I like, that's so kind of you. Wow.'

Chuck grins, clearly pleased I'm pleased. 'The director

would like to meet you as soon as possible. The sooner you can get started the better. We are coming up to exam season and all the schools are very focused on results.'

'Great. When can I meet her?'

'Well, I thought perhaps we could drive over there now. I have three lessons so you'd have to kill a bit of time in Bassano del Grappa, but it's a pretty city and then I could bring you back by mid-afternoon.' He glances over to where I've abandoned my bucket and mop. 'But it looks like you are busy.'

'I'll come now. Well, as soon as I've changed clothes. Can you wait while I do that? Gina can manage.'

'Sure, but what about Roberto?'

'What about him?' I ask as I dash for the door. 'Give me twenty minutes.'

37

'I'm in the middle of the most overwhelming infatuation and I don't know how to stop it,' I blurt down the phone.

'Whoa, slow down, girl. What are you talking about?' asks Alison.

'Chuck, the American, I'm falling for him.'

'The crusty old academic?'

'I never said he was crusty or old. You said that.'

'What is he like then?'

'He's thirty-four and gorgeous. Clever, kind, sexy.'

'What fun!' says Alison. She's either unwilling or unable to get the seriousness of this situation.

'Not really. I think I'm actually falling for him.' I hiss-whisper this confession, even though I'm making the call in the middle of the churchyard, miles away from Raffaella's house or the bar.

'You can't be. He's American, you only ever fancy Italians,' states Alison as a matter of fact.

I realize that this has always been the case but it seems silly when said back to me.

I tell Alison about going out with Chuck on Thursday and how much fun we had. I explain that it was a relaxed, honest evening and a marked contrast to any other evening I've had since I arrived here. I tell her about him helping me find a job and suggesting I study for a formal TEFL qualification. I describe in detail our trip to Bassano del Grappa today to meet the director of the language school. Chuck was so supportive. He gave me all sorts of information about the school so that I could impress at the interview.

'Did you get the job?' interrupts Alison.

'Yes!' I squeal with excitement. 'It's only part-time but it's a start. Eight hours a week. Two mornings' work. At first the director thought I'd only be needed for one morning but we got on really well and she said we'd try two. The school is in this beautiful building. Marble floors, elevated ceilings. They showed me the room I'll be teaching from and it has a balcony. It's gorgeous. I start next Monday!'

'That's wonderful. How did the Wicked Witch of the West and Roberto take the news of your new career?'

'Er, I haven't told them yet.'

'Why's that?'

'Well, it's all happened at such a speed. Chuck only mentioned the possibility of a job on Thursday.'

'Why didn't you discuss it then?'

'Well, I hadn't actually told Roberto that I was out with Chuck so it would have been a bit difficult.' Whereas now it seems impossible.

'My God, you're not kidding about this crush, are you?' Alison falls silent for a second and I let her worry on my behalf. I've been worrying alone all day. 'You know, this is probably not much to do with this Chuck guy *per se*.'

'You think?'

'It's probably got more to do with the fact that he's the first person you've talked to in any sort of meaningful way in two months. He's just a symptom of your loneliness. You'd probably have a crush on a gargoyle right now if it could speak English.'

'Maybe.' I want to believe her. Problem is Chuck is no gargoyle.

I daren't tell her that on the car journey home today I asked him about his past relationships. She might not believe me when I say that I was only interested in proving he's somehow flawed. I was almost sure that he'd have mercilessly played around or that he'd hopelessly lost his heart to someone years ago and is still pining after her. I was looking for something to prove he's a loser.

'Two or three serious-ish girlfriends. One of which I lived with for two years,' he told me with a relaxed shrug.

He's not even secretive. I'm frustrated. His response sounded so normal, so balanced. No sign of axe-wielding tendencies, commitment issues or even good old-fashioned reluctance to communicate.

'Have you ever cheated on anyone?' I probed.

'No,' he said firmly.

'Never?'

'No.' He sounded a bit insulted. 'Have you?'

'No. I really believe in fidelity. If not that, then what? What is the point?'

'Quite.' He sounded frustrated. But it might have been my imagination; he might just have been bewildered about my line of questioning.

'But I bet you slipped straight from one relationship to the next. Too lazy to cook your own dinner, right?' I asked.

'No, actually I really believe in having some space between relationships, so you can learn, or feel gutted or whatever. Don't you?'

'Sounds sensible, but truthfully I've usually lined up the next one before I leave my current.'

As I said this I wanted to swallow my own tongue. What possessed me? I was trying to dig around in his romantic history to establish that *he* is a faulty soul but I managed to sound like a frivolous hussy – by telling the truth. As I fought a blush, Chuck eyed me warily.

'Moving anywhere is difficult,' says Alison, sensibly bringing me back to the here and now. 'There's always a period of adjustment, give it time. Everyone has crushes now and again.' I don't and we both know I don't. I've never looked at another man since I met Roberto. 'It's not like you have any intention of acting on this.'

I'm pleased that Alison states this as a fact. She's not asking me. She knows me well enough to be sure that I am a one-man woman and I'd never think of having a bit of extra-curricular.

OK, so I'm thinking about him all the time and I love his accent and his eyes and I think that absolutely everything he says is spot-on accurate, meaningful and kind, but we can be just good friends, can't we? Of course we can. We have to be. But is it possible for a man and a woman to be just friends? Suddenly I find myself slapped up against the eternal question that has been reflected upon over many a dining table and under many a duvet for centuries.

'The most worrying thing is that this Chuck bloke is the one you are turning to because you are lonely. Where's Roberto in all of this?' asks Alison.

'In the bar. Or at a supplier's. Or at the cash and carry. Or at least somewhere other than with me,' I admit. 'Maybe with Ana-Maria. I mean, I'm trying not to give in to silly, jealous suspicions that have no grounding in any sort of fact but –'

'That's the problem. You guys need a bit of time together. Alone,' she adds meaningfully. 'Time to tell Roberto you feel really hurt that he's never talked about Ana-Maria and that you are concerned that your savings are being sunk in the bar and –'

I cut her off; she's turned into a regular Jiminy Cricket. 'I see what you are saying.'

'Maybe you could go away for a weekend.'

'He wouldn't hear of it. He lives and breathes the bar. He won't take time off.'

'You'll be OK. You two have come through much worse times before. They've always made you stronger.'

'Right,' I mutter.

But in fact she's wrong. Yes, we have come through tough times. Our childless state has been a hideous challenge but can I honestly say that we're stronger because of our troubles? I'm not sure I can. I think our troubles have taken their toll. I know couples who are stronger because they've suffered. I do. And I admire and envy those couples but we're not like that. We're damaged and raw. I'm sure we'd have been a stronger couple if we'd had a bunch of kids snapping at our ankles. Alison is just trying to comfort us both by throwing out such a convenient platitude.

'Look on the bright side – you can be like ordinary couples now and spend your time arguing about Ana-Maria and Chuck. Past loves and present infatuations are very normal things to row about rather than . . .' She breaks off.

'Unlike tearing at each other for lack of a baby,' I finish helpfully.

'Sorry,' she mumbles.

'No, you're right,' I admit. 'Who'd have thought fancying someone other than your spouse would turn out to be a blessing,' I joke.

'That's the spirit. You have to laugh, don't you?'

'Or else you'd cry.'

38

I know that I have zero chance of persuading Roberto to take time off and take me out for dinner. I wish he would. I believe that telling Roberto my news about my imminent employment in a charming rustic trattoria would maximize my chances of the news being received favourably. Besides, since we've arrived here in Italy we've never eaten out alone. In London we had an active social life, we both enjoyed visiting new restaurants. But on the rare occasion we visit a restaurant here, Raffaella always joins us. Alison is right, we do need to spend some time together, *alone*. The only reason I am entertaining silly thoughts about Chuck is that I'm missing Roberto. I'm lonely.

I wonder if I can persuade Roberto to spend Sunday sightseeing. Maybe, if we had a whole day together, we could talk through some of the big issues that we haven't addressed yet. Chuck asked me what our long-term plans for living arrangements are; I was embarrassed to admit that Roberto and I haven't discussed it properly. I'm beginning to think Roberto would be content if we lived with his mother forever. I understand that's not unusual in Italy but it's not my intention. Obviously I need to talk to Roberto about the teaching post but I'll also have to reintroduce the subject of a fair wage at Bruno's. The TEFL course will cost quite a bit and I have to pay Signor Castoro tuition fees; my savings will dwindle to nothing in no time at all. I know we can sort all this out if only we have a little time together.

As luck would have it, the bar is the busiest I've ever seen it and I only have a chance to yell at Roberto over the sticky glasses on the counter as I'm clearing tables.

'Do you think Laurana or one of the other girls could open the bar on Sunday so that we could spend the day together? Maybe go to Verona?' I ask. Roberto shrugs and looks doubtful. 'Well, we could go somewhere closer then. We don't open until six in the evening – we could make sure we were back for opening.'

'But I use Sundays to do all the other things necessary in the bar.'

'Such as?'

He looks impatient. 'Redecorating, accounts, stock-taking.'

'My God, how much stock do we have? You are always stocktaking.'

I can't hang around to grumble as I have to take an order to a table. When I return to the bar Roberto is on the phone. It's another fifteen minutes before we can pick up the conversation.

'I really need to talk to you,' I insist. 'I have news.'

'About your job at the language school?' he asks.

I'm taken aback and suddenly feel uncomfortably hot. 'Yes, actually.' I don't want to sound guilty or meek. It's not as though I've done anything wrong by applying for a job. Yet the way Roberto is looking at me makes me feel as though I've misbehaved.

'I know all about it.' He wipes his hands on a thin cotton towel and turns to me. Aaghh, now I have his full attention; the novelty alone is enough to floor me. I feel I'm liquefying under his intense stare.

'How?'

'Mamma came into the bar this morning and found Gina all alone.'

'Well, I–I can explain that.'

Roberto holds up his hand. 'It's no problem; she is a very capable staff.'

'Exactly.' I've said as much on many an occasion and Roberto is agreeing with me, so why do I feel uneasy?

'Mamma was worried about you.' I bet she was. 'She thought you must be ill but Gina assured her you were quite well and that you had gone to the school in Bassano del Grappa with that American man.'

I'm blushing. Which is as irrational as it is unhelpful. I can imagine the scene now. Raffaella will have interrogated poor Gina, pulled out her fingernails and such. I look around for Gina so that I can give her a sympathetic nod but I notice that she's keeping herself busy and refusing to catch my eye. I don't blame her, she needn't worry, it's not as though she's landed me in trouble. I can't be in trouble, I've done nothing wrong.

'Mamma called the school to find out what is going on.'

'She did what?' A white-hot fury bubbles up inside me. I can't believe what I am hearing. I'm not a child that needs checking up on. How dare Raffaella interfere with my life in such a way? 'You are kidding?' I ask, but I know he's not.

'Mamma has a friend who works in the office at the school. She just wanted to know that you were safe.'

'Bullshit.' I explode. 'Of course I was safe. She was just stirring and interfering. What did she think? That I'd been abducted?'

'She didn't know what to think.' Roberto shrugs and then turns to the optics.

The ginger and clear liquids twinkle in their gleaming bottles. I could do with a double myself. He calmly pours a couple of drinks and stacks them on a tray, then he asks Gina to take them over to the table in the corner. Finally he turns his attention back to me. In the meantime I'm almost hyperventilating with the effort of controlling a killer rage that is slicing its way through every inch of my body.

'She thought there was something –' I stumble for the most appropriate word. I want to remain dignified – 'she thought there was something untoward going on between Chuck and me and she was checking up on us by ringing his place of employment?'

Roberto stares at me. Is he waiting for a declaration of my innocence?

'Well, there's nothing going on between us.' As I say the words my anger starts to subside and guilt starts to creep in. In some small way I can see this from Raffaella's point of view. My own actions have put me in a dim light. I take a deep breath and try to see the humour in the situation. 'Mind you, if there was, poor Chuck. Imagine his boss taking a call from Raffaella demanding to know if her son was being cuckolded.'

Roberto doesn't grab my offer to laugh at the situation. Instead he states, 'Mamma is an old friend with the secretary. So we know that all Chuck Andrews was doing was taking you for an interview.'

'Well, yes.' I don't like the implication but for some reason I can't defend myself.

'I hear congratulations are in order.'

'Yes.' I smile, hoping he's being sincere. Why can't I read him? 'It's just two mornings a week.'

'And you have your lessons with Signor Castoro.'

'Yes.'

'And I understand the school want you to study for some sort of teaching qualification.'

'It won't take long. It's not a degree. Just a certificate in teaching English as a foreign language.'

'Are you planning on working here at all?'

'In the evenings. That's when we are busiest.'

Suddenly, I'm aware of Raffaella. She's right by my side like a brutal and burly executioner; she's just waiting to be given the nod so she can swing the axe. Her eyes are darting from Roberto to me and back again. She spits out a torrent of complaint and anger. I don't need lessons with Signor Castoro to understand the gist of it. Roberto stares at his shoes throughout her outburst and says '*Sì, Mamma*' more frequently than any self-respecting man should say yes to his mother in a lifetime. I wait until the storm passes and Roberto can translate.

'Mamma says you are often more of a hindrance than a help at lunchtime because of the perpetual mix-up you make.' I *really* wish I could refute this. 'She says she doesn't object to you getting a job and that it's fine for you just to work evenings. Besides, there's no school in the summer and that's when trade will really pick up. She says you will be useful when the tourist trade starts, an English speaker will be an advantage then. So I guess the job at the language school is OK. From her point it's allowed.'

Roberto shrugs and offers me a weak smile as though he's just given me a royal pardon, yet we both know he's just been unspeakably rude and unforgivably disloyal.

'Well, that's a relief,' I snap sarcastically. 'I'm thrilled to have your mamma's blessing.' If Roberto can hear the irritation in my voice he chooses to ignore it. We both pick up trays and set off in separate directions to clear the bar.

At 3 a.m. I am still awake. Sleep is eluding me, partly because I am excited about the idea of working away from Bruno's and more pertinently away from Raffaella and partly because I'm hurt and angry. I dash to and fro between the two conflicting emotions. I lie awake staring at the ceiling. Although we live in the town centre, the darkness and stillness are complete because of the heavy shutters that keep out modern intrusions such as street lights or car headlights and it's as though I've been flung back in time by a hundred, or even a thousand, years. The only sounds to lull me are the occasional cat meowing and my husband's breathing. Not that his regular breathing is offering me any respite. The contentment he seems to be exuding through his deep slumber is actively irritating me and I believe it to be directly responsible for the throbbing pain in my lower back. I always get backache when I'm stressed. How dare he sleep so soundly when I feel so restless and alone?

It occurs to me that I'm relieved Raffaella hasn't objected to me taking a job at the language school and simultaneously I'm furious with myself for caring about her reaction at all. Where is my independence?

When I was a little girl and I couldn't sleep due to

nightmares about being lost in the maze in Hampton Court or being hauled away by the child-catcher from *Chitty Chitty Bang Bang*, my mother would crawl into my skinny bed and wrap me in her warmth. She'd tell me to think about nice things instead of the things that worried or scared me. Such simple, effective advice. Thinking nice thoughts always worked and I'd fall asleep thinking about pink tutu skirts and Cadbury's chocolate. I wish I could be wrapped in my mum's warmth right now. How pathetic is that? I'm thirty-two and I'm lying in bed next to my husband of six years and all I want is to be cuddled like a five-year-old. I try to think pleasant thoughts. If I follow Mum's advice it will be a little like her being with me.

Images of the beautiful language school in Bassano del Grappa flash into my mind. The stunning building was strangely peaceful despite being rammed full with garrulous Italian students. I loved the towering ceilings, the walls painted in warm terracotta and the sunny balconies. I try to imagine holding conversational classes with the advanced pupils but suddenly I'm gripped with panic. It seizes me with a Darth Vader-like clasp around my throat. What if I can't think of anything to discuss? What if I can't do this teaching lark and I end up back in the bar with Raffaella? What if I can't get a place on a TEFL course, or worse, I get a place but then fail? I've never had a career, as such. I've never been tested in any form since I was at school. What if I'm not up to being a teacher of any sort? What makes me think I'm up to it? Or anything else for that matter?

I sit up and feel in the dark for the glass of water that's next to my bed. I take small sips and try to breathe slowly. Maybe that nice thought was a little too ambitious. The elegant building is a beautiful thing but the possibility of making a fool of myself professionally isn't so comforting. I should think about something that presents no threat at all, something where there's no possibility of my mind wandering off to the dark side.

Roberto?

No. No way. I can't think pleasant thoughts about him right now. After our exchange in the bar we ignored each other for the rest of the evening. I came to bed first and pretended to be asleep when he finally joined me over an hour later. He sulkily huffed and puffed but I resolutely kept my eyes tight shut. I have nothing to say to him at the moment.

Chuck?

His beaming face pops into my head and the very image seems to massage the tension in my lower back. No. I push the image away even though this requires a superhuman effort. A second later I'm thinking about some of the funny things Chuck said today and I'm giggling to myself. No! It won't do. Chuck cannot be the nice thing that I think of to lull me to sleep. It's inappropriate. I'm married. He's a soon-to-be colleague. He's an entirely prohibited delight. But then I think about his eyelashes; while they are pale, they are tremendously long. When he blinks he causes a breeze. Really – I can feel a tremor as air wafts between us, somehow connecting us. His broad chest and strong forearms fill my head. I wonder what he looks like without a shirt? I'm expecting him to be clearly defined. I wonder what he smells like. I know his cologne and would already be able to pick out that spicy, fresh smell but what does *he* smell like? A vision of my nuzzling under his bear-like arm fights its way into my consciousness and before I know it I'm imagining pushing my face into his groin.

No! This is an entirely unacceptable thought. I am shocked and disappointed with myself. I gasp but the air in my marital bedroom is stale. Tears squeeze out of my eyes. I'm tired. I'm crying because I'm exhausted. I press shut my eyes but it seems as though Chuck is engraved on to my inner lids. He's there, in all his glory; tall, strong and pleasant. His eyes are closed and so his lengthy lashes are resting lightly on his beautiful cheekbones. I am too tired to fight it. I close my eyes too. And actually, I sleep very well.

39

20 *March*

'I'm sorry.'

Still half asleep, I'm not sure if I dreamed these words or whether I've said them myself. I blink against the bright morning light. Roberto is already up and he's opened the shutters. He's standing in front of me, holding a breakfast tray laden with goodies. He repeats himself, 'I'm really sorry, Elizabeth. I've been acting like fool.'

I slither into a sitting-up position but don't reply. I could be imagining this – after all, my night was filled with exceptionally vivid dreams. None of which were about Roberto though. Roberto interprets my silence as a request for more grovelling.

'I've been thinking about the bar and just the bar. The bar has had too much of my attention and you are feeling alone. I know that. Today I am not going to work. You are right, we should have some time together. We should go for a day out.'

'On a Thursday?' It's delivery day.

'Yes.'

'To Verona?' I ask tentatively.

'Good idea. The city of lovers. An appropriate place for us to be today.'

He puts the tray down in front of me and then he pulls back the sheets and jumps back into bed. Roberto starts to butter a slice of toast. I notice that it is white sliced bread, my preference for toast. There are no cooked meats on the tray, thank goodness. He hands me the toast and starts preparing a second slice. I notice that he's also brought me a plate of fresh fruit and tea, rather than coffee. I do love the strong Italian coffee but I have missed my morning brew.

I quietly munch my toast. Roberto takes my silence to be a symptom of my hurt feelings and is increasingly solicitous. Sometimes I think Italian men like petulant women more than affable ones, in the same way some women always fall for bastards. Roberto carefully pours me a cup of tea and pops grapes into my mouth as though I am some sort of indolent emperor. I eat and drink with compliance but can't bring myself to chat.

I'm not sulking or playing for more attention; in fact I am crippled with guilt. In light of Roberto's apology and gentleness, my night of bright and brilliant dreams about Chuck seems like a betrayal. Roberto is staring at me with his chocolate pool eyes and I worry that he can see right through me. It would be awful to think that he can expose every conscious and subconscious thought I've ever had. He pauses in feeding me breakfast to tuck a strand of my hair behind my ear, and when I mutter that my fingers are sticky with butter he sucks them clean as though they are a life source. His intensity disarms me. He waits until I've eaten three slices of toast, most of the fruit and drunk two cups of tea before he slides the tray off me. He elegantly lifts it with one hand and carefully lowers the breakfast debris on to the floor next to the bed. In another swift and comfortable move he slips on top of me and starts to kiss my neck and ears. I love the feeling of his body on top of mine and I smudge into him. I've missed his warmth. Quietly, carefully, we make love, without regard as to whether it is or is not a particularly fertile time in my cycle. The lovemaking is affectionate and familiar. We know each other's bodies and we can gently pleasure each other without stress or struggle. I immerse myself in the calm, relieved to escape the turmoil and complications that normally haunt our days. The effortless nature of the act only leaves me wondering why we don't do it more often.

40

Verona is as beautiful as I could have hoped. It's full of Roman remains, rose-red medieval buildings and romantic dreams of young love. I arrive bouncing with hope and excitement, as Roberto and I have chatted non-stop for the entire journey. I've amused him with stories about our customers and I've had the opportunity to fill him in on the details of my new job. He seems interested and is very encouraging. He's told me a little bit more about his plans for the bar. He wants to landscape the outside area (currently used as a dump for our old furniture, worn tyres and similar junk). He wants an impressive outdoor eating space that will attract families during the daytime and rowdy parties at night. We discuss the menu changes that we might introduce for the summer and Roberto agrees with me that the old-fashioned loos have to be replaced with modern, clean and stylish ones. I have not asked him exactly how he spends his siestas or how he and Ana-Maria split up and made up. I don't want to spoil the atmosphere.

Roberto knows Verona well and quickly finds street parking that is within easy walking distance of the main piazza. Piazza Bra is a large, open space dominated by the Roman amphitheatre. The piazza is rammed with tourists, who are chatting, taking photos, and tripping over pigeons.

'It's so busy,' I say as I jump to dodge a determined group of French schoolchildren who seem intent on knocking me clean over. After being in sleepy Veganze for a couple of months I've forgotten what city life is like.

'This is nothing. Wait until you see the place in July,' comments Roberto. Suddenly, I feel ebullient with the thought of being in Italy in July; this is an enormous relief. Recently I've started to dread the thought of seeing through the month, let alone a lifetime, here. All at once, standing in the middle of this thriving hub, surrounded by noise, chaos and fun, holding the hand of my husband, I feel safe and secure. This is how I imagined our time in Italy would be. I've been so silly thinking about Chuck all the time. I've got that completely out of proportion. We're just going to be pals.

'Shall we take a look around the amphitheatre?' I suggest.

Roberto agrees, although he must have visited it on at least a dozen other occasions. He acts as guide, telling me that the amphitheatre was built in the first century AD and that in the thirteenth century an earthquake destroyed the majority of the exterior arcade but remarkably most of the interior is still intact. We climb up the steeply pitched tiers of pinkish marble seats to enjoy the dizzying views from the top. He holds my hand the entire way, even when it starts to get a bit damp with the effort of the climb.

'It's so wonderful here,' I gush as I flop down on to my bottom and take a moment to catch my breath.

'We should come here for the opera,' says Roberto. I nod enthusiastically, although I'd much prefer a pop concert or even a jazz festival. I don't want to admit as much in case I break the moment; he's trying to be thoughtful and attentive.

We pause for a few minutes. We're sitting facing in the direction the Romans would have faced when they were killing Christians. The thought unnerves me and so I get up and wander to catch a view of the city. Roberto is right by my side.

'Verona it is the largest city in mainland Veneto. Most of the historic heart of Verona is enclosed in a loop of the river Adige,' he says, pointing out the loop in case I'm a total idiot and can't make it out for myself. I can see wonderful churches and other historical buildings scattered liberally throughout the higgledy-piggledy streets. I know we should go and visit one or two of those, Roberto would like it, but my eye is irresistibly drawn to the streets packed with pedestrians, which are bound to be the ones with the best shopping.

'Is that a market?' I try to keep my tone neutral but I do love a bargain. Roberto knows this. He grins and says, 'We can shop if you want to.'

I don't need to be invited twice. I scramble down the steps at quite some speed and in a matter of minutes I'm in the throng of the pedestrian-only street, which is flanked by tempting and elegant shops. Roberto buys a shirt and I buy a new bag. I don't need it and I already have one in the same colour but it's a different shape and the leather smells delicious. The bag is an indulgence, rather than a necessity, and all the more welcome for that.

We head north towards Piazza delle Erbe and we stumble into the market that I spotted from the amphitheatre. There are stalls selling fruit and veg, clothes, belts, shoes and a vast amount of tourist tat. It's the tourist tat that catches my eye because I'm entirely powerless in situations such as these. It's bizarre but true that whenever

I'm on holiday I find snow globes and commemorative tea towels become my 'must have' items. I can't explain or excuse myself; under other circumstances I'm quite rational and stylish. I've learnt that as I can't control my foible, it's best to indulge it. I buy a handful of postcards and, as this is the city of love, I'm drawn to the stalls selling hundreds of red hearts. There are papier-mâché hearts, straw hearts, wooden ones and right at the centre of the stall, hanging far away from grasping hands, there are red glass hearts. They dangle on pretty red ribbons, swaying in the breeze, waiting to be selected like wall-flower virgins at the school disco.

'Let's buy one. Or maybe two,' I suggest.

'What will you do with them?' asks Roberto, who does not share my passion for souvenirs.

'They can go on the Christmas tree.'

'It's not yet April, how can you be thinking of buying Christmas decorations? Besides we don't really decorate trees here in Italy at Christmas.'

I'm stunned and disappointed. I love my Christmas tree at home. Christmas wouldn't be Christmas without the oversized tree dominating the sitting room. I've collected ornaments for years and dress the tree with extreme care and attention. I've brought my favourite ones with me. I file the thought and vow that nearer the time I'll be able to persuade Roberto to have a tree.

'Well, we can hang them in the bar then, or over our bed.'

'Mamma doesn't like nails being hammered into the walls.'

I won't let Roberto's lack of enthusiasm dampen mine. We're having a lovely day and I want us to continue having a lovely day, so I bite my tongue. I turn my attention to the stall-owner who has by this time spotted us debating the attraction of his wares and has come in for the kill.

'Very beautiful, hey? For the young lady?' He looks at Roberto and smiles. Roberto moves his head a fraction to the left and right but the vendor is unperturbed, he's an old pro and can see I'm keen to purchase. 'You like?' He asks, turning his grin and attention to me.

'They are lovely,' I comment as I take hold of the glass heart he's picked out for me.

'Handmade,' he assures me.

I nod appreciatively and ignore Roberto's tuts. 'How much?' I ask.

The vendor names a price which is far above the price chalked on the blackboard pinned above the stall. Roberto points this out, but the old man insists that the cheaper price is for the paper or straw hearts. He passes me one of those but as he does so he shrugs disdainfully, suggesting that I'm going down in his estimation by considering the cheaper goods. How he has managed to make me feel inferior for considering purchasing his wares is a mystery to me, but he has.

'I like the glass one best,' I say as I gingerly hand back the straw heart. The old man grunts his approval and starts to wrap up the glass heart. Roberto sighs but it's not an especially resentful sigh, more an exasperated one. He hands over the exorbitant amount.

'We'll see the same thing for a third of the price on the next street corner,' he states.

'Maybe,' I concede. I don't care. I want *this* particular glass heart, although I know I'm being irrational and

I can't explain why I want this one and no other – it just felt right in my hand. It was warm, not cold as you'd expect a glass ornament to be. Logically, I know this is because it's hung in the sun all morning but I'm not famed for being logical.

As the old man hands over the beautifully wrapped package, he flashes his toothless smile and in broken English says, 'The glass hearts fulfil wish and this one particular fulfil wish for many babies. With this heart comes a big family.'

I take the package from him with trembling hands. How did he know? *How*? Roberto shuffles uncomfortably and keeps his eyes fixed on his shoes. Suddenly, the costly heart seems to be a bargain.

I float through the cobbled streets, without a map or a plan, but simply allowing their loveliness and mysteries to unfold in front of me. The streets are winding and the sun is bright; intermittently we are plunged into shadows and then with a quick turn we are back into the glare. I feel amazing. I ruminate on the wish-granting heart and from time to time surreptitiously stretch my hand into my bag and let my fingers rest lightly on the package.

We stop for lunch in a charming cobbled square. The restaurant we choose is a brightly frescoed building with vivid greenery tumbling down from window-boxes. The idyll is slightly marred, as it takes an age to order our food. Still, I can't be cross when I think of the glass heart nestling in my handbag. Roberto and I fall silent and stare at the fountain in the middle of the square; water is gushing from three spouts and dribbling from a fourth, causing a green slimy line of algae to form down the chin, chubby belly and leg of the cherub. We watch as endless pairs of lovers amble up and throw coins into the pool, undoubtedly making wishes for eternal love.

'How do you think he knew?' I ask Roberto.

'Lucky guess,' says Roberto with a shrug. This isn't the answer I wanted, but at least he hasn't pretended to misunderstand me. Since the old man handed over the fertility heart neither of us has thought of anything else.

'No, he *knew*,' I insist.

'Elizabeth, we are a married couple of a certain age, it doesn't take a genius or a clairvoyant to guess that babies would be a natural next step. The vendor's words mean nothing. The heart is just a toy.'

'But we should hang it above our bed, just in case,' I insist.

Roberto tuts, and for the first time today I see irritation slip into his eyes. Thinking about it, Roberto often seems quite irritated by me. Today has been a notable exception because his eyes have been shining with something I wanted to *believe* was contentment. But the cosy intimacy that has mooched between us all day begins to evaporate. I feel panicked. I want to grasp that shadowy intimacy and hold it tight. We are husband and wife, we should be intimate, we *should* be happy. We shouldn't be so often cross and distant. I can hear my breathing quick and shallow.

I struggle to appear calm as I ask, 'Why don't you want to believe it might be true?'

'Because you believe it too much.'

At that moment Roberto's food arrives and he starts to tuck in. He's eaten his entire plate of spaghetti before my fish is even put down in front of me. I can't blame him, who wants cold food? But I end up feeling desolate and hurried as I munch alone, as I often do here. It's not quite like the experience I imagined. I thought eating was a communal celebration on the Continent. I thought only the Brits abused food by eating pot noodles while watching TV.

As I pick through the bones of the fish, Roberto talks to me about Verona's prosperous economy. The stuff he's telling me might be quite interesting but it smacks of a deliberate change of subject and seems insincere for that.

'We need to visit some bars here and see what the decor trends are, which DJs play at the weekend, what beers are sold, etc.,' he says.

'You want to do a competitive analysis here in Verona?'

'Yes.'

'Today?'

'Yes.'

'But I thought we were having a day off.'

'It's not real work, drinking in bars, is it? Besides, it's impossible for me to switch off entirely now, Elizabeth. The bar is *my* business.'

Maybe, since it's certainly not *our* business. I sip my orange juice and try to resist passing comment. Roberto turns to me and reaches for my hand.

'The teaching will be a good thing for you, Elizabeth,' he says. 'It will give you a passion, other than baby-wanting.'

'You want a baby too.' I try to make my comment sound like a statement rather than a question but I'm not sure I succeed. I've tried not to notice Roberto's reluctance to talk about our lack of family but it's becoming harder to ignore.

'I wanted that, yes.'

'Wanted?' I realize I've shouted when a number of eyes turn towards us. Clearly, in the city of lovers, rows are about as welcome as a nun at a stag party.

'I still want it,' whispers Roberto. He obviously thinks that talking quietly might encourage me to calm down; oddly it has the opposite effect. I'm incensed by his consideration to the strangers around us, as it glaringly exposes his insensitivity towards me. I glare at him. Perhaps if I keep my eyes wide and angry the tears that are threatening won't spill out.

'I just no longer expect it,' he mutters. 'I no longer believe it will be our destiny.'

We sit in silence as I consider the implications of what Roberto has just confessed.

He's given up hope.

He no longer believes we will ever be a family. I'm alone in trying for this. I'm chilled by the thought. The tears I've been hoping to keep at bay throughout lunch finally, silently, roll down my face with the inevitability of a determined tank progressing over the soil of a conquered country. The tears splash on to my lap and are caught by the paper napkin that I'm shredding. I can't bring myself to look at Roberto. He's the cause of my tears, which is bad enough – the humiliation would scar all the more if he witnessed them too. Anyway, I sense that he's not looking at my tears, he's staring out towards the fountain. How long have I been trying to kid myself that we were looking in the same direction? I grab the tattered napkin and scrunch it into a tight ball. My fingernails dig into the palm of my hand. I concentrate on that discomfort in a pathetic effort to distract from the howling pain of realizing exactly what my life amounts to.

A bloody mess.

My husband is fascinated by another woman. I am intrigued by another man. Italy is not the answer to all my problems, I have brought my problems with me from England just as surely as if I packed them with my passport. There is no baby. My husband no longer believes there ever will be one.

How will I ever stand up from this table?

Of course his belief in our chance of having a child makes no material difference, we can still have sex as regularly (or irregularly) as before, but something has irrevocably changed between us. I feel a lump of grief throbbing in the pit of my stomach.

Time shudders on, for how long I don't know. Two minutes? Twenty? I mine into my deepest resource and drag out my dearest belief. I *will* have a baby. I *will* be a mother. With or without Roberto's hope, I have to carry on. I choose one fantasy from my extensive portfolio, the one about shopping with my teenage daughter, and I polish that fantasy. I think about her buoyant grin and my fake exasperation as she tries on yet another funky skirt. For several minutes I visualize the sounds, smells and sights that will accompany this scene and eventually my tears stop and my breathing calms. Finally, I find a reserve of strength and say, 'I want to head to Juliet's home.'

Roberto is still looking at the fountain and has not noticed my distress. 'The so-called Casa di Giulietta is just a tourist trap. The balcony wasn't even added until 1935. You are the English literature expert but even I know that William Shakespeare was dead long before then,' he says with a grin.

Just because he's right doesn't make me feel better towards him for making this observation.

'I want to imagine Romeo standing under her balcony,' I say quietly and firmly. 'I need to believe in the romance.'

Roberto shrugs. 'OK.'

41

'Been busy?' asks Chuck as I hop into his car.

'Sort of. Usual stuff, just working in the bar. Oh, and went to Verona on Thursday.'

'Just you and Roberto?'

'Yes.'

'So did you enjoy the romance, the architecture and the history? It just oozes out of every stone, doesn't it?' comments Chuck.

'I guess,' I smile weakly. His enthusiasm is normally infectious, but the thought of Roberto resigning himself to our infertile state has made me immune.

'Too many pigeons, Pinocchio puppets and pedestrians for you, hey?' asks Chuck, hazarding a guess at my morose state. 'Wasn't it what you expected?'

I play with the idea of telling him why I stayed in my room all day Friday, ignoring the sunshine and the calls that I turn up for my shift in the bar; I lay on my bed and quietly wept until my skin was sore. I tried to repeat my trick of visualizing a moment of maternal bliss but the exercise is becoming harder and harder. Even dreaming gets lonely. I think Chuck would understand. If not him, then who? Not Alison. When I called her, she said that deep down part of me has known that it's been years since Roberto was actively interested in baby-making.

Maybe – but there's a difference between subconsciously accepting a lack of enthusiasm and openly embracing the possibility that he's given the idea up entirely. What a numbing, Armageddon thought; he is despairing of us ever being a family. We should have talked about that. I should have known that. The way I should have known that the vineyard was a bar and that Ana-Maria was an ex-long-term girlfriend. What is happening to us? What has happened?

I am a blank. A nothing. I have no purpose or direction if I'm not trying for a baby; if we aren't going to be a family what are we to be? Roberto seems to think we can be a happy and fulfilled couple just by running the bar but we're not that happy. Quite a lot of the time I'm very unhappy. Most of the time, actually. When have I been truly happy in Italy? The night at Perche No? was fun. But then I got my period. Another full stop.

I want to tell Chuck all of this but if I start talking I know there's a strong possibility that the tears will start to gush again. I can't risk that before work.

'It was fine. I'm just nervous about today.' My excuse is plausible but a jot away from credible. I hope he doesn't call me on it. To avoid him doing so I add, 'I've brought along a couple of English books and magazines to give the conversations a starting point, but I'm not sure they are the right sort of material. The magazines I found under my bed are mostly gossip or fashion mags but I did manage to search out a dog-eared copy of *Newsweek* as well. Roberto picked it up at Heathrow when we flew here.'

He nods approvingly, 'All good stuff. Relevant. Pupils like that. You have nothing to be nervous of. I'll drop you at the secretary's office. She'll give you a list of the names of your students. They are all one-on-one sessions this morning. Your students will love you. You are going to be awesome. I like your skirt by the way. It's er good. It's er short.'

It's impossible not to smile at him.

At lunchtime I wander out into the sunshine leaving the school behind me and bump straight into Chuck.

'Well?' he asks with an enormous grin.

'It was brilliant. I had such a good time. I can't believe I'm being paid to talk to people, especially nice people. I'm teaching one of your ex-pupils actually; Francesca Contadino.'

'Oh yes.' Chuck nods but doesn't add anything more.

Francesca is mesmerizing. She has a neat, hard body and a wide, whooping smile. When I was teaching her I found myself wondering if she and Chuck ever dated. Not that I have any right to feel uncomfortable imagining Chuck kissing every inch of Francesca's stunning hard body. But.

'Who else did you teach?' he asks.

'A woman in her fifties, who wants to travel to Asia. Asia, can you imagine it? You don't think of women her age having a gap year, do you? She's having advanced lessons in English plus she's studying Chinese. She's frighteningly bright. And there were two executives from the Pirelli plant. They need to be fluent for work. Of course, they were both utterly charming and captivating. Italian men their age always are, aren't they?' Chuck is grinning at me although I'm unsure as to exactly why.

'They were *all* lovely,' I add, in case he thinks I have a crush on the businessmen. I wish he knew me better, then he'd know I don't do crushes, or at least didn't.

'Did they like your magazines?'

'Yes. I think next week I might take a manual or even a TV clip and have a discussion around that. I'll get Mum and Dad to send some things over. I think it's important to keep the discussion material varied.'

'You're brilliant, a natural,' says Chuck, and then he envelops me in an enormous hug. He picks me up into the air and shakes me around a little before he carefully lowers me back down to the ground.

'Wow, you are really big, aren't you,' I mutter.

I seem short of breath, which is humiliating. I either look unfit or I look as though I'm some sad old bird who literally pants with excitement when a lump of hunk is in close physical proximity. The shame. The accuracy. I feel the imprint of his arms wrapped around my body way after he's let go. Maybe I should feel bad about that but actually it's hard to dislike.

Chuck grins. 'Do you have time for lunch or do you want me to drive you straight back to Veganze now?'

'You don't have to drive me. I wouldn't dream of putting you out like that. I'll get a bus. You have to teach this afternoon, don't you?'

'Yes, but my next class isn't until four. I'm expecting to hear all about your classes first. I was just hanging around, waiting for you.'

For me. It's tempting. 'Well, I don't have to be at the bar until six.' I check my watch. 'We could eat here and *then* I could get a bus back.'

'We could eat here and *then* I'll run you back. We have plenty of time.' Chuck takes hold of my arm and steers me towards the street. 'I know a great pasta joint.'

Chuck is as good as his word. He does know a great pasta joint. He takes me to a small, slightly scruffy trattoria which I'd have certainly dismissed if I'd been on my own. The paintwork is chipped and the cutlery doesn't match. We sit at heavy wooden tables with paper place settings and napkins. The owner is also the waiter and chef too, apparently. But he embraces his multi-tasking with an unusual buoyancy and verve. He's clearly delighted to see Chuck, who is obviously a regular, and they chat in Italian for a good ten minutes before settling on penne with pesto sauce.

'Did you understand any of that?' asks Chuck, when the proprietor dashes back to the kitchen and we are alone.

'Some. You were talking about the ingredients of the sauces. He persuaded you away from the Bolognese sauce because he was unconvinced by the quality of the tomatoes at market today, plus he mentioned that pesto with penne would be quicker.'

'Wow, well done.'

'I understand more than I can speak.'

'The lessons will help there. It's just a matter of confidence.'

'Of course I might have just made a lucky guess; the chances that you'd be talking about food were pretty high; that's what Italians talk about most of all.'

'I suppose,' concedes Chuck as he snaps a breadstick in half. 'Do you fancy a drink?'

'At lunchtime?'

'Is that wrong?'

'Not if I'm making the rules, but I thought Americans barely drank and certainly not at lunchtime.'

'I'm not thinking of sinking a galleon, just one glass of red now and then. I won't get in the car for a few hours. Drinking and driving is a no-no but that's me, not a national trait. America is a big place. Californians probably do drink less than average but there's a horrendously high occurrence of alcoholism in the mid-west and other places. It's really hard to generalize.' Chuck pauses and then adds, 'You operate hampered by a lot of stereotypes, don't you?'

'What do you mean?'

'Well, you are always saying, "I didn't think Americans did this or that" or "Italians are this or that." You have quite a bank of prejudice.'

'I do not. I am not a prejudiced person at all.'

Chuck shrugs. He pauses while he asks the proprietor to bring us a couple of glasses of wine, then he asks me, 'Do you know any Dutch?'

'Uh uh,' I shake my head. 'The Dutch are hard business people – traders, bankers and such. Not my type.'

'What about the Spanish?'

'I love the Spanish. They are such passionate people. I once worked with a girl who was Spanish; the poor thing was always having rows with her boyfriend.'

Chuck laughs, the way people who think they've just proven a point laugh. 'That was probably to do with her age or his infidelity, or her spending habits, or about a million other things could be the reason, you can't just put it down to her nationality,' he says.

'I can. Anyway assuming *she* spent a lot and *he* was unfaithful is also operating in a stereotype,' I point out.

'Where do you get this stuff from? Unbelievable,' says Chuck, shaking his head with something that looks like disbelief.

'I read a lot,' I tell him proudly.

'Is that instead of living a lot?'

I stare at him warily and try to think how I should answer. I wonder if he's trying to offend me. I decide not, Americans are very polite, they are just a little more straightforward in the way they express themselves than the Brits are. Suddenly I can't see the table because tears are swimming in my eyes.

'Hey, hey, I'm so sorry. I was only teasing. I didn't mean to upset you.'

'It's not you,' I stutter through my tears.

'Then what is it?'

I take a sip of my wine and wonder how much I should say. The morning's teaching distracted me from the pain of Roberto accepting our childlessness but Chuck's off-the-cuff comment has unexpectedly struck a chord and once again I'm face to face with the question: what is it that I've been doing with my life other than waiting? Reading while waiting to start a family seems worthy. But if there's no baby, then what?

'I want a baby.'

'What, now?' Chuck looks confused.

'Now. Soon. Always,' I blurt. 'It's all I've ever seriously wanted but it's not happening.'

I take a large gulp of my wine and then I tell him everything. I tell him that since I was a little girl I've fantasized about having a big family and, when I was fourteen, I honed that desire. For eighteen years I've harboured a dream to live in the middle of a huge, boisterous, Italian family. I tell him how I only ever dated Italians as I ruthlessly pursued that dream, and I tell him how I was so sure that I'd lucked out when I met Roberto and we quickly fell in love. And then I tell him the hard bit; the bit where the fairytale turns into a lonely nightmare. I tell him about the countless examinations and interviews with doctors, specialists and consultants, the herbs, hormones, rituals and tests. I tell him that I used to adore my friends' and brothers' kids but now I find it really tough being around them. I hate myself for not being a bigger person. But I'm not. I'm sad and I'm verging on bitter.

'I hate it when other people expect me to hold their newborns. I know they think they are trying to be decent, offering me some sort of consolation prize. But it's hard. Plus, there are loads of rubbish mothers out there. Everyone knows that. They are put on earth to torture me.'

And finally I tell him the worst thing of all.

'Roberto's given up hope. He said so on Thursday.'

Chuck has stayed silent throughout my lengthy outburst. He did at one point order another glass of wine. Now he stretches across the table and squeezes my hand. Without thinking about it I lace my fingers into his and we hold hands as though we are lovers, not friends.

'But *you* haven't given up hope. Isn't that the important thing? You are strong enough to hope on your own and that might be enough, providing –'

Chuck breaks off. I look at him and he's almost blushing; he's definitely embarrassed. I understand what he's getting at.

'Oh yes, we are still having sex,' I reassure him.

'Well, good, erm.'

'Yes, I continue to hope because there isn't even a specific problem.' I say this with angry disbelief, as though it was the first time I'd ruminated on this fact, not the ten thousandth. Each time I do so the unfairness hits me anew.

'There isn't?' asks Chuck surprised.

'None that the docs can find. Unexplained infertility they call it. The best the doctors can offer us by way of explanation is that our –' I hesitate and wonder how, or even if, I should say this. Sex and baby-making has become quite scientific for Roberto and me. It's normal for us to talk about the most intimate acts without any embarrassment, reverence or mystery. Now I'm talking about baby-making with Chuck I'm suddenly very aware of the reverence and mystery of sex once again. I falter.

'Let's just say everything is functioning and theoretically we are capable, but you know, we're just not that compatible.'

Chuck gets my meaning. 'A friend of mine had the same thing. They tried IVF. They have two kids now.' Chuck sounds so hopeful I could kiss him. It's been forever since anyone was hopeful about my situation.

'IVF? No, Roberto won't think of it. He believes what is meant to be will be and that we oughtn't to interfere with this sort of thing. This one is up to the Big Guy.' I point to the heavens.

'But that's crazy and a bit selfish. You could argue IVF is a modern-day miracle,' says Chuck.

You could argue that and I have. I've used the exact words to no avail. I shrug. 'Who's to say it would work anyway?' I ask. 'The odds are not high.'

'Maybe, but you must resent Roberto for not wanting to try.'

'I do actually.'

I can't believe I've just said this. How disloyal of me. What a revelation. I roll the words around my head. I resent Roberto. For the first time I consciously acknowledge that I'm annoyed with him for refusing to try IVF. I'd *try* anything. I'd *do* anything.

The proprietor reappears; he coughs. Chuck straightens up, letting my hand fall from his grasp.

'*Mi scusi*,' says the waiter as he drops two enormous plates of pasta in front of us with a thud.

Chuck hands me a napkin and I blow my nose. 'Thanks for listening,' I say shyly.

'Thanks for talking. My heart breaks for you, Elizabeth. You'd be a great mum. I know it. And you know what? I really believe you will be one day. Who knows what's out there?' he says enthusiastically.

'Do you think so?' I look up and meet his sparkling green eyes that dance with hope and integrity. I feel doused in his warmth and goodwill.

'I've never wanted kids. It's just not my thing at all. But listening to you talk about them and how much you want them has really moved me.'

'What?' I pull away as he throws his pail of icy water over me.

'I've never understood the longing some people have to reproduce; that whole thing has just passed me by. But my God, Elizabeth, you are so passionate and you've given it so much thought that I really have some insight into *your* longing.'

'But you don't feel it?' I ask with disbelief and an

irrational disappointment. Why should I care if Chuck wants babies or not?

'No, not at all.' He forks a large amount of pasta into his mouth and chews thoughtfully.

'And here's me thinking you were the perfect man,' I joke, even though I'm feeling unreasonably gutted. What the hell is wrong with me?

'You thought I was the perfect man?'

He stops chewing and we stare at one another. The tension between us is palpable. I don't know what to say. There isn't a joke to hide behind.

'I think we should talk about something else now,' I say quietly.

Chuck nods. 'So, tell me all about this morning.'

And I do. Throughout lunch and for the entire afternoon I talk to Chuck about my lessons. I demonstrate how I made one of the Pirelli execs laugh by imitating different regional accents in the UK. My impersonations are really pretty good. Chuck insists on hearing them and nearly snorts water on to the table as he's chortling so hard at my Geordie impression. I say how surprisingly relaxing I find the small classroom I've been assigned; the light tumbles through the windows in thick bands, creating an impression of great space. It was just what I needed today.

The afternoon passes in a heartbeat. Despite, or perhaps even because of, my weepy confession Chuck is easy company and I feel a strange calm when I'm with him – sometimes I'm even joyful, despite the huge disappointment gnawing at my soul. We leisurely wander, exploring a little bit of the town. The sun is doing its best to join the fun. It darts behind a cloud and then reappears again every few minutes, rather like a child playing peek-a-boo. We sit in happy silences and watch the mobile-wielding gangs of Italians chat merrily to one another. Their sociability is delightful.

Undeterred by his insistence that I over-generalize, I sigh and comment, 'You've got to love the Italians.'

'Yes, I've made great friends here. People are very welcoming.'

'And so elegant.' My eyes are drawn to another crowd of tiny-limbed women wearing high boots, carrying over-sized bags and adorned with chunky belts. 'I seriously doubt my ability to ever ape that level of sophistication, which is quite a depressing thought.'

'Come on, we'll go and eat cake. *That* we can do in our own inimitable style.'

The cake will do nothing by way of helping me towards the oh-so-thin limbs that I admire, but I can't resist. The cake-shop window is lit up like a Christmas display. I can't decide on just one so we buy three between us. Chuck forks moist cake into my mouth and I allow myself a moment of undiluted pleasure.

I ask Chuck to drop me off at Bruno's because I've asked Roberto to meet me there rather than at Raffaella's. I want to tell him about my first day's teaching away from Raffaella's censorious gaze. When I'd made the arrangement I'd been unsure as to whether I'd be arriving home triumphant or hanging my head in shame; either way I didn't want to be greeted by Raffaella.

'Oh damn, I can't see his car,' I grumble as we approach the bar.

'Do you want me to take you home? He might be there,' offers Chuck.

'No, he always parks here, there's no space at Raffaella's and I told him to meet me here.'

'Something must have cropped up unexpectedly.'

'Something always does,' I mutter ominously.

'I'm sure he'd have wanted to greet you after your first day of work if he could have. We are quite late. It's my fault.'

Chuck means well but we're both embarrassed by his statement. His thoughtfulness exposes Roberto's lack of it.

I rally. 'No problem, Laurana is probably about. She'll want to hear all about the school. I'll see you Friday, hey?'

'Yeah, I'll run you to and from school, no worries. And if you want to hook up before, call me any time.'

He passes me a piece of paper with his mobile number and his home number written out. I like the way he writes his sevens. His fingers brush against mine and I'm scorched. I'm sure I'm branded like an animal.

I nod, scramble out the car and wave. As I watch his car fade into the haze of the afternoon sun it crosses my mind that the problem is I *don't* have his number. Not at all. Not in the real sense. Is Chuck just the nicest guy you could ever hope to meet, a truly sympathetic friend and gent? Or, does he fancy the very flesh off me and is he therefore likely to jump any moment? It's confusing. And the most confusing thing of all is that I don't know which one I want it to be.

42

There's no sign of Roberto until it's time to cash up. When he finally arrives he looks distracted and apologetic. In front of Laurana I resist the temptation to demand where he's been, because I don't want to let on that I need to keep tabs on him yet can't; both situations are embarrassing.

He makes quite an entrance. 'Girls, how can I thank you enough?' he asks. Flinging his arms wide, he offers up a sheepish smile. He looks every inch the delinquent but repentant teenager facing up to his granny.

'A pay rise,' replies Laurana as quick as a flash. I grin at her. I admire her style. I wish I'd thought of that.

Roberto ignores her comment but instead says, 'You go home now. Are you in the car or do you need a lift?'

'A lift would be nice. Tonight has been quiet, as it is Monday, but sometimes the quiet nights are the longest, wouldn't you agree, Elizabeth?'

I nod and smile. 'Run her home, Roberto. I'll lock up and see you back at the house.'

By the time Roberto returns I've showered and I'm in bed. He pushes open the door with stealth but I sit up and flick on the bedside light.

'I didn't want to wake you,' he says as he unbuttons his shirt.

'I wasn't asleep.'

I hug my knees and wait. I'm not sure what I'm waiting

for most. I can't decide what I want from him first; an interested inquiry about my morning at school or an explanation as to where he's been all afternoon and evening. He clearly can't decide what to say either, so he stays silent while he peels off all his clothes, folds them, puts on pyjamas and finally slips between the sheets.

Eventually he says, 'The nights are getting warmer, aren't they? Soon we will need a fan in here.' Then he rolls on to his side and away from me.

I tell myself to breathe deeply. Without the reminder I might forget to breathe at all, as the dangerous, hot fury bubbling up inside me might suffocate me.

'Are you going to turn your light out?' he asks.

'No.'

'It's late. You should get some sleep. Are you reading?'

'No.' I hear him sigh. He turns his body towards me a fraction but doesn't look at me; instead he stares at the ceiling. 'Do you want us to have sex?'

'NO!' I yell. The fury is unable to be suppressed for a moment longer. Now I have his attention. He sits bolt upright.

'Elizabeth, shush. You'll wake the family. What is the matter?'

'Where have you been today?'

'I've been busy. I had business to attend to. People to see.'

I want to ask him which people he's seen. Has he seen Ana-Maria today? Has he spent all afternoon with her family, reminiscing about old times and laughing over tattered photos? Or worse.

'Laurana said you managed fine in the bar. She said you weren't busy. I knew you'd be OK.'

'We were but that's not the point. I didn't know *you* were OK. I didn't even know where you were.'

'We can't live in one each other's pockets, Elizabeth. We'll go crazy. I didn't realize you needed a minute-by-minute account of my where beings.'

'It's one another's or each other's and it's whereabouts,' I correct automatically.

But put like that I seem weirdly irrational and I begin to lose the certainty of my right to be furious. Of course I don't need a minute-by-minute account but a day-by-day one might be nice. I don't allow myself to say as much because it seems petty. Is it respect for personal space that has led to Roberto forgetting to ask me how my very first day of teaching went? I stubbornly refuse to furnish him with the detail until he makes a polite enquiry, so I swallow all the excited chatter I'd stored throughout the day. I will keep the funny anecdotes and charming details to myself; but swallowing my own happiness tastes disgusting.

'Now can we please get some sleep? I, for one, am very tired.'

'*No*. Why are you so tired? What have you been doing all day?'

Suddenly an image of Roberto and Ana-Maria's tanned limbs entwined in each other and in crisp white sheets forces its way into my head. I see, with frightening clarity, his lips moving towards hers, his hand skimming across her back, down to her pert bottom. I can even see tiny beads of sweat resting on his top lip; a faint glow, betraying his exertion. I shake my head and try to shift the vile images but they stubbornly cling to my subconscious. Whatever I do, I must not bring up Ana-Maria's name.

I'll look jealous and insecure (not a great look). I have no *evidence* that anything untoward is going on. I shouldn't be thinking this about him. I should trust him. No man wants a suspicious and irrational wife. I bite my tongue and try to think of something, anything, to say other than her name. I *must* trust him. I *must* remain calm and logical. I *must* not jump to conclusions.

'Have you been with Ana-Maria today?' I demand, somewhat buggering up Plan A to keep my cool.

'Why do you ask such a thing?'

'Why don't you answer such a thing?'

'You are being foolish.'

'No, I'm not. I didn't ask you if you had sex with Ana-Maria today. Now that would be foolish.' I realize that I sound screechy and breathless. I've slipped into sarcasm. I often do when I'm upset. I always think sarcasm is just a bitter spinster sister of humour. I sometimes use humour to avoid talking directly with my husband too; right now, I can't be that disciplined.

'I'm simply taking an interest. You know, like couples do. You, for instance, could have asked how my day went at school. I wouldn't have thought you foolish, just interested.'

Roberto hates it when I am sarcastic because sometimes it's hard for him to appreciate all the shades and nuances of my irritation, although I think he gets the gist tonight.

He groans and hits his forehead with the flat of his palm. 'The school, I forgot to ask.'

'Yes, you did.' I wait. Surely he knows that this is his chance. An enquiry, even at this late stage, would be appreciated.

'Come on, there's no point in us rowing,' he mutters.

'*Au contraire*. There is every point in us rowing. For a start I can feel better that I've got this off my chest. Why should I be the only one to have a sleepless night?'

He looks confused; the mix of French sarcasm and English idiom has left him behind. This sometimes happens when we row because I speed up my speech pattern and become more colloquial and high-pitched. He finds me difficult to understand. Right now I find him difficult to understand too, but I fear it's more to do with his Y chromosome than his accent. I used to find his inability to follow me charming and the affection his bemused looks inspired was always enough to stop me mid-rant. I'd patiently explain the bizarre idiosyncrasies of the English language and invariably we'd end up laughing and loving. In the past I used to find it impossible to remain angry with him when we were in bed. Now, I stare at his confused face and think he's either being dumb or betraying me.

'OK, I'm sorry I forgot about school. Did you have a good time?'

'Yes, thank you. Excellent.'

'Good. Can we sleep now?' He yawns. His lazy, glazed eyes irritate me; odd, because I've always thought they were like soothing chocolate pools which I could dive into for reassurance or pleasure whenever I needed to. Some faces become contemptible with intimacy.

I stare at him and hope I'm communicating my frustration. It seems unlikely when he rolls over and I'm left glaring at his back. I fully expect my fury to scorch holes in his shoulderblades. How can he be so insensitive? He must know I need more from him than that. I hope the gap in understanding is to do with his language but secretly I question his integrity.

'Do you realize, Elizabeth, if you had checked with the bar diary you would have known where my appointments of today were,' he says to the wall.

I'm not aware there is a bar diary, but feel admitting as much would put me on the back foot and I shouldn't be on the back foot. It's him who forgot to take a polite interest in my new job, it's him that's been out all day (God knows where) and it's him who is harbouring a crush on his adorable ex-girlfriend. Probably.

'If only you took as much interest in the bar as you do in your menstruating cycle, your suntan or even Chuck Andrews,' mutters Roberto. Then he falls asleep or at least pretends to and I'm left well and truly on the back foot.

43

25 March

There are some things in life that are just true. Princess Diana was good with kids, chocolate gives you spots, sale clothes are never available in the right size and I'll never have an affair. Really. I'm not the type. I value loyalty and I actively fantasize about my fortieth wedding anniversary. Plus I love Roberto; he's very lovable.

Except right now of course, when I'm positively furious with him. At the moment Roberto is being bossy, secretive, selfish and cold; which isn't ideal. But relationships, *real* relationships, do have ups and downs. It's unrealistic to expect everything to be sweetness and light absolutely all the time. We are big enough to deal with rough patches. As Alison pointed out, we've had years of rough patches while we've been trying for a baby and we always manage; we struggle through it. It would be pathetic to be frightened or threatened by my silly, inexplicable feelings for Chuck. Even if they are growing like credit card bills in the run-up to Christmas. It would be massively undervaluing my marriage if I imagined that Chuck could ever be a genuine menace. I'm never going to have an affair, as I said, I'm not the type and nor is Chuck come to that. He's honourable and respectful and would never suggest such a thing.

So, I reason, even if Roberto is being a total tosser

at the moment and I'm feeling neglected and lonely, I am still not putting myself at any sort of serious risk by sending Chuck a text and suggesting I catch the bus into Bassano del Grappa to meet him for lunch. I'm just being friendly. My throat is dry and tight and my hands become sticky as I wait to see if he texts me back. After the longest seven minutes of my life, he sends 'Great x.' The inclusion of a kiss sends me dizzy with excitement.

As I wait in the sunshine outside the school, anticipation glides up and down my spine. I haven't mentioned my plan to have lunch with Chuck to anyone at the bar. Roberto and I barely spoke this morning beyond 'Pass the butter', and as usual he had business that took him away from the bar. This morning I worked with Gina; I spent an hour searching for the elusive bar diary but couldn't find it. Gina did say that she was pretty sure she'd seen one hanging around somewhere; she also told me that Roberto had called to say that he is looking at tiles for the bathrooms as per my suggestion. Maybe he is.

I excused myself at eleven, claiming I had homework to complete as a matter of urgency. As Gina doesn't know me too well she didn't realize how improbable this would be and she said she admired my efforts. In fact, I spent the time wandering around the market and selecting picnic food for lunch for Chuck and me. I bought an oily ciabatta, spicy, sunny-coloured couscous, an assortment of cheeses, black and green olives (dripping in oil), some fat ripe nectarines and a couple of small bottles of mineral water (I don't think we are at the bottle-sharing stage). I wanted to buy wine but didn't because Chuck has to teach in the afternoon and it's not fair to tempt him into a woozy head. I considered packing a travel rug but I didn't want to ask Raffaella if I could borrow one, it would lead to too many awkward questions; it's better we find a bench. I am incredibly keyed up about surprising Chuck with the picnic. Picnics are so intimate and romantic. Not that *this* picnic is romantic. This picnic is a thank-you for yesterday's lunch, for helping me find my job in the first place and for listening to me. This picnic is a friendly picnic, nothing more. I'm just saying some picnics can be romantic.

The bell, to signal morning classes are finally over, trills through the cerulean sky. I simmer with expectancy as I watch students flood through the doors and pour haphazardly on to the street. I'm already addicted to the energy that the students exude; it's intoxicating. Like all students throughout the world they look earnest, exuberant, hopeful and horny; it's a great look. I can't think when I last wore it. Eventually I spot Chuck. I only just resist jumping up and down and instead I wave to him from across the street. He beams back and bounds towards me, barely checking for traffic.

'You didn't look for cars,' I scold as he nears me.

'Nice to see you care,' he teases.

I blush. 'Of course I care – I'd have to teach your classes if something happened to you so it's in my interest to keep you safe,' I joke.

It's better not to allow so much as a nod and a wink to the affection that seems to flow between us. If we are going to remain just friends, and we *have* to remain just friends, then there is no room for flirtation or nuance. I can only reconcile my conscience if I'm outstandingly scrupulous about how I behave when I'm with him. Sometimes it doesn't even matter what you are thinking, it's what you do that counts and I'm not going to *do* anything. Besides, who is to say he even likes me *that way*.

As a serial monogamist with a reasonable history I am not one of those dippy women who either profess to know – or maybe genuinely doesn't know – when a man is interested in her in *that way*. I've always known. They usually want you to know so it's hardly a brainteaser. Plus, as a faithful serial monogamist I have never encouraged a guy who I'm not interested in. I'm no saint. If I was ever with a Franco and a Carlo came along who grabbed my attention more, I'd swiftly move on, but I don't overlap and I don't prick-tease. So where is Chuck in all of this?

'What do you want to eat?' he asks. 'I'm starving. I've had a very full timetable this morning, not even time for elevenses.'

'I brought a picnic.' I can't keep the childish pleasure out of my voice. I dangle my rucksack in front of him.

'No way.'

'Way.'

'That's so cool. I love picnics.'

'Me too.' I stare at him and grin like an idiot. He smiles back and his eyes crinkle in a way that makes my stomach (and a bit lower) complete a gymnastic routine worthy of the Olympics. Embarrassed and fearing that somehow he can sense the attraction I feel, I hurry on. 'So where shall we eat?' I swizzle my head from left to right like some sort of frenzied cartoon character – anything's better than catching his eye again.

He's sexy, handsome and bright, which I've come across before; I'm married to a man who can be described in those exact terms, for goodness sake. But more than that, he's also gentle, reasonable and straightforward, which is somehow soothing to be around. And while I continually remind myself that he's a blond American, not a dark Italian, and therefore a million miles away from anything I ever thought would make me happy, I can't help but notice that I am happy when I'm with him. Sometimes I think I'm only ever happy when I'm with him. Oh, I don't know.

Chuck suggests we walk across the historic bridge over the Brenta river in the heart of Bassano itself. We settle on the steps. Chuck tells me that this beautiful bridge was designed by Antonio Palladio; he says it in a way that assumes I'll know who he's on about. I don't and I'm a bit ashamed. When my parents used to force-feed me facts about architecture and history I barely bothered to hide my boredom; now I wish I'd listened a little harder. It would be nice to impress Chuck. Not that Chuck seems to care how much I know about Antonio Palladio – he just seems delighted that I appreciate the views upstream toward the mountains. He always gives me the impression that he approves of me. It's a great feeling to be on the receiving end of.

We try to keep out of the way of the pedestrians marching across the bridge and we turn our attention to the delicious food I've brought.

'Do you like gorgonzola? I've also brought Fontina Val d'Aosta. I've just discovered it. It's delicious, sort of dense, but smooth and slightly elastic. It has a delicate nuttiness with a hint of mild honey. I read that on the label.'

'I love it.' He breaks off a large chunk and starts to munch.

I perhaps haven't thought through this picnic as well as I should have. For a start I haven't packed napkins or a knife. Still, we manage, and I'm relieved when he doesn't nit-pick. Roberto would be horrified at the idea of eating cheese with his fingers on the steps of a bridge. He can be quite fussy about the strangest things. I think breaking huge lumps of bread and slabs of cheese is romantic. I mean *friendly*.

'Is this what you were expecting or were you hoping we'd find a park?' asks Chuck.

I consider. Oddly, I didn't have expectations of how the picnic would pan out. How unlike me. I was so excited about seeing Chuck again and surprising him by doing something nice for him after he's done so much for me but I hadn't thought beyond that.

'This is fine,' I say with a smile and a nod.

'I'd say perfect.'

We sit silently munching. In a way I wish I could describe the silence as uncomfortable but it's actually a pleasant pause. It's like we go back much further than we do.

Eventually Chuck says, 'Do you think you might be interested in discovering more about this city? You know, in your free time or whatever.' He seems less confident than he usually does when we are together, almost tentative. 'The Duomo was built around the year 1000 but renovated in 1417. It's interesting. I could show you around it another time.' I don't answer straight away because I'm chewing a huge lump of bread. Chuck assumes my delay is due to reticence and adds hurriedly, 'I'm not suggesting you come to Bassano del Grappa especially or anything; maybe we could just have a look in your lunch hour, after lessons. It doesn't matter if it's not your thing,' he adds, taking away the offer just moments after he's made it.

I swallow quickly. 'No, yes. That would be great. Totally my thing.' I gush, thrilled with the idea that I might be able to spend more time with him. But then I hesitate. I don't know why I feel I can be so entirely myself with him. More, that I *have* to be entirely myself with him but something compels me to add, 'Actually, churches are not my thing.'

'Well, there's a castle and a museum,' he suggests.

I scrunch up my nose. 'To be honest, I could think of other ways to explore the city.'

'Oh, OK. Well, it doesn't matter.' He looks straight ahead, not at me, and I sense he's embarrassed, perhaps even disappointed. But maybe I'm getting him all wrong, maybe he's looking straight ahead because the views are great.

'But I'd like to do something else with you,' I add quickly. 'There's lots of other stuff. We could shop,' I offer hopefully, then I remember his sex; shopping might not press his buttons. 'Or sunbathe,' I offer. 'Or listen to music, or just talk,' I finish pathetically.

Chuck treats me to a slow grin and all signs of embarrassment and disappointment are banished. 'I like it when we talk,' he says.

'Me too.'

Or even when we are silent. But I force back the words. I am married. And, even if I wasn't, Chuck is not the sort of man who could ever have made me happy. First and foremost he doesn't want kids. Roberto at least wants kids – even if he doesn't believe we'll ever have them. I have no idea why I enjoy Chuck's company as much as I do. Besides – pertinently – I'm married. I've made my choice. OK, so Roberto and I are not in the best place right now but we belong together. Being married trumps comfortable conversations and even comfortable silences with someone else. Those are the rules and there has to be an order to such things.

Yet the air between us is heavy with suggestion, hope and guilt. The air between us knows that given another world, another set of circumstances, there would have been no air between us because I'd be kissing him long and hard and hungrily.

But there *isn't* a different set of circumstances and there *is* air between us. I pull back physically and mentally. I start to pack away the debris from the picnic and efficiently brush away the crumbs that have settled on my jeans. We must remain just friends. There is no space for any other sort of relationship. Anything else is wrong and impossible. I search for something to say that will break the tension and maybe even go the extra mile and put him off me. I can't start something, anything, with this man. It's wrong.

'I'm not keen on schlepping around old churches, or museums or anything, because I'm not a self-improver,' I say defiantly.

'Maybe that's because you are fine as you are,' says Chuck. He looks at me from under his fringe and there's no sign that he's put off.

And I must be a terrible person because I want to punch the air and talk about love.

44

One of the many, many reasons I have always felt that it is unfair that I'm not a mum is that I am a good person. And good people deserve the chance to be mums, obviously. Of course, everyone likes to think they are a good person – no doubt – but I'm pretty sure I am one. I never pass a tin being rattled in the high street; often I scramble to cough up a quid even before I know what charity I'm donating to because I'm certain it must be worthy enough if some poor sod is prepared to stand in the rain collecting. I try to remember birthdays, including all the birthdays of my friends' numerous kids. I never laugh at other people's dancing. I would never dream of parking in one of those places in the supermarket car park that's earmarked for the disabled and I gave all my old videos to a charity shop when I bought DVDs. A good person.

Or, at least, I always have been up to now.

I'm realistic. I know that I'm not an *exceptionally* good person like Mother Teresa was or Bob Geldof is. I'm not even as good as most of my family members or friends, but I'm absolutely certain that I'm not a bad person so I renew all my efforts to ignore this silly, illogical, inconvenient crush I'm developing on Chuck. Because a married woman having a silly, illogical, inconvenient crush on a sexy blond man means that the woman in question must be a *bad* person. Adultery is a *bad* thing. You don't have to be a genius to figure out that much.

I can't banish him from my life. For a start, it's impractical; we now work together and he gives me lifts to and from the school. And anyway I shouldn't need to banish him like I'm some sort of undisciplined, selfish floozy. I can be around him, allow our friendship to deepen and accept it for just that. In time I'm sure he'll reveal himself to be quite ordinary and my silly, inappropriate feelings will doubtless fade. Definitely. Surely. Maybe.

Maybe not.

The problem is the more time I spend with him the more I realize he's far from ordinary. He seems deep. Unexpected. Complex. Real. It's dawning on me that my attraction to Chuck is possibly more than just physical (which would be bad enough); more is bad indeed. The truth is that in some way or other every moment of my day is taken up with Chuck. We see each other every Monday and Friday morning. I look forward to our drives with exactly the same level of anticipation as a four-year-old looks forward to Christmas. He always picks me up at the clock tower in the piazza. I relish those moments when I wait for him and I'm all alone with my expectancy. I guess at what he might be wearing or how he might greet me. Just thinking about him, without angry interruptions from Raffaella or impatient grunts from Roberto, provides me with private feelings of pure joy. Chuck stands out like a flare in a black night. He seems to gleam with health and happiness and the first moment I rest my eyes on him is one of immense, intense pleasure. When I approach the car he usually jumps out, takes my bag off me and briefly kisses me on the cheek. It's comfy. It's scary.

He always pays me a compliment; nothing too full-on or creepy, just 'You look good this morning, very professional' or 'Is that a new dress? Cool.'

Invariably I blush and mutter, 'What, this old thing? No, no, not new, I've had it for years.' Which is, of course, a lie. Getting ready in the morning is no longer a hit or miss affair. I'm starting to understand women who groom. OK, so I'm never going to be mistaken for a WAG but I really like the results of occasionally shaving my legs or slapping on a bit of blusher; making the effort doesn't seem such an effort when Chuck notices even the smallest thing.

The car journeys are a joy. Chuck has got into the habit of always bringing along a bag of fruit for us to munch as breakfast. This way I can duck out of Raffaella's miserably heavy and early salami breakfasts, plus the pears, apples, cherries or mangoes that Chuck offers are fat, ripe and delicious. He buys them from the local market where I bought the olives for our picnic; all the fruit and veg tastes great here, as it's locally produced and organic. Food is a wonderful ice-breaker, it's impossible to be shy after you've seen each other with fruit juice dripping down your chin or a strawberry pip stuck between your front teeth.

Chuck loves his food. His mum bakes cakes but not in a mumsie way. She runs a lucrative business with eight staff producing truly elaborate cakes that sell for a fortune to mums in the posh burbs of San Fran and to dozens of chi-chi pâtisseries, cafés and restaurants. He can chat for ages about things such as cocoa powder and vanilla pods. He can even avoid sounding boring while doing so. His dad is retired now but he used to be a butcher. He's sensitive to my dislike of meat eating and so doesn't go into the same detail about fresh cuts as he does vanilla pods.

'A butcher, a baker, does that mean your brother is a candlestick maker?' I asked with a laugh.

'Sort of. He's a carpenter, so he makes furniture, not candlesticks exactly but almost. My choices aren't so good if you continue with the rhyme though, are they? Rich man, poor man, beggar man, thief.'

'No, only twenty-five per cent chance of avoiding benefit or jail. I'm not sure you are the sort of man my mum and dad would approve of,' I joked.

'My mum and dad would love you, I'd really like you to meet one day,' he replied more seriously, and somehow that comment stopped the laughter, although it left me feeling delighted.

We meet after lessons and have lunch together. Sometimes after lunch we take a walk and I've been out with Chuck and his friends on three occasions in the evenings. We text one another five or six times a day. The texts aren't full of flirty, cheeky innuendos, they are totally blameless and yet thoroughly exciting.

Am in Bar Aderente. Caramel ice cream to die for.

Wish I was there. I'm in kitchen, cleaning under oven!

Uh oh. Will buy litre and freeze it for you for another time.

Thanks!

Have you seen the movie *Pane e Tulipani*? I think you'd like it. It's sweet and hopeful.

No. Have you seen the sunset? It's stunning tonight.

Sometimes he drops by Bruno's, alone or with friends. I'm always pleased to see him. Despite Roberto's coolness and Raffaella's rudeness, Chuck remains the epitome of manners and gives the impression that he is unaware that visiting me runs the risk of a mafia passion killing or, at the very least, Raffaella coughing-up into his drink (I always try to serve him to minimize that risk, plus I've advised him not to take anything from the kitchen). Raffaella has made her dislike of Chuck very obvious. He's never done anything to offend her; in fact I think he's remarkably patient and polite with her. He always talks to her in his impeccable Italian, he asks after her health and the business, he even talks to her old father, but she answers grudgingly and without meeting his eye. I've hinted that maybe Chuck visits so often because he's interested in Laurana or better yet, Paolina, and for this reason alone she tolerates him. She'd rather not have him at the bar at all. Not that she believes he's interested in me in any way beyond friendship, she just dislikes having him around because she's noticed that having him around makes me happy.

He likes reading books about cowboys. He listens to Brit bands and is secretly proud of this small pretension; so he should be when you consider his mates are probably all listening to Bruce Springsteen. He says his favourite movie is *Moulin Rouge* but he might be having me on. He dislikes the sight of blood and he's scared of snakes. He once got knocked over as a kid and was in hospital for weeks (he still has a scar on his shoulderblade – I haven't seen it). His first love was called Lily-Beth. He kissed her when he was seventh grade. He did go to the school prom (I didn't think those things still happened); he bought his date a bunch of sweet peas (he thought it was cool and individual, she thought it was cheap and wanted an orchid, they rowed and didn't dance together). He was voted the guy in his class 'most likely to travel'.

'At least that's what I was voted in the official year-book,' he added.

'Was there an unofficial one?'

'Oh yes.'

'And what were you voted in that one?'

'I can't say.'

I looked at him and grinned widely. 'Come on, you can tell me anything.'

'I'm beginning to understand that, but I fear you might like me a little less if you knew,' he teased. 'One day I'll tell you.' I left it at that because I believe him. One day I'll know.

When my period came it was Chuck who cheered me up. When Roberto vanishes for hours on end I search out Chuck. When Raffaella slights or insults me, Chuck consoles and calms. It's unbearably confusing and inconvenient but I can't regret meeting him. I hope I never do.

I try to throw myself into my work. Teaching and studying gives my week structure and meaning. Developing a routine independent of the family – Raffaella, Bruno's and even Roberto – has clear advantages. Days fly past and weeks seamlessly run away too, until I've been teaching for a month.

Driving home from school one lunchtime, I pretend to Chuck that I've just stumbled upon this realization, when in fact I've been aware of my month anniversary looming for about twenty-eight days. A first monthly salary is a big deal, even if the contents of the packet are still quite modest.

'We should celebrate,' I declare, as though the thought has just occurred to me. It's not that I'm being horribly manipulative, it's just that I don't want to seem over-dependent on him, and admitting that I spend the vast majority of my waking thoughts planning and plotting how to secure more time with him might betray that I am over-dependent. Or manipulative.

Damn.

'Won't you be celebrating with Roberto?' I look at Chuck with exasperation. Is he being dense? We've become good enough friends over the last month for him to know that isn't a probable option.

'Pretty unlikely I would have thought, this being a Friday.'

'Equally unlikely that they'll let you have the night off so that you can come over to my place and I can cook a celebratory meal for you before we hit the bars of Veganze,' says Chuck.

'Are you serious? You want to cook for me?'

'All my friends have to taste my attempts at *penne con gamberi e carciofi* sooner or later. You are lucky you've got away without it for this long.'

'Penne with shrimp and –'

'Artichokes. Are you OK with eating shrimps? I could leave them out.'

'Er, I'm not sure how successful a dish of penne and artichokes will be. Best stick with the shrimps. No worries,

I eat fish, now and again.' I pause and consider the offer for a moment. He's just being friendly. 'I'd love to come to your place.'

I try very hard to sound nonchalant. The thing is I haven't seen inside Chuck's apartment. There's no logical reason for this. He lives alone so there are no flatmates to accommodate, his place is in the centre of town, we often meet up socially but somehow it's never happened. I'm well aware of why. I wonder if he is. If I visit his home we will be right up against the intimacy that, so far, we've managed to ignore – or at least control.

'Do you think you can swing it?'

I know that Raffaella and Roberto will both strongly object to my bunking off bar duties on a Friday but I don't kid myself that they'll miss my company. I am becoming increasingly invisible to my husband and Raffaella just sees me as slave labour.

'They won't be pleased but sod it. I think I deserve some sort of celebration. What time do you want me?'

Chuck pauses and for a nanosecond the car is full of tension. Chuck seems to be biting his lip. I feel the need to rephrase my question as I fight a blush. 'What time do you want me to come round?'

Cough. 'About eight.'

'Can I bring anything?'

'Just yourself. That will be more than enough.'

Just good friends, I mutter to myself as I close the car door. Just good friends. Liar, liar, knickers on fire. They are. I'm so utterly turned on that I could believe that there's a box of fireworks being let off in my scanties. Truthfully, I fancy the hell out of him. Inconceivably, inconveniently, impossibly, the very hell out of him.

45

I stop off at Bar Aderente to have a cappuccino and to call Alison before I get home. I want her advice on how I ought best to negotiate a night off.

Fiona answers Alison's mobile, which is a little disconcerting. We have one of those friendly but semi-formal chats that two people who have never met one another but know lots about one another have on the phone. She tells me that it was unusually hot in London last weekend and that she and Alison picnicked in Hyde Park.

'I'm going to miss London's summer,' I blurt.

'Traffic, trains, overhead aeroplanes?' she asks doubtfully.

'Yes.'

'Fighting for a square inch of space in the local park?'

'Yes.'

'Ugly, burnt flesh bulging over waistbands and flowing over too-tight bras?'

'Yes,' I say firmly.

'You're mad. You are much better off where you are. I bet you're not choked by traffic fumes.'

'No, cigarette smoke, actually,' I say snippily. I know Fiona is trying to be nice. But, irrationally, her insistence that I can't possibly be missing what she has is annoying.

'Oh. Well. Right. Erm. Alison is in the shower. I'll get her to call you when she gets out, should I?'

'Yes, please.'

I hang up and feel a little guilty. It's not Fiona's fault that her love life is marvellous while mine is – well – totally muddled, terrifying and frustrating. And it's not Fiona's fault that Alison is in the shower (actually, indirectly, it might be) and not available to talk when I need her.

I order a wine instead of a cappuccino and take a moment to look around me. The sun is shining down and has done so consistently for a while now; people stroll about with wide open, sanguine faces. At last I can see hues of the Italy I remembered rather than the one that shocked and chilled me back in January. I see charming, rustic buildings adorned with wrought-iron balconies and wooden shutters painted a serious green. But almost instantly it crosses my mind that there are innumerable shuttered buildings within which I have no idea what goes on and I have a feeling I will never know. I see that there are plenty of men running around with colourful bunches of flowers, just as I saw when I was a teenager, but in a flap of a butterfly's wing I also notice that there are a number of women looking cross and duped. How had I missed them before? I can't help but wonder if the flowers are for mistresses or mothers rather than wives.

Generally, Italy seems less overtly sexual than I remember. I am not consistently ambushed by longing gazes from teenage Romeos as I was when I visited as a girl. Truth is men rarely catch my eye unless I'm asking the server for a bill. Only the tragically obvious men-sluts look my way. As a young girl I remember having to fight them off with a stick. I'm depressed at the lack of horniness. I'm older and clearly perceived as such.

Not that it matters. I'm not on the pull. I have Roberto. Indeed it's probably because of the fact that I am with Roberto that men in Veganze stay a respectable distance and that's how it should be. I should not hanker after lecherous looks from leather-jacketed lotharios. It's just that somehow, I thought the all-pervasive sexual atmosphere might help me conceive. Crazy I know, but then once I seriously considered having sex at Stonehenge because I'd heard it helped fertility and that's hardly the thinking of a rational woman either.

I do still see waiters cooing enthusiastically over the babies of their clients and I'm reassured to see that this at least is true to my teenage memories. I watch a family sitting to my left: a full complement of grandparents, a mother, her toddler and her baby. The toddler is opening packets of sugar and pouring them on to the table then tracing patterns into the small mounds of sweetness. Delighted, the grandmother ohs and ahs at the child's creativity. The mother watches, caught between amusement and bewilderment. I imagine that when the old grandmother was a mother she never indulged her daughter in the same way she does her granddaughter. She'd be too worried about the mess being created. It's a grandparent's privilege to be lenient and carefree about the consequence of mess. The mother absentmindedly caresses her baby's head. She moves her hand a few inches and trails it down his back. The target of tenderness shifts again as she plays with his toes. Contented, he gurgles back at her as she lifts him into the sky and then she brings him safe and close for a kiss; she wraps the pair of them in indescribable bliss. They are safely sealed with just a kiss.

I feel a familiar and vicious blow low in my stomach.

Sometimes I think I'm losing all reason. Even the many arches that adorn most Italian towns put me in mind of women blooming with pregnancy. The question I keep coming back to is, if not that, then what? What is the point of it all? What is the point of me? Of everything? The nasty, spiteful question swells into my consciousness with unrelenting frequency. Occasionally the urgency fades – when I'm with Chuck and I'm distracted by feelings of pure happiness or curiosity or even confusion my longing for a family subsides slightly. But it never goes away. On my worse days I consider that my failure to conceive may not be arbitrary bad luck and I wonder if I am worthy to be a mum. Does someone, somewhere, know something I don't? Am I lacking in some way that is glaringly obvious to the fertility gods but not to me?

Madness, I know. Because I'm consumed with this self-doubt and loathing I order myself another drink. It's thirsty work staying sane.

I think I might cry, but luckily am saved by the bell as my phone vibrates on the table.

'Hi, you rang, my lady,' jokes Alison. 'Hang on a minute. Fi, will you make me one too. Yes, and a biscuit. Ta.' Really, what was the point in her calling me if she wants to continue her conversation with Fiona? I wonder irritably. 'Sorry about that. So how are you? It's great to hear from you, we haven't spoken for –'

'Three weeks.'

'Are you keeping count?'

'No.'

Yes. But I don't want to say so. Alison and I have

always said that we think friends who get arsy with one another for not calling are insecure and unfair. Either friend can pick up a phone. It takes two to make a friendship and two to break a friendship. We've never kept tabs on who owes whom a call. At least, that was until Alison stopped calling me.

'We've been so busy,' she says with a giggle.

Alison tells me all about the fantastic things that she and Fiona have been getting up to. I have to confess they seem perfect for one another. They both like cycling, ballet and opera and you don't often come across that level of worthiness. They seem to spend a disproportionate amount of time in galleries and museums and doing 'learny' stuff. I can appreciate that Alison enjoys wandering around Hockney exhibitions way more than she ever enjoyed wandering around Mothercare with me making 'when' lists. Plus they have the whole bed thing; however much I love Alison it has never been in that way. I see that I have to surrender up my role as most important person in Alison's life and I have to surrender with grace.

'Er, look, I was a bit short with Fiona when I rang,' I confess.

'Really?'

I wonder if she knows and Fiona has already mentioned as much. 'I've got a bit on my mind. Will you say sorry and tell her not to take offence?'

'Don't worry, she's cool,' says Alison, reassuring and forgiving me in only a few syllables, as is her way. I miss her keenly. 'So what's on your mind?'

'Chuck.'

'Your hopeless crush?'

'I'm scared I'm beginning to really care for him.'

'Go on.' Alison sounds serious, which is worrying. I was expecting her to dismiss my confession as crazy, sun-induced rambling.

'We share the closeness, confidence and understanding of lovers.'

'But not body fluids?' she checks.

'No.'

'He's your new best friend,' she says enthusiastically. I can hear her relief as clearly as a foghorn. 'That's all.'

'Maybe. But can a man and a woman be best friends?'

'Well, you're straight and I'm a lesbian and we are best friends.'

'I suppose.' I want to be convinced but I'm not.

'Has he declared undying love?'

'No.'

'Well, that's good.'

Is it? 'Yes, it is.' I mutter.

'Everything is as it should be,' she says confidently.

'I shouldn't be wasting so much time thinking about Chuck, I should be thinking about baby-making.'

'Actually, the only good thing I can see in all this is that you are obsessing less about conceiving. This is the first month in years and years when you haven't called me when you got your period.'

Why don't I feel better about her cheery reassurances?

He's exciting and comfortable at the same time. He's transparent and a mystery. I've never come across anything quite like it before. I try to explain as much in a way that's less likely to cause Alison to mock me.

'He listens to me in a way no one else ever has. I have no shyness with him. For example the other week we got talking about how many lovers is an acceptable number to have or at least own up to and I told him the real number.'

'So?' Typical that straightforward Alison would think that is the norm. Maybe women lovers are more forgiving. Men rarely want to know the truth.

'Well, when Roberto and I had that same conversation six and a half years ago I said two.'

'Two?' She nearly chokes.

'Yes. Fourteen less than truthful and two more than he found acceptable.'

'That probably says more about your relationship with Roberto than your relationship with Chuck,' says Alison. 'How's yours and Roberto's sex life currently, by the way?' she asks cheekily.

'My sex life is fine, thank you very much,' I insist, although I know I'm lying so I concede, 'Well, Roberto is still very occupied with the bar most of the time. I don't see that much of him.'

'Have you talked any more about Ana-Maria?'

'No, it's in the past.' I try to sound unconcerned.

'Well, it isn't, is it?' says Alison with a killer tell-it-how-it-is frankness. 'You have a right to know what they fell out about and when.'

'I'm not interested.' I push the thought away by trying to make a joke. 'I'm worried that I'm all the clichés. I'm lonely and displaced. I have a distracted, busy husband and now there's a new exciting stranger. It's bound to end in an affair.'

'Probably. You are rather fond of a cliché.' Alison doesn't sound as though she's kidding. 'It sounds to me like you're homesick,' she declares.

'Impossible. I've always wanted to live here in Italy. All my life.'

'You do have to be careful what you wish for, hasn't anyone ever told you that? It's difficult to sustain pleasure when faced with realities. It's much easier to love fantasies.'

'That is so depressing.'

I feel cross and disappointed, partly because I recognize that what she's saying might have a ring of truth to it and partly because I think she's undermining the importance of what I feel for Chuck.

'I think this Chuck guy might be just part of your homesickness. You think you are attracted to him because you have things in common.'

'That's impossible. I have nothing in common with him. He's American.'

Alison laughs. 'Your famous prejudice and naïvety, I love it.' My irritation with her begins to mount. 'Don't you see, nothing falls into the nice little categories you want them to fall into? If you're homesick you ought to call your folks,' says Alison and then she hangs up.

I ring my mum and dad at 7 p.m. every Sunday night, as regular as clockwork. By calling them on a Friday afternoon I throw them into slight panic. My mother sounds at first fearful and then, after reassurances that I'm fine and Roberto is fine, she sounds expectant. She'd never dream of saying so but I can't help but get the feeling that she thinks I'm ringing with some *important news*. Why else would I call out of the blue? I have often rehearsed the call that I'll make when I do ring to tell my parents that I'm finally going to give them a grandchild.

I imagine I'll be breezy and delightful. I won't mention the years of longing. We'll be happy, happy, happy. If only this was that call. Quickly, I manage their expectations by asking about their neighbours and their garden.

My parents love their garden. Their house is modest but the garden is massive and was the main reason they bought the property a million years ago. The garden boasts a sumptuous blend of creative landscaping, imaginative plantings and fine old trees. As a family we have spent endless joyful hours there playing, chatting, sipping wine, squabbling and putting the world to rights. I suddenly wish I was sitting in their garden right now, glass of Chardonnay in one hand, a novel in the other. As it's nearly May I imagine the various fruit trees will be blossoming and the magnificent wisteria will be cascading down the side of the house.

'It's looking lovely, you should see it. I do hope we don't get another one of those silly hosepipe bans again. Your father has spent the afternoon cutting the grass actually. He's out there raking up the cuttings, even though I've told him to leave them. Max and his family are coming tomorrow, Max could see to it. But your father likes everything neat when you children visit.'

I can almost smell the scent of fresh cut grass drifting towards me. I have a sudden affection for clover, not even the magical four-leaf stuff, just the regular bog-standard three-leaf stuff that grows in abundance in England.

Despite the miles separating us, Mum seems to be following my thought pattern.

'Everything all right, dear?'

'Fine,' I reply cheerily and insincerely.

'Just last night your father and I were discussing whether he is up to a holiday. We'd love to see your new home.'

'That would be nice. You should come before it gets too hot.'

'Yes, or in the autumn.'

I doubt they'll ever come out to see me because they still prefer a holiday in Britain, but it doesn't harm anyone to live with the idea; it's rather comforting all-round. I think my dad could put Raffaella in her place; he abhors bullies.

'You sound a bit down,' says Mum carefully.

I hate being a worry to her. I force myself to sound positive.

'Not at all. I've been teaching for a month today, I'm just debating how best to celebrate.'

'Is Roberto going to take you somewhere special?'

'Probably.' I cross my fingers. It's bad enough that I'm not ringing to tell her I'm pregnant, I can't admit that my celebration dinner is going to be with the hunky American that I have inappropriate feelings for. Sometimes I wish I was totally someone else.

'Your father and I are so pleased that you've found this teaching job, Elizabeth.' She doesn't dare add anything more for fear of offending me or putting me under pressure which I'll resist. We both know I am hideously late in stumbling into a career. I'm grateful that my parents appear to subscribe to the 'better late than never' school of thought. 'Would you like to talk to your dad now, dear?'

'Yes, if he's around.'

'I'll just get him for you.'

I listen to her click-clack through the hall and I imagine her wandering into the garden. My parents only have one telephone, which proudly hangs on the wall in the hallway and has done so for at least thirty years that I can remember. Mum uses a pencil to dial numbers, even though she hasn't got long nails to break; I consider this her only pretension; it's very small and endears her to me, rather than annoys. They refuse to entertain the idea of more phones, or a cordless phone or, God forbid, a mobile. I grin to myself, suddenly feeling irrationally affectionate towards their old-fashioned ways. Parents being constant is a rather marvellous thing.

46

I find Roberto in our bedroom. He's having a lie down.

'Are you feeling OK?' I ask. However rude and neglectful I think Roberto is being right now, I have to admit he's not a lazy man; it's unlike him to be taking a nap in the afternoon.

'I'm fine. Just thinking. I needed to be away from the noise of the bar and Mamma.'

The bar is becoming increasingly popular and it is often busy now, not only in the evening, but during the day too. Roberto is usually very proud of this fact, as it's a clear indication that all his hard work is paying off. Plus I've never, ever heard him hint that he finds his mother's constant, highly-pitched, verbal incontinence annoying – but looking at him now, lying in a darkened room with his arm flung over his eyes – he looks weary. I feel moved.

'Has Raffaella been grumbling about the empty cigarette machine again? I told her the delivery is due today but –'

'No, Mamma has not been grumbling about the empty cigarette machine or anything else for that matter,' he snaps, tossing away any chance of a moment's sympathizing or connection.

I don't believe him for a minute. Raffaella's natural state is moaning. Clearly she's now grating on his nerves too. Would it be so bad to admit as much? We might even be able to laugh about her and ease some of the tension that sits between us like a towering wall.

'It's not disloyal to say to your wife that your mother is naffing you off,' I point out. Roberto stares at me. I shiver. If looks could kill I'd be knocking on those pearly gates right about now. 'I'm just saying –'

I dry up. What am I saying? What's the point? While Roberto won't say or hear a bad word against his mother, I know that the two of them spend many a happy hour chatting over my shortcomings. I can't defend or re-ingratiate myself in a couple of snatched minutes. Why bother trying?

There is one down-side to Chuck visiting Bruno's so frequently; somehow his presence has opened the way for Ana-Maria's recurrent appearances. I have long suspected that Roberto was visiting her somewhere or other but they had the decency to keep their flirtation away from my doorstep; no longer. Now, Ana-Maria pops into the bar almost daily, and while I can't actually object I can't say I'm happy with the situation either.

She is always the epitome of charm with Raffaella and with Roberto's grandpa; they light up like Blackpool when she enters the room. She's confident and friendly with Paolina and perfectly courteous with me. In fact she treats Roberto's family in exactly the same way as Chuck treats them. I can't decide if I find this reassuring or a problem. I know that there is nothing going on between Chuck and me so isn't it reasonable to assume that there's nothing going on between Ana-Maria and Roberto? They are probably just friends – really good friends. Friends that silently have the hots for each other? No, no, no. Not a great line of thought. I push it aside.

Of course I have spent hours carefully examining the relationship between Ana-Maria and my husband, nearly as many hours as I have spent examining my relationship with Chuck. It's impossible not to notice that when Roberto beams at her his whole being is behind the smile. He's attentive towards her. He chats with her. He laughs with her. As I do with Chuck. As we used to with one another – a long time ago. But I have never seen or heard a single action or word that would suggest they are anything more than friends, so how can I possibly resent her? It would be unreasonable.

I sit on the edge of the bed and pull off my trainers and then I fall flat on my back and lie next to Roberto. I scratch my head and wonder what I'll wear tonight, assuming I do manage to make a run for it.

'Who is working tonight?' I try to sound casual.

'Everyone, I'm expecting it to be very busy.'

'Oh.' Nervously, I scratch my shin.

'Why do you keep itching?' Roberto asks.

'Scratching,' I correct. He tuts, and I guess I have to accept that my days of correcting his English are probably at an end. I have no right now that I am in Italy because, despite my lessons, I'd still struggle to master such linguistic nuances as scratch and itch.

'I've been bitten,' I tell him. He looks at me with an impatience that's almost cruel. I realize that my leg has not fallen off and a mozzie bite is not life-threatening but it is very irritating and unsightly; a bit of sympathy wouldn't go amiss. I can't help it if insects find me tasty. 'I'm never normally bitten,' I mumble apologetically.

'You have never been anywhere to be bitten,' he says coolly.

We don't seem to have anything else to say to one another. I'm pondering how best to bring up the subject of my appointment with Chuck when Roberto rolls on to his side to face me.

He puts his hand on my left breast and starts to knead it like a piece of dough.

'Awch, get off.' I push him away impatiently. 'They are sore, I've got my period.' This is actually not true. I'm not even due for a while, but we are past my most fertile time of the month so why bother? I can't find the required energy. I breathe very lightly, nervous that Roberto will notice that I'm lying about my cycle and call me on my lie. Will he remember that I said the same just two weeks ago? Roberto dramatically pulls away from me and sighs.

'Great timing,' he mutters.

His unspoken blame and resentment falls down on me; I think I might buckle under the avalanche of disenchantment. I don't think Roberto is grieving. He's grouchy and horny.

'Well, you can still sort me out,' he adds.

Roberto roughly pulls my hand towards his groin. With his other hand he's undoing his fly buttons. Does this blatant need for sex suggest I have nothing to fear from Ana-Maria? I doubt that men who are playing away bother to pester their wives for a hand job. I should feel relieved.

'No,' I snatch back my hand and fling him a look of disgust and reproach. 'I'm too tired.'

Working as a teacher only demands that I am in a classroom for eight hours every week, but add on another couple of hours travelling and a couple more for lesson planning and marking homework, then two more with Signor Castoro trying to learn the lingo plus a further four or five hours on his homework, take into account that I average six shifts in the bar, sometimes more, I'm doing a sixty-hour week, so saying I'm too tired is not unreasonable. I've used the same excuse quite a lot recently. Thinking about it, it's no surprise that my period came as regular as ever. Night after night I've told him that I'm tired and I've allowed my eyelids to droop. I fall asleep not especially caring what the consequences (or lack of them) might be.

Besides, I just don't see the sense in what he's asking for. I have no moral objection to hand or blow jobs. I accept that many people think they are sexy and exciting but I just can't see the use. It won't lead to a baby, will it? Not that anything else we've ever done has led to a baby either, obviously, but at least there's a chance, however slim.

'There's no point to it,' I insist.

'To make me happy, Elizabeth. To give me pleasure, that is the point.'

'I'm not in the mood.'

'I am,' he says stubbornly.

He really thinks that he can boss me into 'sorting him out', as he so delicately puts it. He really thinks I'll hop on board or just manically wank because it's my wifely duty. The problem is if you think about sex for any amount of time it is impossible not to notice that it's ridiculous. Really, all that up and down, and in and out, and licking. It doesn't bear close inspection and yet infertile couples do nothing other than closely inspect their sex life and the sex act. I can't fail to have noticed its ludicrous aspect. I fume for a moment and then a terrible thought creeps into my head. If I do what he wants he's more likely to agree to my going out tonight.

I gasp at the implication of that mental equation and,

momentarily, I'm appalled at myself. I have never traded sex. Some women do all the time, I know they do, and I'm not talking about terrible deviant women. I'm talking normal, smiley, friendly women. Women who shop in the high street, go to public swimming baths and work in ordinary jobs; women like my friends. Females tell each other a lot and so I know that women agree to sex because it's the quickest way to get to sleep. Or because their husband has finally put up the shelf in the kids' bedroom and sex is the reward. Or as a thank-you for an unexpected act of thoughtfulness. Or to make her man say he loves her. Or to stop him leaving. Or to comfort him because he's lost his job. Or to congratulate him because he's got a promotion. Or sometimes, for hard cash.

There are myriad reasons why people have sex, but not me. To date, I've been pretty straightforward in my motivation. I've only ever had sex with Roberto because I love him or because I want to make a baby. Sorry, I mean *and* because I want to make a baby. Now I am thinking of having sex, albeit a non-invasive sort, so that he'll agree I can go out to meet my friend. Another man, to be exact.

The thought is chilling. Yet I sit up and finish undoing his fly buttons.

'Let's see how much pleasure I can give you then, shall we?' I ask, and I flash a seductive smile which isn't my own. I think I once saw it worn by some *femme fatale* actress in a B movie, or maybe a soap opera.

47

I arrive at Chuck's at 8 p.m. on the dot. He swings open the door and greets me with a massive grin.

'Come in, go through to the kitchen. I'm mid preparations.'

The front door opens into the living room and Chuck gestures towards a door in the right-hand corner which clearly leads through to the kitchen; the billowing steam, music and lights signpost as much.

His flat is what can only be described as compact, yet while there's not much space, there's lots and lots of stuff; it's brimming with life and seems to ask as many questions as it answers about his personality. There are rackets and sports boots casually tossed aside as I might have expected – he always looks as though he's just been throwing a ball around a court. There are artworks from different local cultures hung on every wall; a deep mahogany African mask, some eastern calligraphy on a bamboo scroll, watercolours depicting red, autumnal trees – I'd guess they originated from Canada or New England. There are photos scattered on shelves and on top of the tiny TV. The photos show groups of smiley faces, alien and yet familiar; everyone has similar photos but of a different group of friends. There are photos of far-flung places and of Chuck sky-diving, hang-gliding, mountaineering and other 007 pursuits. I'm exhausted just looking at them. I follow him through to the kitchen, trying not to trip up on his brimming life, and gratefully accept the glass of wine he hands me.

I watch as Chuck efficiently pulls together some pre-supper nibbles. He puts olives, roasted almonds, focaccia, oil and balsamic vinegar on to the table. He lights some candles. The window is open a couple of inches, allowing fresh, warm air to ebb into the flat and bring with it the aroma of basil and thyme, which are growing in pots on the window-sill. The sky is purple and ginger now as the sun is sinking behind the mountains, so the streets are swathed in orange light. Italy may be a very Catholic country but it always puts me in mind of a cheerful bunch of Hari Krishna guys in their orange robes; happily clapping and shaking tambourines.

'I love your flat.'

'It's small but it works for me. It has a great —'

'Feel to it,' I finish his sentence. He nods. 'It feels welcoming. The minute I walked in I could sense that. It feels like a home should feel,' I tell him.

'You're bummed out at being at Raffaella's, aren't you?' asks Chuck.

I'm grateful that he hasn't resorted to bullshit small talk. A true friend meets these things head on.

'Miserable as sin, frankly.'

I think of the cold, austere rooms crammed full of heavy wooden furniture. It's a house full of unwritten rules that are inadvertently broken all too easily. Calling my parents hasn't made me feel less homesick; it's made me feel more. They were both so friendly and forthcoming. They too have lots of rules in their home but they are logical, reasonable rules, like not leaving damp towels on the floor.

'Do you know, every morning I get up and walk into the dining room and feel exactly like a kid joining a new school mid-term,' I say.

'Oh, you mean, like all the other kids have already made best friends —'

'Yes, and they know which teachers shout and give out the most homework.'

'And you think you'll never catch up or fit in?'

'Precisely.'

'Why don't you and Roberto get a place of your own together?'

'I don't think Roberto's ready to cut that umbilical cord yet. Still, give him time; he's only thirty-four,' I add sarcastically.

Chuck looks at the floor; he seems sad. I've embarrassed him. I stare at my wineglass. It's empty already. Well, at least that explains why I've been so indiscreet. Normally I try not to articulate the shadows that lurk in my mind and heart but alcohol has a way of making shadows gather and thicken; they become harder to cold-shoulder. Usually, however frustrated I feel with Roberto, I bite my tongue. My reserve is not motivated by anything noble. I am not being loyal. The reason I haven't hinted at my frustrations with Roberto is that I dare not let the floodgates open. Even in the privacy of my own head I am reluctant to look closely at our increasingly silent and sullen relationship. Besides, it's far better that I use the time I have with Chuck to just forget about the miserable time I'm having when I'm not with him. I must keep my finger in the dam.

'I can't wait to taste this famous *penne con gamberi e carciofi*,' I say, trying to change the subject and atmosphere.

'I hope you like it. I really do.'

The evening passes in a blaze of delicious tastes and smells, clinking glasses and cheerful chatter. The shrimp was a bit dry to be honest, not quite as good as it was billed, but I didn't care. Chuck, however, did care and insists he's never let it overcook before.

'It's your fault, you're so distracting,' he complains.

I think we both know he's paying me a compliment. I am thrilled that I distract him. I want to drive him wild with distraction. Which isn't an especially reasonable or practical thought but then I've had a fair bit to drink.

He's distracting too. He seems taller every time I'm with him. His hair is scruffy and longish, it occasionally brushes his chin and I've started to envy it – I'd like to touch his chin, or any part of him come to that. Our brief moments of physical contact are always totally appropriate to my marital status. They're limited to a hug if he hasn't seen me for a while or the mwah-mwah double kiss that the Italians shower on everyone, when we say goodbye or goodnight. We do not touch any more or less than a couple of old guys who play bowls in the piazza might. Yet every time he touches me a sense of shock and excitement darts up and down my body and when he lets me go I miss him. I have to stop my body from arching after his as he pulls away. I can't imagine the same can be said for the old guys in the piazza.

Tonight, I watch as he impatiently rakes his hair back from his face and I want him to run his fingers over me in the same fast, determined way. I know that this is a terrible thought and as ever I try my best to ignore it. I swear I'll never utter it out loud to anyone, not even Alison, because once a thing is said it's real and can't be taken back. Anyway, I know what Alison would say; she thinks Chuck is simply a distraction because I'm not pregnant and I'm not even –

Happy.

And she might be right, but sometimes I wonder if it's the other way round. Am I unhappy with Roberto because I'm losing my mind and heart to Chuck? I stare at my glass, empty again – it must have a leak and that's why I'm suddenly debating the modern-day equivalent dilemma of chicken or egg. I've been much more disciplined up to now.

It doesn't matter what I think. It's what I do that is important, I remind myself. You can't be unfaithful in thought. What am I thinking? Unfaithful? Who mentioned anything about being unfaithful?

I did.

I take another sip and rest back on the wooden chair. The sky is blue-black now but the air drifting in from the open window is still warm; the music drifting out is mellow piano and horns with the unmistakable voice of Ma Rainey. I am not developing real or deep feelings for Chuck. I can't be. He has long hair. I don't normally go for the gypsy look.

But his unstudied, natural beauty is so attractive. I can't guess at how many hours Roberto spends in front of the mirror, I really can't. Roberto manicures his nails and plucks his eyebrows. Chuck has broad shoulders that taper to slim hips and the sexiest, most adorable bum you could imagine. Tonight, he is wearing a tight T-shirt and some battered Diesel jeans. He's made just the right amount of effort without suggesting he is vain or thinks that he's on a promise. Which he's not. Obviously. He can't be because I wouldn't, couldn't, do anything like that. I'm just saying it's nice he doesn't think he's on a promise.

'I didn't have you down as a blues fan.'

'I'm not, especially. But you said you were and I saw this CD with Bessie Smith, Ida Cox, Victoria Spivey.' He raises his tone at the end of each name, waiting for my face to flicker with recognition. 'I thought I'd buy it just to find out what it is that you like about it.'

'Really?' It's impossible to take that as anything other than a compliment. 'And do you like it?' I ask.

'Yes, though they were a sad bunch these blues ladies, weren't they? You don't get many laughs.'

'The clue is in "blues".'

'I realize that. But why do you like them so much?'

'I don't know. My parents hooked me in. It got me through my melodramatic teen years,' I explain.

'That's so cool. Imagine listening to this stuff when everyone else was listening to George Michael. I bet you were the coolest chick at college.'

'Er, no.'

'You must have been. I mean you didn't have to develop any faux sophistication. You really knew who Bessie Smith, Ida Cox, etc. were.'

'I've never thought of it like that. I always thought I was a little odd.'

'The only thing odd about you is that you don't know how seriously great you are.' And without pausing to let either of us digest that, he adds, 'More wine?'

'Yes please.'

'I'll open another bottle.'

'Good idea.'

He keeps flashing his fabulous smile. It's sincere, it involves his entire face, his eyes, his cheeks, his laugh lines. He's gorgeous.

'Damn it, we've no more wine left, a sorry state of affairs. How are you with spirits?'

One tequila, two tequila, three tequila. Floor.

'Fine,' I lie. Actually I know I should avoid spirits, I don't have the required resilience. I'm usually sick as a dog the day after indulging but I don't want to stop drinking.

As he pours the drinks Chuck says, 'Can I ask you something really personal?'

Yes, yes, I'll have your babies! Obviously that's just the drink talking and thank God it's just the drink talking in my head. 'Go on,' I say more cautiously.

'Can you explain the baby-wanting to me?'

I didn't see that one coming. I stare at him with what is no doubt a mixture of bewilderment and amazement because he feels compelled to add, 'What I mean is, how do you know that a baby will make everything OK?'

I have heard the question asked before. In an un-guarded moment, Alison has asked it with weary exasper-ation, recently Roberto has asked me as a frustrated challenge, other friends – and even acquaintances – have asked me as a conversation starter. Doctors have asked me with calm and neutral tones just before they tell me it isn't going to happen anyway. I find it almost impossible to thoroughly explain the overwhelming instinct that drives this desire – this need – of mine. In truth I've almost stopped trying to explain the undeviating, enduring gut feeling that rules my life.

Chuck's tone is not confrontational but more heartfelt and earnest than I have ever heard before.

'Why do you want to know?' I ask hesitantly.

Chuck comes around to my side of the table; we've been anchored to opposite sides all evening. He places his chair up close to mine. I can see a light sheen on his skin. The kitchen is hot from candles and cooking. He doesn't look yukky and sweaty, more iridescent and dreamlike. 'Make me understand,' he urges quietly.

Can I? 'It's hard,' I stutter.

'Try, for me,' he presses. His eyes are glinting with something beyond curiosity; his eyes are glinting with compassion. He carefully takes hold of my hand. I look at my ringed fingers lying in his tapered and nude ones and I know I should draw back. I should pull away from this daunting intimacy. But I don't want to. It's been forever since anyone invited me to talk like this. In fact has anyone *ever* invited me with the same tenderness and seriousness? I don't think so.

'OK.' I take a deep breath. 'I want a family so much because – at the most simple level – I love babies and I love children. I love everything about them; their cute hair slides and ribbons, their chubby legs, squeaky voices, their honesty, their cheekiness,' I add with a rueful grin. 'And I always thought it would *be,* you know. I've always, always thought that would be my lot in life, since I was not much more than a child myself. I was always the kid trailing neighbours' tiny children around and when they weren't available I played endlessly with dolls. I didn't like being on my own but because of the age gap between me and my brothers I often was. I want lots of kids, close in age so that none of them are ever lonely. Besides, I have all the right skills to be a mum. I'm patient, I'm good at teaching and I love a cuddle. I even have big boobs and big hips. Why do I have those if I'm not going to pop out babies?' I flash Chuck a smirk but I notice that it won't stay on my face. It's as forced as strawberries in December.

He doesn't allow me to dispel the tension with humour. He keeps his charged and forceful eyes focused on mine and nods briefly, urging me to continue.

'But more than that, I want to go on. Do you understand? I want a purpose and a reason to my existence.'

'And you think a baby can do all that?'

'Workaday, perhaps – even pathetic to some – but yes I do. So do millions and millions of others. I know that there are some people who cure diseases and climb mountains and learn to play musical instruments to give them purpose and that's all really admirable, well done them, good luck them, but that isn't for me. I wish it was. I really do,' I say bitterly. I realize I'm becoming agitated and allowing my painful frustration to spit out like fat from a roast. I reach for my glass and drain it. 'As it is, I feel empty and isolated most of the time.'

'Most of the time but not all of the time?' asks Chuck.

'When I'm teaching I feel quite good about myself, it's definitely helped, but at best I see teaching as a honing of skills that I'll use as a mother.' Chuck looks sorrowful. 'I wish a scintillating career could do it for me. I wish I could give up this yearning. I'm becoming a bit of a joke, even to myself, with this relentless longing, but for me a job isn't the answer. Wouldn't it be neat if it was?'

Chuck has filled my glass again.

'What are we drinking?'

'Your last one was ouzo. Another?'

I nod. He joins me. I realize that if I keep drinking I'm going to lose my ability to make sense. If indeed I've done so up to now. I don't care. It doesn't matter. My entire situation doesn't make sense. There's no sense to the fact that I can't have a baby.

Suddenly, I realize I'm crying. Tears and, oh God help me, snot are sliding down my face in torrents. Still, I don't stop talking; I gulp my words through my tears with the same commitment as someone making a deathbed confession speech. I tell Chuck that I think Raffaella blames me for the lack of children and that's why she hates me. I tell him that I fear Roberto must regret marrying me and wish he'd married Ana-Maria instead; she'd probably have produced a football team by now. I explain that I think I'll be seen as an eternal child (a.k.a. a worry) to my parents unless I have a child of my own and can prove I've grown up and I hate upsetting them so much.

My tears flow rapidly throughout this diatribe. He pulls my head on to his shoulder. He doesn't seem to care that my mascara is going to ruin his lovely T-shirt and he isn't the slightest bit squeamish about my running nose or my running commentary. He gently rocks me to and fro and strokes my hair. He doesn't tell me to hush or to calm down.

He murmurs, 'OK, sweetheart, let it all out. There you go. Let it go.'

I realize that he's rubbing my back and as his fingers skim my thin shirt I feel at once comforted and aroused. It's confusing. I'm aware that my lips are very close to his lips. If I moved a fraction I could kiss him. Or, if I didn't have the nerve to actually do that, then at least I'd make it easy for him if he wanted to kiss me and then I could kiss him back. Oh yes I could and I would.

We could run away together and we could have babies. I'm sure my murderous juices wouldn't commit the same crime twice. Chuck and I would be compatible and we could have the big family. Chuck could stop me feeling so sad and alone. He already does. Chuck could give me new hope, a fresh start. The heart-wrenching perfection of how my life could be clouts me and nearly knocks me sideways.

But then I remember, Chuck doesn't want a family. Chuck has never understood the longing some people have to reproduce. It's just not his thing. Oh God. There goes Plan B. I snap my head away from him and stare at him in shock and sorrow. Clearly, I am not about to run away with Chuck and play happy families with him any time soon. The realization that I've been secretly nurturing this fantasy has only finally dawned on me in the instant that it collapsed. But if I'm not about to run away with Chuck then what is the alternative? Staying with Roberto? Childless? And with Raffaella?

''Scuse me,' I slur, pushing past Chuck. 'I feel ill.'

'It's that way to the bathroom.'

48

26 April

My first thought on waking is that Chuck held my hair while I threw up. The shame is enough to make me groan and wiggle back down under the sheets. I can't face the world yet. My head is throbbing, which is as expected as it is unwelcome. My hangover started as I walked home from Chuck's and I'd rather hoped that I would have slept the worst of it off, or at least thrown up enough alcohol to avoid a hideously bad dose of poisoning, but no such luck. The worst thing is, even if my head wasn't throbbing, my soul would still be suffering.

Last night was a revelation. I realize that I've been burying my head in the sand for far too long. The facts are as follows. Fact, I am falling in love with Chuck. It is impossible to continue to kid myself that all I feel for him is friendship. I want him in every way. I want him thoroughly and without limits.

But I can't have him.

This is a completely unacceptable situation and I have to nip it in the bud instantly. Fact. Roberto is my husband. Roberto and I can't have children. Roberto has resigned himself to this; the bar is his baby now but I can't resign myself to it. We were once so hopeful; we used to share a future and view it together expectantly. Ha ha. No pun intended. Now I wonder what will glue us. What will we talk about when we are old? He thinks it will be enough for us to run the family bar. But what is the point of having a successful family business if there is no family? I have to initiate a conversation about other methods of conceiving, beyond crossing fingers and uncrossing legs. Roberto's refusal to discuss IVF is selfish, as Chuck once said.

And immature, egotistical, arrogant and cruel. Chuck didn't say all that. I added those bits.

Roberto is my husband but do I still love him? The question squeezes into my consciousness. I hurl it straight out the door. He's my *husband*. That's enough. It has to be. We have to fix things and think about the future. About a baby.

I roll over to face Roberto. I must still be full of Dutch courage because I decide that there is no time like the present to tackle this. I'm not getting any younger and I know that even IVF isn't guaranteed, it's time-consuming and complicated and we need to start investigating it instantly. However, my show of guts is in vain; his side of the bed is empty. I check the clock. It's only 7 a.m. He can't be up and out yet, can he? What's the rush, it's Saturday. I stretch out on to his side. The sheets are smooth and cool to touch. For a time, it doesn't make sense; due to my alcoholic fuzz it takes me a few moments to compute the obvious. Roberto hasn't slept in our bed.

Where is he? I sit bolt upright. The suddenness of the movement forces waves of nausea to slosh over me. I got home just after midnight last night. I wasn't surprised he wasn't in bed then, I assumed he was still in the bar, but what if he's had an accident? What if he's hurt? I leap out of bed and grab my robe. Barefoot I dash downstairs and into the dining room.

As usual Raffaella and the old grandpa are sat silently chewing their way through their breakfast.

'Have you seen Roberto this morning?' I ask in Italian.

Although it's evident that I'm in a hurry and concerned, Raffaella doesn't answer straight away. Instead she slowly masticates a fatty slice of salami, evidence of which sticks to her chin and rests on her heavy bosom. She's not normally averse to speaking with a full mouth, so I can only assume she's trying to frustrate me. My panic as to Roberto's whereabouts, combined with the ridiculous amount I drank last night, means I'm very likely to cry. I bite my lip and squeeze my eyes shut for a moment to avoid that.

'Why aren't you dressed?' she asks. I peel back my lids and we lock eyes. The air between us seems to freeze. Suddenly, my perfectly respectable robe vanishes and I feel naked. I'm aware that my hair is frizzy on one side and flat on the other. No doubt my mascara is smudged into whorish black patches on my face; I'm guessing this to be the case because I know that there were prints on my pillow. My breath stinks of booze and vomit, I'm barefoot. I'm hardly the epitome of the perfect daughter-in-law. In fact, I look every inch the disappointment Raffaella has always believed me to be.

I decide not to answer the question; my Italian isn't up to the necessary explanation. Instead I state. 'I'm looking for Roberto.'

'He's not here.'

I breathe deeply and try to draw on some hidden reserve of patience. 'Do you know where he is? Did you see him last night? Were you in the bar?' Thoughts of him dead in a ditch are assaulting my mind. Why isn't Raffaella more concerned? Her precious son is missing.

Raffaella stares at me and then slowly and carefully, so that I'm sure to understand, she says, 'He took Ana-Maria home at about nine. I didn't see him after that. I locked up the bar.'

Thoughts of him dead in a ditch vanish in a puff of smoke; although if he has done what I fear he has, I might kill him myself. I don't linger to clock Raffaella's look of triumph, I turn on my heel and run to my bedroom.

Slamming the door behind me I sink on to the bed. What to do? What to do? My hangover seems to have disappeared; the shock of Raffaella's revelation has seen it off. I almost miss it, because without hideous physical feelings of nausea and my thumping head I have to acknowledge what I'm feeling emotionally. I can identify fear and panic. My husband slept out last night. Raffaella seems pretty clear that he was at Ana-Maria's. I reach for my mobile. There will be a message. He'll have explained. There will be a text to reassure me that he slept on her couch and a simple reason for him not coming home. Things can't have gone this far, can they? I don't want to believe that they have. Maybe Ana-Maria's family is away and she didn't like being in the house alone; unlikely though, because she's not twelve. Maybe he took her home but then they had a nightcap and he didn't want to drive; also unlikely, as he could easily walk back from her place. Maybe he didn't sleep at hers at all; maybe he took her home and then went on somewhere else, but where? And why didn't he let me know? My inbox is empty.

I decide I have to find him at once and ask these

questions directly. For months we have skirted around one another, avoiding discussing anything of consequence, even choosing our small talk carefully. Many days have gone by and I've been unsure as to his whereabouts. I haven't demanded to know what he does with his time because I haven't wanted to know. Haven't I cared enough? Or did I care too much?

I have known that he had feelings for Ana-Maria but would he actually be unfaithful? People are, I know. But Roberto? Would he? I pulled away from Chuck. I have not done anything Roberto could reproach me with – however much I've longed to – and I do long to. Not now. Not now. I can't think about Chuck. I am married to Roberto. We made vows and we have a history and I want a future.

I hop into the shower and let water run through my hair and around my body. I don't have time to shampoo though, I just slosh a little body-wash under my pits and bits; all thoughts of wet body-brushing, languishing in luxurious, creamy body-wash and slathering on a post-shower moisturizing cream vanish. Sod grooming; I have a husband to find. I do remember to brush my teeth because the faint smell of vomit is unlikely to help me feel confident when I'm tackling Roberto on his night's conduct.

I rush out of Raffaella's house, trying to ignore the fact that I know she'll be craning to get a sighting of me, hurt and confused. I run to the bar; his car is parked up but he is nowhere to be seen; the place is still locked up. I guess he walked her home. An image of them strolling, hand-in-hand, through the warm amethyst-skied night flourishes in my imagination. I set off towards Ana-Maria's.

It's still very early and the town hasn't come alive yet. Shutters are being dragged back as if the buildings are opening one sleepy eye and then another. I see a couple of delivery people on bikes. They kick up dusty trails in their wake and it's as though the streets are lazily stretching, like people stretching their limbs when they first uncurl from sleep. My dash soon slows to a jog and then I settle into a fast walk. I'm not particularly fit at the best of times and I'm certainly not at my peak on several units of alcohol and only a few hours' sleep. Besides, I need a few moments to gather my thoughts.

I realize that I am walking round to Ana-Maria's fully expecting to hammer on the door and discover my husband sweaty between her sheets. It's a miserable humiliation to bear and I don't want to be out of breath when I howl like a banshee. Why has he thrust this in my face? I was prepared to –

What, go on as before? Bury my head? Ignore the patently obvious?

Yes. Yes I was, if I had to. I might be struggling to make a baby with Roberto but I am damn sure it would be impossible without him.

The walk to Ana-Maria's house only takes ten minutes. A pebble rattles in my shoe. At first it's a distraction, then a discomfort, and finally the pebble takes on disaster status but somehow I can't spare the time to bend and shake out the shoe. I just want to face Roberto.

And then suddenly he is standing in front of me.

And I'm not so sure.

I haven't yet reached Ana-Maria's house but we're close enough for me to reasonably assume that's where he's just come from. We face each other and, for a second, we don't know what to say to one another. He doesn't look abashed or even defensive. In fact he looks very happy. Happier than I've seen him look for a very long time. His happiness hurts me. I must be really pathetic, or jealous and small-minded or just hideously out of my depth, but I hate knowing she's made him happy. Chuck can't make me happy. Chuck doesn't want babies.

'Where did you sleep last night?' I ask.

'Out.' Roberto doesn't stop walking in the direction of Raffaella's. I pull at his arm but he shakes me off with a deft shudder. My touch offends him.

'I realize that. Out where?'

'Not in the street, Elizabeth.' Roberto's strides are long and he's quickly some distance away from me. I have to dash to catch up with him. I fall in step, but galloping along next to him is hardly dignified; besides, it's pretty tricky because I'm fighting an instinct to yell and scream abuse at him and I'm fighting an impulse to batter and claw at him, pulling his neatly pressed shirt off his body.

Within a few minutes we are in Veganze piazza. Roberto stops outside a bar and points to a table.

'Should we take a coffee?' He's probably banking on the fact that I'm less likely to yell obscenities in the street, or maybe he, like me, can't bear the idea of yet another hiss-whispered fight over the bed in our room. It's one of our problems that we have more privacy in public than in the place that we call a home.

We stay silent until the waitress has taken our order. Today we both have a double espresso and Roberto also orders a ricotta lemon cake with blueberry topping. I'm disgusted that he can eat something so sweet and delicious under the circumstances.

'I stayed at Ana-Maria's house last night,' he says as he empties a packet of sugar into his coffee. He seems to need an energy boost. I stare at his wrists. They are elegant; his skin is olive and fine. They have not changed. I've always loved his wrists and hands; now I'm staring at them wondering if last night he laid those hands on Ana-Maria. And how many other days and nights? I want to grab his cake fork and stab his beautiful hands over and over.

'Why?'

'She needed me. Her aunt died, she was very upset. Her family were all away at the funeral. She was alone.'

'She can't have been that upset if she didn't go to the funeral,' I point out.

Roberto does not react to my comment at all. I try to look him in the eye but he's wearing sunglasses and my reflection slides back at me and seems to slip on to the floor. I can't reach him.

'Are you having an affair?' I ask. I assume it's me who does the asking, although the voice sounds disjointed and it could be coming from the crazy guy who bums cigarettes; out of the corner of my eye I can see that he's already making his way around the square.

'Did you have a pleasant evening at Chuck's?' asks Roberto. For a split second I assume that I haven't asked my question out loud at all, then I realize that I did and all Roberto is doing is asking the same one back. He's the master of avoidance. We've both been pretty good at it in the past.

'Chuck and I are just friends.'

'Of course.'

'I did not sleep over at Chuck's.'

'No, it would have caused a scandal. Above all a scandal must be avoided.'

I always believed that if I was ever faced with my husband's infidelity I would react decisively and immediately. Hanging, drawing and quartering was a serious option. Now that I am actually faced with the probability that he is having an affair, I find I am immobile. Do I really want to know? Of course I do. I must. But. If he is and he admits it, we cannot go on as we are. Not that we are in an especially fabulous place right now, we're not, but this morning I'd wanted to talk to him about IVF. As hideous as it is to admit, I realize that a family is still an option if my husband is being secretive, uncommunicative and neglectful but it's not an option if he's in love with someone else. If he leaves me the dark-eyed babies with fat legs and black curls will never exist. I can't let them go. I don't have the time or perhaps even the energy to start all over again. Besides, who would I start again with? Chuck? Not an option. Chuck doesn't want children. *He has never understood the longing some people have to reproduce; that whole thing has just passed him by.* His words echo around my head with tinny bleakness. At least Roberto wants children and I am married to him. I accept the foul inevitability of what I have to do. I have to get over this. I have to fix us. So do I *really* want to know if my husband is having an affair? Do I want to remove that last scrap of belief in what we have? I pause, aware that the next sentence out of my mouth is possibly the most important one I've ever uttered in my life.

'Chuck and I really are just friends and if you've thought otherwise and it's hurt you, then I'm sorry. And if you've done anything, anything at all, in response to believing

Chuck and I are more than just friends, then I'm sorry for that too.'

Roberto looks devastated. 'Look, Elizabeth, the issue is —'

'Shush,' I put my fingers to his lips. 'Don't say anything you might regret. Just give yourself a moment.'

We sit in silence. My hangover has returned and I feel as though someone is trying to turn me inside out. I can't focus either literally or metaphorically. Nothing makes sense. I can't work out if I'm being amazingly mature about my husband's infidelity or a big, pathetic wuss. Am I in shock? I concentrate on the facts that have sustained me through adulthood. I search for the certainty that has been my *raison d'être*. I want a baby. I need Roberto to make a baby. This thing with Ana-Maria is a blip. I have to find a way of believing that the feelings I have for Chuck are pimples on a blip. It is not important. We can work it out. We can sort everything out. I must have a baby.

I repeat these short sentences over and over in my head, like some sort of prayer. The effect is hypnotic, I begin to feel calm. Roberto looks pale and tired.

'The best thing is to put all this silliness behind us,' I say with a bright smile that is unlikely to fool either of us.

I consider kissing his forehead. He'd understand that I was offering him some sign of forgiveness. Of course I don't want this to happen again but I think we can get over it. It's important that he hasn't actually *said* he slept with Ana-Maria; maybe I'm jumping to conclusions. He's *my* husband. Mine. He will be the father of my children.

'I think we should talk about IVF again,' I add.

'Elizabeth —,' Roberto doesn't finish the sentence but

he sounds weary and concerned. He takes hold of my hand. 'I will not consider IVF. We have discussed this.'

'Ages ago.'

'What's changed?'

'Back then I still hoped it would happen naturally, we had time on our side. Now I am desperate. We're desperate. We need a baby.'

'That is the worse time to try. I will not do it.'

I stand up and I feel my legs tremble beneath me. I wonder if he can see me shaking. I put my fingers on the table in an attempt to steady myself.

'You owe me, Roberto. I am your wife.'

49

The problem with my dramatic exit is that I have nowhere to go. The thought is hideously depressing. I rule out the idea of visiting Chuck. I need to be stronger before I can do that. Last night was completely innocent, or at least it was as far as he is concerned. He had no idea that while he was (no doubt) staring at my snot and smudged eye make-up, I was staring into his eyes and imagining kissing him. He was unaware that when I was sobbing about my lack of babies I was simultaneously imagining ravishing him and making an entire Walton family with him. While drinking copious amounts of alcohol made me indiscreet, weepy and finally sick, I can at least take some comfort in the fact that I didn't actually try to snog him. Even so, since he witnessed me bringing up his carefully prepared (although slightly dry) *penne con gamberi e carciofi* over his bathroom tiles I don't think I can call him right now and land this latest drama at his door. He's lovely but I might be pushing my luck.

The school is closed so I can't use it as a bolt-hole. Going back to Raffaella's is out of the question. I consider getting on a bus and visiting another local village. It doesn't matter which one, anywhere other than here. Yet I know that I'll be alone and taking my problems with me. I really need someone to talk to. I can't ring Alison. Alison will probably get on a plane and come and chop off Roberto's bollocks if I tell her what's gone on in the last twenty-four hours. Who to turn to? I stand on the kerb and kick up dust.

'Did you find my brother?' Paolina's voice falls down on me like a sobering slap.

'Yes.'

Paolina has drawn up beside me. She is sitting bolt upright in her tiny but tidy Fiat 500. She seems to have appeared out of thin air. I wonder if she's just chanced upon me or if she's been following me. Could she have seen and heard what's just passed between Roberto and me? Oh God, I hope not. I'd die at the thought of anyone witnessing that.

'Would you like a coffee?' she asks.

'Not really, I've just had one.'

She sighs as though she finds me frustratingly dense. 'I'm offering to take you for a drive.'

'Oh, right, well yes. Where shall we go?'

'Anywhere away from here,' says Paolina. Which is surely my line.

I hop into Paolina's car and for the first ten minutes of the drive we don't exchange a word. We both appear to be entirely focused on our own worlds and I begin to doubt they overlap, which is a relief. It dawns on me that Paolina didn't want to take a drive with me, especially – she simply wanted to escape. I guess she was just passing and stumbled upon me. I understand perfectly and feel closer to her than I've ever felt before. It's weird that self-absorption is what we have in common. I wonder what she's running from, and I think that it's sad that she's also running even though this is her home.

We drive into the country for at least fifteen minutes. I have no idea which direction we've headed in or which village we might end up in. We pull up at an enormous furniture shop. It's fairly typical of furniture shops you find all over the world on random out-of-town roads. It's stuffed full of tables, chairs, beds, sideboards and such, all of which are stacked without rhyme or reason, none of which are especially beautiful or notable. The shop sells the sort of furniture everyone buys saying, 'It will do for now.' As fully functional furniture it never has the courtesy to collapse and demand to be replaced, therefore this furniture stays in homes much longer than it deserves to.

There are one or two other cars already parked up, belonging to early morning shoppers who need a mattress or a dining room table but don't have much cash to splash. Despite the dullness of the furniture available, I envy those families ensconced in their ordinary domestic chores. I'd love to be in a position where the only challenge of the day is choosing firm over soft, walnut over pine. The families each have a couple of kids who are bouncing around the showroom – hiding behind sofas, testing out beds, putting their feet up on chairs and such. I smile at them fondly; Paolina seems not to notice them but walks through the shop straight into a surprising courtyard where there is a coffee shop.

'Wow, I'd never have expected to find a coffee shop here; it's a bit off the beaten track, isn't it?'

'I know a lot of discreet places,' says Paolina, who is hidden behind enormous sunglasses.

'Oh yes, I suppose you do.' Suddenly I feel uncomfortable, I am very aware of her mistress status. Mistresses have never been my favourite people but I feel especially disgruntled by them as a breed this morning. How much does she know? More than me, no doubt. I wonder if she is Ana-Maria's confidante; it seems they might have a lot in common. And yet Paolina has always been fair and fond with me, so maybe I am unfairly judging her.

We take a seat and choose from the menu. I haven't eaten breakfast and now I'm starving. I select a slice of gooey *torta di natale* and a *caffè latte*. When my cake arrives Paolina eyes the delicate coils of pastry which cradle plump raisins and walnuts.

'That looks good,' she comments. 'It's a Calabrian cake originally, you know.'

'Really,' I murmur. What makes her think I care? Even at times like this food is vital and absorbing to Italians. Maybe especially at times like this. The strangeness of the events of the last twenty-four hours allows me to ask, 'Did you come here with your lover?'

'Sometimes.'

It seems an odd place to carry out a clandestine affair. There are plenty of beds, admittedly, but not much chance of using them. As though Paolina is reading my mind she comments, 'We'd come here to talk for ten or fifteen minutes.'

While I don't sympathize with her plight, I admit it's a sad and gritty image. When I imagine anyone having an affair I think of them grabbing frantically at one another's clothes as they swing from crystal chandeliers or I think of them romping in purple silk sheets feeding one another grapes from mouth to mouth. I do not think of them snatching ten minutes' chat at the local furniture emporium.

'Roberto stayed at Ana-Maria's last night.'

I have no idea why I've shared this with Paolina. The

chances are she knew already, but even if she didn't, then what is she supposed to say? He's her brother and anyway she doesn't have any moral objections to infidelity – obviously. Still, I had to tell someone.

Paolina nods cautiously and then asks, 'What do you make of that?'

'He said he was comforting her because some old aunt died. I have no reason to disbelieve him.'

'Her aunt did die,' she confirms.

I take a large bite out of my *torta di natale*. I'm relieved that much of Roberto's story is true. If I have to accept what he has to say it would be an added bonus if I could believe him too.

'Well, clearly, it's an innocent relationship. They're old friends, that's all.' I pause, hoping she'll agree with me; she doesn't. 'I'm sure there will be talk; there's always gossip.' I pause again, hoping she'll contradict me; she doesn't. 'I mean, people always assume the worst but I have no reason to think anything improper is going on.' I wonder how I stumbled upon the word improper. It went out with the ark and seems unreal. I guess my situation is pretty unreal. Here I am sitting with my husband's sister discussing his infidelity. What's the etiquette?

'Did you ask him if the situation is innocent?'

'There has to be trust, Paolina, I can't go accusing him.' I lie because I need as many people to buy into this charade as possible. If other people accept and believe my version of events maybe I will be able to as well.

Paolina raises an eyebrow so high that I can see it above her sunglasses. I wish she would remove them, then I might have some chance at reading her; as it is I haven't a clue what she's thinking, implying or insinuating.

'My boyfriend has left his wife,' says Paolina, matter-of-factly.

I'm grateful that the conversation has moved away from Roberto and me but I don't know what the required response is. Would it be rude to scream, 'Home wrecker!'?

'When?'

'Last week, six weeks after we last broke it up. He said he could not live without me. He's moved into a tiny, rather scruffy apartment in Marostica. He wants me to move in with him.'

'You must be pleased.'

She sighs dramatically, 'Not especially. The problem is that during that time he decided he couldn't live without me, I decided I *could* live without him.'

'Oh.'

'I had just started to see my friends again, which I haven't done for years. It's difficult to stay in touch with friends if you are having an affair. If you can't talk about your love life there's distrust; women expect to gossip about such things. Plus recently, I was focusing better in the office and I found I don't even mind working in the bar now that Roberto has made the place fun. None of these things I did when I was with my lover. But now he keeps telling me we have to be together. He keeps reminding me of the sacrifices he has made for me. I want to tell him that the sacrifices came too late.'

'I don't understand.'

'Nor do I.' Paolina finally takes off her sunglasses; she massages the bridge of her nose. She looks bewildered.

'Perhaps now you can be like an ordinary couple. You can see your friends and work in the bar, etc. but still see him,' I suggest.

'No, I can't. He demands more. The nature of our experience together is so intense. I can't imagine that ordinary couple life you describe.'

'With time, perhaps.'

'I don't even want to settle into an ordinary relationship. I discover that the thing I liked about my lover was the drama, the inconvenience, the tragic excitement. You see?'

'Not really.' The thing is I've always liked things to be uncomplicated. I'm a straightforward kind of girl. Paolina looks at me with faint despair, perhaps even disgust. I've never felt so prosaic. 'What will you do?'

'I fear I will have to stay with him. Mamma will be sad that he was once married but better that than still married, I suppose. My problem is recently I got to wondering, do you think there might have been other men I'd be happy with?' she asks.

'What do you mean?' It must be the hangover or the language barrier but I really can't keep up with this conversation. Where is it going?

'Do you believe in the One?' Paolina stares at me with a scary absorption, as though it is the first time she has ever seen me or even seen anyone at all. She looks desperate and confused. My answer matters to her more than it should.

I try to say yes, I want to say yes, but I find that I can't. Do I still believe in the One? To have been vaguely in love with as many men as I have defies belief. It's a modern phenomenon. It's a modern problem. This one is stunning but unreliable. This one cooks but has no conversation. This one is tight but professes to adore me. This one is gorgeous but not as clever as I'd like him to be. I thought Roberto was the One but it's very confusing, or at least inconvenient, to have been in love with more than one man in a lifetime – let alone acknowledge falling in love with a man other than your husband while still being married. While planning on staying married. It becomes impossible to believe in the One. My mind aches with my inability or inadequacy in answering this question, so instead I ask, 'Do you believe in the One?'

'I did. I thought I had to have Gian Carlo despite an array of the most amazing and wonderful offers that stumbled into my spotlight. I thought it *had* to be him. But what if I was wrong?'

'And?'

'And I broke up his marriage unnecessarily. What if someone else could have made me happy too? Happier.'

We both fall silent and consider the horribleness of that thought. We could have dwelt upon the question indefinitely, only something else, something more terrible, arrests her attention.

'What if no one could? Can?'

'What?'

'What if no one can make me happy? And what if it is some ghastly overrated plot?'

'You've lost me.'

'Love. Being in love. It might not *be*.'

'Oh, it is. You know it is,' I say encouragingly.

'Jesus, Elizabeth, you still have a healthy respect for Father Christmas and the Easter Bunny. You are not what anyone would describe as a rational being.'

I decide to ignore Paolina's sarcasm; she's overwrought.

'So you're not happy that he's left his wife.'

'I feel so guilty. He's so needy.'

'I expect it will work itself out for the best,' I say, although I can't see what the best would be and I fear my platitude is miserably inadequate.

Paolina shrugs. I have a sense that ultimately she's deeply self-sufficient, not a bad thing to be considering who her mother is. I don't imagine Raffaella was the kind of mother who encouraged confidences and moochy, ethereal 'what if' chats. Paolina has had to learn to stand on her own two feet. I have a feeling I'm a sounding board but nothing I can say will influence her in the end.

'So where were you last night when Roberto was doing this comforting of Ana-Maria?' she asks.

I shift on my seat, take a sip of *latte* and consider my answer. I have nothing to be ashamed of, I remind myself. I was with Chuck but Roberto knew that and I came home. I did not sleep over, I did nothing worse than get pissed and slag off my husband; oh yes, and have fantasies about getting naked with my host. I blush. Naturally, Paolina assumes the worst.

'Ah. You were with your American *friend.*' She manages to make the word friend sound especially shady.

'My American friend? He's not a friend. Not in the way you mean.'

'What is he then?'

'He's—he's—he's just someone to talk to.'

'About the weather?' she asks with a cheeky but not censorious grin.

'Sometimes.'

'And other times?'

'About other things. His home town. Our experiences here. How to shop like a local. My fertility.'

'I see.'

'I guess he is a friend. He's nothing more.' Again I blush.

Paolina must have noticed but she just says, 'It's none of my business. I'm sure you are a little homesick. It must be nice talking with a person in your language.'

'It is. I adore Italy. I couldn't wait to be here but I find it doesn't like me.'

'It's a country, Elizabeth, not your aunt. It cannot embrace you. It is a home, like England. And, like England, it has its frustrations and its joys.'

I think of England and have to admit to sometimes loathing the ugly materialism that seems to dominate the south and the chippy depression of the north. The wet weather is dreary. The lack of plumbers and the expensive petrol are annoying. The jealousy and the laziness which seem to be increasingly prevalent are sickening. But at the same time I think of a warm English summer day that gifts a breeze which will carry the smell of freshly cut summer grass and I miss England.

'In what way does Italy let you down?'

It's a good question; I think about it for a moment or two. I am sometimes disappointed that the waiters are rude or that my food arrives at a different time from whoever I am eating with. The loos are shocking. My mother-in-law is a horror. The winters are colder than I expected. The voluble, vivacious, va-va-voom gangs of Italians are harder to penetrate than I had imagined. But on the other hand the delicious smell of strong coffee, sweetened to a treacle sickliness, drifts on the air and I would lick it if I could. The language has been easier to learn than I expected. Paolina and Laurana are brilliantly interesting and honest women who I feel I could call friends, the light is spectacular, the food sublime.

The truth is, mostly I'm disappointed because I haven't had a baby here. The enormity of that precise thought surges through my body. I realize that isn't the country's fault. It isn't a fault that can be pegged on to anything animate or inanimate. I'm so sad that all I can do is shrug.

'Italy has infertile couples too and gay people and broken marriages and hopeful women and resistant men and all the things you find in your England. It is real, not an ideal,' she says carefully.

'Maybe I just need to give it more time,' I say with a shrug.

'Maybe,' says Paolina, but she doesn't sound convinced or convincing.

50

Paolina and I drive back to Veganze. As we approach the piazza she says, 'I throw a coin with you for who is to work at Bruno's today.'

I weigh it up. My hangover is ferocious and all I really want to do is crawl back under the covers but I realize the chances of doing this are slim; I'm pretty sure that Raffaella wouldn't allow me such an indulgence.

'I'll work the shift, keeping busy will be good for me,' I offer. Whereas I get the feeling Paolina requires a little more thinking time, away from here.

'That would be kind. I am going to drive to the hills.' She giggles self-consciously at the element of desperation she is betraying.

I smile sympathetically. 'Everyone needs to do that from time to time. Good luck.'

'You too.' Paolina stretches towards me, places her hand on top of mine and gently squeezes.

I do not know what to expect when I open the door to the bar. I don't think it would be too dramatic to say that I feel I'm knocking on the gates of hell, especially as Beelzebub greets me.

'I no expect you today,' says Raffaella.

'Well, we're made of pretty tough stuff, us Blighty folk,' I murmur. 'It will take more than a public humiliation and a stinking hangover to keep me away.'

'*Che cosa?*' she demands. I knew that she wouldn't

understand my mutterings in English, it's one of the few secret pleasures I can indulge in. I turn to her with a bright but entirely false smile and ask in Italian, 'So what do you need me to do?'

Raffaella's face contracts with irritation and cruelty. Clearly she was hoping that I wouldn't have the guts to face her or anyone else today. In fact, I bet she hoped that I was at home packing my suitcase and planning to hotfoot it back to the UK pronto. Part of me wishes I could do that. Right now I'd love to be sitting in my mum and dad's front room talking about the weather or the garden and sipping Earl Grey tea, or I'd love to be in a noisy bar with Alison and her new lady sipping cocktails and slipping into oblivion. But each root of comfort would only sustain me until the teapot was drained or the hangover set in. I know Mum and Dad would remind me that I'm married to Roberto and I therefore have a responsibility to be at his side and try to work things out with him. They wouldn't approve of me throwing in the towel. Even Alison would remind me that up until these last few months I've always firmly believed Roberto was my dream man.

Truthfully, I would like to be at the side of my dream man too, only he's vanished. And I don't just mean that he's not in the bar. The Roberto I met in the street this morning was a stranger. Even when we are standing side by side we are entirely separate.

'Where's Roberto?' I ask.

'I don't know. Probably, my son with Ana-Maria,' replies Raffaella. Sadly my Italian has improved enough to know I'm not misunderstanding her. I sigh at this latest low in our relationship. Even my mother-in-law no longer sees the necessity to hide the details of Roberto's situation from me. This is my moment to tell her that she can't say Ana-Maria's name to me. This is my moment to spin into a crimson fury and demand that she and her rat son treat me with a little respect. I'm mute.

'You must clean the bathrooms. We have no cleaner today,' she says.

I pick up the bucket, mop and bleach and give in to the inevitability that I'm going to be cleaning loos again. Whatever happened to my self-esteem?

When Roberto arrives an hour later he treats me with polite but cool indifference. He comments that I've made a good job of the bathrooms and that it's decent of me to take Paolina's shift. We move around one another as though we are new acquaintances – and not too fond at that. We are careful not to offend or insult one another. Roberto helps me understand the customers' orders but I realize his efforts to clear up any potential ambivalence are to protect the customer from receiving an unwanted meal, rather than from any real concern for my confusion or embarrassment. We are careful to avoid accidental contact such as grazing fingers when passing a wineglass or physically bumping into one another as we squeeze behind the bar. It crosses my mind that I'll have to increase the physical contact somewhat if I'm hoping to conceive with this man. It would be easy to despair of my plan to stay with Roberto and make our marriage work when his phone beeps to signal incoming texts three times. On the third occasion he takes himself outside to make a call. He doesn't even have the decency to look subdued; he practically skips away.

'Is Ana-Maria coming in today?' I ask when he returns.

'That is a provocative question. A stupid question,' he hisses. The cool cover that he's maintained all morning is blown away in a single puff.

'Not at all, it was a totally straightforward question.' I play dumb.

'No, of course she is not coming into the bar,' he snaps, and then he turns on his heel and strides into the kitchen.

Should I take that as proof positive that they are actually having an affair now? If their situation really was above board then why wouldn't she come into the bar? She normally does. I piece the jigsaw together. My best guess is that they have been craving one another for quite some time now. In the beginning they might have told themselves that their relationship was innocent – just good friends – but as they have spent more and more time with one another they have fallen back in love. Last night they gave in to the inevitability and did the deed; in many ways I'm surprised it's taken them so long. I recall Roberto lying in our darkened bedroom. I assumed he was fed up with his mother or stressed out over the bar, but was he battling with his conscience? Could I have pulled him back from the brink if I hadn't been thinking about negotiating my night out with Chuck?

I wander outside the bar and plonk myself on to the nearest chair I can find. It's metal and uncomfortable – I haven't had a chance to put out the cushions yet. My inadequacies are stacking up. Panicked, I consider that I must be a terrible wife; my husband is shagging his ex *and* I've forgotten to make the outside eating area chairs comfy and welcoming. The irrational parallel I am drawing between these shortcomings suggests that I am indeed in shock.

My husband has slept with someone else.

No, no, it's impossible. I won't believe it of him. I can't believe it of him. But then am I really so naïve that I can believe otherwise? It's clear he adores her company and they have history. It's not impossible that they're having an affair; it is entirely probable. Yet saying the words in my head is an isolated act, quite distinct and alone from feeling it in my heart or believing it in my being. My Roberto. Would he? Could he? Before we came here I'd have sworn that he was one hundred per cent faithful and happy, but –

But since coming here I don't think either of us has been particularly happy. I pause and try to pursue that thought with some conviction. One thing at a time. Think of one thing at a time.

Perhaps we weren't that happy in London either. The only difference being that there we both had other and sufficient distractions so that it was possible to ignore our growing gulf. I had Alison and the worldwide web with its endless hocus-pocus cures and remedies for my child-lessness. I had workmates and my family, I had hope. And Roberto had his career and – oh, I don't know. Thinking about it now, other than work Roberto didn't have much that was independent of me when we were in England. He liked visiting my brothers and my parents and he liked to come along to the pub with my mates. Anyway, I always said he should consider them '*our*' mates and I'm sure he did, didn't he? When we met he had a number of Italian pals living in London but slowly, one by one, they drifted back to their mammas and fresh pasta. He used to play football in the park on a Sunday morning, but thinking back, those kickabouts fell away a couple of years ago. I hadn't really noticed; to be honest I was quite glad to have him returned to me on a Sunday morning. It's a great day for brunch or shopping.

Did Roberto ever feel lonely in London the way I do in Veganze? He never said so. But then there were other things we didn't talk about too.

I remember that day when he came home from work and he'd been fired. He had literature from estate agents stuffed in his laptop bag, yet we'd never discussed moving. Obviously his plans were aborted, but if they hadn't been, when was he planning to include me in that scheme? I'd have wanted some say in where we lived next. Was his secret search for a new home a wonderful, thoughtful surprise or was it a desperate attempt to change the dynamics in our home life? And before then, long before then, the day he stopped talking about trying for a baby. He shagged me within an inch of my life, he forced every sinew and nerve and seemed to be truly willing a baby into being but when a baby didn't emerge we never even offered one another a conciliatory pat on the back. I hit the web in search of other routes to life and he – well, he gave up.

I feel sick and I don't think it's anything to do with the hangover. I'd thought that as our marriage had been perfectly happy, and had just recently run into turbulent water, we'd get to dry land if we steered straight and carefully. I was planning on sticking a band-aid over the graze known as Ana-Maria.

But if there's even more to it than that, if there are longer-lying concerns, then I'm not so sure a band-aid will cover it.

What to do? What to do? I want a baby. I yearn, hanker,

need, require a baby. I don't have time or energy or nerve to start again with someone else. I don't have the luxury of calling my marriage what it is; a squalid, cluttered sham. I have no choice. I have to pretend that I haven't yet reached the obvious conclusion. I have to feign blissful ignorance or the whole paper house collapses around my ears. At least Ana-Maria has the decency to stay away today. If they don't rub my nose in it, if they are discreet, perhaps I can live with it – at least for as long as it takes for it to go away, and it would go away if we had a baby. I know it would. Roberto wouldn't be unfaithful if he was a father – would he? No, he wouldn't; I'm almost certain. Everything would be better then. I don't have to dignify it by acknowledging it. I turn towards the bar. Raffaella is standing in the doorway, arms folded across her enormous chest (quite a feat), and she's staring at me. I turn away instantly; I will not catch her eye. She's been watching me all morning and is waiting for me to crack. The witch.

My nose is tingling as I fight tears. Is my plan to stay here and put up with whatever Roberto doles out to me realistic? How much humiliation can I bear? What if his infatuation with Ana-Maria is more than that? What if he is in love with her and he doesn't love me any more? It's not a bizarre thought. There hasn't been much show of affection, let alone love, since I arrived here. But he's *my* husband.

And what of Chuck? So far I have managed to operate in Veganze like a human being because of his tenderness and his interest. Will I manage without him? I have to. I cannot think of Chuck. I am married. It's not right to feel the way I do about him.

'Dime for them.'

'Sorry?' I look up and am face to face with Chuck.

'A dime for your thoughts. Isn't that what you Brits say, a penny for your thoughts?'

'Yes, we do.'

'Maybe I should have offered a euro.'

'Chuck, about last night. I wanted to apologize –'

He puts up his hand and shakes his head slowly from side to side. His mannerisms aren't patronizing; he looks amused and warm. 'No need, Elizabeth. Every friendship has to be cemented by the regurgitated contents of an abused stomach at some point. I take it as a compliment that you are so relaxed with me. Although, don't make a habit of it.'

I blush, he's being so nice. It's a stark contrast to how I've been treated all morning and suddenly I fear that I might not be able to subdue my tears any longer. It's ironic that Raffaella's witchy snarls and cross looks and Roberto's indifference haven't been able to move me as much as Chuck's concern.

'I didn't think you were working today.'

'No, I wasn't supposed to be, I'm covering a shift for Paolina. She has some stuff going on.'

'Don't we all.'

'Do you want a coke?'

'That would be good.'

I make him stay put. I like being outside even though I've forgotten my sunglasses and the sun is blazing brightly now. I fetch us a coke each and slide his towards him with an unexpected amount of flair.

'It's on the house,' I say loudly.

Raffaella tuts and pointedly huffs and puffs as she

retreats back inside; she has yet to acknowledge Chuck even though he's thrown several cheery comments her way. I'm grateful that he's shown his face today. Of course it is fantastic to see him because he always makes me feel relaxed and cheerful, but by coming in and continuing our friendship as normal he's telling the whole world we have nothing to hide. I'm not expecting the relaxed and cheerful thing today, not under the circumstances, but if he makes me feel more valued than dog faeces on the bottom of a shoe, then that's progress.

'So what are your plans for the day?' I ask.

'Well, I was coming in to try to persuade you to come out with me. I was figuring you'd need to clear your head, but as you're working I see that won't be happening.'

'Sorry,' I shrug.

There's nothing I'd like more than to go out with Chuck today but I know that it would be a mistake. I'm feeling emotional and vulnerable. My husband is all but having sex on the bar in front of me. He's treating me with disdain and disrespect, whereas Chuck is . . . well, Chuck is hot. He's sitting in front of me and treating me with nothing but sympathy and kindness. Plus, he's hot, did I mention that? I realize that every day that I have spent with Chuck has been a risk, a gamble. There was always a thinly veiled possibility that I'd finally admit to myself what has been obvious for three months: I like him more than I like my husband right now. I am falling in love with him. Yes, he's hot, but he's also generous with his time and his thoughts. He's interesting, clever, new, honest, unknown, exciting. However, Roberto *is* my husband. Roberto is the man I am going to make babies with. We are going through a rough patch, that's all. We can get through it, I'm pretty sure. We just need to spend some serious time together and get back on track.

The worst thing I could do right now is spend more time with Chuck.

'I can't come out with you today, Chuck. In fact, I don't think I can see you again.' I force myself to meet his eyes. Smack, how can they surprise me every time? I watch as Chuck's eyes cloud. Normally so wide and hopeful, they darken in front of me; he looks confused and hurt.

'Have I done something wrong? Was the *penne con gamberi e carciofi* that bad? Look, I can cook other dishes, or we can go to restaurants.' He's like me; he uses humour to deflect.

I smile. 'Not at all – well, actually it was a little dry but that's not it.'

'Are you embarrassed because of the sick-up thing?'

'No, well, yes again, but that's not it either.' Chuck opens his arms wide and then lets them drop to his side in a gesture which clearly conveys he's stumped and waiting for a response. I guess I owe him that much. He's been a great friend, my best here in Italy. I can't just cut loose without offering any sort of explanation.

'Roberto stayed out with Ana-Maria last night.'

'Oh.'

'I guess my marriage is in more trouble than I thought. I mean I'm not saying they are actually having sex –' I pause, I hope he doesn't call me on that. 'I guess I'm just saying that I shouldn't be spending so much time with you and he shouldn't be spending so much time with her and we just need some time together. I want to make it work with him. I want his babies. I –'

Chuck cuts across me. For the first time ever he doesn't seem to want to hear what I have to say.

'Absolutely. I totally understand. You are husband and wife and I've never wanted to come between that,' he says earnestly.

I stare at him and try to ignore the throb of disappointment that is swelling in my gut. Never?

'I am so sorry if I've been in the way. Consider me gone.'

And with that he stands up and walks away without so much as throwing a regretful look over his shoulder.

19 May

It hurts. Getting used to the fact that Chuck is not going to be in my life any more hurts. I've only known him a few months. Yet I'm floored to discover it's pretty tricky getting up in the mornings now I don't have him to look forward to. I'm surprised when I realize that he's my first thought, every day. In fact, as he also makes regular appearances in my dreams too, it's becoming problematic distinguishing between the two conditions. They blur into one another, leaving me feeling fragile and confused.

I catch the bus to work now. It's always crowded, and the driver speeds as though he's a contestant in a Grand Prix, so I don't enjoy the journeys in the slightest and invariably feel quite nervous by the time I arrive at school. I've tried buying my own brown paper bag of fruit, in case it's the breakfasts I miss, but I rarely have an appetite. Invariably I forget about my purchase and it over-ripens, swells and splits in my school bag; the sickly sweet smell alerts me and I remember to throw it in the bin. I always claim a window seat and I make an effort to concentrate on the beautiful countryside. Indeed, the blazes of bougainvillea that cling to the teal mountainside are stunning. The scarlet flashes catch my eye as the bus speeds past. I try to ponder what goes on in both the tiny and the rather grand dusty terracotta or peach-coloured buildings, but I've found I'm much more drawn to looking at the cars sharing the road. I strain for a fleeting glimpse of Chuck's car. It's a reasonable assumption that the bus will pass him at some point; we are going in the same direction. In fact, on about a dozen occasions I swear I see him, but on second glance it never turns out to be Chuck. A similar car perhaps but a man with darker hair is driving, or a chubbier man, or a smaller man, or even a handsome man but not the handsome man I'm looking for.

I do glimpse him for real from time to time at school. His blond head rises above the sea of darker crowns even on the busiest stairwell. I once waved at him but I don't think he saw me. At least, he didn't wave back. When I'm working in the bar my neck becomes sore because I jerk my head towards the door hundreds of times per evening just in case he chooses that moment to throw caution to the wind, ignore my relationship embargo and pop by anyway. The excitement of hearing the door creak is tremendous as I enjoy an infinitesimal moment of hope that I might see him. The disappointment, because it never is him, is crushing.

Stupidly, I find myself dawdling past his apartment and I can't help but notice whether a window is open or closed, if a shutter is up or down and whether his car is parked on the street or whether it's absent. More often than not the windows are closed, the shutters down and the car is nowhere to be seen. I torture myself with imaginings of where he might be. What if he's out with another woman? Well, not *another* woman technically. If he is out with a woman then she would be his woman, she could only be *another* woman if there was an initial woman and there isn't. We were just friends. I remind myself that it's natural that Chuck is out, no doubt with a new girlfriend; I was taking up far too much of his time – unfairly. Still, something stings.

On the rare occasion that I notice his window open I dart into the shadows, like some character from a Bond movie. I'd die if he caught me lurking on the sun-bleached streets outside his house. What would he think? Obviously the only natural conclusion to draw would be that I'm some sort of Billy-no-mates, weirdo stalker, which would be accurate. Once I thought I heard the slow, sad chords of Ida Cox drifting from his open kitchen window, but I might have been mistaken.

I have to give Chuck credit; he clearly respects me enough to have taken me at my word. That or I didn't mean much to him at all and hurling out our friendship has been easy for him. Either way, there's no denying it, he's given me space. Acres of it, oceans of it. Space that I'd hoped to fill with my relationship with Roberto.

Fat chance.

I have made myself available for Roberto. I have renewed my efforts to communicate, share interests and act supportively but I get the feeling I'm on a one-way street to nowhere.

Despite feeling as rough as the bottom of a budgie's birdcage on the Saturday evening, following my dinner with Chuck and Roberto's sleepover party at Ana-Maria's, I decided that Roberto and I had to go out for the evening – on a date.

Paolina returned from the hills, and while I don't know if she had categorically resolved anything while gazing down from those majestic heights, she looked fresher on return and was happy to give Roberto and me the night off. Roberto took less persuading to take time away from the bar than he had ever done before. I wanted to be encouraged by that but I couldn't help but feel his actions were the actions of a guilty man.

We both dressed carefully. I wore the long white linen gypsy dress that I'd bought when I thought I might be crushing grapes with my feet. I painstakingly applied full make-up and hoped it could somehow shield me. Maybe I should have bought one of those festival masks from Venice; it might have come in useful – I needed something to hide behind. Roberto wore a shirt I'd never seen before. We took a cab to Valdagno and we travelled in the loudest silence I've ever endured. When we arrived at the cosy trattoria Roberto asked the waiter for a quiet, corner table, which I found encouraging. Although by the time the evening was over I think we both secretly believed that it might have been wiser to sit near a boisterous party of twelve; perhaps their noise would have cloaked our conversational lapses.

I had resolved not to talk about Ana-Maria. I don't have to dignify the situation by talking about it. I will not allow her to become important. Instead I asked lots of questions about the bar. I faked an avid interest in the takings, the music, and the choice of decor. I reiterated some of my own suggestions and Roberto responded to them enthusiastically; I did not chide him and remind him that it wasn't the first time I'd shared with him my ideas about cool bathrooms and happy hours, instead I assured him I'd go online and look up suppliers of glass basins.

I insisted we order multiple courses, although it quickly became apparent that neither of us had big appetites that night. Plump scallops, vibrant sun-blush tomatoes and shiny fat olives were disrespectfully poked and prodded but not eaten. We ordered an expensive bottle of wine and under normal circumstances I'd have happily cracked open a second, but I realized that I couldn't risk getting squiffy. I have never done anything especially terrible while under the influence (except throw up in Chuck's loo, but the sooner I forget all about that night the better), but then I haven't done anything especially admirable while under the influence either. With Herculean effort I could just about keep my evil insecurities subdued beneath a swathe of calm. Alcohol would encourage me to slip into a filthy pit of jealousy, fear and unhappiness. I realized that I had to be very careful, very careful indeed.

The conversation between us pit-pattered back and forth, rarely drying up completely but never flowing with any conviction. I just wanted things to be like they were before. No, that's not quite right; I wanted them to be as I believed they could be. I wanted us to eat our meal together and then for us to dash home for rampant, *fruitful* sex. But if that was not to be, I at least wanted to introduce the subject of IVF.

The breadstick scratched the roof of my mouth. Really, I shouldn't have been picking at it; there were so many more delicious choices lying in front of me – barely touched. I'd intended to be bubbly and vibrant. I'd wanted to logically discuss this matter calmly, judiciously and, most importantly, effectively. My tongue lay fat and useless.

Eventually I muttered, 'I think I need to register at the local doctor's.'

'Are you ill?' Roberto asked, momentarily pausing from

mopping up his creamy sauce with inch-thick chunks of bread.

'No, but I think it would be a good idea for him to know me and know my history; know *our* history, in fact.' I looked at Roberto meaningfully. I wasn't sure if he would feign ignorance at what I was getting at or fly off the handle and insist I never speak of such things again. When did I stop knowing him? He surprised me by shrugging.

'If you want to.'

Encouraged, I added, 'I want – I need to talk to him about IVF.'

Roberto carefully put down his bread, picked up his napkin and wiped his mouth. He stared at me for what felt like a week and then said, 'I will not consider it, Elizabeth. I have said so much before.'

He seemed strangely intimidating, and movie images of mafia gangsters threatening cement shoes sprang to my mind.

I drew breath and reminded him, 'But you owe me, Roberto. *Now* you owe me.'

I have registered at the local doctor's and I have had my first appointment with him, where I passed over my medical records and, with the assistance of Paolina, who acted as a marvellous interpreter, added the human detail to the printed notes.

The doctor immediately agreed to refer me to the fertility expert in Bassano del Grappa who advises on IVF procedure. The appointment is likely to come through within the month. He was pleasant and reassuring.

I tried to be encouraged but found it impossible to be

as cheery as I wanted to be. I could not banish my doubts and nervousness. The doctor assumed I was losing hope, rather than plotting how best to extract sperm from an unwilling husband. Unsurprisingly, we haven't had sex since he spent the evening away from home. I keep meaning to. I want to, by way of proving that I trust him, but something stops me. He's no keener; we sleep clinging to the opposite sides of the bed.

'I am sure you and your husband have many avenues to explore before you give up hope,' the doctor said with a confident beam.

I didn't mention Roberto's position on IVF; it would have spoilt the moment.

I have not seen Ana-Maria; she no longer comes into the bar. Roberto is still often absent for hours on end at any time of the day or evening. I regularly hunt out the bar diary, which is now left conspicuously behind the whisky, and I make an obvious effort to check it for appointments whenever he's not around; he has made an equally striking effort to ensure there are appointments detailed in the diary to explain his absences. I'm grateful to him for colluding in what I fear to be an illusion of innocence. Sometimes he writes contact numbers, sometimes he doesn't. I have never called him on one of those numbers or on his mobile. I cannot hint that I might suspect an affair because once acknowledged it can't be avoided; ignored it will go away. I'm sure it will. I need to give the impression I believe in him and that I trust him. But this can only be achieved if I don't slap-bang right up against anything that might prove otherwise.

52

23 May

Some things are constant. Not love – apparently – or friendship, or even dreams, so I suppose I ought to take some sort of perverse comfort in the fact that Raffaella continues to be as invidious as ever. Her loathing of me is, at least, constant. In the beginning she had dozens of ways to make it clear that she did not consider me family; now it appears she has thousands.

Before, she plucked Roberto's dirty clothes out of the basket and ignored mine, preferring to run a wash on half full rather than to help me out; now she contrives to always be using the machine whenever I have time away from the bar, so that I have to put on a load in the middle of the night or use the town's launderette. In the past she insisted on preparing meat dishes; now she doesn't even put a place setting at the table for me. She has never paid me a wage, and recently she has repeatedly asked Roberto if we can contribute more of our savings towards the bar's refit. I told him that I didn't want all our savings used up this way. I'm aware that we may very well need funds for the IVF treatment. He said I wasn't to worry, but I do worry, so I withdrew half of the savings and opened a new account in my own name. I have yet to find the moment to tell him this.

This morning I returned from the language school and

dragged my feet towards Raffaella's place. I have a serious amount of homework to do for Signor Castoro and I can't decide where I ought to study. Foolishly I have left it until now, Friday, to attempt – just as I did when I was a kid at school and left homework until the last moment. The bar is too noisy and distracting nowadays; of course I'm pleased that it's no longer a ghost town, but it used to be a convenient and private place to hide. I know that if I sit in the piazza and try to study my mind will drift and my eyes will close. The Italian sun shines constantly and confidently now. The hot weather is great on so many levels (nice tan, long nails, better wardrobe), but not especially conducive to work. My alternative is studying in my bedroom at Raffaella's. Even when temperatures are soaring that place causes me to shiver. I sigh and cross my fingers that she'll be in the bar or at the market haggling with some poor soul about the cost of asparagus.

As Raffaella's comes into view I immediately spot that she's home (bad news) and that she's being industrious (disastrous news). My experience of Raffaella being industrious is that she's even grumpier and bossier than usual, and she actually does very little herself but anyone within a five-mile radius gets dumped with a long list of chores. When she decided that she was going to grow her own vegetables last month, I discovered that this meant I was in for four days' back-breaking hard labour with a spade. Raffaella is clearly having some sort of clear-out. As I approach the house I watch her dragging cardboard boxes and black plastic sacks of junk out into the yard.

'*Buon giorno*,' I call politely and insincerely. I only do so because I don't know the Italian for drop dead. Raffaella doesn't reply but unusually she does at least acknowledge me. In fact she throws out something like a smile; a sneer I suppose. My Italian has improved enough so that I can now speak to her; she still often chooses not to understand me, but not today.

'What are you doing?'

'I am discarding rubbish. Making more space.'

'A clear-out is always very refreshing, isn't it?' I comment breezily. I should know; it was me who had to drag about a zillion bags of broken picture frames and moth-eaten tablecloths from the attic to make a nice room for Raffaella. 'Which room are you clearing?'

'Yours.'

'Mine?'

'I see you have not unpacked your cases yet. I think you no want all the extra stuff you bring with you. My son he is forever tripping up on it. I decide to throw it away.'

'What?' I grab a plastic sack off her and frantically root inside. Oh my God! She is throwing out my wardrobe. I scramble through the soulless sack to discover several of my favourite tops and skirts. I pick up another bag and find dresses, jeans and underwear. Raffaella turns away and goes back into the house, presumably to find more of my worldly goods. Stunned, I quickly and haphazardly root through the half-dozen bags and three cardboard boxes that are casually tossed by the bins. It only takes moments for me to establish that she has thrown out about three-quarters of everything I own. Besides clothes, the nasty witch has thrown out make-up, CDs, books, my Christmas tree decorations, even my deodorant! I am staggered and bewildered into a shocked silence and for a few minutes I stand by the bins, guarding my possessions; it is all I can do to instruct myself to breathe. What the hell is going on? Have I died? This sure seems a lot like hell, and seeing my worldly goods piled in chaotic heaps next to the bins makes me feel eerily obliterated.

I want to run indoors and demand to know what Raffaella thinks she is doing. I want to yell and scream and even hit her. Yes, I am that vile. I want to hit an old woman, I am so furious and miserable and tiny. I don't charge indoors to lay out my mother-in-law. For one thing I daren't risk leaving my stuff, in case it is nicked or collected by the bin men. For another, even in this state of vile fury and misery I know that I'd never be able to look my parents in the eye again if I resorted to battering the old cow.

I struggle to pick up all the bags at once and I drag them back into the kitchen. Raffaella is nowhere to be seen, so I dash back outside to collect the remaining three boxes. I carefully stack them on top of one another. It's a precarious balancing act but I want to take them all inside in one trip as I daren't risk leaving my other things unattended for too long. Irrationally I have visions of her setting fire to them in the kitchen. I feel like some heroine in a movie playing a homeless refugee desperately trying to hang on to her chattels and dignity. I'm aware that in those movies the heroine usually starts with everything and loses the lot; it's not a helpful thought.

By the time I get inside the house I'm panting under the weight of the boxes. Roberto often accuses me of reading light novels – well, let me say, there's nothing light about them when you are lugging a box of them across the yard.

Raffaella is calmly sitting in the kitchen now. She's

drinking coffee and munching on an apple. She looks self-satisfied, almost serene.

'What the hell do you think you are doing?' I demand. I am not serene. I am blazing.

'I clean up my son's room. You no do so. I have to do it.'

'You threw my clothes in the bin.'

'You have many. Too many.'

'And my books, my hairbrush and my ... my ... mascara.' I spit out the words as I grab items from the bags and boxes and slam them on to the large kitchen table.

Raffaella takes another bite of her apple; a fly settles on her hand. I want to bat away the fly and I want to shove the apple down her throat. Whole.

'My son is used to a tidy home,' she comments calmly. 'I discuss the clean with my son.'

Is it possible that she really doesn't know what she has done wrong? Can she honestly believe that it's acceptable to throw out my possessions? No. No she cannot. Raffaella has declared outright war; a nuclear wipe-out, in fact, with all the associated carnage. Packing my suitcase and buying me a plane ticket home would have been less of an avowal of her hatred for me.

I decide to cut to the chase. I stare at her, although she's keen to keep her currant-like eyes averted; she concentrates on carefully slicing another chunk of apple and eats it off the knife. Her hands are mottled with liver spots and her skin looks too loose for her bones. I should pity this old woman but I don't harbour any sentimentality or affection for her; I loathe her.

'Listen to me, Raffaella, because I'm only going to say

this once.' My voice is low and yet the rage is palpable. I breathe deeply and try with every iota of self-control I possess to refrain from ripping off her head. 'I am Roberto's wife and I am not going anywhere. Do you understand? I am not giving him up to you. So never, ever touch my things again. For that matter, do not even go into my bedroom again.' I feel proud and relieved that I've reached the end of the sentence without cracking or crying.

'It is my house,' she replies confidently. Now she meets my eye. Having wanted this I suddenly feel petrified. She's not abashed, or ashamed or repentant. She's evil. Pure evil and I'm terrified. A realization creeps upon me and wraps its cold, bony bleakness around my heart.

I might not win this.

After I have returned all my possessions to my bedroom I march around to the bar and demand that Roberto comes for lunch with me. He sees that I am livid with rage and therefore agrees instantly; he knows a scene is not great for business.

Over an enormous plate of spinach and ricotta lasagne (which I don't touch) I tell Roberto of Raffaella's latest insult.

'No, Mamma did not mean to offend you. She wanted to help. Maybe she got carried away. You should perhaps have unpacked your clothes. The suitcases are a nuisance.'

'I couldn't unpack; we haven't got any wardrobe space!' I yell with indignation. 'Roberto, you know that your mother was being a bitch. She hates me. She's hated me from day one and she wants to make my life hell on earth. Plus, she's succeeding.'

Roberto sighs but has the decency to give up defending his mother. 'I'll put a lock on the door.'

'It's not enough; she'll pick it if she wants to or just break the door down.' I believe the woman has no limits.

'Can't you try to get along with her?'

'I've tried. You know I have.'

'Try harder.'

I glare at him. 'We have to get our own place.'

'We can't afford it.'

'We can, we'll use our savings.'

'That's money we need for the bar refit.'

'Who says so?' My voice squeaks with indignation. I gawp at Roberto. This is becoming impossible. Why won't he listen to me? I hope to God that he'll see sense. I reach towards his hand but he pulls back and picks up the menu.

'Do you want cake?'

The Italians, men and women alike, enjoy cakes in a way that puts me in mind of a time I never knew in Britain; an innocent pre-world war time. I've often watched them, at about four or five in the afternoon, dress up and wander to Panifico Pasticceria to choose a slice of heaven. I've noticed that it can take an Italian an hour to eat just one slice of cake. They savour every morsel and it's a delight to watch, quite different from the greedy gobbling that you see at Gregg's bakers back home. The Italians know how to celebrate food, and life becomes a party every afternoon because of that. I love the way they buy packages of freshly baked pieces to give to friends on Sunday mornings. The gifts are not dumped in greasy paper bags but presented in cardboard boxes which are adorned with masses of twirling colourful ribbons. Today I cannot be distracted. Even by cake.

'Do you know, the worst of it was that she implied she had not only a right to do this terrible thing to me but that she had your blessing too!' I groan.

'Believe me, Elizabeth, she tell me she is going to clean our room but I had no idea she would throw out your clothes.'

'Of course I believe you.' Although I find it depressing that we are in a position that he has to protest his innocence over such a bizarre incident. 'It was the way she called you "my son" throughout. *Mio figlio, mio figlio.* She always does that. It's so annoying.'

'I am her son.'

'You are also my husband but I don't call you *my husband* all the time, I call you Roberto.'

'It's a language thing,' says Roberto with a dismissive wave of his hand. 'What you call it? A language barrier.'

'It's certainly something to do with territories,' I mutter ominously.

'OK. Maybe,' he concedes. 'But the fact remains I have been her son longer than I have been your husband; maybe it's habit. In another thirty years you will forget my name and only describe me in terms of how I relate to you.'

'No, I won't.'

We wait. He's hoping the conversation is closed, I'm wondering how I make my way into a trickier one. I take the bull by the horns. We're not in Spain but still the metaphor seems relevant enough.

'This morning I got a letter confirming the appointment date to see the fertility specialist.'

'This is horseshit, Elizabeth. I tell you I will not see an IVF doctor. I will not do it.' Roberto slams his fist on to the table. The espresso cups leap off the saucers and land with a clatter. A fork falls on to the ground.

'Why not?' I yell back with exasperation. 'Is it the fact that it's not a guaranteed method? Are you worried I'm going to be disappointed? I know there's no certainties but I'd rather try than not.' Roberto stays silent. 'Just tell me, just talk to me. I don't understand why you won't even discuss it. Is it the health risks? To me? For the child?' He moves his head a fraction, not necessarily in response to what I am asking, more of an exasperated shrug.

The warm sun is stroking my cheek and luckily catches my tears of vexation and self-pity before Roberto notices them. The waiter comes and clears our table. He looks at me in an increasingly familiar, mildly chastising way and asks why I haven't eaten much of my lasagne. I assure him it was delicious but that I'm full. The truth is my throat is constricted with tension and I can barely swallow. He offers me three alternative dishes. Each time I have to disappoint the concerned waiter and insist that I've eaten enough. Finally, he tuts and walks away, shaking his head, looking as though I've just kicked his puppy. I feel an overwhelming sense of being a massive disappointment. And not just to the waiter. Normally I'm amused by this excessive concern, which is always shown by waiters when a plate is returned anything other than licked clean. On one occasion a chef came out of the kitchen to ask me why I hadn't finished his Sicilian artichoke fettuccine. Today I find the concern overwhelming, almost intrusive, and can barely stay civil. Roberto and I sit in a gloomy silence and I begin to wonder how long we can both endure it.

Roberto stands up and casually tosses his wallet on the table. 'I need to pee, pay the bill –' then as an afterthought – 'please.'

His wallet is as familiar as my own purse. I bought him it for our last wedding anniversary, which was approximately a million years ago. From the outside the wallet looks like a straight, smart, regular wallet; inside there is a cartoon illustration of a buxom, blonde beauty drawn in the style that was popular in adverts in the nineteen-fifties. The tongue-in-cheek twist always raises a smile. The leather feels warm and comfortable under my touch. Automatically I root through, looking for euros, barely noticing the contents of the wallet as it is so familiar to me: credit cards, notes, a photo of me, condom.

Condom?

I freeze. The shock of such an alien item snuggling in Roberto's wallet slaps me so viciously that I can almost feel the angry sting on my cheek. Why does he have a condom in his wallet? Stupid question. I don't suppose he's planning on filling it with water and dropping it from the clock tower. *We've* never used contraception, obviously.

In the cruellest moment of my life so far, I simultaneously understand two things. Roberto is definitely sleeping with Ana-Maria. There is no longer any margin for error or self-delusion. And secondly, he wants me to know that this is the case.

53

There is not a fraction of a second when I doubt where I need to go now. My only concern is that he won't be home. I hammer on his door, I know his timetable inside out and know that he will have stopped teaching at 12.15 p.m., but maybe he hasn't come straight back to Veganze, maybe he's gone away for the weekend. I pray this isn't the case and pound my fists with an unseemly desperation against the dark wood. Just as I'm about to run around the back of the apartment to check if his car is parked up, Chuck pokes his head out of the window; he looks concerned that I'm some sort of life-threatening lunatic. It's true to say I am out of my mind. He lets me in and I leap up the stairs two at a time; the door to his apartment is open. He's standing there, waiting for me, looking anxious and wary.

'Roberto is having sex with Ana-Maria,' I pant. I'm not used to exercise; legging it across the piazza and around to Chuck's has cost me.

'Right,' Chuck says hesitantly. I study his face. Did he know? Had he guessed?

'I suppose everyone in the town has put two and two together before I have,' I say carefully. 'The difference being, I didn't want to know,' I add.

'I'm sorry,' he says sincerely.

I push him back inside his apartment and slam the door closed behind us. I place my finger on his lips.

'*You* have nothing to be sorry for.'

His lips feel like warm plump cushions under my fingertips. He doesn't brush me away, instead he gently touches my cheek and while the touch is feather-light I feel pinned down, almost tied to him. Suddenly I know certain things quite clearly. I know that Chuck has been my best friend since I arrived here, my only friend, much more than a friend. I know he doesn't want babies but right this second that doesn't matter to me, my marriage is a decaying mess. I need to feel love. I know I want to kiss Chuck.

I kiss him. He kisses back. Carefully at first, eyes open and staring at me, but quickly he ups tempo and starts to kiss me long and hard. His kiss is burly and dark and overwhelming. Deeper and more adult than I was anticipating. His kisses feel as surprising and exotic as my very first kiss but as sexy and confident as I could have hoped. We kiss forever. He kisses my lips and my jaw, my cheeks, my eyelids, my ears, my neck. We lose track of time and just roam. The kissing is all-consuming; the anger, pain and humiliation that I have endured today, and for months, sluice away and I find it impossible to think of anything other than Chuck's lips. Until he eventually yanks his T-shirt over his head in one rapid, impressive movement, then I think about his body. His torso is beautiful. I knew he had wide shoulders and golden skin but who could have guessed at the tightly defined abs? And who would have known that a tiny sprinkling of freckles would make me melt.

Unexpectedly all that has gone before this is shadowy. I begin to believe that other kisses and other men, even

Roberto, were in anticipation of this. And all the words Chuck and I have exchanged, and all those we've failed to articulate, seem unessential. We're stripped and left in an open silence; exposed by our want and need of each other. Embarrassingly, my knees buckle with the enormity of what is inevitably going to happen next between us. I wobble but I don't want to stop it or even delay it a moment longer. We fall towards the floor, not even bothering to make it the few extra metres to the sofa or bedroom.

I notice the floorboards are dusty; a tiny spider scuttles out of the shadows, across the hall and then once again out of sight. The sun is flooding in through the sitting room window, and it cascades in a stripe across the hallway; Chuck has not pulled the shutters. The warmth fills the air. It's not pleasant, it's cloying and sweaty, but I don't care. I don't need silk sheets or candlelight for this. I can hear traffic buzzing and tooting and voices laughing and shouting in the distance. It seems like the right music to me, more real than even the blues ladies who normally accompany my romantic and amorous moments by crooning out a sad or dreamy ballad.

It's frenzied and fast and startling. Chuck's lips tangle into mine and we're kissing so deeply I can't tell us apart. I inch up my skirt and yank at my tiny panties, he grapples with his flies and then almost instantly sinks into me. There's no uncomfortable pain, no shock. My body accepts him as though it's been waiting for him. And maybe I have. I gape at him and he stares back. We hold each other in that look and never lose sight of what we are doing and who we are doing it with. Not for a second.

It feels astonishing. It feels crucial. It feels true. He's grunting and quivering and I'm moaning and shaking. We sound like the animals we are and I feel whole.

Of course the spirit of the sex means it's over in minutes. The urgency and unexpected nature dictated as much, but I feel released and fulfilled in a way that I'd stopped believing was possible. Our sex was not about making babies, it was not about fury, or revenge, or fear, or duty.

Which leads me to the question, what was it about?

The same thought must be nagging Chuck too, because as he goes to find tissues for us both he calls back from the bathroom.

'I need to know, Elizabeth, just for the record so to speak. Do you want me because you want me? Or do you want me because you are angry with your husband?'

I stand up and run to my lover. I throw my arms around him and push my body close up to his, not caring if my pretty summer dress becomes sticky with his love.

I hold his face in between my hands, look him in the eye and admit, 'When I saw the condom in Roberto's wallet I felt shocked and exposed but I was surprised to find that a big part of me felt relieved. I have wanted you for months now. I'm not angry with Roberto. I'm grateful to him. I get it now. This is the first favour he's done me in a long time.'

54

I don't want to stay in Veganze for a moment longer than necessary. The idea of hiding in Chuck's apartment is only appealing until I realize that there would be a point when I'd have to leave, or worse, I might be rooted out. Chuck says I'm not to panic. He runs me a deep bubble bath and tells me to enjoy a soak. I'm touched that he's remembered that one of my many grumbles about living with Raffaella is that she won't allow anything other than showers, as she insists it's a waste of hot water. Showering is my preferred daily method of hygiene, but sinking into a deep, creamy bath is something I love to do at least once a month by way of winding down. This is my first bath since I got here. As I wallow in the sensation of bubbles popping around me, Chuck packs a bag and makes a few calls.

Without discussing it, we are both aware of the impossibility of my going back to Raffaella's to pick up any of my things, although the chances are I'd probably find the lot stacked against the bins once again. Even so, I can't risk the horror of the rows that would certainly ensue. Of course those rows must come, but not yet. As if reading my mind, Chuck says, 'We'll buy you anything you need.'

'I don't need anything. I don't care,' I tell him firmly.

I probably should be more concerned than I am about the turn my life has taken in the last hour but for some reason I cannot summon the required hysteria. Oddly,

I feel that everything is as it should be; which is impossible, isn't it? My husband is having a long-term affair with his first love, I'm an adulterer, I'm homeless and I own nothing other than the clothes I stand up in, at least temporarily. How can this be as it should be? And yet it is. As I slide into the car next to Chuck I know I have everything I need right now.

We decide to go to Venice. I feel it will be my first time, because the visit with Ana-Maria and Roberto was not pleasurable and anyway it's now exposed as a farce. As Chuck and I drive, we chatter. Not about what has just happened or anything enormous at all, but about the things we've always chattered about when we travel side by side. We talk about the landscape, what's on the radio, our families and the things we'd like to do when we get to our destination. We do not talk about Roberto and Ana-Maria or even our loving. Neither of us knows what to say about any of that just now. The urgent loving on his hall floor recedes and yet is ever-present. I feel a live current zap between us and we are now connected in that ethereal, elusive and permanent way lovers are. The fact that our relationship is in every other way unchanged is a source of total joy to me. I've always believed that true lovers are best friends. Roberto and I have continued having sex for months after we stopped being friends. That sad reality blisters my mouth like an acidic wash.

This time, Venice is everything I hoped it would be. This time I don't feel rushed or pressured, I feel free and overwhelmed. I understand why, for centuries, writers have agonized over finding just the right words to express satisfactorily the splendour and uniqueness of the city. This place is a one-off. Even in late May when temperatures are rising and tourists are teeming, Venice has a wistful, fairytale quality that astounds me. It's rather odd that the reality of Venice on a sweltering, congested day doesn't disappoint me. I'm excited by it. So many things in Italy have not been as I imagined they would be and I have resented that. But I had not imagined that the shops in Venice would be full of flashing plastic gondolas or that there would be incongruous lines of cheap, nylon football shirts running the length of the Rialto – and I don't mind. They don't blot my romantic notions because I've never had a romantic notion about Chuck and me being in Venice. Our magic can't wear thin because he is unexpected. I wanted him but as a married woman I never seriously entertained the possibility of having him. So every moment we have together is a delicious surprise.

Roberto let me go. Or chucked me away. Depending on your viewpoint. It doesn't matter. The outcome is the same. I'm free to be, rather than to dream. A unique freedom.

We spend a lazy afternoon initially wandering around San Marco, the heart of the city. Surprisingly, I still do not think about Roberto and Ana-Maria, or Raffaella, or the bar. I have spent months agonizing over these individuals; I find I don't have any more energy to devote to their latest atrocities. My head can't take the weight of the situation on board. Instead I breathe in the moment. I enjoy the café orchestras and laugh at the cooing pigeons landing on people's shoulders and outstretched arms; I jump when they fly low past my head. Already fat, the pigeons scrounge food like church mice, continually scratching the pavement with their tiny claws. I marvel at the constant traffic of waiters serving alfresco diners.

Plates and glassware chink, people chatter, laugh, whistle and shout. It's boisterous and chaotic but it's alive.

Without my noticing it happening, Venice becomes slightly calmer and cooler and is slowly bathed in an indigo light as the orange glow of the sinking sun fades and is replaced by a crisp and confident moon.

'What next?' asks Chuck. It's a big question. Somehow I understand that he doesn't just mean ice-cream or cola?

'Sod it, I haven't thought about next.'

We have exhausted San Marco and we've wandered through the backwaters and boatyards of the quieter districts. We've ambled around the eastern district, Castello. A place that smelt of hard graft, a place whose charm comes from the fact that it is lived in. We've strolled to the south and stumbled upon the bohemian-chic Dorsoduro, which is crammed with artistic treasures, and then we've sauntered north. We've paused in the peaceful atmosphere of Cannaregio and marvelled at the delightful off-the-beaten-track churches. I particularly enjoyed them because, like me, Chuck is happy to have a quick look, buy a postcard and then move on. Mum and Dad would always squash any enthusiasm I had for a place by lingering an hour over every statue of Mary.

We've spent most of the early evening in the shaded narrow corridors but it's only now, when the moon is up, that I feel my first shiver. I lean my elbows on the iron railing of a bridge and gaze out on to the canals, enchanted. Chuck hands me the zip-up top we bought earlier and I pop it on.

I watch as middle-aged, affluent tourists drift by on gondolas. We've resisted the cliché. It's possible to enjoy the stars glistening in the navy sky without shelling out the hundred quid. Besides, as I haven't even got my handbag with me, Chuck has paid for everything today from the delicious lunch to the bird-feed for the pigeons in the square. There was a truly odd moment when he bought me the zip-up, knickers and a toothbrush. The familiarity between us is like that of a six-month relationship and yet we'd shagged for the first time only six hours before. I might have expected that him picking out panties for me was going to seem a bit peculiar, but the weird thing was, it wasn't peculiar at all. Our sudden intimacy seems balanced and appropriate.

'I think we need a drink,' he suggests.

We find a quiet bar with outside seating and order a carafe of house red and some chocolate ice-cream; we had a late lunch and ate well then, so neither of us fancies a proper meal. The red wine is full and intense. I savour it, as it's my first drink of the day. Without discussing it, Chuck and I seemed to agree that it would be better to choose lemonade at lunch. I needed a clear head. Now, as the day is coming to a close, Chuck judges it perfectly and realizes that I need a loose tongue.

'Are we running away?' I ask.

'Temporarily, yes,' he states. 'I think you need some space.'

Momentarily I panic. Have I read today all wrong? I thought Chuck and I were connected. In a tricky position – yes – but somehow connected. I thought he understood that. Maybe I was just a quick and easy lay to him. Well, I was in fact exactly that. But I'd thought – hoped – that I was more. What if he has got a girlfriend? We haven't spoken for a month. It's possible. I should have established the facts before I jumped his bones. Funnily enough

I never worried about that at the time. There were brief moments, before I put an embargo on our friendship, when I thought maybe Chuck had feelings for me – it was almost impossible to know for certain because I was with Roberto. What am I talking about? I'm still with Roberto. Not in the same way, of course, but –

Aaghh, this is all so complicated. The floodgate has opened. Everything that I've been ignoring all day threatens to drown me now. I take a deep breath. I know that I have to ask some difficult questions and perhaps face some unsavoury truths but it's better than the alternative. Roberto and I always skirted around the tricky issues, and in the end not only did we not know how to talk to one another, we couldn't remember why we'd bother. I can't – won't – let the same thing happen with Chuck.

Another deep breath. 'If you think I need space, what was the episode in your hallway about?' I ask.

'Not space from me,' says Chuck, partly amused, partly disbelieving. 'Well, at least not unless you want it,' he adds, showing his own insecurity.

'No, no, not at all,' I gabble, 'I definitely don't want space from you. I had that over the last month and it was terrible.' I realize that right now I'm not exactly following the rulebook on how to play it cool but I don't think this is the time for games.

'That said, I'm not a fan of people jumping from one relationship to the next,' adds Chuck, warily.

'I've never done anything other.'

'I know,' he says ominously. 'You told me.' That's the problem with having a relationship with your best friend, they know everything about you. 'Personally I think it does a person good to have time in between one relationship and the next. Time to reflect and learn from what's happened.'

'Yeah, but you are American,' I say, in an attempt to laugh off his comment.

He puts his fingers on my lips to shush me, echoing my action earlier today. Remembering the lusty, needy sex makes me shiver, but in a good way.

'I'm just saying this probably isn't the wisest thing either of us has ever done,' he says.

My heart sloshes down through my flip-flops and lands in a squelching mess on the cobbled pavement. He's back-pedalling.

Then he adds, 'But I can't see that there is an alternative for us. I've looked for an alternative ever since I met you. I wanted to find a way not to end up like this but here we are and I just can't bring myself to be regretful about it.' He holds his hands in the air as if surrendering to the situation.

My heart jumps right back up again and settles in my mouth. He's not back-pedalling! He's taking the brakes off. Speechless with delight, I lean into him and kiss him hard.

55

The second time we make love is quite unlike the first. This time we both know it isn't the last.

We talked until the sun disappeared and the sky was coal-black. We talked in the shadows and warm air and when the air became chilled we moved inside the bar and talked and drank some more. The floor-to-ceiling wooden double doors were spread open and I longed to open my legs too.

I told him some of my ambitions and frustrations with teaching and because I'd drunk a stack of wine it became impossible to distinguish between the two. They jealously meshed into one another, making no sense. I talked about Alison and we speculated about whether Fiona and she would go the distance. Chuck talked about his mates here in Italy and his best buddy back home. He asked me some odd trivial things like when did I pass my driving test and have I ever been to a football match – except he says soccer.

He laughs at me and with me; when he does so his entire face explodes with a life-seizing guffaw that I adore. He contradicts me and agrees with me. He informs and makes mistakes. He's astoundingly authentic.

After our ice-cream and two bottles of wine we asked the waiter if he knew of a hotel that might have a room. We both feared that the only hotel that would have space at this time of year would be a flea-pit. The waiter shrugged and looked doubtful but said that we could try his girlfriend's cousin's place, which was back around the San Marco's square and Rialto bridge area. He scribbled the address on a piece of paper and wished us luck.

'It probably busy. Is very good hotel, very popular but you can only try. If you no try you no get,' he said wisely.

The best we were hoping for was an overpriced down-market tourist trap, but despite the odds it was a gem of a place and surprisingly reasonable. Al Sole Hotel is a beautiful fifteenth-century terracotta building which nestles in the ancient Palazzo Marcello. We stumbled into the reception fully expecting to be turned away, but we were told that they had just received a last-minute cancellation and amazingly they did have a room for us. In fact it was one of their better rooms, boasting a stunning view of the Tolentini Canal.

Some things are meant to be.

We lie on the heavily embroidered bedcovers and kiss one another, over and over again, for the longest time. I'm trying not to draw comparisons – it's never helpful – but I can't remember the last time Roberto and I kissed like that. We barely bother with a perfunctory peck on the cheek nowadays. I know Chuck is concerned that I am moving away from a monumental relationship with indecent haste, but the more I am with him the more I realize how dead my relationship with Roberto is and has been for quite some time. I just haven't wanted to admit it to anyone, least of all myself. As Chuck kisses me he caresses my arms, my legs, my shoulders, my back, and each stroke seems to brush away my sense of loneliness. With each startling contact I feel the frustration slip from my body and the disappointment drip out of my mind.

His fingers fix me, comfort me, and most thrilling of all, they excite me.

We shed our clothes unselfconsciously and lose ourselves in one another. Unhurriedly, so, so gradually, he kisses and licks and nibbles until I yelp with gratification. Slowly, slowly his tongue roves over my body and he uncovers unexpected places of pleasure that make me moan and whimper simultaneously. He pays attention to my wrists, the insides of my elbows, the backs of my knees. He nibbles my thighs and sucks my fingers. I think of nothing other than the texture of his skin, the smell of him and the taste of him, and he seems to be entirely concerned with making me squirm with delight. He explores my nipples, my stomach and my bush with a frank interest that borders on reverence. Soon limbs, sheets and sensations become entwined and muddled, yet I encounter an unexpected impression of lucidity and conviction. I like it here with Chuck. It feels good. It feels utterly right even when I weave my fingers through his blond hair and gasp with surprise that it is light hair in my hand, not dark.

When I think that I can't take any more and that I'll explode with longing if he continues his gentle exploration, he changes tempo. Suddenly, he thrusts, he plunges, he fills me. I groan with a searing mix of hurt and hope as I let this other man into my life.

I am done in with delight.

I want to reciprocate. I want to give him as much as he's given me, although I'm not sure it's even possible. I push him on to his back, wiggle down and take his cock into my mouth. He makes me feel so sexy; an acknowledged goddess. He sighs, writhes, slithers and groans until finally he shakes and becomes breathless, then lets out a loud moan which is bordering on the embarrassing and will probably have alarmed the people occupying the room next door. Through the open window I hear a cheer. I doubt it is related to our performance but it makes me smile anyway. Exhausted and replete, I tumble off his hot body and tuck myself under his arm.

'I wish I'd met you before,' I whisper.

'Where – among the fourteen lovers your husband is unaware of – would you like me to have fallen?'

'Anywhere,' I say with a bittersweet smile. 'Everywhere.'

My hair is damp with exertion and is sticking to my neck, my nipples are moist with his kisses and my thighs with his love. I smell of him and he smells of me but I feel immaculate. I feel sexy and wanted. Thrilled and thrilling. We hold one another, close, until our breathing becomes peaceful; we inhale and exhale in harmony. I am myself.

56

27 May

We make love for four days. We do eat, and drink, and walk, and talk in those four days, but even when we are doing those more mundane things we are making love.

Sometimes we ride fierce and fast, other times we choose stretched and slow. The temperature outside soars, and sweat runs down his back or slides between my buttocks, making our skin seem glittery and dazzling. He seems mesmerized by my large breasts, which bat him in the face when I ride on top. He laughs when I apologize for them.

'They are gorgeous, what are you apologizing for?'

'I've always hated my big boobs,' I admit.

'Well, I love them.'

'And they look even worse when I have a tan.' I panic at a vision of my big white udders slapping around my brown stomach when I get a tan this summer. I'm pretty sure Chuck will say I look fine but I'm not sure I'll be able to believe him. 'I've always wanted to sunbathe topless because if I get a tan my tan-lines make my boobs look even bigger.'

'That's crazy,' he teases. 'Next you'll be asking does my bum look big in these strap marks? You are absolutely beautiful, Elizabeth. How can you be anything other than proud of your body? You ought to be more confident and sure of yourself; if you want to sunbathe topless you should.'

Easier said than done. Whenever I'm with Chuck I can genuinely feel my esteem rise, but it's starting at a pretty low level after months with Roberto's and Raffaella's attacks.

'No, it's impossible with such huge breasts, it's too overt, too explicit. All I want is an even tan but their size says more than that, whether I like it or not.' Chuck kisses my left boob and for a moment I don't think it is such a terrible part of my body. 'It's OK for women with goose bumps for breasts, nothing they do appears overtly sexual. I envy them. Plus men always think women with small boobs are brighter than women with big chests.'

At this Chuck nearly chokes on my nipple as he laughs out loud.

'How do you work in a world so full of clichéd prejudices? Big breasts are vulgar. Italians are enigmatic. Americans are ignorant. Mother-in-laws are wicked. You have it all wrong.'

'Not all of it,' I say sulkily. I'm uncomfortable with him contradicting me and yet, thinking about it, Alison and my family contradict me from time to time. Actually, Alison contradicts me just about all the time. Perhaps it's a way of showing they care what I think. They care about me enough to want to help me to get it right. Maybe debate is OK. It's better than diktats at least.

'How does it work in your world then, Chuck?' I ask curiously.

'There are myriad possibilities,' he says with a smile.

It's a hopeful thought.

He leaves me gasping, astonished, vulnerable, venerated.

I feel him in every crevasse and contour of my being. His large and lovely body takes possession as I come again, and again and again. With each wave of bliss that gushes between my legs my past is condensed and my future looms large. I begin to wonder how I could have lived thus far without this precise blend of passion and reassurance.

'When did you start to want me in this way?' I ask curiously.

'From the very moment I saw you I thought you were hot.'

'Really?' I sit bolt upright with excitement.

'Really,' he confirms calmly.

'I had no idea.'

'It would have been very wrong of me to give you any idea because within about a nanosecond of meeting you, you told me to back off.'

'I did not!'

'Yes, you did. You told me that your husband's family owned Bruno's. Bringing a husband into the conversation so early on was a pretty clear signal and I liked that about you. I like faithful women.' We both fall silent as we guiltily consider that I'm being unfaithful right now. 'And I like it even better when hot women are unfaithful with me,' says Chuck with a laugh which breaks the tension.

I consider hitting him with a pillow but can't bear the idea of behaving like someone in an advert for mattress sales, so I resist. Chuck kisses me carefully and slowly for quite some time. When he pulls away he continues, 'I didn't expect to think about you again after that first encounter in the piazza but then I found myself repeatedly going there on the offchance I'd see you. I didn't plan to seduce you away from your husband; I thought I could be a good buddy to you. That's all I hoped for. It was weird – I just felt I needed to be near you. Anyway, whenever I turned up at the bar you'd invariably be in rubber gloves, cleaning crap for him. I thought you were madly in love with him.'

'But then?'

'But then as I got closer to you I saw that you were unhappy. I think I saw it before you did.' He stares at me, examining the effect his words are having on me. I know he's trying to tread softly, softly.

'Did you know Roberto was having an affair?'

He looks away. 'I heard rumours, but there are always rumours.'

'Did you believe the rumours?'

'It didn't matter what I believed. It was all up to you. You had to come to me. All I could do was wait for you.'

We like waking up early and eating breakfast on the balcony. The early morning sun shimmers on the canal, like a million diamonds, shafts of stars, or perhaps fairy dust. Then we take a walk. By midday the water is calm and more prosaic and we usually go to bed to make our own magic. In the evening the water is lit by boats and waterside restaurants. Boats slice through the sea, leaving lines of waves behind them. It puts me in mind of the lines of faux-clouds that planes leave in the sky. Imitation waves. Imitation clouds. These manmade attempts appear ludicrous or heroic, depending on my mindset. We seem tiny and enormous by turn. Chuck catches me gazing out the window. He wraps his arms around my waist.

'Weren't we lucky to get this view,' he comments.

'Yes, it's a beautiful background to a nervous break-down.'

'Are you having a nervous breakdown?'

'No,' I admit, and pause before I add, 'but I feel I ought to be. It would be more respectable.'

'To hell with that.'

We revel in our salacious indolence. He combs his fingers through my hair and I muse, 'If only I could keep one inch of you all to myself. So that I could keep hold of it even when you go out of the room and I'd never be alone.' One inch is not so much to ask from such a big guy.

'Which inch would you pick?'

'The tip of your penis, obviously.' We both laugh, but I know really that I'd choose his lips that kiss and contradict me.

I can smell my own sex even when we are walking through the streets of Venice or dawdling around a museum; it smells superb. Chuck fills me with possibility and confidence. It was supposed to feel odd. That's what I'd have thought likely, after years of making love with one man; a different man should feel anomalous.

But it doesn't.

It seems like his broad, powerful body was created especially to delight me. I begin to believe I was born a woman for this man.

'I feel wise and naïve at the same time when I'm with you.'

'What do you mean?'

'When I was twenty-seven I loved telling people I was twenty-seven and married, by which I meant established. What a child I must have seemed. Now I am a child that is thirty-two. I feel anything is possible again.'

I question him continuously, discovering the mammoth

things as well as the minutiae that make him who he is. I want to know everything about Chuck Andrews. I'm interested in his values, dreams, family and friends. I watch him all the time; sometimes he catches me staring at him and grins self-consciously. I study the tiniest detail. The way his hair parts, the mole on his neck, even the curve of his fingernails. I like knowing everything about him. I like everything I know about him.

57

28 May

'What did the unofficial yearbook say about you?' I ask.

It's the fifth day of our lovefest. This is a thought that has popped into my head from time to time and can now be voiced.

We are leaning over one of a million small bridges, staring out at the Tolentini Canal watching the afternoon sun joyfully skip on the water. There are two gondolas, moored. Despite being painted black they ooze glamour. One boat has ruby-red seats, the other has calm, regal blue; both boats are decorated with golden crests belonging to another age. Water laps and they bob, occasionally drifting into one another; as they gently nudge I am put in mind of lovers stealing quick kisses.

'The man most likely to seduce married women,' he says with a shy sigh.

'You are kidding, right?' I ask anxiously.

'No, 'fraid not.'

'Why did it say that? Did you have a reputation? Have you done this before?' I demand.

'Shush, calm down. I had a crush on one of the teachers in high school, that's all. Yes, she was married, but of course nothing ever happened. It was just the kids teasing me. I couldn't tell you when you first asked because you'd have taken it the wrong way. You'd have read more into it than it deserved.' Chuck shrugs.

'I guess.'

We both turn back to watching the bobbing boats but I feel a new tension in the air. He coughs.

'But while we are on the subject, there is something I need to tell you.' Chuck puts his arm around me and draws me closer. Oddly, despite the warm temperature and his closeness, I feel a chill. 'I don't want you to panic or freak out when I tell you this.'

'You're scaring me,' I say with a grin that doesn't make any real impression on my face or psyche. I don't want to hear anything other than words of love from this man and somehow I don't think he's about to whisper sweet nothings.

'You asked me if I've done this before and by this I assume you mean –' he falters.

'Had a relationship with a married woman,' I say bluntly. I don't want any room for error.

Chuck nods stiffly. 'When I first arrived in Veganze, I did have a fling with a married woman.'

'You what?' I wiggle out from under his arm.

'It isn't as bad as it sounds,' he says quickly, as his empty arms drop to his side.

'It sounds terrible,' I yell, scaring a pigeon; it takes off in a fluster of flapping wings. I'm tempted to do the same. Chuck must sense my instinct to flee because he grabs my wrists and holds them tightly. He pulls me close to him and looks me in the eye.

'Sweetheart, you have every right to be pissed off and scared, but hear me out. I really want to be honest with you. I arrived in Italy and I knew no one. I guess I was lonely. She was gorgeous.' Hearing him describe another woman as gorgeous causes me to shudder. 'First off, I didn't even know she was married and by the time I found out I was too far in.'

'You said it was a fling. How deep were you flung?' I demand angrily.

Chuck lets go of my wrists and runs his hands through his hair. Once again he turns to look out over the bridge and away from me as he confesses, 'We were seeing each other for about six months, I suppose, in total.'

'Six months!' All thoughts of Chuck being a kind and wonderful man flood from my head. He's a vile home-wrecker. A *serial* vile home-wrecker? I stare at him with something that must be approaching disgust, because he rushes on to justify his immorality.

'When I did find out that she was married she insisted that her marriage was dead and that she was only staying with him for the sake of her family.'

'She had children!' I want to punch him. Maybe I am over-reacting but I really don't think I can stand any more shocks. I thought Chuck was so decent and straight-forward. My confidence in our relationship, so recently towering, begins to topple. I *need* him to be decent and straightforward; I'm not strong enough yet to deal with any more duplicity – not after Roberto.

'No, no.' Chuck looks pained and panicked. 'I'm not explaining this at all well. When I mentioned family I meant her parents. Her father was a judge and her hus-band was a local politician. She said that her family wouldn't be able to rise above the scandal of her divorcing even though it was what both she and her husband wanted. It sounded plausible at the time.'

He must have been in love with her. Only love makes us blind to such clichés and lies. Chuck is a good-looking, intelligent man in his thirties – of course I should expect him to have been in love before; it would be weirder if he hadn't, but hearing about it is miserable.

'She told me that she and her husband had come to some arrangement. She fed me a load of lies. I believed her for a time and I cared for her for a time, then I stopped believing her and stopped caring for her so I finished it.'

I look warily at Chuck. I want to believe him but my faith in constancy has taken such a massive bruising of late. I'm not sure if I can. I'm not sure if I have that sort of trust left.

'Why did you wait until now to tell me about this woman?' I ask suspiciously.

'I wanted to tell you before, but I felt such a fool and I thought you'd think less of me. I know you worked so hard to keep your marriage going under terrible conditions. I know you place enormous store on the institution. So do I, come to that. Whatever you might be thinking now.'

I want to believe him but a smidgen of doubt has snook into my consciousness. I can't help but wonder if Chuck genuinely respected my vows or whether he was scared of making the same mistake twice. I look at him hoping to see the glow that surrounded him just ten minutes ago when I believed he was unique and noble. He looks nervous and mortal.

'I thought if you knew about Ornella you'd despise me.'

I despise her. I don't even want to hear her name. The ferocity of my jealousy is stunning. Roberto was as good as shagging Ana-Maria in front of me and yet I feel more resentment and envy towards this awful Ornella – not much more than a foolish indiscretion in Chuck's past – than I ever felt towards Ana-Maria.

'So why tell me now? Why not leave me in blissful ignorance?'

'For one thing there's always a risk of someone else telling you. I really don't want you to think I'm some sort of weirdo with a thing for married women, but more important than the risk of gossip I believe that there shouldn't be any secrets between us; there shouldn't be any taboo subjects. We're better than that.'

He's right of course, although it's exhausting that honesty always seems to involve a certain risk or backlash. I want to demand reassurances off Chuck. I want him to promise that he will tie himself to my side forever and never hurt and expose me but, instead, love and protect me. Forever and then some. But I can't demand that. It's not fair. Chuck must not end up paying for Roberto's mistakes. I rally. I take a deep breath and scramble to muster every last ounce of dignity and trust.

'OK, it was a long time ago. Thanks for telling me. It doesn't matter.'

I bury my head on his chest to give myself a moment to comprehend what's been said and a moment to calm myself. He closes his large hands around me and strokes my hair.

'You're not worried, are you?' he asks with concern.

'No.' A little.

'There's no reason,' he says confidently. 'I'm yours. This is all about you. This is not some sort of game to me.'

We go back to the hotel and make love with a level of intensity that I had no idea existed. With every caress and kiss and thrust and fall Chuck seems to be trying to reassure me that what's past is past. I shove Ornella out of my head and allow myself to sink into his lavish attentions. After hours of love I find that all I am concerned with is becoming familiar with the exact quality of his full, warm lips, the soft cushions of his fingertips and the coarse, dense hairs on his legs. I want to envelop everything. I want to hold tight. I want to gobble him up.

58

We lie in the darkened bedroom, lit only by the moonlight that cascades through the window. My eyes sting and my lids droop but I don't want to fall asleep yet. All my life I've fallen into deep slumber after orgasm; like some sort of bloke. This orgasm sleep pattern is only a problem now that I want to talk throughout the night.

'It's funny, isn't it, that lovers even on different sides of the world look at the moon and they say they see the same moon and feel some sort of connection,' I muse.

I really ought to be more self-conscious over these amateur attempts at discussing the questions that occupied the metaphysical poets centuries ago, but I'm not. I feel free to chatter about anything from Victoria Beckham's new hair length to the moon. It surprises me that I even know who the metaphysical poets are and what they discussed. It goes to show that some of my mum and dad's force-fed knowledge is lodged in the dark nooks and crannies of my brain, after all. They'd be chuffed that I'm thinking in the abstract. To be fair, they are chuffed if I think of anything.

'Why is that funny?' he asks.

'Because it's true. It *is* the same moon and yet the sun is different everywhere. No one ever swears their undying love on the sun or looks at the sun and wonders whether their lover is staring at the same sun.'

The Italian sun is more ferocious than I remembered,

and sometimes I find myself longing for the insipid British rays. I nuzzle into his shoulder, smudging my existence into his. He pulls me a fraction closer still.

'You are such a hopeless romantic,' he teases.

'In fact, I am a very hopeful romantic,' I reply seriously.

'I suppose so.' He coughs, and instinctively I know that he's not about to suggest we order more champagne. I hope this isn't going to be another 'I slept with another married woman' confession – another, other married woman. I'm just coming to terms with this afternoon's confession. He starts tentatively, 'Elizabeth, the hotel manager says that this room is booked from tomorrow.'

'Oh, will we have to change rooms?' I ask.

'There are no other rooms.'

I freeze, and although I know he's not going to agree I suggest, 'So we should try to find a new hotel.'

Chuck sighs, kisses my forehead and says, 'It's time to go back, Elizabeth. We have to face the music. You've rested from the shock of Roberto and Ana-Maria's affair and Raffaella's bullying. You have even had enough time to make quite a complication of your own.' He pauses to kiss me and then continues, 'We need to get back and start to sort things out.' I try to shake my head but he insists. 'If nothing else we need to go back to work. We left the school in the lurch.'

I know he's right but I can't risk a reply. I'll howl if I do, and snot and saliva and stuff just aren't attractive. I force myself to nod tightly, then I roll away from him and try to feign sleep. I'm so angry with him for bringing our idyll to an end. Why can't we just continue as we are? As I ask myself the question I already know the answer. We would run out of money, we'd die of exhaustion (hey, but what a way to go, shagged to death), we'd lose our jobs, Alison and my parents would send out a search party. Obviously I haven't rung them in the past week. I left my mobile at Veganze but I couldn't call even from a public box; I haven't been able to find the words. I'm a coward and don't want to deal with any of this.

I can't imagine standing face to face with Roberto. What am I going to say to him? What has he to say to me? We are over, completely so, I realize that, but splitting up is enormous. We've been together for six years, my family think of him as one of theirs. Obviously his mother will be throwing a party, but even so, it's complicated. And what next for me? Staying in Italy seems ludicrous if I am not here with my Italian husband. But what is there to go back to in England other than a cramped flat where you can touch all four walls in the bathroom when sitting on the loo?

And Chuck? Where does Chuck fit into all of this? If I go back to England then we have no future together. Not that either of us has talked about a future.

I roll over and face Chuck. He's staring at me but he doesn't say a word. He's like that; he says his piece and then leaves it up to me to make what I will of his opinions. I like it that he doesn't go in for macho posturing and angry insistent decrees. I consider that it's probable he has kissed every inch of my body in the last five days; I know for certain that he's touched me in ways I hadn't thought possible. Maybe some women would have acted with more thought and restraint than I have. Some women would have held back their bodies and their hearts and calmly discussed the consequences of starting a relationship at this point. But I am not a prudent or discreet person. I never have been, and there are some tricks you just can't teach an old dog.

But what of babies?

The thought pops into my head and thumps me in the gut. It's lucky that I am lying down because I genuinely believe that I might collapse under the weight of that thought. I have betrayed my unborn babies. How could I have forgotten about them? What sort of mother am I? Well, one without kids obviously. It must be some sort of record, because almost a week has gone by without my longing for a baby. In the past six years I'm not sure a day has gone by without my brain and heart being seized with imaginings of having a child. But the longing for a family, while subdued by a week of incomparable passion, has not disappeared. I know myself well enough to understand that no matter what, my future *must* have a child in it. But Chuck doesn't want children. What did he say to me that day when we had lunch together in Bassano del Grappa? *I've never wanted babies. It's just not my thing at all.*

How can I reconcile these polar-opposite essentials?

Chuck trails his index finger up and down my arm and at some point I must fall asleep, too weary to chew it over any longer. I only realize as much when I wake with a violent jolt.

'Something made you jump. Something frightened you when you were sleeping,' he murmurs. He kisses my eyelids and I wonder if he's been awake and watching me all night.

'Myself,' I mutter.

'You're afraid of yourself?'

'Terrified.' I pause. The blackness of the room gives

me the cloak I require. 'I married the wrong one,' I confess.

'There isn't just one. There are countless opportunities.'

'That's horrible.'

'No, it's wonderful.'

'So you and I?'

'Just another combination.'

I feel his smile move the air between us. It's possible he finds that thought comforting. I'm petrified.

59

29 May

We pack, pay, leave and travel home without drifting into any emotional depths; in fact we're awkward and reticent with one another. I guess it's to be expected; we're both, in our own way, terrified. But the distance between us is upsetting. I want us to ride above the expected. I want us to be stronger, more enormous and resilient than that.

Chuck tries to play the blues ladies' CD in the car but I switch it off.

'It's too sad,' I mutter.

He nods briefly.

When we arrive in Veganze I ask Chuck to drop me off at the bar because that's where I'm most likely to find Roberto.

'Would you like me to come in with you?' he offers.

'No, I have to do this on my own.'

'I'll call you later this evening,' offers Chuck.

'I'd better call you. I'll be able to choose the moment. It would be awful if you called in the middle of –' I trail off. He nods tightly. We both know that the entire situation is awful.

'But if you need me. If it turns ugly,' Chuck says.

I nod my understanding. My plan is to go in and tell Roberto it's over, call him a few names, tell him a couple of home truths about his mother and then pack some clean knickers, grab some toiletries and leave. My mouth feels like I've swallowed a bucket full of sand. As much as I want to make light of this I realize it's a hideous situation.

Roberto's car is parked outside the bar so neither Chuck nor I make a move to kiss one another. I'd like to. I want to. I almost need to. Kissing him would give me the requisite strength to burn the bridges with bravado but it would be appalling to be caught snogging him outside the bar. I have visions of Raffaella banging her walking-stick on his car window, not that she actually carries a walking-stick – other than in my mind, where it occasionally morphs into a broomstick. Hastily I pull away from Chuck to stop myself giving into the urge. He looks hurt but I'm sure he understands. I scramble for the door handle and hop out of the car as quickly as I can.

'I'll call you,' I assure him.

The regular oldies are sat in convivial huddles outside the bar. One or two touch their caps and smile by way of greeting. I'm relieved that no one has thrown rotting fruit or demanded that I'm branded with a scarlet letter A for adulterer. I had imagined that Raffaella would have pounced on my unexpected and sudden absence as opportunity to tell the town that she'd been right about me all along – unsuitable, flighty. I notice that there are some groups of younger patrons too; they sit in noisy gangs enjoying a mid-morning brioche. I'm glad trade is good for Roberto. Oddly, now I have Chuck I am less resentful of the bar. Having Chuck's – what? Love? We never talked about the Big L word. Let's just say having Chuck's affection and support makes me able to be a bigger person.

It's so bright outside that the bar seems pitch black.

As I enter I take a moment to let my eyes become accustomed to the darkness. I can make out a few shadowy groups and couples sat at the corner tables and on the comfy couches. Gina and Laurana are behind the bar. Laurana rushes towards me and gives me a big hug.

'Hey, you. We've been worried, where have you been?' The concern is apparent in her eyes and voice. I feel an unexpected twinge of guilt. I suppose I should have called someone to say I was OK.

I smile and squeeze her hand. 'I'll explain later. Is Roberto here?'

'He's in the kitchen.'

Without further ado I walk determinedly towards the kitchen and Roberto.

'Hello.'

'Elizabeth, where in hell have you been? We had no way of getting hold of you. You did not take your bag or your phone. The school did not know where you are.'

Roberto's eyes are flashing with frustration that other people might have taken for concern, but I know that his heart is throbbing with insincerity and I'm not moved.

'You are having an affair with Ana-Maria. I don't want to hide from it any more.'

'We cannot talk about that now.'

'There's never a good time for you, is there? Are you in love?' I pause; he hangs his head. 'What was your plan? Did you think you'd run us both in parallel for decades? Or did you plant the condom where I'd find it because you are too much of a coward to tell me how you feel about another woman?'

'Elizabeth!' Roberto's eyes appear to be pleading but I'm now immune to his Latin charm. I no longer want to fall under that spell. I just want answers. I just want our relationship to be given an honest and dignified burial.

'Oh sod it, Roberto, just admit it. We're an infertile couple who've been trying for babies for six years; you don't need to wear a condom when you are having sex with me.' A bolt of injustice darts through me. 'In fact, how dare you deny me IVF saying it's up to the big guy but then use contraception with your mistress? That's hardly very Catholic, is it?' He stares at me with eyes that beseech me to shut up but I have no intention of doing so. 'I need to know when it started? Was it that first night that you stayed out or was that just the most insolent?' I glare at him but he stays mute. 'Have you been sleeping with her since we arrived here?' My tone is mock patient but he knows me well enough to know that I am boiling. Then a disturbing thought creeps into my mind. 'Did you give *her* the flowers on Valentine's day? The ones Paolina saw you buy? The ones you said were for your mother?' My tone is once again angry and I can't or won't hide my fury.

I suddenly realize that for months every word said between us has had another thought behind it, which confuses an already hideously murky issue. I need some straight talking.

'Elizabeth. You must sit down.'

'You no longer have any right to tell me what to do,' I say and stubbornly refuse the stool he's offering. I feel stronger standing up; sitting down would put me at a psychological disadvantage.

'I have something important to say,' he adds.

'I don't want any more lies or bullshit. Just be straight with me.'

'Why do you always do this?'

'Do what?'

'It's difficult to live with your wife holding a gun to your head, full of emotional bullets that she so clearly wants to shoot. You are always like this. Your way or no way.'

'I just want answers.'

'Elizabeth, this isn't the time to talk about us!'

'When would be a good time for you, exactly? Clearly never in the last five months.' He shakes his head, wearily. He definitely isn't up for a fight, although I'm raring to go.

'It's done, Roberto. We can't go on like this. You are in love with someone else and well, I think that I – '.

'Elizabeth, stop this now. Don't say anything else.'

Thinking of Chuck fills me with renewed confidence.

'I have to say something. We've been avoiding issues for too long. I need to tell you. It's not just you who is in love with someone else.' He doesn't deserve my consideration but thinking about Chuck makes me big enough to give it to him anyway. 'I'm sorry, Roberto, but then maybe this is going to help you, there's Chuck now.' Roberto stares at me as though I have just urinated in his eye and I suppose I have. Quietly I add, 'We should let each other go, Roberto.'

He remains silent. I should by now be expecting his silence. I should know that confrontation isn't his thing. I realize I'm asking a Roman Catholic for a divorce and the notion is probably unthinkable for him, but continuing to live a lie is unimaginable to me.

'Say something, Roberto,' I plead.

'Your father's dead.'

Physically my body responds before my mind or heart can process what Roberto's just said. My stomach dissolves, my nose itches so viciously I can hardly breathe as tears scratch my eyes.

'What?' Roberto is holding my arm. He leads me to the stool and he gently pushes me into a sitting position. Like a rag doll I allow him to mould and fold me.

'Max has called. It happened on Saturday.'

'On Saturday,' I repeat but I still don't understand.

'A heart attack. He did not suffer.'

'It's all over?' I ask.

'For him, yes.'

60

Within four hours of Roberto telling me that my father has slipped off this planet to God knows where, I am sitting on a plane to England. Paolina packed a bag for me when Max initially rang Roberto with the news. Five days ago. I glean that they've been talking every few hours, waiting for me to reappear. Max had a selection of flights lined up for when I finally did. I marvel at his presence of mind. How had he, in this moment of unprecedented turmoil, managed to think about my flights? I wonder at his composure and practicality. It's a good thing he is the oldest. If I was the oldest and I had a younger sibling in a foreign country, I'd probably do something gross and unforgivable like forget to tell them their dad is dead because I'd be too shocked and scared to know what to do next.

Since I heard that my dad is dead I haven't thought about anything. My mind cannot deal with even the simplest of questions Roberto throws at me. Where is my passport? I don't know. The dressing table drawer I think, or maybe somewhere else. Do I want a magazine for the flight? Paolina asks, or a drink? I don't know what, or even if, I replied, but she scuttled off to buy them in any case. I suppose it was something for her to do. I did manage to scribble a note to Chuck telling him what I can hardly believe. I explain that I have to go to England immediately and ask him to phone me tonight. I gave the note to Gina and asked her to take it to him because I can't slip away. I don't think my legs would carry me even if I could find an acceptable excuse. Everyone is busy. They are moving around me so quickly that I'm dizzy. I feel sick. Everyone has motion except my dad. He is dead. Roberto told me.

I can barely remember the car journey to the airport; I know that Roberto and Paolina were there and that it was the longest journey of my life and yet it must have been over in a flash because I can't remember any conversations that may have taken place. The neck of my T-shirt is damp, I can't think why, then I notice that I am crying; I hadn't realized. Paolina gave me a packet of tissues. My body is in shock and my mind is numb. He's dead. Finished. Stopped. I say the words over and over but I don't understand them. How can this be possible? How can he be dead? He was alive when I last saw him. The ludicrousness of that thought makes me spurt out a sound somewhere between a laugh of derision and a howl of incomprehension. I drink a brandy on the plane because the air hostess says it's good for shock. The man sat next to me reads *The Times*. My father reads *The Times*.

Or at least, he used to.

61

I arrive into Birmingham airport and Max is waiting for me. I must look terrible because he just hugs me and doesn't ask where I've been since Saturday. What am I going to say when someone does ask? As they surely will. How can I explain my absence? How can I justify it?

We don't get home until after 6 p.m. The house is full of people and yet we all know that it's empty. A couple of neighbours, the woman who does the flowers at the church, my brothers, their wives and kids are already gathered. I suppose they've all been waiting for me.

I hug Mum but she doesn't let me linger. There is no great moment when she flings herself into my arms and collapses. She doesn't hang on to me and rack with sobs. She's never been needy and my father's death can't change that. Thank God. I'm relieved that I've finally stopped crying for the moment so I can meet her dignity with a semblance of my own.

'I expect you'd like a cup of tea, coming all this way. How was the flight?'

Mum makes me a cup of tea and serves it in a dainty cup and saucer, which I recognize as her 'best set'. It normally stays in the dresser. She tries to force a sandwich on me. I'm not hungry, but I let her make it because she's an unstoppable force when it comes to feeding and watering her family, which was one of the reasons Dad was so fat. I breathe deeply and I'm grateful that no one can read my mind. I'm not blaming Mum. I'm just saying he was fat. I'm not blaming him for being fat. I'm just saying. I cease with that line of thought. It's uncomfortable and unnecessary.

'The kids are on school holidays so we had to bring them, no one to leave them with because we didn't know how long we'd be staying,' whispers Sophie, Max's wife. I'm unsure as to whether she's having a pop at me. My disappearing act has inconvenienced everyone. They must be curious as to where I have been.

One of the neighbours compliments me on my tan and asks if I'm enjoying Italy. I nod but can't think of any way to elaborate. It's not the moment to be waxing lyrical about the terracotta buildings and sublime cooking. I shove the sandwich into my mouth to avoid further conversation. It's like chewing sandpaper. The tea is too strong to drink. I sit like a stranger with the tea cup and plate balanced carefully on my lap. Someone asks when Roberto is coming. I glance around the room trying to ascertain who asked the question. I wonder who will answer it. He should be coming. People will expect it. People who don't know that we both have lovers and our marriage is a sham. I consider that he might come anyway; it would be the decent thing to do. My father would appreciate it. My father would expect it. Voices are blurring and blending together – I can't tell if it was Thomas or Mrs Finley who wants to know about Roberto. Everyone is staring at me waiting for a response.

'Not sure,' I mutter.

'She left in such a hurry. I don't suppose you had time to discuss it, did you?' says Mum, jumping to my rescue. I nod and I'm appreciative. I have no idea how she knew

I didn't want to answer that question but I'm so grateful. 'Poor Elizabeth was on a retreat when her dad died. We haven't been able to get hold of her,' she adds. Ah, so that's what Roberto said. I'm thankful; this isn't the moment to introduce the topic of Chuck. I suppose it was in Roberto's interest too. It would have hurt his pride admitting to his mother-in-law and brothers-in-law that he was clueless as to his wife's whereabouts. Mum doesn't look at me while she furnishes Mrs Finley with this explanation; I somehow sense that she doesn't believe it.

'Really, a retreat?' says Mrs Finley, seizing the opportunity to fill a silence. Her gusto is understandable but cringe-making. 'Was it a religious retreat, dear? Have you got religion since you moved to Italy? They do have lovely churches, don't they?'

'Yes, but – no, it was more of a health break,' I mutter. I'm uncomfortable with lying but I'm not sure what else I can do now the lie is in motion.

'A spa?' She probes.

Unexpectedly a sound somewhere between a cry for mercy and a squeal of embarrassment escapes from my lips. Three people rush to pass me a tissue and mutter about my being shocked. I start to sob quietly as I think of my dad. He's dead.

A conversation starts up discussing who is sleeping where. Some are staying in the local B & B, someone else is on a mattress in the spare room. There's no bed in there now, just Mum's sewing machine. I realize I don't care. I'll sleep where they tell me to sleep. It doesn't matter.

What was the last thing I said to Dad? I talked to him

about installing broadband. I remember I felt vaguely irritated by him because he couldn't get the hang of sending and receiving e-mail and I'd told him a thousand times that it was the easiest way to stay in touch. He asked what was wrong with the good old-fashioned method of talking on the phone. I couldn't tell him that my phone calls were more or less monitored and that Raffaella thought eavesdropping was a birthright.

My dad probably died thinking that I couldn't be bothered to pick up the phone and talk to him.

The doorbell rings; everyone jumps up to answer it but Mum tells us to stay where we are, she'll get it, so we all resume our position like obedient schoolchildren. It's becoming difficult to remember who is supposed to be looking after whom. That is until I watch her leave the room and I notice how slight she is. Was she that thin last January when I came up for the afternoon to say goodbye to them before Roberto and I dashed off to Italy? Or has she lost part of herself since she found Dad dead in front of the fridge? Did she drop a dress size instantly in grief? Shrinking seems more than possible to me, it seems probable.

Mum looks like a very old woman. I whisper as much to Thomas, who shrugs and says, 'She is an old woman, Elizabeth. She's seventy-six.' His response seems brutal. Facts can be. 'Dad was eighty-one. It's a good age.'

'But I had hoped for longer,' I mumble. 'People live well into their nineties now, don't they?'

'Yes, some do, and others die in their thirties,' he points out. As a doctor I suppose he sees much more than I have ever seen and understands much more than I'll ever understand. But if he says Dad had a good innings I might kill him with my bare hands. I sit on my hands and tell myself throttling my brother would not help anyone.

How had I failed to compute that my father was getting so old? That he was so near the end? It shouldn't take a genius. How had I gone to Italy and left him here to die?

People come and go all evening but I don't move from my spot on the sofa. Eventually I realize that there's only Eddie, my eldest nephew, Mum and me left. Eddie is fourteen and pretty much a man now. He's going to sleep on the sofa-bed. I'm glad of his adolescent presence. He's naturally buoyant about everything (other than his own love life) and therefore a great comfort to have around. Mum takes my plate out of my hand. I'm not sure if it's the one she gave me when I arrived and whether I've been holding it for hours or whether I've been given more food during the evening.

From the front room window I can see a pink glow shining up from behind the houses across the street. I've looked out at the same view for years and yet now it is completely altered. Everything seems changed.

'We're having a lovely summer,' says Mum, appearing from nowhere. I see that she has taken her shoes off and has put on her house slippers, a sign that she isn't expecting any more guests, it's just family now. 'It was sunny on Saturday too. He had a beautiful day to die.'

I turn to my tiny mum and put my arms around her. I'm taller than she is, I have been for a while, but as I'm still in shoes I seem to tower above her and it's like holding a child. I gently rock her backwards and forwards and stroke her back like she has stroked mine on a million occasions over the years.

'I'm going to miss him so much,' she says quietly.

I suck on the roof of my mouth, determined not to cry again. 'I know you are.'

She pulls away from me and stretches to her full height. 'Still, we've been very lucky. We've had so many years.'

All at once, she's taller than me again.

62

I crawl into bed at 11 p.m. and reach for my mobile. Despite all the sadness I feel a relief, almost excitement, at the thought of speaking to Chuck. In among all this grief and grimness I'm sure his voice will help. Before I even get a chance to call him I see that there is a text message from him. The love! I open it eagerly, anticipating his comfort.

Got your message. I'll give you space. Sorry.

I think I might throw up. I fling back the covers and jump out of bed only to flop back on to it again in an instant. I reread the text over and over again. How insensitive. How cruel. What the hell is going on? Space? I don't want space. I want him to gather me up in his muscled arms and hold me tight. I realize that it might be unrealistic to expect him to arrive on a white charger, this clearly isn't the best moment to meet my family, but what does he mean he'll give me space?

I call him immediately but only get the engaged signal.

I reread the message again to see if there is any way I could have misinterpreted what he meant, but I can't kid myself, it is unequivocal. I asked him to call me; he's texted to say he has no intention of doing that tonight or perhaps ever.

I press redial. He'll be able to explain himself. I'm sure of it. Bugger, it's still engaged. I can hardly breathe as despair chokes me. For ten minutes I continually press redial, over and over again. The line is permanently engaged. The tone sends shafts of fury through my already horribly tense body. Doesn't he have call waiting? Can't he recognize my number? Is he avoiding my call?

I wonder if I should text back. No. Why the hell should I? It's me who needs support right now. It's me with a dead father and a dead marriage. Why hasn't he called? What the hell does this text mean? At the first sign of difficulty he's buggered off. Deserted me. At least Roberto stuck around through *years* of problems before he backed off. I press redial one more time. It's still engaged. Who the hell is he talking to that is this important? Why hasn't he kept the line clear for my call? It is all too much. My despair instantly morphs into rage.

How fucking stupid am I? How could I ever have imagined that I'd persuade Chuck to have babies with me? How could I ever have imagined that he'd make a responsible father? Shame sluices over me. What made me, even for a second, think that Chuck might be more important to me than having babies? I am blind. Obviously, I have no idea about men and am a lousy judge of character. With Roberto, and now Chuck, I didn't want to see the glaringly evident signs. Only yesterday Chuck told me that he had a thing for married women. Maybe the fun is in the chase for him. He's probably already talking to his next victim with a ring on her third finger on her left hand.

But he seemed so sincere.

I fight a flashback. I try not to remember waking up in Chuck's arms and carefully, always reluctantly, peeling away from him. I try not to think of our hot flesh stuck together in a way that made me think I'd found home. Twice in one very, very long day I feel an unbearable sense of loss.

He *seemed* sincere but he's not. If he was sincere he would be on the phone, hunting for the best words to murmur to console me. His words would have undoubtedly healed; being sure of that is worse than doubting it. I open my bedroom window and fling away my mobile. It makes a satisfying smashing sound as it lands in the road. I see splinters of plastic spray a foot in the air. I bang the window closed, proud that I have removed any temptation to call Chuck. However sincere he seemed in the past, I will not call and beg him to explain away his cold betrayal at this crucial time. It's crystal clear.

Oh fuck, for a pitiless, vicious instant I wish I'd written down his number.

63

Death comes with many terrible practicalities. For Mum, it started the moment she came home from choir practice and she found Dad dead on the floor in the kitchen.

'I'd been gone about two hours, dear. Maybe two and a quarter, not more.' She found his enormous bulk in front of the fridge; the door was open and there was a hazelnut yogurt spilt on to the floor. She didn't know what to do next. Should she call an ambulance? He was clearly dead – they couldn't do anything to revive him – so was a doctor a better idea? She decided it was, despite it being after 9 p.m. She knew their local GP, Doctor Hudson, a nice man in his fifties who has been looking after my father for years.

'You see, I did realize that I couldn't just lie down and sleep next to him, dear, however much I wanted to. It wasn't something that could be left until the morning, was it?'

'No,' I agree. Although we are both wondering, 'Why not?' There was no rush. My dad was dead. Her husband was dead. He'd still be dead in the morning. But of course she had to call the doctor; it's the right thing to do.

'I didn't know whether to clear up the yogurt so that no one slipped on it. I thought I ought to because I like the house to look nice when guests are coming round, especially doctors, I always make an effort for the doctor, Elizabeth, you know that. But I wasn't sure. On those

TV programmes they say not to touch anything, don't they?'

'That's only in murders, Gran,' says Eddie. He's heard his gran's story twenty or so times already and he thinks it's about time he ought to inject a little sense into her ramblings. Mum looks at Eddie and feels an overwhelming love for the son of her son burn in the pit of her gut, so she lets him say the stuff everyone else is thinking and she doesn't take offence.

'Did you clear up the yogurt, Mum?' I ask, as I have every time she's repeated the story to friends and neighbours and wellwishers who have popped by.

'Yes, dear. Some had spilt on to your father's jumper so I gave that a little rub with a J-cloth. He wouldn't have liked people to see him that way.'

Besides the signing of the death certificate, which was in this case straightforward, there are innumerable decisions to be made around the funeral. Most of which have been discussed over the last five days, but nothing is finalized.

'We were waiting for you, dear. I knew you'd have strong views on how it should all be done,' says Mum, showing a confidence in me that I don't deserve.

I find I am called upon to have an opinion on flowers, readings, hymns and prayers. The fog of shock slowly dissipates and I accept that Dad is dead. He must be, because while he is all we talk about, he hasn't popped out of his study and asked me if I'm still keeping up with the story line on *The Archers*, as I keep expecting him to do. Mum is being phenomenally strong in front of friends and neighbours and keeps busy making endless cups of tea and finalizing the plans for the funeral on

Monday. I fumble along next to her, a pale imitation. I offer tea but then forget to put the kettle on. I put biscuits on a plate but fail to pass them round.

Mum keeps turning to me and saying things like, 'Burial not cremation for your dad.' I nod and presume it was once discussed between them. 'We thought it best that we only have one wreath from us all. Your dad wouldn't have liked the money wasted on lots of flowers, would he? He liked to see flowers in a garden – growing.' Nod. 'We can ask people to make donations to a charity instead. That's what people do nowadays, isn't it?' And I nod again. Although I have no idea what Dad would have thought about his wreath or even what charity we are going to donate money to.

'Your dad would have wanted "The Lord is My Shepherd", wouldn't he?' I nod but I'm not sure. Maybe he would have liked to hear some Duke Ellington. For some reason I can't offer this view, even though Mum had been sure I'd have strong opinions on the arrangements. I sense that I'm letting her down. 'Most people know that one,' adds Mum. I suppose so.

'Your dad would have wanted a decent spread. Lots of prawns and generous cuts of meat. Maybe salmon, not just egg sandwiches.' I agree that much is true, I'm sure of it. I nod with a little more enthusiasm, glad to be on steady ground.

'When will you be going to see him?' she asks.

The ground trembles once more. What? While so far the arrangements for the funeral have not challenged me, this question stops me in my tracks. I hadn't thought of going to see Dad in the house of rest. The funeral director, with his large, clean and soft hands came to our home to finalize all the arrangements. I hadn't entertained the thought of visiting a funeral parlour until I was the one on the slab. Mum has visited Dad twice; she sees these few days before the funeral as her last few with him. I think she'd like to stay suspended in this state of uncertainty for as long as possible. If there was a way of embalming his body and visiting him on a daily basis until the end of her days, she would do it. It crosses my mind that she'd have made a good wife for a jailbird. I, however, am counting the hours until Dad is in the ground. I'm cold and numb and need to feel something other than nothing. Since the first day I arrived here I haven't cried. I wanted to be dignified and grown-up, so for twenty-four hours I fought the tears and now they won't come at all. I'm weirdly looking forward to the funeral. I need to cry. I want to get it over with.

'I find it very comforting. Talking to him as he lies there. It's not that different from when he was alive, just a little quieter,' says Mum. She smiles at her own attempt at a joke.

'What do you talk to him about?' I ask.

'You, Max, Thomas, the grandkids.'

'Well, I'm sure you've given him all the news, Mum. I'm not sure I need to go,' I reply weakly.

'I tell him what I know, Elizabeth,' says Mum, and then she stares at me for an uncomfortably long time. 'That's the most I can do.'

64

2 June

Everyone you'd expect is there except him, and yet my father has never been more present.

The funeral takes place on an average British summer's day, that is to say it's overcast and a bit chilly but at least it's not raining.

I was overwhelmed with relief and gratitude when Roberto called to say he would be flying in for the funeral. Our conversation was brief and perfunctory but I was not expecting it to be anything more. In light of Chuck's recent behaviour Roberto's commitment to doing the right thing seems magnificent. Chuck clearly intends to give me quite a lot of space. I've heard nothing from him. I realize that since I've destroyed my mobile the only way he could get hold of me is to get my mother's telephone number. He'd have to ask Roberto or Paolina for it. Quite an ask, I admit. Too much of an ask, clearly. I thrash between fury, sadness and despair. I'm bewildered as to why Chuck has decided to treat me with such cold and final indifference.

'Thank you, Roberto, it will mean a lot to my mum and it would have meant a lot to my dad.'

It also means a lot to me. If Roberto had failed to materialize at the funeral, questions would have been asked and I'm not ready to give any answers yet. I know that we are over but I'm not prepared to break the news to Mum at the moment. She's going to be angry and disappointed and sad too, no doubt. She has enough to deal with right now.

'Your father was always a gentleman,' said Roberto. 'I want to buy my respects.'

'Pay,' I corrected him. Many people have said the same thing; my father was esteemed and cherished.

'I won't be able to stay though. I'll fly back the same day I arrive,' Roberto added. And for that I'm even more grateful to him. I could not have stood the pretence of us sharing a bed.

Roberto times his arrival so that he doesn't have to linger in our kitchen all morning. He appears from nowhere, at just the correct moment, and seamlessly slips into the funeral car with Mum and me so we can travel to the church together. Max and Thomas are travelling in another car each, with their wives and kids. I smile thankfully at Roberto. He looks handsome and composed in his black Armani suit, and his fine-looking male presence is required in our car; alone, Mum and I look fragile. Roberto holds Mum's arm as she walks up the aisle towards the enormous mahogany box which stores Dad. This is thoughtful of him; she needs him more than I do. During the service he squeezes my hand, once, briefly but meaningfully, and I squeeze his back. I wonder what he feels standing in the church where we married. I feel nothing in relation to us; all my thoughts are on Dad.

The funeral is all one can hope a funeral to be. The service is relevant and not too long. My parents are churchgoers, so the Vicar can speak with confidence about the achievements and character of Ernest Gardiner.

The mood is dignified but not at all despairing. Thomas reads from the Bible, as it's been agreed that my father would not have approved of anything modern, like a poem. Although I wondered if he would have liked to hear some Wordsworth or even Blake; uncertain, I never voiced my thought. I wish I'd known him better. I should have known him better. The church is packed, and as my eyes sweep over the rows of earnest and sombre faces, I recognize a few. The headmaster from my old school, some buddies of Dad's who have been dotted around our home since time began, Charlie Rotheroe, the guy who runs the garden centre where Dad used to potter, Mr Walker from the newsagent's. My parents, having lived in the same area forever, have many friends and a surprisingly active social life.

Afterwards, at the hotel where we are having the refreshments, I'm introduced to dozens of people from the golf, cinema and bridge club. Someone from the neighbourhood watch group says what a marvellous and committed chairman he was. Someone else from the local Rainbow Club thanks me because my father had driven disabled kids to and from the library every week for twenty years. I'd forgotten he did that. He never made much of a deal out of his voluntary work. I shake hands with countless smiling wellwishers who insist that I must keep in touch, who are assured I'm proud of him, who remind me that he had a good life. I try and fail to commit names to faces. I drink three glasses of sherry which grate in my throat and I am unsuccessful in getting a bite to my lips despite the wonderful 'spread' my Mum has ordered. I stay dry-eyed. Most do. Everyone agrees that he did have a good innings, and I haven't the energy to challenge anyone that I wanted him to have even more than that.

After about the millionth clammy handshake at the reception I suddenly have an overwhelming urge to escape the crowds. I slip out of the patio doors into the green and calming outdoors. The hotel garden is in full bloom. Pink and peach roses coyly dance in front of me. Their petals are wet and I'm unsure if it's rained or if there is a sprinkler system. I bury my nose into one of the flowerheads and take a deep breath in. I can smell my father. Or at least I am reminded of him; he was a fanatical and skilled gardener and the smell of roses on a summer wind will always belong to him. As will the smell of Imperial Leather soap, shoe polish and Vick's chest rub.

'Hello.'

'*Ciao*, Roberto.' I turn to face him.

'How are you?'

'Let's just say that if I smoked this is when I'd need a cigarette break.'

He nods but looks uncertain. I doubt he understands why I'm weary of the wellwishers.

'Your father had many friends.'

'Yes. I don't know any of them well.'

'Still, a popular man. You must be proud.'

'I'm sad,' I say simply and sullenly. I haven't the vigour to appear reassured by platitudes.

Roberto shifts from foot to foot, awkward and clueless.

'I have to catch the plane home in three hours.'

'Yes.'

'Paolina sent her love. Everyone sent their condolences.'

'Thank you.' I can't envisage Raffaella sending good wishes but I'm concentrating on being polite and detached and so don't bother to say so.

I want to ask him about Chuck. But what's the etiquette? How can I ask my husband if he's had any word from my lover? Ex-lover. I know it's pointless and imbecilic of me but I long for Chuck's big, calm presence. I think that it is the only thing that has even the slightest chance of making me feel in the least bit better. Not the presence of the sender of heartless texts Chuck, the other Chuck. The supportive and sexy Chuck. Where has he gone? How is it possible that he vanished in an instant? I sigh. I have to harden my heart. The point is he has vanished. It's just one more thing that I don't quite understand. One more thing that seems unfair.

'I have to go back. You understand. The bar, my mamma.' If Roberto means Ana-Maria he has the decency not to say so.

'I have to stay,' I say simply.

'I realize. You need to help your mother.'

'I need to help myself too.'

Roberto looks chastised. He takes a deep breath and then bravely grasps the nettle. 'The baby-trying killed us.'

'No. No,' I mutter, although I know he might be right.

'It did. You know it,' he says firmly. Roberto walks towards me and takes hold of one of my hands. I ought to pull away from him. His deceitful touch ought to burn and offend but it doesn't; it feels familiar and comfortable. I leave my freckled hand in his large brown paw. He kisses my fingers. The kisses are not amorous; his is the most sorrowful gesture I've ever experienced, and considering I'm at my father's funeral that is saying something.

'Timetables and herbs. Sticks in the bathroom that you pee on.' Roberto shakes his head. 'It is not how I want my love.'

I feel a fat tear betray me by sliding down my cheek. I don't move to rub it away because I don't want to draw attention to it. I will the tear to evaporate and not shame me. The last thing I want now is Roberto feeling sorry for me. I feel sorry enough.

'Plus after some time, I realized that I did not want it as much as you. I did not want a *bambino* above everything else. And that got me thinking about us. Many times you muttered in your sleep and I feel sorry for your loneliness. The guilt was extraordinary. I came to wonder if we could ever be happy. I hoped we could be. That's why I wanted a clear start in Italy, but it quickly became apparent to me there that if I did not give you a *bambino* you would never see me as a whole man. I would never be enough for you.'

'And you are enough for Ana-Maria?' My comment is petty and jealous, but I feel irate and deceived that Roberto is blaming our marriage breakdown on our poor unborn babies. Surely the fact that he and his ex have been shagging one another senseless for God knows how long is a contributing factor.

'Ana-Maria would love me with or without babies. You can't say the same.'

'I –' The word 'can' is strangled in my throat. No, I can't say the same. Poor Roberto. Poor me.

I let my hand slip from his grip. It's easier than I imagined.

'I'll call you. There is much to discuss.'

Roberto means there are practicalities to settle – the sale of the flat, a divorce, telling our families. He does not mean we have a reconciliation to discuss. Neither of us has the energy or the inclination to try for that. Our marriage slithers from my grasp. I feel like I'm standing on wet sand and the tide is coming in. With each crashing wave I lose my footing and I'm stumbling. I'm not sure if I can remain upright but I have to because if I fall, I'll drown.

65

20 June

Alison lands on my mum's doorstep although I didn't invite her. She's angry with me, which I mind less than I would normally, because I'm angry with myself too and I think she has a point.

'Why the hell didn't you call?'

She pulls me into a tight hug but I can still feel her fury throb through her jacket. It puts me in mind of the hug Mum gave me when as a seven-year-old I disappeared to a friend's house for three hours without telling her. When she found me she was torn between relief and rage. She grasped me into such a tight hug she left marks on my chubby, childish upper arms. When Alison releases me I want to check for light bruises.

'Why didn't you call me and tell me your dad had died?'

'I broke my mobile.'

'So why didn't you use a landline?' she asks in an accusing tone.

I shrug and avoid answering by asking, 'Who did call you?'

'Roberto.'

Recently Roberto has been eclipsed by thoughts of my dad and Chuck; his name said aloud in Mum's hallway seems alien. I stare at Alison to try and compute that I'm still someone's wife, albeit someone's estranged, soon-to-be-ex, wife. I've moved on from Roberto but since I've moved on to two men that have also gone from my life, it doesn't feel much like progress.

'He's worried about you.'

'Who is?' I ask, as a moment of hope flickers somewhere it shouldn't.

'Roberto.' Alison can't keep the exasperation from her voice. Of course, how would Alison know if Chuck was worried about me? A ridiculous notion. I shouldn't have entertained it for even a nanosecond. 'Then I called your mum and she's worried about you too –' Alison takes a sweeping head-to-toe glance of me – 'and judging from your current sartorial elegance they have every right to be worried.'

I am wearing my pyjamas although it's nearly noon and I'm wearing a dark brown robe that belongs to my mum. It's damned ugly at the best of times, and as I've customized it with innumerable splodges and stains (mostly from sloppy food like Weetabix) it's safe to say this isn't the best of times. I haven't brushed my teeth this morning and I haven't brushed my hair since I washed it last, which was – oh, I don't know when. A week ago? Ten days ago.

After the funeral everyone went home, glad to rush back to their lives full of washing loads and electricity bills, because there's nothing like a funeral to help you appreciate the tiresome normality of the life you live. It was assumed by everyone, from my brothers to Charlie Rotheroe, the guy who runs the garden centre, that I'd keep Mum company in these her darkest hours. As the only daughter, with no career and no children, I am perfectly placed to devote myself to comforting her. Even I can see the logic behind the supposition.

I've failed miserably.

I am unable to muster the necessary 'life goes on' attitude that I know is required. Because does it? Will mine? I can see that Max's and Thomas's lives may go on; they have children and spouses to run through their homes and their veins like the lifeblood they are. But I haven't got that sort of comfort and nor does Mum. I look at Mum and can't believe anything other than that the best years of her life are over. She's had the era that was full of noise and vibrancy, love and joy. Her youth once teemed with timetables and rotas and small imperative demands that she had to meet. She's guided her children through school and music practice, she's listened to their faltering voices piecing together vowel sounds until they were skilled enough to read complex medical journals and the *FT* (at least, until Max and Thomas could do that – she might be waiting a little longer if she's hoping for the same thing from me). Slight, pretty and hopeful, she's glided up the aisle to take her handsome beau and then five decades later she's eased up the same aisle, drenched in sadness, to bid farewell to his huge, familiar mass.

What words can I offer my mum as comfort? The best is past, and I know it to be so with a cold and concrete conviction because we are the same. I can't see a future for me either. After years of planning, predicting, hoping and longing, I now realize that I am more like my mother than my brothers. Our similarities depress and shame me but I cannot be false enough with either her or myself to pretend that the future is anything other than austere.

At night I fall into the deepest well of self-pity. Then not only am I dejected and mortified at my inability to comfort my mother – I actually resent her. I'm almost jealous of her. At least Mum once enjoyed a young family. At least she dwelt in love, to an old age, with my dad. These possibilities are lost to me.

Chuck.

During the day I wander zombie-like through the house. Mutely, I accept the tomato soup and soft-boiled eggs that my mum prepares. As she hands me the invalid food that she used to make when I was a kid with tonsillitis I see her eyes brim with concern and my feelings of self-abhorrence grow; not only am I unable to help her but I'm adding to her woes by being a worry. I realize she's lost her husband and she's old and I ought to be taking her on jaunty trips to Royal Horticultural Society gardens or to National Trust houses for a mooch and tea and scones, but I can't. I wish I was a better person, but the most I can manage is to put the kettle on and shuffle down to the corner shop to buy Jaffa Cakes when required.

'Go and get showered instantly,' says Alison. 'You smell horrible. Then we are going for a walk and a talk.'

I moan and pout but she glares at me and I know that she's a force to be reckoned with whereas I am minuscule and weak right now, so I do as I'm told.

I do feel better after my shower. Mum has left out a warm, fluffy towel and a new, posh hair conditioner. I take my time, luxuriating in the creamy bubbles popping between my fingers. The hot jets massage my shoulders and back. I turn round and open my mouth; the water pours in and out again, dribbling down my chin. I close my eyes as the water drills against my lids. At least in the shower it's impossible to tell when I'm crying.

When I finally emerge I find Alison and Mum sitting around the kitchen table. I hesitate before entering the room, shy and unsure how to announce myself although I know I'm the one they are waiting for. The June sunlight blazes in through the open back door. I can hear the neighbour's kids in their garden; they are arguing over something or other. Their indignant and self-righteous voices whiz over the fence and mingle with the more sombre but equally earnest tones of Radio 4 presenters, which are constant in our kitchen. The sweet aroma of over-fat roses flows into the house. I glance out of the window. The garden is in full bloom now, in fact the petals will soon drift loose from the stems, fall to the ground and start to decay, sending up an altogether headier, slightly sickly stench. I feel a little sad that I've let the beauty of the garden slip past me unnoticed this year. Mum and Dad have a fabulous garden which is carefully planned to look resplendent all year round. The crocuses and daffodils dance buoyantly in cheerful gangs of colour in the borders in spring, the Japanese maples are resplendent, defiantly spattering scarlet and orange against the grey mornings in autumn, the evergreens look dignified under glistening frosts or dustings of snow in the winter months, but for me the unequivocal high point of the year is the summer, when the rose beds are mesmerizing. I adore the silky, delicate petals clustering together in such perfect forms. In that instant I regret that I have stayed stuffed in my room for the lion's share of the past month, rather than enjoying the fresh air and blooms. I think of

Dad and the fact that he's missed his beloved roses too. Worse, he won't ever see them again. I'm freshly stabbed with anguish and grief.

Mum and Alison are clearly not swamped in the same distress just at this moment, they are chatting, and Mum suddenly breaks into peals of laughter at something Alison has said. It's only hearing her laughter that I realize how absent it's been in the last three weeks. I really should be trying harder to distract her and not wallow so much.

'What's funny?' I ask as I take a place in between them.

Alison pushes a mug towards me and a plate of chocolate digestives. I double take at the sight of the mug. Mum must feel really comfortable with Alison, normally she insists on cups and saucers – we only have mugs in the house at all because I like to use one first thing in the morning. Alison stayed here with us when I got married, as she was chief bridesmaid, and they've met a number of times when Mum and Dad visited me in London, but I hadn't appreciated just how well they got on with one another.

'Fiona, Alison's girlfriend, is funny,' says Mum in reply to my question. Again I'm startled. While I've never hidden from my parents the fact that Alison is gay, it's never been openly referred to. I don't swear in front of them either, I'm an eternal eight-year-old in their presence.

'Share the joke then,' I say, trying to sound jovial. I'm aware that if I don't make an effort to act semi-human Alison will be down on me like a ton of bricks.

'Fiona wants a baby,' giggles Mum. 'And she's trying to persuade Alison that it's a good idea so she's started this campaign. She's been leaving little hints around the house. Alison found a pair of Gap baby socks in the bed but as she didn't have her lenses in, she thought it was a mouse and hit the poor defenceless socks with her shoe!' Mum starts to chuckle again as she imagines the scenario. I can't see the funny side. I stare at Alison in disbelief.

'You're kidding, right?'

'No, I honestly thought we had mice.'

'I mean about her wanting a baby.'

Alison looks mildly uncomfortable. 'I think she's serious.'

'But you've only known each other five minutes,' I say irately.

'Elizabeth, don't be rude,' admonishes Mum. She pushes the plate of biscuits back towards Alison. 'Do you want another or will it be Fiona who is eating for two?'

She giggles again, probably fired up by how risqué the conversation is. And given my mum thinks two-piece bikinis are a new and scandalous invention, talking to my best friend about whether she or her lesbian lover will be carrying the child they may conceive (presumably with the help of a turkey baster) *is* being risqué.

'Well, nothing is decided. There's a lot to talk about. We're just mulling over the idea, but I think Fiona would be doing the heavy work.'

Alison grins at me, almost as though she's expecting my congratulations. I stare at her, truly bewildered. Alison doesn't like kids. Alison is a career woman. Alison is a lesbian and yet despite all these things she's probably going to have a baby before I am. Of course she bloody is! The Pope is probably going to have a baby before I am! I'm sure that Alison can feel my malevolence surge over the plate of biscuits, waiting to hit her between the eyes, because she refuses to meet my gaze. It's not that I object to lesbians bringing up children, of course not, it's just I thought Alison was immune to the charms of a mewing and snuffling tot. I thought when absolutely every other friend of mine had a Russian Doll set of offspring, Alison, at least, would remain childless. In my bleakest moment it's been a comfort that, if the worst came to the absolute worst, we would be able to lunch together when we were in our forties and be safe in the knowledge that we would not have to sit through endless shows of photos of children. Our handbags would be devoid of Calpol sachets, our purses empty of small pieces of broken plastic toys.

But it appears not.

'Come on, you,' says Alison, getting to her feet and nudging me quite hard in the arm. 'Your mum has some overdue library books that need returning. Let's wander into town and stretch our legs.'

66

The books that need returning to the library are Dad's. Mum has many interests, but code-cracking during WWII and golf courses in north-west Scotland do not number among them. I hand the books over with reluctance. I want to hold on to them because I can imagine my father slowly pulling books from the library shelf, deliberately leafing through them and then finally, after great consideration, making his selection. I wonder if he read them. Did he have time? Anger flares up inside my stomach as I think of all the things that are interrupted by death. Dad never took a world cruise, he never saw Britain host the Olympics, he never held a child I'd given birth to.

Alison doesn't allow me to linger; after I've paid the fine on the overdue books she drags me off to a coffee shop and insists we both have gooey cakes.

'So?' she demands, the moment we are furnished with homemade lemonade and Victoria sponge. I tuck in; unfortunately grief has not subdued my appetite.

The 'so' is all encompassing. She's expecting me to explain why I didn't call her to tell her about Dad's death or to invite her to the funeral. Plus, depending on what Mum and Roberto have said, she's probably also wondering where I was when I went AWOL for the week before that, while my family were desperately trying to find me so that they could bury my father. She might want to know why I'm barely speaking or sleeping and why I have no plans at all to return to Italy.

I haven't the energy to fudge. I tell her in gruesome detail about my terrible time in Italy; the *full* extent of Raffaella's meanness and Roberto's coldness, culminating in her flinging away my belongings and him carrying condoms. I tell her about running away with Chuck and having wild abandoned sex with him for nearly a week and I tell her about my final conversation with Roberto, the one where we let each other go. I don't tell her about Chuck's text. Right at this point, that's one humiliation too many, even to share with my best friend.

'So what next?' she asks with a huge deep breath.

'I don't know. I'm disgusted with myself. I've messed everything up,' I moan. My shame at buggering up my life leaves me feeling physically sick on a more or less continuous basis.

'Well, it's not *all* your fault,' she says carefully. She places a heavy emphasis on *all*. Therefore assuring me that she certainly thinks some of it is.

'Alison, my dad was lying cold in front of an open fridge with hazelnut yogurt on his sweater and I was dripping with cum,' I wail. The guilt is intense. I can't forgive myself.

'Maybe you shouldn't have been having it away with the chunk of hunk, but I don't understand what difference it made to the situation with your dad. Even if you had been sitting with Roberto when Max rang with the sad news, it would have been too late. Your dad was already dead. It was over,' she finishes gently.

Intellectually I know that this is true, but I can't stop the guilt pumping around my body like a venomous poison.

426

'I should never have gone to Italy.'

'Nonsense. Your father was no doubt thrilled with your choice to travel.'

'No, I should have moved back home and spent more time with Mum and Dad. That's what I will do now.'

'Whoa, hang on girl. First of all I don't think your mum would want you to do that, especially if you are going to insist on moping round the house all day, every day, getting under her feet. Really, you're nothing but a nuisance at the moment. But even if you were being her lifeline, your mum wouldn't expect you to put your life on hold and look after her forever. She's never said she wants that, has she?'

'Well, no, but –'

'She's always struck me as an especially independent sort of woman.'

'Well, yes – but.'

'And what of Chuck?'

My cup slips a fraction, my hands are strangely clammy. 'What of him?' I ask cautiously.

'Well, the way you describe him sounds pretty full on. Doesn't he fall under the category of unfinished business?'

I pause. Yes, yes, of course he does. But then no, no, absolutely not. I realize I have no alternative other than to tell her about the text and the ensuing silence.

'What odd behaviour,' she says carefully.

'Odd!' I marvel at her understatement. 'He behaved like a total bastard.'

'But up until that moment he'd behaved like a total dream.'

'That just makes it harder to bear.'

'Some people aren't very good around death. Maybe

he just panicked and didn't know what to say to you.' Alison trails off; we both know her excuses for his behaviour sound lame.

'This is going to make him sound hideous. I can hardly believe it myself but I've given his actions a lot of thought and the only conclusion I can reach is that everything worked out quite conveniently for Chuck.'

'What do you mean?' asks Alison, intrigued.

While I've been slouching in my PJs seemingly gormless and inert, my mind has been whirling.

'Chuck was about to ditch me anyway. He used the timing of my dad's death to make a swift exit. He was not prepared to support me, follow me or fight for me because he knows that we have no possibility of making it as a couple. Chuck doesn't see a future for us.' I pause, take a deep breath and then admit, 'You see, he doesn't want kids. I do. End of.' I try to sound breezy and matter of fact as I push on. 'He never misled me; I can't even have the satisfaction of accusing him of that. He told me he didn't want kids well before I launched myself at him. He told me that he'd never intended to seduce me and was going to leave well alone if I hadn't run to him.'

Yes, he also told me he thought I was hot, and yes, he obviously had a good time in Venice too, but I have to remember that he never talked about a future. He never said he loved me.

'You really believe that?' asks Alison.

'I do. He's a classic commitment-phobic. He even admitted that he had a thing for married women; that is classic commitment-phobic behaviour, isn't it? Still, no matter, he was a distraction, that's all. You said as much yourself. You said I'd have fallen for a gargoyle, I was

428

that lonely in Italy. Now I'm home he'll vanish.' I cross my fingers as I say this and hope I won't burn in hell.

'Unless I was wrong, of course,' Alison says carefully.

'You're never wrong.'

'I'm often wrong. Or I change my mind. It's normal.' Alison pauses. 'Have you talked to him since you received the text?'

'Er, no. I told you, I broke my mobile.' I fight a blush as the memory of my flinging the phone bursts to the front of my mind. Maybe I was a little hasty. 'He can't call me and I don't have his apartment or mobile number. I never memorized it. Who does nowadays? I don't know how to get hold of him, even if I wanted to.'

'So you do want to,' says Alison, with more insight than I appreciate right now.

'No.' Yes. At least, sometimes I do. At night when I'm lying alone, I do.

'You could call the language school. You'd be able to find that number.'

It's a thought. Hope surges through my body. In a gnat's breath despondency catches up. What would be the point?

'I just have to start thinking of Chuck as a recreational fuck. You know – the one you're entitled to if you discover your husband is an adulterous bastard,' I bluster.

Alison looks doubtful.

She's right not to believe me. I am lying to her and I am lying to myself. Being with Chuck was not just a meaningless and vengeful act. It was something extraordinary. I thought *he* was something extraordinary. The week in Venice was a natural culmination to the months of deepening friendship and as such it was of great importance to me. With Chuck I felt entirely thrilled and thrilling and thoroughly known and knowing. While the week was possibly the most dreamy and romantic of my life, it was also the most vivid, intense and authentic. I wanted him with a ferocity that was beyond plans or propriety.

Sometimes when we made love it was all about answering to the primitive and visceral, other times it was bizarrely dreamlike and quintessentially quixotic. We were enveloped in a significance that made us into who I'm sure we are supposed to be. We fell apart from the crowd, even though the city was heaving with other lovers. We were different and separate from everything and everyone else and yet at the same time we were intrinsic and vital to the universe. For once I understood why I was born a woman. All the months and years of baby-trying and failing had made me doubt there was a reason, but for that all-too-brief week I had some sense of understanding. I evolved.

But thinking about Chuck, reminiscing about Chuck, elaborating fantasies involving Chuck, is not allowed. He's given me space. Heaps of it.

Suddenly, I feel like an empty plastic cup floating on an ocean. Lost, ugly and disposable. What a glum world if Chuck isn't in it. I sigh and rally. That isn't a helpful thought. I have to push on. I beam at Alison and say, 'If your firstborn is a girl, I'm expecting you to name her Elizabeth.'

Alison laughs, easily distracted by her own happiness.

67

21 June

Through the open window I watch Mum potter in the garden. For the millionth time that morning I find my gaze pulled towards Dad's office. His computer is in there. It's no good. I can't fight it any longer. I'm just not that strong. It only takes seconds to find the telephone number of the language school in Bassano del Grappa. Without pausing to talk myself out of it this time, I do what I know I've been wanting to do since I smashed my phone. I call to ask for Chuck.

The phone is picked up by the school secretary. Knowing she is a friend of Raffaella's makes this call a million times harder.

'I sorry, Elizabet –' she does not pronounce the 'h' – 'the teachers are all on the holiday now. Exams have started with supervisors from different schools. Our teachers all away having fun.'

'Oh yes, of course.' I fight back the disappointment. Hot tears burn my eyes. Too late. Too bloody late. What sort of fun is he having? Who with? I take a deep breath. 'Are there any messages for me?' I ask.

'Yes.' My heart leaps. 'From the Director.' And plummets again. 'She want your address to send wages and papers.'

'Anything else? Anyone else?' I ask, but I know I sound as hopeless as I feel.

'Nothing.' She's firm and final.

I give my home address and telephone number. I summon every ounce of courage and simultaneously throw away my last speck of dignity when I add, 'You can pass on this address to any of the staff, if they ask for it.'

'OK.'

There's nothing more to say. 'Well, 'bye then.'

'Good bye, Elizabet.'

68

'It's amazing, the World Wide Web, isn't it?' says Mum.

She pronounces each W carefully and excitedly. She throws me a sunny beam as she directs her mouse towards the favourites list, where she has already stored a number of sites. I can't believe that it's only nine in the morning and she's up, dressed and on the web.

'No one ever stops saying that, Mum. Do you want any breakfast?'

'I've had mine but I'll join you in a cup of tea if you are putting the kettle on.'

'Will do.'

I've turned a corner since Alison's visit and I'm making a supreme effort to be the model daughter. It's not so tricky, because Mum's relief that I'm no longer languishing in bed and her gratitude when I spend any time with her is transparent and touching.

We've visited a National Trust house and its attached teashops, we've taken strolls along the side of the golf course towards the river and we regularly potter into town, often spending hours at the local library. We walk, arms linked, chatter ebbing and flowing between us. Mum primarily has two lines of conversation; what should we have to eat for the next meal and Dad. She slips between the banal and the profound with an enviable ease.

'What do you think, a nice bit of ham? No, you wouldn't want ham, would you dear, being a vegetarian. Your dad liked ham. We've a lovely butcher, Mr Parsons. Dave Parsons. He came to your dad's funeral. Did you see him?'

'I don't know him, Mum. I wouldn't have recognized him.'

'No, of course not. Silly me. How about a quiche?'

I find I have a limit when it comes to her conversations of choice. My father is in my mind, almost all the time, but I don't often think of the old gent who spent hours pontificating on the pros and cons of a light supper versus a big meal. No, I spend time thinking about the man as I remember him best. The man who remained calm and reasonable throughout my countless teenage tantrums, the man who walked me up the aisle whispering to me that – above all – I should enjoy my day, and the man who didn't quite understand broadband.

It was remembering the last conversation I had with my father that prompted me to introduce my mother to the web. Perhaps my acts of daughterly devotion are too little and too late, but I have an overwhelming urge and need to make some recompense.

It transpires that Mum is secretly and latently techie and she is delighted when she discovers the internet. She peruses her favourite shops for hours although she insists that she'd never buy clothes without trying them on first, she arranges to have her heavy groceries delivered once a fortnight from the supermarket and she creates her own blog. Eddie, and to a lesser extent Max and Thomas, encourage her remotely by sending her brief but regular notes. Each time she sees the little envelope icon pop on to the screen she squeals with delight and starts to compose.

As I place the cup of tea down next to Mum, I read over her shoulder.

> Elizabeth and I tried a new cheese at supper yesterday it was Fontina Val d'Aosta. She says she discovered it in Italy . . .

With Chuck. It's been a month since I called the school and left my phone number but still no word from him.

I shunt the thought out of my head and ask Mum, 'So what should we do today?'

'Well, I'm going out in a moment, dear. I'm spending the day with Joan Hawkins. We're having lunch together and then a group of us are going to play a hand of bridge this afternoon.'

I stop chewing my toast. 'But what about me?'

'I don't know, dear. What are your plans?'

'Well, my plans *were* to look after you. To keep you company.'

Mum picks up her cup of tea with her old lady hand. Every time I see that thin-skinned, blue-veined hand I'm taken aback.

'I don't need looking after, darling, and I have friends to keep me company.'

I stare at her but she refuses to meet my eye. She stands up and walks to the window. I follow her gaze; it rests on Mr Hopper who lives over the road; he's washing his car. My parents live in a quiet cul-de-sac. Most of their neighbours have lived in the same house for twenty or thirty years, like my parents have. Had. What tense do I use when I'm thinking about Mum and Dad? Mum is still present but Dad is past. I sigh but the air all around me is fusty. Mum must be thinking the same thing because she opens the window and waves to Mr Hooper. He calls to her and offers to wash her car. She says that's very kind but there's no need, she'll take it to the garage and have it done there.

'He's too old to be washing cars,' she quietly mutters to me.

'What should I do today?' I ask again.

'Oh, darling,' chuckles Mum, 'that takes me back. That was the anthem of school holidays when you were a child. You had so many lovely toys, and jigsaws and friends, but you never knew what to do with yourself.'

'That's normal for a kid, though,' I defend. Remembering instantly the exact way I'd groan, 'I'm booooored.'

'Yes, dear. It's absolutely normal for a *child*.' With that Mum turns back to her e-mail.

Mum leaves the house just after ten. I'm at a loss now she has independently struck out. I can see a long day stretching out in front of me and I'm unsure as to how I'll fill it. Panic seizes my throat and my gut. I feel nauseous with terror. Will every day of my life be like this from now on? Will I always wake and face a great big nothing? A huge void where my life should be? I don't understand how everything has unravelled so speedily.

My days in London weren't considered especially meaningful by lots of people, I know that. People like Roberto, my parents, brothers and Alison thought I should be doing more than waiting on tables and waiting to get pregnant, but I never agreed with them. My life seemed full to me. I think Chuck had it right, not everyone can have or even wants a hot-shot career. But I did want a baby, *so much*, and focusing on that was everything to me. OK, so all my days in Italy weren't exactly what you'd call happy; but I still believed I was moving towards my life's goal and that was enough to get me up and out of bed in the morning. Then there was Chuck. Aaghh. Mistake. Thinking of those blissful days I spent with Chuck is a mistake.

I go back upstairs to my bedroom to gather some dirty laundry. OK, I'll give myself three minutes. Three minutes of undiluted pleasure when I remember how it was. I lie down on my unmade bed. I remember how our bodies, sheets, logic and meaning were entwined and perplexed, but when he asked, 'Do you like that?' I felt an unmatched sense of lucidity and conviction. I liked it there, so, so much. I remember lying flat on my back and staring down at my body and his blond head. It bobbed fractionally as he lapped his tongue and sent me into new realms of bliss. I think about his laughter and it rings through my body like pealing church bells. I think of his quick and generous smile and sparks explode just below my stomach.

OK, enough. I *have* to stop thinking about him.

Venice with all its magical, fairytale beauty seems a million miles away from my current world. As I lie in my floral bedroom stuffed with childhood toys and childhood memories I find it increasingly difficult to believe in Venice. Funny, after years and years of being a dreamer I find I can no longer kid myself. Venice was not a Once Upon a Time which would ultimately lead to a Happily Ever After. It was not the start of an amazing romance, but rather a bitter tragedy. Obviously Chuck did not feel as I felt, and the indefinable, exquisite joy that sent me spinning when I was with him was a one-way feeling. I was just another mountain to climb; an experience that he needed to tick off like the bungee-jumping, sky-diving and other boy's-own activities that are recorded in the photos in his flat. It must be so, because how else can I explain his silence? Being here in middle England, with my grieving mum, it's almost impossible to believe that for a time I was brimming with hope and contentment. Now my body aches with sadness.

It's a beautiful day, and the sun is doing its best to cheer me up although its glare exposes the dust nestling in every corner and on every surface of my room; it's a pig-sty. Since Dad's death I've fought a hideous sluggishness, everything seems to require so much effort. More effort than I can generally muster. I suppose it wouldn't kill me to have a tidy-up. Cleaning became quite therapeutic for me when I was in Italy. You could have eaten off the floor in Bruno's during those lonely early weeks, before I met Chuck.

Mum arrives home at 6 p.m. on the dot, as I knew she would because that's teatime for my parents. I've prepared a salad but it's not just garden lettuce, slices of tomato and cucumber; I've bought rocket, pine nuts, balsamic vinegar, walnuts, pears, blue cheese and a crusty loaf. I laid the table carefully with a cloth, mats and napkins, the way Mum likes to see a table set. I even cut some roses from the garden and put them in a vase as a centrepiece. They smell delicious.

'You've been to the shops,' says Mum, unable to hide the delight and relief in her voice. I get a sense that she was testing me by leaving me on my own and that I've passed.

'Yes, I picked up one or two things.'

'Did you get all of this from the corner shop?'

'No, I got the bus into town.' Mum beams. 'We were out of furniture polish,' I explain.

'You've tidied up?' The delight and relief up-weights to astonishment.

'Yup, a bit.'

In fact I've worked like a frenzied dervish. I hadn't planned to do so much. Initially I thought I might pop on a load of washing, maybe clear the magazines off my bedroom floor. But the work was absorbing and I soon found myself reaching for the vacuum and the rubber gloves. Keeping busy helped shift the feeling of being sick with terror at being alone. I opened all the windows and allowed the summer air to run through the house. It is in fact impossible to be thoroughly miserable when a warm summer breeze catches the ends of your hair and lifts it a little; I know, I've tried and failed.

'Do you fancy a cup of tea?' asks Mum.

'No, I fancy a glass of wine.' I produce the bottle I've bought and wave it at her.

'It's a bit early,' says Mum, looking doubtful. She normally waits until after seven before she allows herself a gin and tonic or a glass of Chardonnay.

'Come on, Mum,' I tempt.

'OK, you deserve it,' she grins mischievously.

Mum tucks into my salad and makes a generous number of appreciative noises. She's blown away by my simple salad dressing and briefly I feel like Nigella Lawson.

I like watching my mum eat the food I've prepared. It's a joy to look after someone. My pleasure in this is one of the reasons I've always thought I'd make a good mum. Roberto and I have never had the sort of marriage where I cooked for him. For one thing, he was the better cook and if anyone did the cooking it would be him. Besides, generally, we ate out at the weekends and during the week we kept different hours. He ate his lunch in the office and I ate mine at home. Then I'd have my supper at work and he'd have his at home. I've never considered how little time we actually spent together but it appears to have been very little indeed. I suppose that was why the person who knew me best was Alison, and then when we moved to Italy it was Chuck – those were the people I spent my time with. Of course, in Italy, cooking was Raffaella's domain. Thinking about that causes me to shiver.

'What's up, love? Someone walk over your grave?' asks Mum.

'She's probably dancing on it,' I reply with as rueful a grin as I can muster. I notice concern flicker across Mum's face. Up until now we've eaten in companionable silence. But as the sun begins to fade and the day cools, the birds start to noisily shoo one another to bed; their calls can be heard through the open window. Mum and I listen to them but think about each other.

'You have made such an effort, dear. I really appreciate it,' she says as she slices her fork into the summer pudding.

'I didn't make this, I bought it,' I confess.

'Still,' she beams. I smile back. 'I've been worried about you. You've taken your dad's death very hard. Harder than I might have imagined,' says Mum as she dollops more crème fraîche on to her pudding.

Guiltily, I look at my plate. Suddenly I feel sick again and don't think I can finish the large portion I served up. Is it fair to allow Mum to think all my sadness is to do with my grief for Dad? It seems dishonest. Maybe it's time I told her that Roberto and I have separated. She seems stronger than I could have hoped.

I start carefully, 'I do feel terrible about Dad.'

'We all miss him.'

'I think I wasted a lot of time I had with him.'

'There's never been enough time. I felt that when I lost my parents and I was older than you are now when I lost them. I feel it with your dad too, even though we had fifty-three married years together. I'm perhaps greedy.' She smiles; her smile is wistful. 'Time seems like the enemy now but time is going to be our friend. Time will eventually take away this pain and we'll be left with the memories. The good memories.'

But how can she be sure? What if time fades those memories too? I already can't quite remember Dad's face, not unless I'm looking at a photograph of him. It's too soon for him to become hazy. What if I don't have enough memories to sustain me? Icy-fingered fear wraps around my throat and tightens its grip. And what of Chuck, do I have enough memories?

'You're doing the right thing today,' says Mum, patting my hand. 'Keeping busy helps. It's the only tool we have. Really, dear, you should be thinking about getting back to Italy and getting back into your ordinary routine.'

'I can't do that.'

'Yes, you can. I am fine here. You don't have to feel you have to look after me forever. Don't you miss Italy? Wouldn't it be fantastic to be there now?'

I imagine the sun drilling down on my face and shoulders, I think of the stunning monuments, streets and works of art that I hadn't finished exploring, I think about the colourful, cheerful bars and yes, I miss Italy more than a little. But then I think of Roberto and Raffaella and my blood freezes. I think of the scrunched sheets in the Al Sole Hotel in Venice and my heart shatters. I say nothing.

'Don't you miss Roberto?' Mum stares at me for a long time. Up to now she's conducted most of our conversation without making eye contact.

'Roberto and I have split up,' I splurge.

Mum gasps and puts her hand to her mouth as people do in Agatha Christie movies when the villain is revealed.

'I am so sorry,' she says sincerely.

'Yeah, me too,' I manage.

'Why?'

'There were lots of reasons. Lots of problems. In the end, I suppose it was because we didn't love each other enough to make it work. Isn't that always the final analysis?'

I want to tell her the details but can't bring myself to land that much on her plate. There might be a time when it's right to spill all the gore, but it's not now over summer pudding and crème fraîche. Yet there is something I can't hold back. Something I've wanted to yell out since Chuck gave me the vast eternity of unwanted space.

'How will I have a baby on my own, Mum?'

Tears squeeze out of my eyes. I brush them away impatiently. It was hard enough maintaining hope for a family for the long years when Roberto and I were struggling to conceive. It was a leap to believe I might one day have a child with Chuck, considering his starting point was that he was totally disinterested in having kids, but now it's impossible. I am on my own.

69

I wake up with an unfair hangover. Unfair because I only had two glasses of wine; surprisingly Mum had the extra one in the bottle but this morning I feel as though I've been on a high-intensity pub crawl. What was the expression Chuck used? Sunk a galleon. That's about right.

Yet despite the vague queasiness, emotionally I feel better than I've felt for weeks. I feel a ton weight has lifted now my mother knows about Roberto.

Straight after breakfast, while Mum is pottering in the garden, I call Roberto at the bar. I decide that trying to reach him there is far safer than trying him at Raffaella's. I don't mind if Paolina or Laurana answers but I'd hate it if Raffaella did. In fact I decide that I'll put the phone down if she answers – I don't want to have to talk to that evil witch. I consider it one of the perks of divorcing that I won't ever have to make polite small talk with her again.

'*Pronto.*' I instantly recognize Paolina's voice. '*Chi e?*' she asks. Her voice is efficient and suggests she's in a hurry.

'*Ciao*, Paolina, it's Elizabeth.'

Instantly, her voice softens, '*Di mi.*'

'I'm OK.'

'I'm so pleased to hear it.'

'You?'

444

'Getting by. Sorting things out.'

Suddenly I'm interested in how, or even if, she has resolved things with her lover. I'm not sure if I have the nerve to ask her outright. I don't want to seem impertinent but I'd like her to know that I'm concerned for her.

'Where are you living now?' I hedge.

'Still with Mamma.'

'Oh.'

She understands what I'm getting at. 'He went back to his wife,' she states calmly.

'He did?' I can't keep the surprise out of my voice. The man's a yo-yo. Paolina allows a silence to settle between us and I know the ball is in my court. She's too proud to volunteer more information unprompted. 'Are you sad?'

'No. It is what I wanted. I am free now.'

'Oh well, good,' I say hesitantly. 'I'm glad you're happy.'

'I'm not that yet but I will be.' I smile to myself. Her answer is so Italian. Direct yet winking at the enigmatic. Practical but nodding towards the romantic. After many months of absence I recognize a surge of affection for the nation once again.

'Actually, I have been away. I went away just after you did. I stayed in Padova with a friend. A real friend, not a fictional friend made up to cover for me. I needed time away from Veganze to think. There was too much drama here. Not my own drama even.'

'I can imagine.'

'Mostly you were the cause.'

'I can imagine.'

She laughs. 'And you? How are you, sincerely?' she asks.

'I'm getting there too. I'm calling to talk to Roberto.'

'Yes, I thought this. He's not here.'

'Where is he?'

'On holiday, by the sea.'

A new wave of fury souses me. 'He's taken time off?' I demand.

'Yes.'

'With Ana-Maria, presumably.'

'You know how things are.'

I can almost hear her shrug. What can I say? What can she say? Yes, I know my husband is in love with another woman. I know I spent almost a week in Venice making sweet, sweet love to another man and I know I was calling to ask for a divorce, but really, a holiday! He hardly ever took so much as an afternoon off to be with me.

'Did your mother throw out all my belongings?' I ask.

'No, she tried, Roberto would not allow it.'

'Small mercies I suppose.'

'Yes,' she says awkwardly.

I'm trying to stay reasonable but my emotions are all over the place. Not surprising, considering the last few months. One moment I'm calm, the next furious, then I'm weepy, then resolute again. I'm exhausting to be with. It's exhausting to be me. Anger is snapping at my heels once again.

'I'm still furious about the way he allowed me to find out about the affair. He didn't even have the guts to tell me he wanted out.'

'Would you have heard him?' asks Paolina, calmly.

'Yes! Is this the Italian way, to deny everything to the end? To still be lying and pretending even when there is nothing left worth lying for? Explain it to me, Paolina. Tell me something that will make sense of this.'

'It's not the Italian way; it is Roberto's way. You were so busy marrying the Italian you never knew the man. My brother is not a terrible person. He's a good person who has made mistakes. Like you.' She pauses and I try to digest what she is saying. 'Neither of you wanted to talk about how things really were. You prefer instead to believe things were as you hoped them to be or how you hoped they could become.'

I grip the phone handset so tightly my knuckles turn white. How dare she? What gives her the right to say such things? Just because she's my sister-in-law, and his sister, and she's known me for nearly seven years and I asked her advice doesn't mean –

– That I wanted to hear it.

I start to giggle uncontrollably. Isn't that my problem? Hasn't it always been? The anger gurgles out of me. Recognizing the truth of the situation has loosened a tight knot of resentment that sat in my stomach.

'What is funny?' Paolina asks.

'I am,' I reply honestly. 'Look, Paolina, I'd really love to talk to you for longer but this is my mum's phone so I'll have to go soon. I wonder could you parcel up some more of my things and send them back to me? I'll pay you of course.'

'No problem. I'll do that. Maybe you will call me more often, hey?'

'I'd like that,' I reply firmly.

'I'd like it too. Really,' she says with sincerity. 'Sometimes you can call me to talk about the meaning of life and others just to tell me the small things that are happening to you.'

'Yes, I will.' I assure her.

'Because we are alike, no?'

'In what way?'

'OK, so you are the wife and I am the mistress but we both wasted too much time on the wrong man. Chasing the dream, refusing to see the reality. I love my brother but I think you are doing the right thing now, Elizabeth, and I send you love.'

Then she hangs up before I can reply and I am left in a great big pool of Italian love. It really is quite unlike any other sort.

70

31 July

Mum and I visit the library regularly now; we both love a good read but our tastes, and even our selection methods, vary enormously. I make directly for romantic contemporary fiction; I judge a book by its cover and I can select four novels within ten minutes. Mum browses a different category every time she visits. She drifts around archaeology one week and explores natural science the next.

Last Wednesday, the day of my phone call with Paolina, Mum and I went to the library together. As she entered she muttered, 'I think I'll have a quick look at the nutrition section today, darling, and then you'll find me in classics.' Then she disappeared for over an hour. I had time to make my choice and read all the notices on the cork pinboard. I was only devoting half of my attention to the familiar and useful but not especially compelling notices (swimming lessons for adults and children, cleaners wanted, cleaners available, cats missing, kittens looking for a good home), the other half was glued on to a baby sleeping in its stroller just a metre or so from me. A boy; so sweet, with Bambi-like eyelashes resting on his cheeks.

TEFL training throughout the summer, at the local sixth-form college; places still available.

That notice caused my stomach to hiccup as I was instantly reminded of Chuck handing me a bundle of internet printouts on the very same subject. That was really sweet of him; so many sweet memories – it's not helpful.

I'm not sure why I jotted down the website address, but I did. That night when I went online I typed in the college address while telling myself I had no serious interest in the qualification. As I filled out an application form and e-mailed it back to the administration tutor I reminded myself that there was no point in doing a TEFL course – I'm not going anywhere. The next day when I got an e-mail confirming my interview date I intended to politely decline, but then I thought it just might be something to do other than wait for Mum to choose books or return from bridge and choir practice. I remembered the amazing buzz I'd got when I did teach for that all too brief month in Bassano del Grappa and decided that it couldn't do any harm to just go for a chat. I probably wouldn't get the place anyway.

'Mum! Mum! You are not going to believe it, they offered me a place on the spot.'

Mum dashes towards me and flings her arms around my neck. She pulls me, with surprising strength, into the tightest hug. 'I am so pleased! I knew you'd get it.'

'Did you? I'm surprised.'

'Funny girl. They'd have been mad to turn you down. I bet you are a natural teacher.'

Chuck had said the same thing. 'Do you think?' I feel a blush creep up my cheeks; I'm not great at handling compliments.

'When do you start?'

'They had a cancellation for the course that starts on the fourth of August, so next Monday, I guess.' I giggle nervously, suddenly overwhelmed by the looming change.

'Darling, I am so proud of you.'

'It's a month-long intensive course, six days a week, and it's expensive. It will finally clear me out of my savings.' All the reasons not to do the course scramble into my mind as my nerves start to wake up.

'Don't worry about the money, Elizabeth, you can stay here and I'll help out in any way you need,' says Mum generously. 'Besides, qualifications are a fine thing to spend savings on; much better than clothes.'

Not that I've bought clothes since Moses was a lad. I haven't worn anything pretty or trendy for weeks. As I'm not working I haven't been in a position to flash the cash. To my eternal shame I've found myself wearing Mum's T-shirts and, on cooler days, her cardigans too. I keep telling myself it doesn't matter; I have no one to impress around here, but it's impossible to feel good about yourself when you are wearing a top which belongs to a seventy-six-year-old. Especially one that has little to recommend it other than the fact that it was purchased in a three-pack (one mustard, one beige and one olive). I've worn my mum's trainers in the garden; they must have been bought as a statement against the dictatorship of fashion, because they are so ugly the dog runs away from them. At first I didn't much notice or care what I was wearing, it seemed trivial in the face of losing Dad, but since I spoke to Paolina, I've got to admit, I've started to look forward to my parcel arriving.

'Oh, speaking of clothes, Paolina called this morning

when you were at your interview. She says she's despatched your things but she wanted to check that you are going to be in this afternoon because you have to sign for the crate.'

'Yes!' I do a little dance around the kitchen. 'I can't wait.'

Mum smiles patiently and doesn't take offence at my obvious glee at casting off her garments.

'Things are looking up for you, aren't they?'

'I suppose.' I freeze and instantly pull my face into a more sober expression.

'It's OK, you are allowed to be happy,' says Mum, patting my hand. 'Your dad didn't like glum faces. Now what do you fancy for lunch?'

71

Mum and I are just clearing away the pots from lunch when the doorbell rings.

'That might be my delivery,' I yell and dash to answer it. I fling open the door with anticipation.

'Chuck?'

He's standing on my mum's doorstep in all his blond gloriousness. I wipe my eyes, like a cartoon character. I can't believe this. I'm so shocked that I nearly burst into tears. I fight them back; crying at this moment would only confuse and I, for one, am already totally bewildered.

'What the hell are you doing here?' I hadn't actually planned to say that aloud.

'I'm returning your belongings,' he says simply. My gaze drops to the floor where there is a heaving, over-packed suitcase. I recognize it as my own. 'Paolina came round to my apartment and she said that you'd asked for her to return your belongings. I offered to bring them. I came on the first flight I could get. Look, can we talk about this inside?'

I am literally unable to function. What is a reasonable response to finding your lover on your doorstep after two months of silence? Ex-lover. *Ex*, I remind myself. The one who was really keen on space. Should I pour scorn in his face and bring my knee up to hurt him in the bollocks? That seems quite restrained to me. Yet I find I'm unable to hurt him.

Mum bustles down the hallway.

'Who is it, dear?' I can't find my tongue to even make the necessary introductions.

'Mrs Gardiner, I presume,' says Chuck, holding out his hand.

'Yes.' Mum beams at him, no doubt instantly wooed by his sparkling eyes, his height, his accent and his manners. It's not just a family trait. I think most women would fall. Looking at him for the first time after a long time I have to admit he is still pretty wow even if he is a flighty, shallow, commitment-phobic rat.

'I'm Chuck Andrews.' Mum's face does not flicker with any sign of recognition; of course not, I've never mentioned Chuck's name to her. He studies her and realizes as much. Did I imagine that or did he look disappointed? The egotistical bastard probably hoped that I've been weeping and wailing about him for two months and that my mum would know exactly who he is. Well, I'm glad I've had the restraint to weep and wail in private and deny him that pleasure at least!

Although he doesn't sound like an egotistical bastard. In fact, he doesn't look much changed at all. He seems just as sincere and sexy as he did in Venice – a little less giddy on happiness perhaps. How is it possible that he's unchanged? Shouldn't there be some sort of external alteration to signpost his cruelty? It's clear that he is the consummate wolf in sheep's clothing, when, totally unperturbed, he confidently continues, 'I'm a colleague of your daughter's. I'm returning her belongings. I –'

'Oh, come in, come in, Mr Andrews.'

'Chuck, please.'

'Come in, Chuck. Goodness, Elizabeth, where are your

manners? This lovely young man has just dragged your heavy suitcase all the way from Italy and you are keeping him on the doorstep.' She glares at me.

Because I can't see an alternative, I step back and let Mum lead him through to the front room. Somehow I manage to resist sticking my foot out to trip him up. The hall wallpaper morphs around me. I think I'm going to pass out. God, my stomach has turned gymnastic. I need the loo. I need the door. What the hell is he doing here? I've heard nothing for two months and then suddenly he's on my doorstep. I thought I was getting used to his absence but his presence is something I doubt I'm strong enough to deal with. Isn't he a little late with his excuses? If indeed he's coming armed with excuses. He seems oddly unapologetic so far. The arrogance!

I look into the hall mirror and bitterly regret the choice of shirt this morning. It actually belongs to my mother. Could things be worse? Plus, why the hell didn't I put on any make-up today? I was trying to look studious for the interview. Why couldn't I see I just look hideous?

Mum comes back out of the front room and stares at me.

'What's the matter, dear?'

I stay silent. Where to begin? I should have told her about Chuck, then she could have protected me from this; she wouldn't have invited him in and made him cosy in the front room. Now who is going to protect me? I'm not able to look after myself, that much is obvious. I can't even put one foot in front of another.

I try to remain calm. Just because he's here with my suitcase doesn't necessarily mean anything important. He's probably just passing through and this is just a friendly,

I'm-so-not-interested-in-you-in-that-way-I-can-barely-remember-us-ever-being-anything-other-than-colleagues visit. I wish I could be equally disinterested.

But then I wouldn't give up the memories of him for the world.

My head is about to explode. I wish it would. If my brain was splattered across Mum's really rather awful floral wallpaper then I wouldn't have to think about any of this.

'Go and sit with your guest, Elizabeth. I'll make some tea.' She practically pushes me through the door.

'Hi.' Chuck throws out a weak smile as I stumble into the room.

'Hi,' I murmur.

I stand with my back against the door, ensuring a swift exit if need be. It's so disorientating having him sat here on my mum's Dralon sofa. The sofa is a million years old and she should probably get a new one; it's lumpy and springs jut out at weird angles like broken bones pushing out of flesh. It has this way of swallowing anyone who tries to perch tentatively on the edge, which somehow suggests we have a sofa with a mischievous streak. Chuck hasn't tried to perch on the edge; he's flung himself back as though surrendering to it. Smart move. He actually looks quite comfortable. How dare he? It's so disconcerting, especially considering I feel about as comfortable as someone who is wearing a dress two sizes too small on a first date. He looks large in Mum's small room; powerful. I feel hemmed in; weak. We should have gone into the garden. There's nowhere to hide here. Nowhere to run to.

'I am very sorry about your father.' He coughs. I feel his gaze hammer down on me but I can't meet his eyes.

'Yes, you said sorry, in your *text*,' I snap. The implication being, of course, that a text is the most gross way to pass on condolences, even if I was a vague acquaintance; it's completely unforgivable considering what we meant to one another – at least, what I thought we meant to one another.

Chuck seems to catch the anger in my voice and looks at me with confusion but doesn't say anything. What? He expected me to be delighted that he abandoned me in my saddest and most needy time? Mum's mantelpiece clock ticks and adds to the tension. The normally soothing tick-tock sounds as threatening as the sort of drumbeat that escorts a person to the gallows. I decide that polite small talk is out of the question. I'd prefer to fling a few pointed jibes that might lead to some answers.

'Thanks for the space, Chuck. I've been using it really well,' I mutter sarcastically.

'Good,' he replies, with an evenness that is irritating. He coughs again. 'So what have you been doing with yourself since Venice?'

Unfair! Just hearing the word Venice causes me to flush scarlet. For me, the very word conjures vivid images of him riding and writhing on top of me, below me, beside me. Does it do the same for him? I force myself to look up from my feet, where I've been resolutely staring, and I steal a glance in his direction. He's sitting a little further forward on the sofa now; not quite as relaxed. His elbows are resting on his spread knees. He is staring **right** at me. Our eyes meet for the first time. His gaze slices through me and I'm certain that he can read my mind and soul, making it impossible and quite pointless for me to try to lie.

'Grieving,' I state plainly.

His head falls into his hands. 'Of course. I'm sorry and –' he sighs deeply – 'I'm sorry that things didn't work out as you hoped with Roberto.'

What? I'm lost. What does he mean things didn't work out as I hoped with Roberto? They did – in a way – in the end. Roberto and I don't belong together. I thought that much was clear in Venice. Before I have time to say anything, he continues.

'I know there's no reason for me to assume you are in the least bit interested in what *I've* been doing in the last couple of months, but I'll fill you in all the same.'

His tone sounds both supercilious and indignant. I really resent it. No, I am not interested! Well, actually, I am – very; although I would rather eat sewage than admit as much. But what is it with his sarky, superior attitude? Shouldn't he be humble and apologetic? God, how could I have missed the extent of this man's conceit and selfishness?

'After I got your message from Gina, I moved to Bassano del Grappa and I moved in with Francesca.'

'Francesca!' I can't keep the hurt and shock out of my voice. 'You did *what*?'

My God, it's worse than I imagined. I had sometimes worried there might be an unspoken attraction between those two but I never suspected that he'd actually been having an affair with her! But then why the hell not? They are both perfectly amazing: beautiful, accomplished, thrilling. They suit each other. I hate her.

'I couldn't stay in Veganze and risk bumping into you every day,' he says. Bumping into *me* in Veganze? Why would he think that was likely or even possible? 'I moved back to Veganze two weeks ago.'

I can't stop myself sliding into sarcasm. 'Oh, another one of your famously lengthy relationships,' I mutter.

'Sorry?' asks Chuck in a tone that suggests he's anything but. 'I wasn't having a relationship with Francesca. She was a friend to me.' He stares at me with something approaching disbelief or maybe disgust. 'Just a friend. *I'm* not the one famed for bouncing from one relationship to the next, am I? You are,' he points out with a cold anger.

'Yup, that's me. And you are the one with a thing for married women,' I shout back.

'Well, I hear that you've finally decided that you are no longer that,' he counters, his anger up a notch.

'I should be safe from your advances then.' I'm a hair's breadth away from full throttle.

We stare at each other with patent fury. I'm so deep in a pit of frustration and loathing it takes me a moment to digest exactly what he's just said.

'What do you mean I've *finally* decided I'm no longer a married woman?' I ask.

'Sorry, cheap shot.' Chuck seems to be trying to recover some of his poise. He pulls his fingers through his hair in the familiar way that tugs on my innards. Damn, he's sexy. Even now. Even in the throes of a terminal argument, I can't help but notice his qualities. 'Elizabeth, to be straight, I'm fed up with you running backwards and forwards to Roberto. I thought in Venice you'd made your mind up that you wanted to be with me. So when I got your message, I was –' he stops and looks round the room; he's choosing his words carefully. After an age he chooses – 'disappointed.'

Suddenly I feel as though I'm on the waltzers. Shapes are moving and morphing in front of me. I can see Chuck and I can hear him but I can't understand him. My world is shifting underneath me.

'My note said my dad was dead and asked you to phone me,' I blurt.

Chuck looks as though someone has just punched him. The colour bleeds from his face – I expect to look down and see it lying in a pool of shock on Mum's carpet. Suddenly, a fraction of a second after I've joined the dots, his face floods again – this time with hope and excitement.

'I didn't get a *note*. Gina just gave me a verbal message – supposedly from you. She said that your dad had died and that you were going home for a few days but that I mustn't call you. That you didn't want to hear from me again, especially not when you came back to Italy.'

'She said what? Why would Gina do that?'

Of course there are many reasons why she might have wanted to ruin things between Chuck and me. Maybe she was trying to be loyal to Roberto, or maybe she fancied Chuck for herself and wanted me out the way. I have no idea. People do terrible things from time to time; that much I'm certain of.

'She said you were going to try to work things out with Roberto.' Chuck is grinning now. 'That's why I sent you the text saying I'd give you space. That's why I went to stay with Francesca.' My legs turn to liquid. 'I had to respect what you'd asked for, even if I didn't think it was the right thing. It was fucking agony. I hated the choice you'd made. I wanted to call you. I so nearly did on loads and loads of occasions but it seemed wrong considering Roberto is your husband and you'd just lost your pop. I knew it would be crap of me to lay on any more pressure, however much I wanted to.'

'Loads and loads?' I ask, giggling, finally allowing my body and brain to compute this terrible deceit. Hope starts to swell in my stomach. 'You thought I'd chosen Roberto?'

'Yes. When I returned from Francesca's neither you nor Roberto were anywhere to be seen. Until Paolina visited I assumed you were away together. She told me he was with Ana-Maria.' Chuck shoots me a look of concern but I beam at him, hoping he understands that I don't give a damn where Roberto is or who he's with. 'I had no idea you were in England.'

I am about to dash across the room and fling myself at Chuck. I am about to allow the horrible, relentless pain and disappointment of his 'desertion' to slide away from me forever, when I see his grin slip.

'Why didn't you just call me and ask about the text if it didn't make sense to you?' he asks.

'Because I thought you were a commitment-phobic. I started thinking about your other affair with a married woman and your reluctance to have kids.' I trail off. I realize my reasons for not contacting him are faithless and ignoble in comparison to his reasons for giving me space.

Chuck looks shocked. Pained. 'You don't have a very high opinion of me, do you?'

'It's not that,' I bluster. 'I threw away my phone. I didn't . . .'

'What?'

'I didn't have your number. I did call the school.' Eventually.

I stutter on, 'But exams had started. I'd left it too late.' I begin to get an idea what he must be thinking and feeling. Suddenly, comprehending our situation from his point of view, I realize that I've been a selfish moron. I *should* have called after receiving the text. Think of all the hurt and confusion I could have saved us both from. I should have had more faith in him and myself; enough to know that what we had in Venice was real. I should have given him the opportunity to clear up this hideous mess. Why didn't I trust more? Looking at him now, in his tight T-shirt and battered jeans, wearing an expression of confusion and indignation, he's really never looked so entirely honourable and irresistible. I, by contrast, feel grubby and uncomfortable. I don't dash across the room and fling myself at him. I remain rooted.

I'm grateful that Mum pushes open the door and comes into the room with a tea tray heaving with cups and saucers, milk and sugar. I wonder how much she's heard.

'So, are you here on holiday?' she asks Chuck brightly.

For a moment he looks dazed and I doubt his ability to answer her, then he seems to pull himself together and says, 'More of an exploration; I'm looking for answers.'

He eyes me meaningfully. If Mum thinks his reply is eccentric she doesn't show it. No doubt she puts it down to him being American. She fusses about how Chuck takes his tea. I notice she hasn't used bags but rather she's treating him to the authentic experience. I watch as her strainer catches the leaves.

I stay silent and Chuck only just manages to respond to her jabbering so the conversation is painful and stilted. Mum must think so too, because after a few minutes she says, 'I'll get some cakes, shall I? I baked a sponge this morning. Let's cut into it.' She gets up and bustles through to the kitchen again.

Chuck flops and rests against the sofa back. He dramatically slaps his forehead.

'I've just worked it out. All of it. Looking at you now, the penny has dropped. God, I'm dim. I see, now, why you accepted my seemingly sudden departure with such indecent ease.' He stands up and starts to stride around the room. It's a small room and he's a big guy, so every two or three paces he has to change direction. I can't keep up with him, mentally or physically. 'I don't think I've ever been so insulted in all my life. You didn't think I'd be up to it.'

'Up to what?'

'You thought you'd just bring this baby up on your own, did you? Without even so much as mentioning its existence to me?' His voice is unnaturally high with indignation.

'What baby? What are you on about?'

'There are laws, you know. I have my rights. I want to be part of the baby's life, no matter what I said before. You are not going to exclude me from this,' he shouts. 'I want in.'

Mum must have heard him in the kitchen; actually Mr Hooper must have heard him from across the street. I'm too confused to try to temper my response, I shout back.

'In what?'

'I want to be involved in bringing up my baby.'

'What baby?'

'The one you are carrying?'

I stare at him utterly aghast. This is too much of an emotional roller-coaster for me. I can't get a grip on our reality. 'I'm not pregnant,' I splutter.

'You are,' he says, but this time he doesn't shout, he

sounds less certain. He pauses and then adds, 'Aren't you?'

'No,' I say indignantly.

'Oh.' He looks crestfallen. His face crumples like student sheets at the end of term. But I must have that wrong. Why would he be disappointed? He doesn't want babies with me or anyone. He said so.

'Why did you think I was pregnant? That's crazy. Are you saying I'm fat?' I'm mesmerized by this latest turn. The man is mad. I'd never imagined that I might have rocked his boat so entirely but I clearly have. He's losing his reason. Gina's trickery, the sudden revelation, the long journey perhaps – it's all been too much for him. He's being so irrational.

'Well, you are a little curvier than when we last met. Quite a lot actually –' he says apologetically.

'Thank you very much!'

'But it's not just that, you also seem altered. You're glowing. Sort of serene. I thought – look, sorry. I don't know why I jumped to that conclusion. I just kind of sensed something about you. Or I thought I did. Look, forget it. Can we start this conversation again, please?'

'You have more to say to me than that I'm fat?' I demand crossly.

'Elizabeth, please.' He's clearly mortified.

Mum comes back into the room this time with a tea tray heaving with goodies: besides the sponge she's also brought a plate of biscuits and another one of muffins. I know the biscuits and muffins are shop-bought but I'm prepared to keep her secret.

'Everything all right?' she asks, showing that she knows clearly everything is far from it.

Chuck sits back down. In fact, he almost collapses with weariness or maybe embarrassment. I don't know what to think or say, so I sulkily leave the onus of conversation to them again.

Chuck starts politely, if not a little predictably, with a comment about the goodies. I can't believe he thought I was pregnant. Am I that fat? I know I've put on a few pounds. I have been doing quite a lot of comfort eating but how hideously insensitive to mention it! And what a moment to choose. First I think he's a heartless commit-ment-phobic and he thinks I'm a fickle prick-tease; we no sooner get that sorted than he judges me to be faithless and I see him as deranged. Where the hell do we go from here?

'This looks lovely, Mrs Gardiner.'

'Thank you, dear.'

'My mum is a baker.'

'Is she? Oh dear, I feel I'm about to be scrutinized.'

'I'm sure your cakes are lovely. Elizabeth is proof they are delicious.' As soon as he says it, his face turns scarlet with a new flame of blush.

'Will you stop with the fat digs,' I yell at him.

'I'm not trying to have a dig. I was just taken aback. I thought one thing. You said it wasn't so. I'm –'

'Relieved, no doubt you are relieved. Because babies aren't part of your plan, are they?' I snap.

'I never said relieved,' he protests.

'What's this about a baby?' asks Mum.

Because I'm in turmoil and not capable of thinking straight, I blurt, 'He thought I was pregnant with his baby.'

'*His* baby?' Mum cries with astonishment. 'How could you be pregnant with *his* baby?'

'That's not the bit we are debating, Mum,' I say snippily, aware – too late – that I've opened a can of worms. 'The bit I'm taking umbrage with, right now, is that Chuck has come all the way from Italy to tell me that I'm *fat*.'

Mum's face creases with concern. 'I thought you were pregnant too,' she says. 'But I thought it was Roberto's baby. I've been wondering when you were going to talk to me about it. I thought the problem was you were having a baby with a husband you no longer loved, but are you now telling me that the problem is you are having a baby with a man who isn't your husband?' Mum looks horrified.

'I'm not having a baby!' I yell.

'Oh, well, sorry,' says Mum. 'But you've been grumbling about feeling sick. Your clothes are too tight, your emotions are all over the place.'

I look down at the skirt I am wearing today. It's held up with a safety pin because I couldn't get the button fastened. I had to let the shirt hang out; the shirt that strained across my enormous boobs, that is. I've always had big boobs but recently mine have defied belief and they are quite tender too. I thought I was due but I haven't had a period since I've been at Mum's. No period. No sodding period. Oh my God! Without another word I push past Mum and dash out of the front room, nearly upturning the tea tray burdened with goodies. I grab my bag and run, feet slapping hard on the pavement all the way into the village and into the chemist.

72

I run back from the chemist with a pregnancy kit in my hand; I couldn't be bothered to wait for the gawky girl to put it in a bag or give me my change. I run all the way home, feet slamming so hard that they throb, heart pounding in my chest with a wildness that makes me think I might be sick. Mum is right, I have been feeling sick so often recently. Could it be . . . Could it? I offer prayers up to anyone who will listen, anyone who can influence; my dad, God, the lady in the white coat on the fertility website. Please, please, please, I beg.

Mum and Chuck are both standing in the front garden, both anxiously staring up the street, waiting for my return. Mum looks excited. I can't read Chuck's expression. He thought I was pregnant. He saw it first. If I am, that is. Oh God, oh God, please, please. I dare not want it this much. I dare not believe it. I feel closer to the possibility than ever, but will I survive a disappointment if I'm not?

I don't stop in the garden to so much as acknowledge my anxious loved ones. I push straight past and run upstairs into the bathroom. Chuck is hot on my heels but I slam the door in his face and lock it.

I know how these tests work. I've used them dozens of times before. I've spent hundreds and hundreds of pounds on them. I rip the cardboard and hold the stick in my hand. This is it. I pee and pray at the same time. I think God will forgive me the inappropriateness of that.

'Elizabeth, can you hear me?' asks Chuck. I sit on the side of the bath and wait the longest 120 seconds in history. I can't make my lips form an answer. I nod mutely and therefore, unhelpfully. Chuck goes on regardless. 'Elizabeth, sweetheart, I just want to say, whatever the result, it doesn't matter. I want you and I want babies, if that's what you want. Hell, I want them anyway, and if this doesn't give the result you need don't worry, we'll try again. We'll keep trying and trying. It will be fun.' He laughs but his laugh is desperate and nervous. 'We'll have a family, Elizabeth. I promise you. We'll do IVF. We'll adopt. The stuff I said before, well, that was before.'

I turn the lock and open the door to face him. 'Before what?' I ask.

'Before I fell in love with you.'

Epilogue

She is it. She is all. She is more than even I could have hoped for. She makes me want to sing, and laugh, and dance, and live. Live so, so well. She is meaning and sense to me. She was worth the wait. Every moment of it.

Truly, my greatest delight is covering her with kisses. I love to kiss her rosy cheeks, her plump belly, her smooth legs. My lips melt on her soft and velvety skin and it feels as though I'm dipping my face into a bowl of fresh cream. I drink in her smell, it's more scrumptious than freshly baked cake or Italian coffee and it's more pure, fresh and intoxicating than even the full-bloom roses in my mum's garden. Well, most of the time it is; sometimes she carries a faint whiff of vomit or worse.

I am not alone in delighting in Lily; wherever we go she draws a crowd. The *passeggiata* takes three times as long as it used to when I was pregnant and Chuck and I did the same route around the cobbled streets of Bologna. Now, people are always stopping us to have a look in the pram. They 'oh' and 'ah' about her blonde curls and sparkly green eyes, they comment on her keenness to kick off even the lightest blanket and loll in the warm evening sun, they delight in her grin which, like her daddy's, when cracked engulfs her entire face. She's played to the crowd from day one. I think she's going to be a terrible flirt when she gets older; I'm already resigned to spending most of her teen years worrying about her skirt length.

She coos, and burbles, and throws out gummy smiles to anyone who takes a peek. People are always pressing helium balloons, flowers and tiny fluffy toys on us – complete strangers. I was right about one thing, Italians do love babies.

'I adore these warm evenings that allow the entire family to take a jaunty walk to the town centre,' I say to Chuck, not for the first time.

'Yeah, it's something to do, since the TV is so crap.'

I grin at him. I know he is hellbent on keeping me focused on the reality of our lives here and not allowing me to become unrealistically dreamy or to over-idealize – there lies a path of disappointment, he warns. I can't take him too seriously; I mean, what is not to love?

The cobbled streets are drenched in blond sunlight. Bologna's compact historic core is medieval in plan, so there is a rich scattering of churches, monuments and museums. I'm slowly making my way around them. I've overcome my initial belief that if you've seen one old church you've seen them all. I've discovered that the more you know about these places, the more interesting they become. Plus, I spend a significant amount of time just wandering along the elegant, porticoed streets that radiate from the two main piazzas – dipping into the gorgeous shops for a browse or to spend. My all-time favourite occupation is still sitting in a piazza, either Piazza Maggiore or Piazza del Nettuno, and sipping delectably strong coffee. This is now especially amazing because of the attention Lily draws; I am never alone – there's always someone who wants to chat, keen to know how old she is or if she's a good eater or sleeper.

Not that I have so much time to waste nowadays. Time

flies. Lily is a good sleeper but she's a picky eater. She's keen to nibble on my boob but does not take her fill, so just about every twenty minutes I seem to be whipping them out. Looking after her is obviously my number one priority and the sweetest way for me to spend time but I also like to slip in the odd hour teaching. Chuck bought a language school here in Bologna, which we run together. Sometimes I have to pinch myself. I find it hard to compute that I help run a business, a reasonably successful business if the last year is anything to go by. A business I care passionately about. Who would have thought it? Chuck bears the lion's share of the work but I've been helpful with the administration and advertising, and since I now have a formal TEFL qualification I've been able to help out in the classrooms reasonably regularly too. Since Lily arrived I've cut back my hours but I still manage ten hours a week when she's napping after lunch. I take her into my classroom and she sleeps right alongside me while I teach. That arrangement can't go on forever of course, but I delight in the Italians' flexibility in this matter. My pupils are always thrilled to see her. As I mentioned, she's a crowd-pleaser and Italians like babies.

It hasn't all been plain sailing. It seemed like Chuck and I were just getting used to one another when Lily arrived and threw our recently negotiated relationship into disarray. Mostly we all delight one another, nine times out of ten the discoveries I make about Chuck, or being a mother, send me into orbits of ecstasy, but from time to time we're unpleasantly surprised with each other. I was taken aback to find that Chuck snores, irritated that he does not put down the loo seat after use and stunned when he totally refused to be in attendance at Lily's birth because of his dislike of the sight of blood. He says it drives him insane that I never put lids back on bottles – whether that's water bottles, cosmetics or tomato ketchup – and my failing to do so has led to more than one spillage and row. He thinks I should do more exercise and I think he'd go as far as to secretly describe me as a bit unfit. But we are both working on these small shortcomings. I'm trying to find a way to incorporate exercise into my daily routine and I've got Chuck to agree to at least come into the delivery room for baby number two – he can always make a run for it if things get gruesome.

These differences don't matter a jot to us. Initially some people worried that we were rushing into this relationship, but we noticed that the people we're closest to, and who knew us best, wholeheartedly gave their support. Mum, Alison, Thomas and Paolina practically insisted we should be together, arguing that we are made for one another. Not that anyone else's opinion was ever going to sway us either way. Chuck and I have done enough being apart to know that we want and need to be together.

We are a family. We are solid and realistic. The realism came quite quickly and naturally after a tricky pregnancy, a twenty-seven-hour labour and countless sleepless nights with a tiny baby. Sometimes it seems that we haven't had much room at all for endless tender declarations, hearts and flowers. Chuck did hang the glass heart from Verona above our bed, which was fabulously thoughtful, but most of his romantic gestures tend to be rooted in a heavy dose of practicality nowadays. He often runs me a deep bath and he occasionally lights candles too; he tries to let me snatch extra sleep by getting up with Lily whenever he can; he buys me fresh fruit from the market and tells me the nutritional value of a pear versus a pineapple or a banana. I distribute leaflets advertising the school as I push the pram around town, I mark school work if I see he has a mountain of it and would really prefer to just take off for an hour on his bike. We sometimes have minuscule domestics about whose turn it is to change Lily; but that's a dream come true for me.

We exist in this way, simply happy. It's not just that I don't have time to day-dream any more, it's more that I don't have the need. The here and now is enough.

TELL ME SOMETHING

Bonus material

Reading Group Questions

- In what ways do you think Elizabeth's priorities shifted as the novel progressed?

- Did you, to any extent, see Elizabeth's overwhelming desire to start a family as a symptom of her difficulties with Roberto, rather than a cause?

- How differently did you feel the Italian and English families in the novel were portrayed? Did it strike you that one had a particularly better quality of life than the other?

- How do you feel the author handled the female friendships in the novel? Did the relationship between Elizabeth and Alison feel balanced?

- Did you think Elizabeth was justified in her decision to escape Veganze before she'd confronted Roberto?

- How far did you sympathise with Paolina's predicament?

- How did you react to Roberto's attitude to his and Elizabeth's difficulties in conceiving? Did you feel he was being unfair?

- Do you think the novel supports Chuck's assertion that for every person there is an infinite number of relationships that can work?

- How far do you think the characters of Roberto and Chuck fit Elizabeth's notions of Italian and American stereotypes? Do you agree with her?

- Did you feel any empathy towards the character of Raffaella?

Have you read all of Adele's fabulously addictive novels?

ABOUT LAST NIGHT

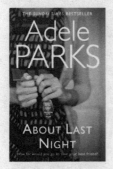

There is nothing best friends Steph and Pip wouldn't do for one another. That is, until Steph begs Pip to lie to the police as she's desperately trying to conceal not one but two scandalous secrets to protect her family. Her perfect life will be torn apart unless Pip agrees to this lie. But lying will jeopardise everything Pip's recently achieved after years of struggle. It's a big ask. How far would you go to save your best friend?

MEN I'VE LOVED BEFORE

Nat doesn't want babies; she accepts this is unusual but not unnatural. She has her reasons; deeply private and personal which she doesn't feel able to share. Luckily her husband Neil has always been in complete agreement, but when he begins to show signs of changing his mind, Nat is faced with a terrible dilemma. She begins to question if the man she has married is really the man she's meant to be with . . .

YOUNG WIVES' TALES

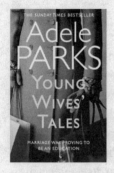

Lucy stole her friend Rose's 'happily ever after' because she wanted Rose's husband – and Lucy always gets what she wants. Big mistake. Rose was the ideal wife and is the ideal mother; Lucy was the perfect mistress. Now neither can find domestic bliss playing each other's roles. They need more than blind belief to negotiate their way through modern life. And there are more twists in the tale to come . . .

HUSBANDS

Love triangles are always complex but in Bella's case things are particularly so as she is *married* to both men in her triangle. She plans never to reveal her first marriage to husband number two Phillip – after all, Stevie is no longer part of her life. That is until, inconveniently, her best friend introduces her new man to Bella and it's none other than husband number one. Could things get more complicated? Well, only if Bella and Stevie fall for one another again . . .

STILL THINKING OF YOU

Tash and Rich are wild about each other; their relationship is honest, fresh and magical, so they dash towards a romantic elopement in the French Alps. However, five of Rich's old university friends crash the wedding holiday and they bring with them a whole load of ancient baggage. Can Tash hold on to Rich when she's challenged by years of complicated yet binding history and a dense web of dark secrets and intrigues? Does she even want to?

THE OTHER WOMAN'S SHOES

The Evergreen sisters have always been opposites with little in common. Until one day, Eliza walks out on her boyfriend the very same day Martha's husband leaves her. Now the Evergreen sisters are united by separation, suddenly free to pursue the lifestyles they think they always wanted. So, when both find exactly what they're looking for, everybody's happy . . . aren't they? Or does chasing love only get more complicated when you're wearing another woman's shoes?

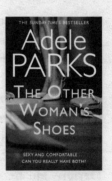

LARGER THAN LIFE

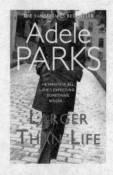

Georgina fell in love with Hugh the moment she first saw him and she's never loved another man. Unfortunately, for all that time he's been someone else's husband and father. After years of waiting on the sidelines, Georgina finally gets him when his marriage breaks down. But her dream come true turns into a nightmare when she falls pregnant and Hugh makes it clear he's been there, done that and doesn't want to do it all again. Georgina has to ask herself, is this baby bigger than the biggest love of her life?

GAME OVER

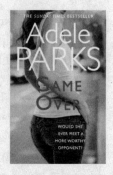

Cas Perry doesn't want a relationship. When her father walked out on her and her mother she decided love and marriage simply weren't worth the heartache. Cas, immoral most of the time and amoral when it comes to business, ruthlessly manipulates everyone she comes into contact with. Until she meets Darren. He believes in love, marriage, fidelity and constancy, so can he believe in Cas? Is it possible the world is a better place than she imagined? And if it is, after a lifetime of playing games, is this discovery too late?

PLAYING AWAY

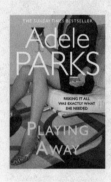

Connie has been happily married for a year. But she's just met John Harding. Imagine the sexiest man you can think of. He's a walking stag weekend. He's a funny, disrespectful, fast, confident, irreverent pub crawl. He is also completely unscrupulous. He is about to destroy Connie's peace of mind and her grand plan for living happily ever after with her loving husband Luke. Written through the eyes of the adulteress, *Playing Away* is the closest thing you'll get to an affair without actually having one.

Can she find Happily Ever After in a world where there isn't room for fairy tales?

Read on for a preview of
Adele Parks' novel
LOVE LIES

Prologue
Scott

'Do I smell, Mark?'
　'No.'
　'You'd tell me if I did, right?'
　'I would.'
　'Is my hairline receding?'
　'No.'
　'You're sure I'm not going bald?'
　'Yes.'
　'Do you think I'll lose my teeth?'
　'Only if someone punches you.'
　'My nan got gum disease.'
　'We've got great dentists. Scott, you are coming down and this is just another one of your irrational worry sessions. We can waste a lot of time doing this, mate.'
　'Mark, do you think I'll end up broke? You know, blow it all.'
　'No, we've sorted out your finances. You're never going to suffer from poverty – other than poverty of spirit. No matter how many TVs you throw out of hotel windows.'

1. Fern

I have taken a bullet. I live an ordinary life. I've almost accepted it. Almost.

I ought to clarify I don't always go around thinking big, profound thoughts like that. Quite a lot of the time I amuse my brain cells by thinking about which movie star is shagging which other movie star (and do they have better sex than us mere mortals), or whether I can get away with not washing my hair if I'm inventive enough with my up-do (thus securing an extra thirty minutes in bed in the morning). My idea of deep is wondering whether organic food is worth the huge price tag or whether it's all just a ghastly marketing con. But today I am twenty-nine years, eleven months and three weeks old. I can no longer keep the big thoughts at bay.

Let me clarify, when I say ordinary, I mean normal, average, run of the mill, commonplace. Mundane. Clear?

I know, I know. I should be grateful. Ordinary has its up-side. I could be some human mutant with skin stretchy enough to be able to wrap my lower lip over the top of my head, *or* an über-fertile woman prone to giving birth to sextuplets and now be a proud mother of thirty-six indistinguishable, media-loving brats *or* someone who really does train-spot. Then my life would be considerably worse than the one I am leading, but even knowing this is not as much comfort as it should be.

I live my ordinary life with Adam. My boyfriend of four years. I hesitate to refer to him as my partner because that would suggest some sort of equality or responsibility in the relationship and, frankly, both things are notably lacking. I organize the paying of all the bills (although he does cough up his share when prompted). I buy groceries, cook, clean, remember the birthdays of his family members, buy wedding gifts for our friends, arrange travel and accommodation if we ever do manage to grab a weekend away, I even put the pizza delivery people's number on speed dial. Adam alphabetically arranges his CDs and vinyls in neat rows, all the way along our sitting-room shelves.

Yes, we do share a flat. A two-bedroom flat in Clapham. Not the posh bit of Clapham, sadly. The bit where the neighbours think old pee-stained mattresses and settees, spurting their cheap foam innards, are acceptable alternatives to rose bushes in the front garden. Despite sharing a flat, I also hesitate to refer to Adam as my live-in lover because that would suggest an element of passion and that's notably lacking too, of late. Our relationship is more prose than poetry. It wasn't always that way.

We used to be wild about each other. We used to swing from chandeliers, or as good as. There was a time when we couldn't keep our hands off one another. Which led to some, er, shall we say interesting situations. I'm not trying to brag. I just want to paint a fair picture. We are certified members of the mile-high club and we have made love under canvas, in a swimming-pool and once in a botanic garden (Kew). We made love frequently and in many, many different ways; slowly and carefully, fast and needy. In the past we often came at the same time. Now, it's unusual if we both are in the room at the same time.

I used to think we were going somewhere. It looks like we've arrived. This is my stop. I have to get off the train and take a long hard look at the station. It's not one with hanging baskets full of cascading begonia and there isn't one of those lovely large clocks with Roman numerals. There's nothing romantic or pretty about my station at all. My station is littered with discarded polystyrene cups and spotted with blobs of chewing-gum.

Frankly, it's depressing.

We don't own our flat. We don't even have an exclusive flat-share. My best friend, Jess, also rents with us. Normally, I acknowledge that this is no bad thing. She is (largely) single and so we are each other's on-tap company on those nights when she doesn't have a date and Adam is at work.

Adam is in the music business. Don't get excited. He's not a rock star, or a manager, or producer, or anything remotely glamorous and promising. He's a rigger; which, if I've understood things correctly, is one step up from the coach driver on a tour but not as important as the people who work in catering. He freelances, and while he must be quite good at his job (offers of employment are regular) it's clear he's never going to be a millionaire. For that matter, he's never going to have so much as a savings account.

This didn't used to bother me. I'm a florist and work in someone else's shop: Ben's Bunches and Bouquets or Ben's B&B for short. Ben, who is as camp as a glow-in-the-dark feather duster, is an absolute angel of a boss but I only earn a modest wage. Jess works in a bookshop and, after thirteen years' service, she has just reached the dizzy heights of store manager. We're not the type of people to be motivated by money (one of my other great friends, Lisa, is married to a City lawyer and he's rich but we think he's nice *despite* that). I don't resent Adam's lack of cash. I resent his lack of ... oh, what's the word?

Commitment.

His inability to grow up. To move on. It is Adam who has jammed our brakes at the ordinary station because he's a settler. He lacks ambition. When challenged, he says he's content and throws me a look of bewilderment that's vaguely critical. He thinks I'm unreasonable because I yearn for more than a tiny two-bedroom flat-share (all we can afford despite working endless, incompatible hours). I long for something more than Monday to Wednesday evenings in front of the TV, Thursday nights at the supermarket, Friday and Saturday nights at the local and Sundays (our one day a week off together) sleeping off a hangover.

Recently, I've been overwhelmed with despair as I've come to understand that not only do I currently have very little in my life to feel energized about but, with the exception of hoping my lottery numbers come up, I have absolutely nothing to look forward to in the future. This is it for me. The sum total.

When I was a tiny kid I once saw a deeply unsuitable sci-fi TV show where the goodies were trapped in a room and the walls were closing in on them, about to crush them to death. The same menace was used in *Star Wars*

Episode IV but Princess Leia had it really bad because she was knee deep in garbage too. I found the concept truly horrifying and suffered from nightmares for months. Lately, as I watch the (supposedly) best years of my life amble off into the dim distance, I've started to experience the same nightmare again. I wake up sweating with the taste of fear in my mouth. I'm going to be squashed to death by the walls of a tiny room.

In the beginning I was impressed by Adam's *joie de vivre*; his jaunty carelessness was part of the attraction. I loved it that he would find the time to listen to some demo disc from a yet to be discovered band. A demo disc that he'd scrounged from a no one and would pass on to Someone; not because of the lure of brash financial gain but just because he thought this band might be the next 'it' – more, he thought they *deserved* to be the next 'it'. I didn't care that I didn't actually understand what he was on about when he said something like, 'This band is totally thrashing with PJ Harvey-meets-Throwing Muses Fire, yet it's so completely purring with hectic pop.' I wonder if he cared that I just smiled and said nothing. Maybe my lack of knowledge about the pop scene has been interpreted as a lack of interest, because Adam's stopped urging me to listen to lyrics that are 'all about a breakneck chase through messy relationships'. I think he's accepted that my music tastes are mainstream. It's a shame in a way, because while I didn't understand what he was on about I did respect that he was on about *something*. I loved it that Adam had this extraordinary passion and I believed it would lead to something big. Problem being I never actually defined exactly what that something big might be – and nor did Adam. Yes, he pointed one or two promising bands in the right direction and they went on to greater things. But Adam's stayed still. Ground to a halt.

Thinking about it, it's a good thing that Adam has stopped asking me to join him at the gigs of struggling bands which take place in tiny underground bars that flout the no-smoking laws. I wouldn't want to go to those sorts of places any more. When you are twenty-five it's easy to be impressed by passion, creative flair, free spirits, etc. etc. When you are pushing thirty it's hard to resist being contemptuous about the very things that attracted you. Why is that? One of life's not so funny jokes, I guess.

On evenings like this one it's particularly hard to remember why I thought dating a gig rigger was ever a good idea. On evenings when Jess is out on a proper date (at some fancy restaurant somewhere) with some guy who has potential (a hot merchant banker that she met last Saturday) and I'm left alone with nothing more than a scribbled note (attached to the fridge by a Simpson's magnet which we got free in a cereal box), I struggle.

I'd especially asked Adam to stay home tonight. I'd said to him that I wanted to talk. Well, to be accurate, I pinned up a note to that effect on the fridge this morning; we didn't actually speak. Adam was working at a gig in Brixton last night and he didn't get home until three this morning. My boss Ben and I take it in turns to go to the New Covent Garden flower market each morning and today it was my turn, so I had to leave the flat by 4 a.m. I didn't have the heart to wake Adam so I left a note. It was clear enough.

We need to talk. Don't go out tonight. Don't accept any work. This is important. I'd underlined the words 'need', 'don't' (both of them) and 'important'. I thought I'd communicated my exasperation, urgency and desperation. Apparently not. Adam's reply note reads: *Got a sniff of a big job coming up. Lots of green ones, Fern-girl. Would love to gas tonight but no can do. Later. Luv u.*

When I first read the note I kicked the table leg, which was stupid because not only did I knock over a milk carton which means I now have to clean up the spillage but I hurt my foot. It's Adam I want to hurt.

I drag my eyes around the flat. It's a bit like rubbing salt into an open wound. If I was sensible now I'd just pick up my bag and phone a mate (or use any other lifeline) and I'd head back into town for a meal and a chat. It's a rare lovely summer evening. We could sit on the pavement outside a cheap restaurant and drink house wine. But I don't call anyone. Actually, I can't. Jess and Lisa are the only two people I could face seeing when I'm in this sort of mood and I know neither is available. I have other buddies but they are either friends Adam and I share (and therefore not useful when I want to let off steam about his inability to grow up and commit) or they are my good-time-only friends (also not useful when I'm steaming).

Jess is on her date and Lisa can never do a spur-of-the-moment night out. She has two kids under the age of three. A night out requires a serious time-line leading up to the occasion and military precision planning on the actual night. She grumbles about the lack of spontaneity in her life but Jess and I refuse to take her grumbles seriously; we both know that not only has she everything she ever wanted, she also has exactly what we want too.

So, it's a night in the flat with just the washing up to keep me company – the flat that epitomizes all that is wrong with where I am at, just one week before my thirtieth birthday. Great.

Jess and I have tried to make the flat as stylish as possible on our limited budgets. We regularly visit Ikea and we're forever lighting scented candles that we buy from the supermarket. However, all our good work can be undone in a matter of minutes if Adam is left un-supervised – in many ways he's a lot like a Labrador puppy. Because he, and many of his mates, work nights they often waste away a day hanging around our flat. When Jess and I leave for work the place usually looks reasonably smart. Not posh, I realize, but clean and tidy. When we come home it looks like a particularly vicious hurricane has dashed through.

Today the place looks especially squalid. The curtains are drawn even though it's a bright summer evening. My guess is that Adam and his mates have been watching DVDs all day. A guess that is confirmed when I find several discs flung across the floor, giving the flat the appearance of a bad dose of chicken pox. There is a collection of beer cans abandoned on every available surface. Most of the cans have stubbed-out fag ends precariously balanced on top, which I hate because our flat is supposed to be a non-smoking space. The scatter cushions have been well and truly scattered in messy heaps on the floor (men just don't get it – cushions are not to be used, they're for decoration) and I'm annoyed to notice something has been spilt on one of them (coffee, I think). The room smells of stale, male sweat; this might be a hangover from the numerous bodies that have been rotting here today, but more likely the hideous stench is coming from the pile of skankie trainers that are heaped next to the TV. Why Adam insists on taking his shoes off in the sitting-room, and then leaving them there for eternity, is beyond me.

I draw back the curtains, fling open the window and start to gather up the empty cans and cups. I work efficiently, as irritation often makes me noticeably more competent. Ben has commented that I pull together the most beautiful bouquets just after I've had to deal with a particularly tetchy customer. 'Darling, temper works so well for you. You are a true artist and these lilies are your brushes; this vase your canvas.' (Ben honestly believes he's a secret love great-grandchild of Oscar Wilde.) I throw the trainers to the back of Adam's wardrobe, I put the soiled cushion cover in the wash basket and while I'm there I sort out a quick load of darks and pop a wash on. I wipe surfaces, dust and drag out the vacuum cleaner. It is only once the room is shiny and clean that I allow myself a glass of wine. I think a large one is required.

I carry the goldfish-bowl-size glass of Chardonnay back into the sitting-room, plonk myself on the settee and start to flick through the TV channels. Annoyingly (and predictably, considering my tense mood) nothing grabs my attention. Maybe some music will help. I flick through my CDs. As I've confessed, my tastes are mainstream and my CD collection is probably identical to tens of thousands of other women, my age, up and down the country. In my teens I was an Oasis girl, who wasn't? I have a bit of Röyksopp and Groove Armada that I listened to in my early twenties, especially when I was in the mood for luuurve. There was a big loungy vibe going on at the time, or at least I think there was – there was in my flat. More recently I've bought CDs by the Arctic Monkeys, White Stripes, Chemical Brothers and Scouting for Girls. I buy these CDs on average six months after they've been big in the charts. Hidden in a box near our CD racks I also have Diana Ross and Dido, who I listened to approximately once a month throughout the first half of my twenties (whenever I broke up with my latest squeeze). I hate it that being with Adam has somehow made me apologetic about my collection. It's brought me hours of entertainment, consolation and fun. Surely that's what music is about. Half the stuff Adam listens to sounds trashy, loud and overly aggressive or just plain old depressing, if you ask me. But then, he doesn't ask me. Not any more.

I opt to listen to one of Scottie Taylor's CDs. Scottie Taylor is, in my opinion, the greatest entertainer Britain has produced ever, and the biggest pop phenomenon we've had since the Beatles. I'd never dare make huge sweeping statements about anything to do with the pop industry in front of Adam but I'm on fairly solid ground with this one. For one, Adam is not here (which is why I've been driven to drink and the imaginary arms of Scottie Taylor), and for two, this opinion is pretty much accepted as fact. You could ask any woman in Britain, aged between fifteen and fifty, and she'd agree.

Scottie is the man every woman wants to fix and fuck.

He shot to fame fifteen years ago when he was just seventeen years old. Women my age have grown up with him; he's an institution. He was recruited by a pop mogul to join a girl band, X-treme, an obvious publicity stunt when X-treme were battling for chart supremacy against the Spice Girls. Despite the gimmick of introducing Scottie to the band, X-treme died a death and no one can even name any of the other band members now. I think one of them (the redhead) is a presenter on a Sky shopping channel, I spotted her when I was mindlessly flicking once; she's put on a lot of weight. The other three are occasionally papped coming out of the Priory or Primark. But none of them have even dared threaten a comeback tour. It's generally accepted there wasn't a platform to come back from. It was different for Scottie. As X-treme became more ex-dream, Scottie became bigger and bigger. After just two pop hits with the band he was approached by a new manager and went solo. As Scottie climbed to number one, you could hear the nails being hammered into X-treme's coffin.

He's an incredibly talented songwriter and vocalist but besides that he's needy, sexy, beautiful and has the most filthy grin in history. Despite sleeping with pretty much every gorgeous woman in the pop world, plus a fair number of models and film stars, he is resolutely single and as such the perfect fantasy man. Just what I need right now to ease the tedium of being ignored by Adam.

I put on his latest CD and turn the volume up high.

The thing is, it can go either way with music. Sometimes it's life-affirming and uplifting; other times it can plunge you into the deepest, darkest doldrums. By the time I've downed two-thirds of the bottle of Chardonnay I'm beginning to feel horny and hurt; a lethal combination. Scottie is crooning some love ballad, or more accurately some hate ballad. Something about knowing when love has made a dash for the door and love not living here any more. I start to swirl the lyric around my mind with the same seriousness I would if I was grappling with the monumental questions like: Why are we here? Why don't you ever see a baby pigeon? Why are yawns contagious?

The hardest thing to bear about my live-in relationship with Adam is not the mess he makes, or the unsociable hours he works, or his lack of focus on his career. The hardest thing is I love him and I have to wonder, does he still love me? That's why I'm often grumpy and bored. I don't feel special. I think there's a serious danger that our love has made a dash for the door. I sometimes think Adam and I are more used to each other than mad about each other. How depressing. The orange glow of an August sunset fills the room with a pale amber hue and yet I feel distinct shivers scuttle up and down my spine.

2. Fern

I can't help thinking that if Adam loved me as much as I love him, or as much as he used to, or as much as I want him to, or whatever, then things would be different. Things would feel more exquisitely special, distinctly not ordinary. Plus he'd follow basic instructions. I mean he'd stay in on the one night of the week that I ask him to, wouldn't he? He'd occasionally squirt a bit of Fairy liquid over the dishes in the sink or put his smelly trainers in the wardrobe, wouldn't he? He'd ask me to marry him.

Wouldn't he?

There, I've said it. It's out there. I am that pathetic, that old-fashioned, that un-liberated. I want the man I love, who I've been with for four years, to ask me to marry him. Tell me, ladies and gentlemen, am I so unreasonable?

Part of me is ashamed that after everything the bra-burning brigade did on behalf of my sex, I still can't shift the secret belief that if Adam proposed my life would be somehow more luminous, glorious and triumphant than it currently is. I know, I know, it's an illogical thought. Since his inadequacies are stacking up like the interest on a credit card in January, it does not make sense that I want to shackle myself to him on a permanent basis. The fact that I am irritated he no longer looks me in the eye when he's talking to me (what am I on about? He rarely talks to me!). The fact that the very sight of his favourite old baggy sweatshirt now brings me out in a rash (and yet I'd previously considered it to be cuddly and snuggly – right up there with my baby blanket in terms of offering comfort). The fact that the way he chews his food, cuts his nails in bed and leaves the seat up in the loo makes me want to hold his head under water and wait for the bubbles to stop surfacing ought to add up to something other than my desire for a huge, floaty meringue number. But it doesn't.

No matter how annoying Adam can be I find I am irrationally besieged by a belief (which grips me with the same severity as religious doctrine grabs some folk) that marrying him will somehow change things for the better between us.

I know, I know. Once again the facts would point in another direction. I've never met a woman who can, hand on heart, say this is the case. The vast majority of women insinuate (or openly state depending on their level of inebriation) that marriage only leads to a deepening of cracks in a relationship. Where there was a hairline fracture, throw in a dozen years of matrimony and you find an enormous chasm, a veritable gulf. Even the very happily married tend to look back fondly at the days gone by, the days of dating, when the most monumental decision a couple ever have to make is which movie to see – as opposed to endlessly debating domestic dross. Can we afford a new mattress? Is it worth insuring the house contents? Is it stupidly irresponsible to go with the quote from the *first* plumber who turned up to look at the leaky radiator – after all, it's taken six weeks to get a plumber to show, can we really wait for two more?

And yet I want a proposal.

I think I need to make it clear at this point that I am not one of those women who always wanted to get married. As a child I owned Airhostess Barbie, not Bridal Barbie. I had no ambitions to endlessly re-enact a marriage between said doll and her eunuch boyfriend, Ken. Nor did I dance around the kitchen with a tea towel tied to my head and a sheet around my waist singing 'Some Day My Prince Will Come' (although my older sister Fiona did this until she was about fifteen). In fact I spent most of my late teens and early twenties avoiding any sort of proper relationship. I thought a guy was being unreasonably controlling and presumptuous if he insisted on knowing my surname before making a dishonest woman of me. I was a good-time girl rather than a good girl. I never bought into the nonsense that sex was in any way tied up with responsibility, disgrace, doubt, guilt or even love. As far as I was concerned sex was all about hedonistic pleasure and fun – lots and lots of fun. I suppose sexist propaganda would have it that I ought to hang my head in shame, wear sackcloth and frequently beat myself rather than own up to the fact that in my past I've rarely dignified any relationship with longevity. But I won't. I can't be that much of a hypocrite.

Then there was Adam.

I met Adam in the same way I usually met guys back then (he was the mate of a bloke I was shagging at the time). It wasn't love at first sight or anything really corny like that – it was laugh at first sight. Not that I was laughing at him, I wasn't; I laughed right along with him, everyone did. He was a riot. He's one of those walking bag of gags lads. He's full of witty one-liners, bizarre facts and decent jokes. No one delivers a punch line like Adam. We flirted from the word go but Adam kept me at arm's length until my fling with his mate drew its last breath. Then he asked me to go to Glastonbury music fest with him. And that was it – we were an item.

I never so much as looked at another man from that moment on. Seriously, he held me captive. I realized that I hadn't simply been a slut (as I believed and my mum feared), I just hadn't met the right guy. Simple as that. As nice and old-fashioned as that.

I've loved being faithful to Adam. It hasn't been a struggle. Having sown my wild oats it was a joy to sink into a relationship where it really didn't matter if I occasionally wore cotton M&S knickers rather than lacy thongs – he'd still want to rip them off me.

Adam and I laughed our way through the first couple of years and we laughed our way into this flat-share and for quite some months after that. But we haven't been doing a great deal of laughing of late. In fact there hasn't been so much as a chuckle, a guffaw or a weak giggle. Neither of us is the rowing sort, so silence and tension have become our staple.

I call Adam to find out what time he expects to be back so I can gauge whether it's worth waiting up for him. Even before I press the dial button part of me knows this is likely to be a pointless exercise. Invariably, even if Adam is able to give an expected time of arrival, he's about as reliable as a politician a week before elections; besides that, he often doesn't answer his phone anyway. He's either up a ladder rigging lights or down a cellar listening to a band and so he can't reach his phone or the signal can't reach him. It's an accurate metaphor for our relationship. I'm therefore pleasantly surprised when he picks up.

'Hi, I was just wondering where you are and what you are up to,' I say, trying to sound as friendly and non-naggy as I'm able.

'Hey, Fern-girl. I'm coming right back to you.'

'Are you?' A rush of excitement floods into my stomach, pushing aside the irritation I've felt all evening.

'Yup.'

The doorbell rings. 'Hang on, someone is at the door, hold the line,' I say.

I open the door and Adam is stood facing me, holding his phone to his ear and grinning.

'Lost my key,' he says as he snaps closed his mobile and then briefly kisses me on the forehead.

'Lost or forgotten?' I demand. The rush of excitement at seeing him is instantly drowned by a fresh flash of irritation. Living with him is a bit like sitting in a ducking chair. *Oh, I can breathe; everything is going to be fine. No, I'm under water once more. I'm going to drown.* If he's lost his key again then we'll have to pay for the locks to be changed for the second time in six months. It's such an unnecessary expense, all that's required is a little thought. But, if he's simply forgotten to take it out with him I'll be just as irritated. I mean, it's not rocket science, is it? You go out, you come in again, to do that you need a key, put key in pocket.

Adam shrugs. 'Think they are in my other jeans.'

'I hope so,' I mutter as I head for our bedroom to

check in his jeans pocket. The jeans are on the floor in a crumpled heap. Luckily, I do find his keys, along with a stick of gum and his Oyster card. I walk back into the kitchen dangling the keys off my finger; half triumphant, half vexed. Nowadays I often rage with conflicting emotions when I'm around Adam. I wish it wasn't so. I wish things were simpler.